OPEN AND ENTER

The ancient shaman's song that starts the dreamwalk . . . the succubus that surfs the Internet . . . the shy suburban teen just learning to fly . . . the *bruja*'s revenge on a child-molester . . . the African wise woman in the American Civil War . . . the bloodstone spell for birth and death . . . an antiquarian's laptop that calls up an ancient and awesome evil . . .

Here are the stories that will take you beyond
THE SHIMMERING DOOR

THE
SHIMMERING DOOR

EDITED BY KATHARINE KERR

HarperPrism
An Imprint of HarperPaperbacks

HarperPaperbacks
A Division of HarperCollins*Publishers*
10 East 53rd Street, New York, N.Y. 10022-5299

Individual story copyrights apeear on pages 433-434

HarperPrism is an imprint of HarperPaperbacks.

ISBN: 0-06-105342-2

HarperCollins®, ☖ ®, HarperPaperbacks™, and HarperPrism®
are trademarks of HarperCollins*Publishers* Inc.

HarperPaperbacks may be purchased for educational, business, or sales promotional use. For information, please write:
Special Markets Department, HarperCollins*Publishers*,
10 East 53rd Street, New York, N.Y. 10022-5299.

Printed in the United States of America

Cover photograph by FPG Int./Paul Avis

First printing: August 1996

Designed by Michele Bonomo

Library of Congress Cataloging-in-Publication Data

The shimmering door / edited by Katharine Kerr.
    p. cm.
    ISBN 0-06-105342-2 (pbk.)
     1. Fantastic fiction, American. 2. Magic—Fiction.
     3. Witchcraft—Fiction. 4. American fiction—20th century.
  I. Kerr, Katharine.
  PS648.F3S56 1996
  813'.0876608--dc20   96-16517
                     CIP

Visit HarperPaperbacks on the World Wide Web at
http://www.harpercollins.com/paperbacks

96 97 98 99 ❖ 10 9 8 7 6 5 4 3 2 1

This book owes a great deal to Jo Clayton. When, last year, I was drowning in personal problems, she took this particular project in hand and kept it alive. Without all her help I might never have finished it at all. Thanks, Jo. I owe you a lot myself. Here's the book. Please do consider it yours.

TABLE OF CONTENTS

NIGHT

INTRODUCTION

Twenty thousand years ago, deep in the shaft of the Lascaux caves, they recorded his death. His arms flung out, he lies stiffly on the ground in front of the bison that has just gored him. He still wears his bird mask, and beside him lies his staff, topped with the image of a bird. His magic failed, it seems, at the last moment. Seven thousand years later, in another cave, the one we call Les Trois Frères, they show us another shaman. Draped in animal skins, tailed like a wolf, wearing the mask and antlers of a stag, he stares out at us while he dances at the edge of the herd. They painted Bison Man in the same cave, too. They? Who? For all of us who hail from Europe, they are the ancestors. At the dawn of what makes us ourselves, there were sorcerers.

Or so I like to define these motifs, as a magic staff, as a shaman whose totem or fetch was a bird. Despite the overconfident pronouncements of some archaeologists, we really cannot be certain that the man with the head of a bird or the one draped with a deer's whole hide are sorcerers. Priests, some say, but again, can we be certain? We cannot even know if the ancestors separated religion from magic, if they saw any difference between sorcerer and priest, wisewoman and priestess. The evidence gathered in studies like Mircea Eliade's *Shamanism* makes it unlikely that they did. Others call the figures gods, but had European humanity created gods to love and worship then, back in our own Dreamtime? We cannot know.

One thing, however, that Bird Man and Stag Dancer cannot possibly be is ordinary human beings. When they donned their masks and skins, they were marking themselves as something separate, someone set apart. They were partaking of an experience different from that of the ordinary hunters who cluster in the cave paintings, little figures hastily sketched beside their prey. I cannot help but think, even though I'm thinking with my heart, that if we call them sorcerers and shamans, we won't be far wrong.

The figure of the shaman—the magician, the wisewoman, the witch, the sorcerer—recurs constantly in Western lore, art and literature both, from then on. As far as I know, the lore of the Far East and Africa contains them as well, as does that of many Native American peoples. (At times like these I really have to berate my own shallow knowledge of non-Western cultures.) Throughout prehistory, on into recorded thought, scratched onto rocks or carved in temples, images of magic and those who work it abound, even if the sorcerers in some of these cases are termed priests instead. The same thing occurs in literature, whether in preliterate poems like the *Iliad* or sophisticated compositions like Malory's *Le Morte d'Arthur.* Sorcerers appear in entertainments, like Merlin in the Arthurian tales, and in serious works, such as Ficino's natural philosophers, the precursors of modern scientists.

That last phrase may be giving some of you pause. Let's consider it for a moment. These days the reputation of sorcerers has fallen upon hard times, even in the world of genre fiction, where such critics as we have sneer at their doings in works labeled "fantasy" as opposed to works labeled "science fiction." Science, runs the common belief, is true and good, while magic is false and bad. The two have separate laws, even, mutually contradictory and eternally opposed. Thus works of fantasy, such as the volume you have in your hands at the moment, must somehow belong in a completely different category than works of science fiction, where those who work marvels are scientists and technicians, never the outmoded sorcerer or witch.

But is this true? And what, really, is sorcery?

Within Western culture, magic and the sorcerer have had a very long and venerable history. Until late in the seventeenth century, what we call magic and science fell under the same heading, both being merely different parts of a discipline called "natural philosophy." The natural philosopher studied Nature in all her manifestations and did so in an organized and careful way that became the foundation of the scientific method. Most of you probably know that even scientists admit that in alchemy lie the foundations of modern chemistry. Alchemists inherited a set of assumptions about the nature of certain substances, then derived a series of experiments to assess the truth of these assumptions. Those that could not be proved were laid aside. Those proven they codified to stand as the basis of further research.

Similarly, other topics of natural philosophy included a set of assumptions which then generated certain beliefs in a rational manner. Thus Dr. John Dee could spend part of his time laying down the mathematical foundations of sidereal navigation and another part learning the Enochian tongue from an angel in a scrying glass. Dee's records of these conversations with the angel are complete, methodical, and well organized—scientific, we might well say, in their execution. Unfortunately, since for the raw data Dr. Dee depended on the dubious talents of a medium with a drinking problem, we may doubt the validity of his results even while admiring his method.

Dr. Dee's experiments with the angel mark him as a sorcerer, one of the last great sorcerers, we might even say. His area of study, magic or sorcery, has little to do with folk superstitions but much to do with religion. What these two undertakings, magic and religion, share is the idea that if a person trains and concentrates their powers of thought, their thoughts can cause effects outside of their own bodies, i.e., thought, properly cultivated, can make changes in the outside world. In religion this is called prayer—somehow the gods hear your thoughts and make the changes for you. Our sorcerers, however, can bring these changes about through their own powers alone.

All through Western culture this belief in the power of thought has been coupled with a belief in other planes of existence, each containing other forms of life as natural to their plane as we are to ours, the physical plane. Obviously, religion shares this belief as well. A corollary of this belief is that a properly trained and qualified person, the sorcerer, can communicate with these beings. In religious thought, however, it's always the other beings, angels and gods, that initiate any contact between our plane and theirs. The sorcerers believe the opposite, that they can learn the techniques and develop the powers that will open the gates between the planes at their will, not the will of the Others.

The literature of magic also emphasizes that the ability to work magic, the talent to learn to control your thought and mind to this pitch, is very rare. Because the talents are rare, magic is rare. Because magic could be dangerous, the would-be student has to prove himself worthy of learning.

All the magical practices in our Western magical literature descend from these core beliefs—the power of thought, the existence of other planes, and the necessity of inborn talent for magic—in a fairly logical and rational manner, given their assumptions. Once the budding discipline of science found that these assumptions could not be proven by the methods of science, magic fell into disrepute, the province of fools and peasants, outright charlatans and the credulous, or so we are led to believe. That those who continued to practice and believe in magic after the triumph of science were all fools and rabble is one of our own assumptions that needs some testing and reexamination, but such an exercise lies outside the scope of this introduction.

There's certainly no doubt that magic is enjoying something of a revival these days, both in the form of New Age ideas (most of which are ancient, actually), and in fantasy literature. Tales of magic intrigue and enchant us once again. Sorcerers once more stand at the edge of the village to remind us that a strange world lies outside its walls. For those of you who find them and their craft fascinating, I have assembled this book of tales.

All of the men and women described herein have learned their art slowly and painstakingly, have risked much and suffered much to perfect it over long years of work. It seemed fitting, then, to organize the tales about them around the central image of time passing, of a sorcerous life as a day in a much broader year than the ones the rest of us know. A would-be sorcerer starts out as innocent as the dawn, but all the old tales agree that in the end, sorcery brings with it the weariness of midnight.

The tales herein are fantasy in one form or another, but I like to think that they contain truth as well—facts that cannot be quantified, experiments that cannot be reproduced, perhaps, because they come from the human mind and heart, but truths that are valid all the same. Many of them take place in ancient times or in places that never were; others find sorcery in settings as common as a flea-bitten Texas town. Not all of the stories are serious, mind you, just as not all truths are grim. I've not been above including a few good comic pieces on our sorcerous themes.

May you find them all worthy of your time in your own day's journey.

Katharine Kerr

THE SHIMMERING DOOR

MORNING

*The learning time when all things are new and
most of life is still to come.*

WATER PATTERNS
JO CLAYTON

Jo Clayton lives in Portland, Oregon, with a calico monitor ornament named Tigerlily, who pretends to be a cat, and a sealpoint siamese named Owl, who has a habit of levitating into small high places and yowling till Jo fetches a stepladder and reaches for him, at which point he jumps down and wanders away. While listening to the rain and laughing at the cats, she manages to write science fiction and fantasy novels and a few short stories.

1

Whyisthatkidalwayscrying ifyoudontshuthimupiwill

The sounds came flying at him, pelting him like small black pebbles, stinging when they hit. He howled louder, spitting blobs of sound to knock them away.

A shape bent over him. He knew the shape. It was edged with red spikes. It was always edged with red. It reached for him. There was pressure on his body, his arms were locked against his sides. The shape lifted him, started shaking him. He wailed his fear, brown jags that broke into the pattern of dark and light over him, lifting him, shaking him. Fear was red and yellow laced through him; he screamed and blue came washing over brown, over red and yellow. He slipped through from the grip that held him, fell bouncing on the softness, splashing on the softness.

Kerjal swore, turned away, wiping his hands down his sides. He didn't want to see his firstborn rocking like some damn fish in a cradle filled with water.

Betta scurried past him, hand raised to her face. The red marks of his fingers and the swollen eye were a reproach to him, but he wasn't about to admit even to himself that he regretted what he'd done. He went out, scowling. There was work in the fields; he couldn't waste time on a whiny child and a sniveling woman.

2

Wizard Viritagh knelt and carefully spread the leaves apart so he wouldn't dislodge the unripe pollen that clung to the center ribs. "Do you see the nubbin, Karsti?"

His daughter squatted beside him, her cap of dark brown hair as shaggy as a hedgehog's back. She nodded. "The little greeny brown thing way down at the bottom."

He eased the leaves back into their spiral dome. "Tell me about this plant."

She looked up, squinting against the sunlight streaming through the break in the canopy, love dots dappling her smooth brown skin. She was eight, his hope for a child of his blood to follow his path. His sons were good boys, and he loved them dearly, but they had other roads to walk.

"The plant is yormedo. When the pollen is ripe and mixed with the pulp of the fruit of the marel tree, it makes a strong yellow dye. When the pollen sacs have not yet burst, an infusion of the leaves has several properties, differing according to the age of the leaves and the number of boilings. One boiling makes a mild febrifuge. Two boilings makes a strong purgative." She grinned, her eyes inverted smiles. "Whatever's inside comes out fast anyway it can."

He laughed and rubbed her head. "And you better not try that again, my girl. I've never seen a man so surprised."

She sniffed. "He was a bad man."

"I know, Karsti, and that's why all I did was make you clean it up. Go on."

"Three boilings makes a poison that kills by convulsions. When the nubbin is ripe and ground into a paste, it brings visions and dreams, but is very dangerous for anyone who doesn't understand dreamwalking."

"And how do you tell yormedo from paguero or chamel or zombat?"

"Yormedo has one central rib to each leaf with pollen or pollen sacs dotted along it. Its leaves usually curve inward to form a dome. Paguero's leaves also curve in, but they have three ribs and the pollen sacs grow on a stem that rises from the central well. The leaves of chamel and zombat look just like those of the yormedo, but they curve outward. When are you going to take me on a dreamwalk, Da?"

Viritagh got to his feet, closed his fingers about his daughter's small hand as she rose beside him. "I've talked it over with your mother. The summer solstice is next week and the Wounded Moon will be full the same day and all the signs I've read are good. It will be then."

"Ah." She was silent for several steps. "Does it matter if I'm scared, Da?"

"I was trembling in my boots when your Grandda took me on my first stroll. I'll tell you what he told me. Hold steady and stay the course, and I'll be there beside you every step even when you think you're alone."

3

"His eyes don't follow the rattle." The HerbWife shook the painted gourd again, then set it on the table Betta had fetched from the kitchen. "But he hasn't the look of the blind."

"No no, Telyon, he's not blind, he's just stubborn. Wait. I'll show you." Betta moved to the chest at the end of the bed, took out a necklace of bright glass beads the size of acorns, red and yellow, green and blue, white and black. She dangled the necklace above the cradle, and the baby kicked and reached for it with an urgency startling in its contrast to his lethargy a moment before. He made angry animal sounds as she held it just beyond his reach. Before he could start howling she lowered the necklace until it was lying coiled on his stomach.

He closed his fist about one of the beads, pulled the necklace to his mouth and started gumming it in an oddly rhythmic pattern, rolling his head to his left, then to his right, moving one bead over with each turn.

The HerbWife watched in silence for several minutes, then she said, "Is he often like that?"

"Doing things over and over and over till it drives you crazy watching him? Yes. Oh, yes."

"You have the cornmeal and the dried ehkai leaves?"

"In bowls in the kitchen."

"Good. Get the necklace away from him and bring him to the threshing floor."

"Hoy! He's slippery as a fish."

"He gets that way when he's frightened or angry."

The cornmeal was laid out in a complex pattern of signs, some of which were filled with stones, some with bits of glass, some with leaves or small polished squares of wood. A three-legged bronze brazier stood in the center with a handful of glowing coals piled at the center of the dish.

The HerbWife gripped the child tightly and moved with care between the lines. He was attracted by the red shine of the coals and wriggling energetically as he reached for them. She managed to drop the ehkai leaves into the brazier without letting him slip away, then held him pressed against her as she chanted the Words to bring the smoke alive.

She tried to pass him through it.

And suddenly her hands were holding only water and he was tumbling toward the coals.

The threshing floor exploded upward, a geyser broad as a man's thigh blowing higher than the hayloft.

A moment later it was a new spring filling the hole where the floor had been.

Betta ran into the bedroom, stopped, collapsed against the Herb-Wife, limp with relief. Telyon was in his cradle gumming at the necklace and staring at something only he could see.

"Hoy! How did you know?"

"He's jumped like that before, only not so far, usually when Kerjal's shaking him."

"Your son is a Water Caller, Betta-nai. With rain so scarce the past two years and the signs saying there's worse to come, he is more precious than a mountain of jade. Tell no one outside the village what he is, or they will try to steal him."

"Aaahhhhhhh."

"There is bad with the good, Betta-nai. He will be mute and will probably never know what words are. You'll have to train him as you would a dog."

4

Viritagh snapped his fingers and fire surged about the coals in the brazier. On the far side of the fire, his daughter's face leaped from the darkness, her eyes shiny with excitement. "When you set your foot on the dreamroad, Karsta Viridatter, you begin a march that will use your whole life. It will be hard and lonely, and there will be much sorrow. Do you understand this?"

She nodded gravely. "Yes, Father."

"You must tell me now. In your own heart, do you wish this?"

"In my own heart, the need to do this is like the need to breathe."

He relaxed, smiled at her, then felt around on the floor behind him till he found a little book; he set it on his knee, leaned toward her. "Do you have any questions? Ask anything, Karsti, this is the time for it."

"Why haven't you taught me the chants? I've learned all the rest, haven't I?"

"Ah. This is not something we talk about, Karsti, except with those that already know. I can't teach you my real chants because they're mine. They won't work for you. The ones I sing aloud are for clients to hear. They expect me to do it and wouldn't feel right if I didn't, but they're as useless for magic as the beads your mother braids in my hair when I dress for a meeting. The real words, the Power Words, you'll have to find those for yourself as you walk the dreamroad and learn the disciplines." He chuckled. "And some of them will be so embarrassing, your soul will itch when you have to say them."

"Why, Da?"

"I don't know, just seems to work out that way. Sorcerers, mages, wizards, witches, it's the same for all of us. I've got a gift for you, Karsti." He reached across the dying flames, gave her the book. "This is your Word Book. I've written the public chants in the first pages. You can play with those, change them however seems best to you. The others, though, they will be your True Words, the soul of your magic. Sleep with the book, Karsti. In a few weeks it will know you that way, and you'll never lose it. Umm, one last thing. I disguise my own True Words a bit to save me shame should someone happen to see them. Just shift each glyph down two in the list." He groped again, came up with the pouch of nubbin dust. "Are you ready?"

"I'm ready."

He filled his palm with the dust, cast it on the fire. "Breathe deep, Karsta Viridatter. You won't see me, but I'll be with you always. If you need me, call my name. Otherwise, follow your heart and do what it tells you."

She was standing on the shore looking out across the water. The ocean laughed at her and sighed and heaved its skin into foam-crested waves. She hesitated a moment. Her father's voice sounded in her mind's ear: Follow your heart. "Yes!" She ran leaping from crest to crest, laughing with the joy of it.

A dolphin leaped beside her, looking at her with a boy's bold eyes. It squealed her name—Aaars teee—and startled her so much she lost her footing, fell on her back. A wave crashed over her, filling her eyes, nose, mouth, with bitter brine.

She shouted a Word! and it blasted her from the water into a blow-hole in black lava, a cave in the side of a fire-mountain somewhere.

She blushed beet red as she remembered her first Word and knew she would never, ever tell it to anyone, especially not her father.

A chuckle brought her swinging around.

An old woman wrapped in shawls sat in a massive chair carved from the black lava. Her ancient wrinkled face was black as the stone around her, her eyes were yellow as sunlight, her gray hair twisted into a long braid and pinned in a pile atop her head.

Karsta bowed as her mother had taught her, hands pressed together, head dipping low. "Grandma-lustry."

"I am Sibyl, Karsta Viridatter. Blessings, child. You've walked with full heart and gained your first Word." She chuckled as Karsta blushed again. "Ah well, Words of Power are like that. I've a message that you must carry to your father. Will you do it?"

Karsta bowed again, wondering why her and not her father.

A chuckle as if the Sibyl read her mind.

"A polite child. I give it to you because that is how I choose to do it. Say this:

> *Sun-fires fry*
> *The Land goes dry*
> *Waterthieves rule*
> *Wisdom's a tool*
> *That turns in the hand*
> *When the land burns*
> *Wizard should watch*
> *His Wizardly nose*
> *What he could catch*
> *Would spoil his repose*
> *Like goes to like*
> *Else the pattern's not run*
> *Don't ask me why*
> *My babble is done.*"

She chuckled again at the look on Karsta's face. "Get used to it, luv. What your father told you is true. They'll expect it from you, your clients will. Bad verse is a comfort like an old worn blanket. Now go." She leaned forward, pursed her wrinkled lips, and blew. . . .

And Karsta sat up blinking, looking through a smoky haze at her father's anxious face.

5

As the months spread into years and the drought bit deeper into the land, Telyon grew and learned. He could dress himself, feed himself, understand enough of what others said to know they disliked the sounds he made when he tried to talk. He stayed mute except when he was angry and wanted to disturb someone.

Sounds hurt him, less than when he was a baby, but they still scraped like nettles along his nerves. When he was three he learned that he could make them stop hurting if he concentrated intensely on the color patterns they made behind his eyes. Patterns in front of his eyes were mind-traps—he lost himself in them, patterns of movement, patterns of texture, patterns of color, of light and shadow—but those behind the eyes calmed and comforted him.

With the distraction of the hurt gone, he began to understand that those sound-generated colors meant something. Water was blue. Running water had a blue ground with ripples of white darting across it. Stagnant mossy water, rain, all the different sorts of water acquired patterns. Mother was a plaid of reds and purples with a diagonal line of gold slashing across the squares. Father was white on white with jags of red and large patches of black. The cat that slept on the windowsill was a mix of water and daylight, sinuous lines of blue and gold. He found more and more patterns and he tucked them away in his capacious memory. His words.

The villagers used him to call water to their dried-out wells. They caught him in a silver web and lowered him into the well, leaving him there until the water came. At first he screamed from fear and anger, tried to leap away, but something about the net trapped him where he was. When his rage and need brought water, they pulled him up, petted him, and tried to give him sweets. He bit their fingers and peed on them.

When he was five, he sat for hours staring at his mother as she sewed beads onto his father's shirts. They were prosperous now, important people in the village, and there was need to dress the part.

Every time she took out her bead work, he came and squatted on the rug beside her, eyes fixed on the beads and the silver glitter of the needle as it moved in and out of the cloth ground, watched the patterns she sewed take their slow shape.

When he thought he knew how the needle went, he pulled at her skirt and gobbled at her until she found a scrap of cloth, threaded a beading needle, and gave him a cupful of beads.

Though he was so clumsy at other things that they made him angry with his own flesh, his fingers turned deft when they sewed beads to cloth.

The first picture he made was his name. Not the name his mother and all the others called him, but the secret name that only he knew. When he was finished he wasn't satisfied with what he'd done and tore the threads out, carefully collecting every bead so he could use them again.

As the months passed and turned into another year, the villagers learned to pay him in beads. He showed them the colors he wanted and how many, then they lowered him in a sling until he called the water, gave him the beads he wanted when they pulled him up again. He went home and worked on his Words, stringing them together into a Word Book that only he could read. And the village and the farms around it were a green jewel in the heart of desolation.

6

"They say it's the Land God's doing. We don't believe them. They've got a Water Thief. We want you to point him out to us, that's all."

The speaker was a wiry thin man. His skin was shiny with ancient grime, his eyes red-rimmed with weariness. His hair and beard were neatly combed, but they, too, hadn't been washed in a long long time. His silent companion standing by the door might have been his twin.

Sitting in the apprentice's corner, Karsta took shallow breaths and was grateful for the window at her shoulder and the breeze that wandered in now and again.

Wizard Viritagh sat cross-legged on an embroidered leather pillow, the beads braided into his hair clacking gently with every move of his head. He cupped his hands, looked into them for several breaths, then looked up at the men. "Water Thief," he said. "That is a serious thing. How do you know?"

The man by the door stepped forward. "My well was deep and it had a bit of water yet, enough for drinking. My wife and my eldest daughter were filling the water jars. Between one lowering of the bucket and the next, the water was gone. I went down to see. The sides and bottom of the well were dust dry. You know that's not natural." He stepped back and returned to staring morosely at the floor.

The first speaker nodded. "And that is only one such story. Twenty villages could tell the same tale."

"It is sufficient." Viritagh brought his hands up, pressed fingertip to fingertip while the palms were about an inch apart. He unfocused his eyes and stared past the clients as if he looked on sights they couldn't see.

In her corner, Karsta noted these things and the effect they had on the visitors, tucked the observations away for further thought.

Viritagh sighed, moved his eyes back to the face of the man who'd done the most talking. "What you ask I will not do." He raised a hand as the man leaned forward, his mouth coming open. "Wait. This I will do. I will go to Kekavayt, discover the Water Thief, and remove him from the Plainlands."

"What you gonna do with him?"

"That is not your concern. I will swear that I will make sure he does not return to the Plainlands, but that is all. If that is not sufficient, you must find another wizard."

The man by the door leaned forward, caught the other's arm. "Turv . . . "

"Shut your mouth, fool." He straightened his shoulders. "We have to talk. We'll be back."

After the door clicked shut, Karsta said, "Da."

He smiled at her. "Why?"

"Uh-huh." She stood and stretched, the cloak that concealed her shape falling back from her shoulders; she was tall enough now that she could hitch a hip on the windowsill. She leaned against the frame, frowning. "Is it because they meant to kill him? The Water Thief, I mean."

"No, Karsti. Because they didn't." He smiled at the puzzlement in her eyes. "Think about it."

7

Telyon lifted his head. His mouth dropped open, and he began grunting and gabbling. His mother set down her sewing and began talking at him.

b a b y d o n t d o th a t y ou kn o w y ou r f a th e r d o e s n t l i k e
y o u t r y i n g t o t a l k h e w i l l b e b a c k a n y m i n u t e b a b y
p l e a se s t o p

For a moment he lost his concentration enough to let the sounds of
her voice get to him, hurt him, scramble the world around him even
further so everything was confusing and painful. He howled, trying to
knock the little black pebbles away from him long enough to let him
concentrate again.

b a b y wh a t s w r o n g wh a t c a n i d o

Arms flailing, howling, he ran at her, jumped on her, hit at her, trying to get her to stop talking. Stop talking. Stop talking.

Hands caught him, flung him away.

wh a t y ou d o i n g y ou l i tt le b a s t a r d y ou re c r a z y th a t s
wh a t

Whimpering, grunting, he banged his head against the wall, banged
it, banged it, banged it, banged . . .

8

Karsta straightened, sat on her heels. "That can't be right," she said.
"He's a child. And a mute."

Viritagh passed his hand across the basin and the water surface wrinkled, breaking the image, then smoothed again. "A sorcerer without
Words. Water Affined. No wonder he sucked the Plainlands dry." He
laughed, but it wasn't a happy sound. "Wizard should watch/His Wiz-
ardly nose/What he could catch/Would spoil his repose."

"We have to take him away from his folks."

It wasn't a question, but he nodded. "He's controllable now, but if
his strength keeps growing . . . without teaching . . . no training in
control . . . " He passed a hand across his face. "I don't know what
to do, Karsti, I truly don't." He lifted the silver basin, emptied it
onto dry, cracked soil under trees that seemed like cardboard repli-
cas of real trees, no color and no strength and no life in them. He
polished it with a clean rag and gave it to Karsta to put back in the
carry sack.

" 'Like goes to like/else the pattern's not run.' Maybe the Sibyl meant
we should take the boy to a sorcerer so he could get the training. His
poor mother. You're going to tell her?"

"Yes. When it's done and can't be undone." He looked at her, looked
away. "It's a terrible thing, taking a child away."

"You said it was a hard road, Da." She took the waterskin from the broken-off branch where she'd hung it, drank a mouthful, and held out the skin to her father.

He shook his head. "We're doing no good here, just disturbing the boy and making his life more difficult. Take my hand, Karsti."

She sighed. "Sometimes I wish I could learn sliding faster, Da."

"Things come in their times, rushing them is foolish."

"My head knows, I wish my heart would listen." She slipped the strap of the waterskin over her shoulder and held out her hand. "I'm ready."

Their camp was beside a trickle of water on a hillside west of the Plainlands. Karsta left her father staring into the tiny flames of a smokeless fire kindled from very dry wood and climbed to the top of a rockfall. She settled herself on a boulder that seemed stable enough and sat looking out across the plain.

Kekavayt village land was a shimmer of green in the center of a vast round of lifeless yellows and browns, of deserted villages where an oven wind blew dead leaves along empty streets and across the mummified corpses of cows and goats. From where she sat, the villages were only irregular patterns of shadow and the bodies were invisible, but the scenes from the scrying bowl were burnt into her head.

"Like to like," she murmured. "Sorcerer to sorcerer?" She'd met others in the profession since that first walk on the dreamroad, enough to know that placing a mute child with a teacher was not going to be an easy task. She thought about taking the boy to their home in the mountains. Everything in her shouted NO!

"Like to like." She stared at the plain sweltering under a white-hot sun. "Like. To. Like. Water!" She scrambled to her feet, in her excitement nearly tumbling down after the stones she kicked loose. "Water. That's the LIKE she meant."

9

The water in the basin tossed as if a miniature storm blew high crashing waves, color fought with color, dark muddy angry colors. "It's the sorcerer in him," Viritagh murmured. "He's sleeping, I think, but it's fighting me. Remember, Karsti, a wizard up close can outpower a sorcerer if he . . . " He grinned and fluttered a hand at her without taking his eyes off the basin. "Or she can pin the sorcerer down. Trouble is, he can be across the horizon before you finish the ties. Usually."

He bent closer to the basin and whispered Words she didn't try to hear.

Gradually the water stilled and cleared to show the boy curled in a knot, his eyes squeezed shut, his mouth working.

Viritagh whispered again, and gradually the boy relaxed, his breathing slowed, and the scowl vanished from his face.

"Good. That should hold him long enough." He set the bowl on the ground, careful not to disturb the water. "Karsti, you sure they'll come when you call?"

"They always do when I walk the dreamroad. I don't see why they won't when I'm there in body. Bravvy's got more curiosity than a cat and his Mum doesn't like him to get too far off." She held out her hand. "Let's go."

Viritagh watched his daughter run across the waves, the young dolphin leaping and squealing beside her, the older one holding back, watching also. He smiled at her and thought she smiled back, both of them parents, proud and anxious at the same time.

Karsta circled back after that short burst of play, knelt on the water, her head close to the older dolphin. After a moment she stood and waved.

He waved back and went for the boy.

10

Telyon woke in blueness, rocking.

At first he nestled next to the large sleek form beside him, then his hands started moving, searching. All he felt was water. The beads were gone. His Word Book was gone. He gabbled his shapeless sounds while his mind cried out in color patterns, M y W o R d S i W a N t M y W o R d S.

New patterns slipped into his mind, cool and soothing as the seawater he lay in.

Y o U r W o R d S d O w A i t U p O n T h e S a N d F o R wh E n Y o U w A n T th E m C o M e P l A y U n T i L i T s T i M e.

A blue-and-gray tail splashed water into his face, the smaller of the two shapes leaped up and danced on that tail a moment then went leaping away. He felt something strange, hot and strong bubbling up through him. For the first time in his short life, he laughed; then he shifted shape and went racing after the dolphin boy.

WATER EVERYWHERE

NINA KIRIKI HOFFMAN

Nina Kiriki Hoffman lives in Oregon's Willamette Valley where she spends a month or two each year housebound from grass pollen. She has written a novel, The Thread That Binds the Bones, and has achieved considerable recognition for her short stories.

After school Meredith responded to the river's call. Its voice had been murmuring to her through history and math, science and French and lunch. She walked through town and made her way to the water.

The autumn sky promised rain, and the wind whispered of cold coming down from the top of the world, sliding over oceans and mountains, sampling tinted moisture as it came. Meredith, fourteen, was just starting to understand the language of water; she was training in its special disciplines with her *miksash,* her godfather, Uncle Hal. They spent an hour every day near the creek that ran through Chapel Hollow, listening to water murmuring about rocks and soil and little live things, about the taste of distant mountains and clouds. Underneath everything, water sent out constant greetings to itself wherever it was, including within her.

The river had a deeper song than the creek, more powerful and dark, though here near the shore it was almost gentle. She sat on the pebbled slope and took off her shoes and socks, then edged down and dipped her toes into the Columbia. Water welcomed her with a cold smooth embrace. She wiggled her toes, imagining she was tickling water, wondering if it would laugh. It clung to her. Presently it whispered,—Do you give yourself to us?—

She hugged herself and looked out at the river, wide and brown and quiet, an eternity of water. Give herself to it? She would be lost, the way she was lost at home among all her cousins and uncles and aunts and grandparents.

The chill in her toes was spreading, numbing her feet and ankles. She could almost feel herself dissolving. "No," she said, gripping her shoulders tight. "I want to just stay me."

—We release you freely as we took you.—

Uncle Hal had told her that was one thing about water: in liquid state, it accepted anything, it released anything; if it was boiling, steam, or frozen, other aspects of its character surfaced. "Water carries, water drowns; water gives and takes. Water burns and water preserves. Water sustains everything."

Listening to him, Meredith had decided water was the best discipline to have. But when she said as much to Uncle Hal, he had smiled and shook his head. "All disciplines have their strengths, and none could exist without the others. Whatever the Powers give us is wonderful." Then he grinned wider. "However, Sign Water gives you *krifting* and dreamworks, beguiling and trancing, and—" His smile faded. "That was unworthy, Meredith. Just remember water is wonderful."

She wiggled her toes some more. If she gave herself to water, would she fall apart the way splashed water sent out a million drops? If she splattered apart, how would she ever gather together again? Uncle Hal had talked to her about relating to water, using its powers, but never about giving herself to it. She murmured to water, "I don't really want to get away, I just don't want to surrender to you utterly."

"What are you talking about?" asked a voice from behind her.

Meredith glanced back to discover one of her classmates, a town girl named Ruthie, standing booted and jacketed on the bank above her. Meredith's face went stone still, while inside her the voice of one of her other teachers, Great-aunt Fayella, whispered, "Those *tanganar* towns-people are tricky. They'll come close to you sometimes, unless you keep them properly scared away, and they'll be wanting things. They may put on a pleasant face, but always, always remember, underneath they hate you, and they'd kill you if they could."

When Meredith turned to look at her, Ruthie said, "Oh!" Her eyes widened. "I'm sorry! I thought you were Pearl!"

Pearl Delarue did have dark hair about the length and style of Meredith's, and they were the same size. "It's all right," Meredith said gruffly.

"Honestly?" Ruthie said.

"It's honestly all right," said Meredith. She hadn't spoken to Ruthie in years, but she remembered first grade, when they had had desks next to each other in the back row and they had whispered a lot. During recess they had hidden among the trees and compared toys. Ruthie's Barbie had delighted Meredith as much as Meredith's *kletah,* her wooden spirit guardian, had delighted Ruthie. "You *dress* yours?" Meredith had asked Ruthie. "You *feed* yours?" Ruthie had asked Meredith. They learned that they both slept with their toys. Meredith couldn't remember when she and Ruthie had stopped talking to each other.

Ruthie twisted her black braid in her hand, as she had been doing for as long as Meredith had known her. "Can I come down?" she asked.

Meredith looked out at the river. The ripples were oily and quiet. Water did not speak to her. She patted the pebbled slope next to her.

Ruthie scrambled down to sit beside her. They sat a while, staring at the distant shore on the Washington side of the river.

"Are you—uh—Changing now?" Ruthie asked after a long silence.

"Yes," said Meredith without looking at her.

"Does it hurt?"

Thinking of the five-night fever that pulled water out of her, of the juices and broth Uncle Hal had fed into her, of the strange pepper-and-steel taste of Change-drink he had given her, Meredith glanced at Ruthie. "Not much, so far," she said. What she had experienced, what she had seen and heard, had not hurt; it had just *felt.*

Ruthie's dark eyes met Meredith's gaze. Meredith hadn't realized how much she had missed that. No town person would meet her eyes anymore now that she was dangerous. "I'm Sign Water. That's supposed to be the easiest *plakanesh.* I was sick, but it just made me weak. I had visions. Now I get dreams a lot, and hear voices."

"Is that why you were talking to the water?"

"Yeah." Meredith wiggled her toes. "It's weird. Like I have other eyes and ears opening up. I hear things and see things somehow, but I don't know what they mean yet. Sometimes I feel like a baby."

Ruthie grinned a little, then looked away.

"What?" said Meredith, remembering Fayella's words, wondering if Ruthie had some buried reason for coming down to talk to her, when everybody knew that in their teens the townspeople and the Hollow people sorted themselves out and became different from each other. Sometimes they hurt each other. Did Ruthie really want to kill her?

"I was just thinking. A lot of the time my cat is looking at something, but when I look I can't figure out what it is. I wish I could see through her eyes. And dogs. They can smell things like they know what's going on in the next county. Is it like that?"

"Sort of." Meredith smiled. She had two cousins who went animal; it was their job, taking care of the sheep and cows, herding the deer. They changed into animals to learn what was bothering the stock. It was mostly a power of Sign Earth. Neither of them talked much about what it felt like, and for the first time, Meredith wondered.

"Can you—can you fly?"

Meredith looked at Ruthie, who looked back. There were rules at the Hollow against talking about such things to outsiders, but Ruthie had grown up in Arcadia, and everybody who had grown up in Arcadia knew quite a bit about the people who lived in the Hollow.

"I want to," said Meredith. "Uncle Hal says I probably will, once I understand how water gets from the river up to the clouds. I've been working on it, but water goes into this other form that speaks a language I don't know yet." She glanced up and a drop hit her nose.

Soon more drops were falling around them, slapping the pebbles and the river's surface and wetting their clothes. Meredith gave her toes a final wiggle and pulled her feet up, sliding wet socks onto them. Ruthie put the hood of her jacket up and pushed her hands into her pockets.

"How are you going to get home?" Ruthie asked. "You missed the school bus. Aren't you freezing? You don't even have a jacket."

"The cold is . . . the cold is . . . " Meredith paused, trying to think about it. The raindrops were cold against her and her wet feet were cold, and yet the cold was an embrace, a shield, almost a friend. Water.

Water was her friend, but there was no river direct to her home. Home was twenty miles away. She put on her shoes, checked her watch. "Melantha's still at her fiddle lesson. Aunt Kiara will stop by to pick her up in ten minutes, and I'll catch a ride with her."

"Oh," said Ruthie.

Meredith got to her feet. Until Ruthie had asked her she hadn't even thought about getting home. It was complicated because the Hollow had no phones, but often someone from the Hollow was here in Arcadia doing errands. Cousin Dirk, a lawyer, even had an office in town, with a *tanganar* receptionist, but he was only in the office a couple days a week. Meredith held out a hand and helped Ruthie up.

"Meredith?" Ruthie said, brushing off the seat of her pants. Rain fell all about them, kissing them with brief cold pats.—We touch you we touch everything we seep into everything we find the lowest level we enter everything we leave everything behind we fall we fall we melt we rise we rise we travel we embrace we change we do not change—sang the drops.

"Yes?" Meredith said, only half hearing Ruthie.

"I'm glad we talked."

"I am too," said Meredith impulsively, and then Fayella's words spoke in her mind in a loud voice edged with command.—Keep them away from you! They want something from you. They want to kill you. You cannot trust them. They will hurt you unless you own them. Stay away from them!—Meredith shook her head, trying to get the voice out of it. She looked at Ruthie and felt the warm sugar sweetness of sitting under green leaves on a spring afternoon fingering Barbie's clothes, and talking, talking, talking. "I miss you," she said in a strangled voice to Ruthie.

"I miss you too," said Ruthie, but then her eyes focused past Meredith, and her face went frightened and pale.

Ruthie turned and ran away up the bank.

Meredith looked behind her and saw her Cousin Carroll standing on the shore only a few feet away. He stood relaxed, tall and blond and slouched, hands buried in his pockets; yet tension radiated from him. She had never noticed that before, had always thought he was cool and lazy and mean. How did she know he was tense? She searched his face, sniffed the air, listened for a hint, then realized: the rain was whispering it to her. He smiled and strolled to join her. "I don't think you have the technique down," he said. "You're not supposed to scare them. Yet."

She frowned at him. "What are you doing here?"

"That's no way to talk to an elder," he said.

He was right; he was the most powerful member of his generation, intimidating people in their thirties and forties, though he was only twenty-two. He had a reputation for playing practical jokes that hurt, and until she and her sign could work together, she was wide-open to them. She had been fortunate until now; mostly she had escaped his notice. She stared down at the pebbles.

"Better," he said. "I was watching that beautiful girl. Would you like her to come live with us?"

Meredith looked up at him. Fayella had been encouraging them to kidnap people and bring them to the Hollow, to make up for the way Family members had been dying for the last twenty years, young and not well. There was too much maintenance work and not enough hands to do it. Fayella had been teaching them all about fetchcasting and telling them to keep their eyes open for strong friendly strangers who had no family to worry if they should disappear. "No!" she said. They were not to take town people. "Ruthie lives here! She has six brothers and sisters, and parents, and her grandma lives with them. She's off-limits!"

"Limits are made to be broken." He smiled.

"You're just saying that to be mean," said Meredith, meeting his gaze with her own, but feeling scared.

Carroll glanced after Ruthie, though she was out of sight. "No, I'm not. I find her very beautiful—young and so full of promise. If it were possible, I would invite her to come with us. But you're right. I'm not ready to defy custom so completely yet. Would you like me to take you home?"

She felt suspicious. She had never known Carroll to do favors for anyone, though he did his job of hunting and gathering well and without complaint. She sighed. "Yes, please," she said.

"I'm going to be quite small while I fly, so I think you would be better as something very portable," he said, smiling at her, and lifting his hands to cast. At the first flickering of his fingers, she felt a crushing pressure from all directions; every bone in her body felt as if it was cracking and grinding to powder, her muscles turning to jelly. When the pressure stopped she could not see, hear, smell, speak, taste, or feel. Locked in darkness, initially she just waited. It was not the first time somebody else in her family had transformed her, but it was the worst shape, whatever it was, that she had ever been in. She could not even tell for sure if time was passing; she had no reference points.

After three forevers she thought perhaps there was something she could do to escape. Water, she thought, questing for her element, listening with her other ears, searching with her other eyes.

Water was everywhere.

Water flowed hot near her, though held away by meshed and layered barriers. Water was also trapped in the barriers, present but unmoving.—Help me,—she whispered without a mouth to the flowing heat.

It heard her and, though its river was flowing and passing, coming toward her, going away, water reached out with a part of itself that was not physical, the flowing energy from the side-by-side place, and stroked her. At last she could feel: warmth and comfort. Help. Water washed away the restraints holding her into this uncomfortable form, whispering,—Child of ours, how can you be stone? If you give yourself to us, you can be water instead.—

She thought of the geometry of a splash, of scattered drops that never collected in the same place again. She though of how the river was always coming toward and going away, how water was everything that moved. She thought about lying formless in crushing darkness.—I give myself to you,—she said. It couldn't be any worse than being the way she was.

With a great rushing and pushing outward, she changed away from the form into which Carroll had packed her. She was many and one at the same time, clinging to herself, releasing herself; flowing, soaking, alive to the air, which was cool, and the fabric—she realized she had been a stone in Carroll's pocket, for now she was soaking into his pants, touching him intimately and impersonally as she ran down his legs, and all she cared about was that his flesh was warm and the water under it was still speaking encouragingly to her, even as gravity invited her downward and Carroll danced with surprise.—Cling to what you want, release what you wish to get away from,—whispered the water in Carroll's blood.

She flooded out of Carroll's clothes, releasing the fibers, and ran away from his skin, letting go of the hairs that invited her to cling and linger. She spread on the stone floor.

Stone whispered,—Do you want me to swallow you? I would welcome you inside.—

Without a mouth, she replied,—No, thank you. I don't want to disappear.—She could feel the porous nature of the rock beneath her, every opening tickling her with invitation, but after she spoke, stone closed its many mouths and lay smooth and solid under her.

—Thank you,—she whispered. She knew she was one body of water and many drops; but she wasn't sure all her drops would come back to her body if she let them seep down to mingle with stone. The sensations she was feeling were too new to trust. Uncle Hal, in their many sessions by the creek, had never told her about the possibility of *becoming* water; she didn't know any of the rules.

She lay quiet. It was such a relief not to be cramped down into herself, instead to lie here large as she wanted to be. She knew from speaking to the stone floor that she was in the kitchen cavern at Chapel Hollow now, so Carroll had actually brought her home somehow.

Fabric entered her, full of invitations to join with it, soak in and make it large and heavy. At first she reached up into it, loving the stimulation of weaving in among its threads, seeping into the threads themselves, meshing with them as if they became her skin and bones; but then the cloth lifted away, separating her from part of herself. The self in the cloth released its hold on the threads and flowed back down through the air to join her on the floor.

She realized that some of her was warming and leaving her, rising through air. But instead of feeling that she was losing herself, she felt as if she were spreading wider, being more; the part of her in the air was telling her where things were in the room, what the ceiling felt like, and how many small warm creatures full of water were there, watching, how everything breathed and how water moved in and out on those breaths. Air whispered,—With fire's aid, I can carry you.—

—Fire, please help. Air, please help,—murmured Meredith.—Stone, thank you for your help. I release you freely.—

Fire sent warmth to her and air held out many hands to help lift her. She slipped into a diffuse state, floating up toward the ceiling, spreading wide and touching other water already present. Now she could sense with other eyes and ears that people moved through the kitchen; stone had formed one big table and many chairs, and people, warm walking reservoirs, were rippling the air with talk. She couldn't understand what they were saying, but she knew some of it was loud because the waves coming from their mouths were stronger.

She reached out wider and spread all the way to the meal preparation area in the kitchen's far end, where other people stirred, some letting water out of things, some mingling water with other things and heating it over fire.

Above the fire she felt excited, and near the heat of bodies she could move quickly. Breath tugged at her, but she let other water flow past her into bodies. Where the room was cool, she felt slow and as if she wanted to lean into gravity's embrace again and collect herself.

For a while she stayed where she was, experiencing heat and space and diffusion, using her new strange senses without understanding everything they were telling her. One part of her breathed continuing prayers of thanks to water, fire, air, and to stone, which enclosed the volume of space where she was. The rest was busy just being.

But at last she decided she wanted to be herself again. She wondered with sleepy alarm if that was something she could manage.—Water—she whispered.—Thank you for teaching me to be like you. Can I become like myself again?—

—This is yourself.—

—Can you teach me to take human form again?—

Water laughed, as if she had tickled it.—Freely we accepted you and freely we release you.—

Stone was cool under her feet—she had feet again—at her back a fire burned, pressing heat into her skin—her hair was wet and heavy on her head—she could smell meat roasting and herbs and onions simmering, and knew she was hungry—people were arguing down the cavern, Great-aunt Agatha's voice rising louder than the others—someone near her gasped.

"Miss Meredith!"

Still breathing as if it were something she barely knew how to do, Meredith turned to face Delia, the oldest fetch at the Hollow. They were near the big cooking fireplace in the food prep area.

"Miss Meredith, what—" Delia glanced at Meredith's face, then down, then up again. Meredith looked down and discovered she was naked and somewhat damp. She bit her lower lip.

Delia took off her apron and held it out, hesitating as if unsure how her action would be interpreted.

"Thanks," said Meredith, accepting the apron. Water was locked into its fibers, but when Meredith whispered to it the water slipped out and stretched the fabric into a thin wide cloak. She wrapped it around her.

"What—" Delia said, then put a hand over her mouth.

Meredith cocked her head and looked at Delia. Delia had been a safe person here in the Hollow, where most of Meredith's relatives had their scary sides. Delia had scolded occasionally, but more often she praised and patted. Delia had never acted frightened of Meredith before. Then again, Meredith had never seen anyone pull a piece of fabric into a new shape. How had she known how to do it? "It's kind of complicated," she said.

"You've Changed," said Delia.

"Maybe," said Meredith. "I guess . . . " She tried to smile. "I guess that might have been *plakanesh.*" She looked up at the ceiling, remembering being everywhere in the room. She had Changed, but her relationship with Delia didn't have to. She had Changed, but Ruthie might still be her friend, or be her friend again, if she was careful. She had Changed. She didn't have to let Change consume everything about her, the way she had seen it treat others, turning them unfriendly or distant or strange. Water changed, yet it stayed the same.

Delia reached into a pocket, came out with a wax paper–wrapped piece of hard taffy. *"Kisranev,"* she said, and offered a smile.

"Thanks," said Meredith, startled. She took the candy, then glanced over her shoulder at the conference table.

"How could you be so irresponsible?" cried Aunt Agatha's voice. "Have you forgotten what Family means?"

"It's about you," Delia murmured. "They said Carroll lost you, and they've been trying to find you for the last half hour."

Meredith grinned. "Guess I better go get found. Thanks, Delia. Thanks for *ranevkis*."

With the taste of sugar sweetening her mouth, Delia's congratulations still sounding in her ear, and Delia's thin wet apron wrapped around her, Meredith walked toward her family. Water murmured from everything, air, stone, even in the smoke of fire. All of its words were friendly.

"You *forgot* my daughter? You *lost* my daughter? How could you?" cried Meredith's mother. "You transformed her! You held connection to her! Where is she?"

"I tell you I don't know," Carroll said in an angry voice.

"I'm here. I'm okay," Meredith said, stepping up to the table.

"Meredith!" "Where were you?" She lost herself in their concern and dismay, looking over her mother's head at Carroll, remembering that even his blood had been her friend.

She thought of relaxing shape and finding Ruthie again after years of holding to the restrictive form assigned to her by Family, and of how water had freed her from being locked into rock. If anyone worked change on her again, she could work her own change to water and find her way home.—I accept you freely. I release you freely,—thought Meredith. She felt one of her feet dissolving into water, thought sternly at it until it turned back into a foot. Maybe not too freely. Not just yet. Some things were worth hanging on to.

She pressed her smile against her mother's shoulder.

La Curandera

Margaret Ball

Margaret Ball lives in Austin, Texas, with her husband, two children, three cats, a dog, and a hermit crab. She has a B.A. in mathematics and a Ph.D. in linguistics from the University of Texas. Recent publications include The Shadow Gate *(1991),* Flameweaver *(1991),* Changeweaver *(1992) and* No Earthly Sunne *(1994), all from Baen. She has also coauthored* Partnership *with Anne McCaffrey. When not writing she plays the flute, makes quilts, and raises children at home in her spare time.*

Coming out of school, Jen kept her head down like always. Don't mess with nobody and nobody won't mess with you, Phil always told her. It didn't work any better here than it had in her old school. She looked at the sidewalk and held her books against her chest and tried not to hear the boys snickering behind her. Two of them had cornered her in the breezeway that morning. "Just want to see if they're real," one of them said. And they wouldn't let her past until old lady Whittaker came out and told them all three to stop scuffling around and get to homeroom.

Now that Mexican girl was walking beside her, talking as if she couldn't tell Jen only wanted to be let alone. "What're you gonna do for the science fair?" Teresa asked.

"Haven't thought of anything yet," Jen mumbled.

"Me neither." Teresa shifted her notebook to the other arm. She had a brown paper sack in that hand. "I was gonna stay and look in the library, try and get some ideas. But today I gotta go up the hill and take some stuff to my aunt."

"Hey-hey-hey, Teresa baby, you gonna ask the witch for a love potion?" Clayton hooted, with his hands cupped around his mouth.

Teresa flushed and looked away. "*Tia Caterina* isn't a witch," she explained in a low voice, as though she thought Jen might take Clayton's teasing seriously. "She's a *curandera*."

"A . . . healer?" Jen translated hesitantly.

Teresa giggled. "That's all old superstition. Me and my folks, we don't believe in it. Of course when my cousin Monica was tryin' to have a baby . . . " She went off into a long involved story about how her cousin tried this and tried that and you couldn't really be sure what worked, but Monica swore up and down it was *Tia* Caterina's herbs, finishing with, "Anyway, she lives up on La Loma, you probably wouldn't want to go up there." Teresa jerked her chin towards the back of the school, where rows of shabby unpainted frame houses lined treeless streets that looked exactly as flat as everything else in this piece of West Texas.

Loma meant hill in Spanish, Jen knew that much. "Where's the hill?"

Teresa giggled. "Well, I guess you gotta live here four or five years before you can see it, but it does slope a little bit."

Would it be pushy to tell Teresa she'd like to walk with her? Or was the other girl just trying to get rid of her politely? It didn't make any difference, Jen realized, because here was Phil's dirty white pickup truck pulling up beside them. Becca leaned out of the back, curls bouncing, shouting, "Jen-Jen-Jenny, come *on*, Daddy Phil's been waiting and waiting!"

Jen looked at Phil's face. He was hunched over the wheel, thin shoulders tense. Was he mad at her for keeping him waiting? She opened the door and climbed up into the high front seat of the pickup. The upholstery on this side was frayed, and springs poked into her bottom when she tried to sit near the window, so she had to scoot over close to the gearshift. As soon as she'd closed the door Phil stepped on the gas and the pickup chugged away from the curb.

The reflection of Phil's rimless glasses gleamed in the windshield. Sparks of light shot off the bumper of the car ahead of them. "Any luck with a job today?" Jen asked, then bit her lip: wrong thing to say. She knew that even before Phil's hands clenched white over the steering wheel.

"I'm not taking no stoop labor work like some damn uneducated Meskin," Phil said, not looking at her. "Stupid town, no work fit for a white man to do. An educated man that reads books. How's a man going to get anywhere in a dump like this." It wasn't a question.

The cab was full of Phil's books, battered paperbacks from the Book Swap Shop in Houston. Mostly Mack Bolan series. He let Jen look at those and his *Soldier of Fortune* magazines if she wanted to, but he yelled at her if she picked up the ones with the other kind of covers, the smiling ladies with not much on. Jen didn't care, she didn't want to read any of his books. The war stories were dumb, all about people shooting each other and blowing up buildings. If Jen wanted to kill somebody, she wouldn't be stupid enough to make a big noise and a mess while she did it; she'd use something quiet and secret, like poison. As for the other kind of books, she knew all she needed to know about that stuff, too.

She turned her mind off and stared slack-jawed at the shimmering waves of hot air rising off the street. Phil went on about this stupid hick town with no decent jobs for an educated man, and she didn't say *You made us move here from Houston because you said the Meskins and niggers were taking all the jobs there.* She thought it, though. She thought it so loud, seemed like Phil would have to pick the words right out of her head if he ever shut up for a minute.

In the back of the truck, Becca hung on to the side and made train noises. When Jen twisted her head to look back, she could see Becca's curly hair blowing in the wind the pickup made, blowing out so hard it was almost straight. She wished she were back there with Becca, pretending to be a train or Superman and letting the wind blow everything else out of her mind.

Something brushed her thigh and Jen twitched, tried to cram both her legs sidewise out of Phil's way.

"God's sakes, kid, I'm just tryin' to change gears. Can't you sit still and not bother me?"

Jen slid sideways until the seam of her jeans caught on the spring that poked up in the worn-out upholstery.

"Ruinin' good clothes now." Phil swerved, cut off a cherry red Isuzu, slammed his hand on the horn for no reason that Jen could see. "Get back over here where you won't tear your jeans."

Reluctantly she moved back toward Phil. This time he let his hand rest on her leg after he downshifted. "I'll get in back," she said.

The last traffic light in town turned red in front of them. Phil jammed on the brakes. "You just do that little thing. If'n you can't sit still like a big girl, you can ride in the back and Becca can come up here with me."

"I'll stay," Jen said quickly.

Phil laughed under his breath and took off without waiting for the light to change. He swerved between cars ahead, needing both hands on the wheel now. Jen tried to think of something neutral to say, something that would engage his attention and make him be pleased with her for a change. "I think I made a friend at school today."

"You did! What kind of a friend? If you've been hanging out with those boys I saw you with this morning—"

"A girlfriend," Jen interrupted. She was interrupting herself more than Phil, before she could say *If you saw them, why didn't you make them stop?* "Her name's Teresa Ramos. We have science together. And you know what, Phil, she said a funny thing this afternoon—"

"I don't want you hangin' around with no dirty greasers," Phil interrupted. Jen bit her lip. She'd wanted to tell him what Teresa said about La Loma, about how you had to live out in West Texas four or five years before it started looking like a hill to you, but somehow she'd started wrong and made Phil mad again.

"I'm not hanging out with her exactly," she said instead. "She just walked up and started talking to me after school. I couldn't do anything about it."

"Yeah. Well, I guess you gotta go to school with them, but you don't gotta act like they're as good as we are. Govmint oughta ship all them lazy Meskins back over the river where they come from stead of letting them come here and live off our welfare and our food stamps. And taking all the jobs that oughta go to a white man." Phil's hand slipped down to squeeze Jen's thigh rhythmically while he talked. She stared into the white glare of the dusty road. Out here at the edge of town the pavement ran out before the houses did. Like the town didn't ever really come to an end, it just slowly dried up and blew away: first blacktop streets lined with stores and houses, then a gravel road and a few unpainted frame houses, then white dust that rose in slow lazy puffs around them like the smoke from a pile of burning trash.

Jen and Becca didn't have proper beds yet, just two folding cots that Mama borrowed from a lady down the street until Phil found work and they could get them some good furniture. Becca's cot was so flimsy that it squeaked every time she took a deep breath. Jen lay in the dark listening to Becca breathing and sleeping and the rhythmic squeak, squeak, squeak of the cot's metal frame. What time was it, eleven, twelve? Mama's shift waiting tables at the Bide-A-Spell Inn wouldn't be over until two o'clock. She'd know it was almost time for Mama to be home when she heard the sound of Phil's pickup starting, when he went to go get her.

The line of light under the door widened, stretched out into a triangle of lamplight spilled across the bare uneven boards. Becca mumbled something and flung up one plump hand over her eyes.

"Hush, Becca," Jen whispered, "it's all right. Go to sleep."

Phil shut the door and tiptoed forward to sit on the edge of Jen's cot. His weight tipped the frame to one side. "You oughta be asleep by now."

Jen closed her eyes and tried to breathe deep like Becca, slow and deep and even, matching the steady rhythm of little squeaks from Becca's cot.

"That's good, that's my good girl." A hand stroked her shoulder, moved downward.

Slow and deep and even.

Both cots squeaked regularly.

After a while the weight on her moved away. Jen kept her eyes closed. She heard steps and the door and then there was nothing in the room but her and Becca and the friendly shadows. If she could stay in the shadows, she would be safe. Nothing but shadows. Nothing happening. Nothing happened.

A long while later she heard the pickup start.

Mornings were a rush, her and Becca both trying to get washed and dressed and out of the house without waking Mama, and Phil cursing them both under his breath. If they had an alarm clock, Jen could get up earlier and they could walk to school. She always overslept in the morning. She felt so tired, too. She didn't know why, it wasn't like she stayed up late watching TV or anything.

Running a comb through her short hair, she stared into the cracked greenish bathroom mirror. A green girl stared back at her, pale and quiet. Jen felt like there should be a mark on her forehead, something that told everybody she wasn't a real person. Maybe there was something like that, and she was the only one who couldn't see it. She squinted into the mirror until she felt like she was going into that green place. She could stay there and send the reflection to school instead. Who'd know the difference? They were both imitation people.

She drifted through the day in that mood. Nothing mattered, nobody could touch her, she was only a reflection, she wasn't really there at all. She sat in the back row and doodled through all the classes. Make an elaborate J, draw a box around it, then fill in the whole box with solid black pencil strokes. As if the J had never even been there.

She dawdled after the last bell, waiting for the hall to clear, and Miz Broussard caught her. "Wait a minute, Jennifer," she said. "I would like to talk with you about your science project."

Jen looked down at the brown tile floor. Talking was dangerous. It could pull her out of the safe place she'd found, the mirror place.

"Jennifer," Broussard repeated. She was a tiny woman, no taller than Jen, even with that big knot of wiry black hair piled on top of her head. Had to look up just a little to meet Jen's eyes. "Is that what they call you?" she asked. "Or Jenny?"

"Jen." Short as it could be, shrink it down to nothing.

"Jen, your family just moved here from Houston, is that right?"

Jen barely nodded.

"You seem to be having, I don't know, a difficult time adjusting. I feel as though you're not really *there* in class. Is there anything I can help with?"

Jen looked down and picked at the dry skin flaking off her arm. What did she mean, *help?*

"I have a terrible time with dry skin too," Broussard said, startling Jen so that she stopped digging her nails into her arm. "When we first moved here, oh my!" She laughed under her breath. "We come from Louisiana, you know. My first year out here, I thought I just might dry up and blow away."

"I feel that way sometimes," Jen said, surprising herself. She remembered the white clouds of dust rising around Phil's pickup, the dry baking heat of the sun on the roof.

"You can be rubbing in hand lotion all day long and it seems like it doesn't help. I don't know, you get used to it, but I think this country doesn't like people. Or plants. The more I water my petunias, the more they just turn up their toes and die on me. I've got a whole graveyard of murdered pot plants at home."

Jen had to work to keep from grinning at that. "It might make a good science project," she said tentatively. "If a person could, I don't know, start two plants and leave one out in the dry air all the time and find some way to keep the other one moist. I mean, maybe it's not enough just to feed and water them. Maybe they need the right atmosphere."

Mrs. Broussard's whole face sparkled, and she nodded so energetically that two of her bone hairpins poked themselves out of the coiling black bun. "That's a great idea! Why don't you come along to the lab with me right now, and we'll see if there aren't some supplies that could help you get started."

The hall was empty by now. Phil would be waiting, getting mad. Or maybe not waiting. Jen pushed the thought out of her mind. She felt happy and interested in something for the first time in so long, walking down the hall with Broussard, talking like one real person to another.

"Plastic sheeting—"

"—but transparent, not the black kind—"

"—and I could use an old Windex bottle for a mister—"

Miz Whittaker plowed down the hall like a big old calico print balloon. Jen tried not to see her, but she planted herself right in front of the two of them.

"Mary Louise Broussard, I have to warn you about this little girl," Whittaker rumbled.

She started telling about yesterday in the breezeway, only different, making it sound like Jen had *wanted* to be stuck out there with those boys. Jen could feel her face getting hot. She'd left her schoolbooks in the locker. She crossed her arms over her chest, but it didn't help. So much for Broussard. She wasn't going to want to talk to somebody who was already labeled, like, a bad character or something. She sure wasn't going to listen to anything a person might say.

"Excuse me," she interrupted. "My stepfather's waiting outside. I gotta go."

She took off down the hall without looking back, not quite running, not even caring that she was going the wrong way to meet Phil out front of the school. The hot afternoon light outside shimmered on the polished hall floor, made it look like she was running over a brown lake full of autumn light. Then she was in the light, sun and fire blazing all around her, and it didn't help; she still felt cold and dark inside. Years and years of invisible black marks washed over her: *dirty girl crazy Jen space case I have to warn you about this little girl* "and it never changes!" she whispered. "Never stops, never changes!" All the crazy stupid worthless things she'd ever done or said came and sat on her shoulder, the way Phil looked disgusted when she did something wrong like hanging out with Mexicans, the boys crowding her in the hall and the hands coming out of nowhere, and then Miz Whittaker staring at her chest like it was her idea to be, what did the teacher last year call it, *early developer,* like it was something dirty. Maybe it was. Maybe that was how those boys and Miz Whittaker and everybody could *tell* about her, there was just something wrong with her that couldn't ever be fixed, so it was all right whatever they wanted to do, it didn't count didn't happen she couldn't stop it.

Then she thought of one way she could make all of it stop, right now, and she stood still in the white-bright glare of the afternoon sun and looked around her, real carefully. She'd already come a good part of the way she would need to go, running out the back of the school like that as if she didn't know Phil would be waiting for her, didn't know which way was home. All around her now were brown yards in which the grass had given up, discouraged by months of hot dry sun, and brown frame houses with porches that sagged down close to the burnt brown grass.

A brown baby in a diaper sucked its fingers on the porch nearest her, staring at her with big black eyes. Window air conditioners and fans whirred up and down the block, and cicadas buzzed. From somewhere farther away she could hear the sound of music, the tinny sound of a radio tuned to the Spanish-language station. The house on the corner had a sign on the porch, Tien-something . . . so faded she couldn't read the letters. A girl with a baby on her hip pushed open the screen door and came out with a brown paper sack in her free hand. It must be some kind of store. And it was okay for girls to go in there.

When she opened the screen door, the buzz of conversation stopped. Three old men turned their heads and stared at her.

"Could you tell me where *Tia* Caterina lives?" Jen asked.

Teresa's *tia* wasn't any older than Mama, maybe younger. There were wings of white hair at her forehead, but her skin was smooth and her eyes looked livelier than Mama's—like life hadn't worn her out yet. She wasn't dressed like a witch, either. She was just a plump middle-aged woman with smooth skin and shiny dark hair, wearing a powder blue polyester skirt and blouse that were a little too tight around her waist, and shiny black patent leather sandals that were also a little too tight on her small feet.

And the house, the one room they were sitting in, anyway, didn't look like what Jen had expected either. Not that it looked like anything she'd ever seen before. Every inch of the walls was covered with pictures, mostly pretty young women with their eyes raised to heaven. The young women wore trailing shawls over their heads, usually blue but sometimes red or pink, and their cheeks were softly tinted and there were sequins and glitter glued on the pictured shawls. Around the faces there were other pictures: hearts with knives in them, and crosses, and suns with bright golden rays shooting out.

The two small tables were covered with similar things—velvet cloths with trailing fringes, candles grouped in twos and threes, little statues that looked like the pretty women in the pictures. Or maybe they were dolls. Jen wasn't sure; a couple of the statues had real clothes on, stiff with sequins and gilt braid, like queen or braid dolls.

"You gone tell me what you come for?" said *Tia* Caterina after Jen had had a good long chance to examine the room.

"I don't think you can give it to me," Jen said. She looked again at one of the pictures, a particularly gruesome one of a three-dimensional heart pierced with a dagger and dripping very realistic blood. That looked sinister enough. Maybe this woman was a witch after all. "Do you know about herbs and things?"

"I know a little," *Tia* Caterina said. "What is your sickness?"

"Nothing. I just want to find out something. For a science project at school," Jen improvised. She rushed on before she could think better of it. "Do you, like, know about anything that grows around here that's poisonous? I mean, that would kill people?"

The *curandera* laughed. "You want me to think you come to *Tia* Caterina for help with a science project? An Anglo child from the Anglo school!" She laughed again. "Tell me what you really want, now. It is for a joke? The other kids dared you to come here, hmm?"

"It's not a joke," Jen said. "Teresa Ramos told me about you. She said you help people."

"Sometimes I do," *Tia* Caterina said, "but I am not a *bruja*, and I do not give poisons to children."

"I promise you it wouldn't hurt anybody else."

"Can you be sure of that?"

The *curandera* stared into her eyes. Jen was about to nod yes, she was sure, when for some reason she thought about riding home with Phil yesterday. *If'n you can't sit still like a big girl, you can ride in the back and Becca can come up here with me.*

"But what else can I do?" she cried. "I try to stop it and it just goes on and on and it gets worse and everybody can tell—"

"Tell what?"

"That there's something wrong with me," Jen whispered, "I shouldn't be here . . . Born rotten, Phil says. . . ."

"You hurt somebody bad?"

"No," Jen said, "but I've wanted to."

"Never mind *wanted*. What you done that's so bad?"

Jen shook her head slowly. Tears blurred her vision; she dragged the back of her hand across her face, but the tears kept coming. "Not what I've done. What I am." *No good, crazy, trashy, bad attitude, I have to warn you about this little girl.* "It goes on and on and never stops and I thought I found a way to stop it but you won't help me. Teresa said you help people. I guess she was wrong."

She started to stand up, but *Tia* Caterina laid one hand very lightly on her shoulder. "When you go to an Anglo doctor, you tell him what medicine you need?"

Jen shook her head.

"Okay, and you don't tell *Tia* Caterina neither, understand? I got to find out what ails you, then I'll know what can help. First we better find out if you got *mal ojo* or *susto* or you been *embrujada.* Anybody been praising you lately, saying good things with a bad heart, saying things that sound good from far away but not touching you? No? Then it's not *mal ojo.*"

Tia Caterina asked several more questions, then stepped into the hall and came back with an egg in her hand. She passed it over Jen's head and face, down one arm and up the other. Jen stared at it but it just looked like an ordinary egg to her. *Tia* Caterina smiled as if she knew what Jen was thinking, but she didn't stop moving the egg around, always just a half inch away from touching Jen. When it reached Jen's midsection there was a cracking sound, though Jen hadn't seen *Tia* Caterina's hand squeezing, and some of the egg white spilled out of the cracked shell. *Tia* Caterina caught the runny egg white in a bowl that Jen hadn't noticed a moment before, dropped the cracked egg into the bowl, and set it on one of the little tables.

"You got the bad kind of *susto,*" she announced, "the kind somebody else put on your spirit. We got to spin that out of you again, put it back where it belongs." She handed Jen a kind of greeting card with a frame of blue and red flowers and some words written in the middle. "We gone use *Las Doce Verdades,* the Twelve Truths. Got it in English here for you. Study this good, because when we get started I gone need you to say this with me. And you don't stop, no matter what happens, until we finish."

Jen had to hold the card almost up to her nose to read the spidery script. *Tia* Caterina gave her a minute to study it while she lit three white candles, murmuring something Jen couldn't understand. Then she seated herself again facing Jen. This time she was holding a long needle that flashed in the candlelight.

"Don't worry, I'm not gone to stick you!" she said with a laugh. "You study that card good?"

"Yes, but—I'm not a Catholic, you know," Jen said uncertainly.

Tia Caterina smiled. "Don't matter. The saints can work their miracles whether you believe in them or not. You think they need you to make them real? Now you read that card! You start with the first one, then you say number two and number one, then number three and so forth, until we done all twelve, you understand?" And she started saying the words in Spanish, half-singing them, motioning at Jen to keep up in English from the words on her printed card.

"Una es la Casa Santa de Jerusalem, donde Jesucristo . . . "

". . . where Jesus Christ lives and reigns forevermore," Jen read.

"Me ayuden y me protejan, amen."

"Help me and protect me, amen. Two for the two tables of Moses, one for the Holy House of Jerusalem . . . "

Tia Caterina was twirling the silver needle while she chanted the Twelve Truths. Jen thought she saw something black and sticky clinging to the needle. She gasped, but the *curandera* was moving right along to the Third Truth, and Jen had to squint at her card to keep up. When they got to "Seven is for the seven last words," she saw that the needle was almost all covered with black thread now. The thread looped down from the tip of the needle in a long curve, down and then up and through her shirt. She could feel a tugging deep inside her.

"Me ayuden y me protejan, amen."

"Help me and protect me, amen. Nine is for the nine months that most holy Mary carried Jesus Christ in her womb, eight is for the eight sorrows . . . "

The tugging hurt. No, it didn't. It felt . . . strange. Empty. When Jen looked at the black thread she could remember how it felt when she was coming here. Hopeless. Bad. *No good, crazy Jen, space case, trashy . . .*

The thread was stuck. *Tia* Caterina yanked at it and pointed to the card in Jen's hand. She'd forgotten to read, hearing only the black thread, feeling only the acid that dripped out of it. "Ten for the Ten Commandments, nine for the nine months, eight for the eight sorrows . . . " *Tia* Caterina nodded approval and twirled the needle around and around while the black sticky thread poured out of Jen, faster and thicker, until Jen thought she must be all empty inside. She was afraid to look; it made her sick and dizzy. They were on the last line now. "The twelve apostles, the eleven thousand virgins, the Ten Commandments, the nine months, the eight sorrows, the seven words, the six candlesticks, the five wounds, the four Gospels, the three divine persons, the two tables of Moses, and the

Holy House of Jerusalem where Jesus Christ lives and reigns forever-more, *me ayuden y me protejan,* amen."

There was a sharp tearing feeling inside her. For a moment Jen thought she was going to faint, or bleed to death, or both. Then she looked down. *Tia* Caterina was winding the last of the black thread into a neat, glossy, black ball. Only the shining silver tip of the needle showed.

"You gone be tired now," said *Tia* Caterina, handing Jen the ball. It felt sticky, but it didn't burn her skin the way she imagined the black acid eating her up from inside. "But you don't sleep until you get rid of this thing, else it'll crawl back inside you. Understand?"

"You mean, throw it away?" Jen looked around the little room for a wastebasket.

Tia Caterina shook her head. "I've done my part. Now you got to help yourself. This isn't yours. You give it back to whoever it belongs to. Then you'll be through. Oh, it'll come back, bits and pieces, times when you're tired or lonesome. But you just keep saying the *Doce Verdades* and spinning it out of you, you'll be all right. You know how now. You have to name it, you have to give it back, you have to call for help. You know what to do."

Jen wasn't sure of that. She didn't even know how to pay *Tia* Caterina, or if she should pay her. She walked through the dusty downslope of La Loma, heading back past the school for the other side of town, where the streets were just as unpaved and the houses were just as shabby. The black ball stuck to her palm. There were clouds covering the sky now, and a smell like rain in the air, but she felt twice as hot and sweaty as before. Small breezes sprang up, whipped scraps of paper across the dry brown yards and tugged at her skirts and didn't cool anything off.

When she got home at last, the house was empty and eerily silent. Mama must have taken Becca to work with her because Jen wasn't there to watch her. The pickup truck was gone, too.

Jen was too tired to think. She wanted to wash the dust and sweat off, but she couldn't figure out how to take a bath without putting down the black ball. So she sat at the card table where they had their meals, counting on the uncomfortable folding chair to keep her awake. Her head was almost down to the table when the pickup screeched into the dusty driveway and a door slammed.

As Phil came yelling in the front door, Jen jumped to her feet and made it out the back. He was nasty-drunk, mean drunk, and she knew better than to let him corner her in that mood. He followed her, shouting about sluts and trash and running around in Meskin slums and how it was time somebody took her in hand and taught her a good lesson. He grabbed for her arm and Jen dodged just in time. She was fixing to take off along the alley when the black ball got heavier, so heavy she could hardly move, like it was sticking her to this spot.

Everything slowed down. The clouds were heavy overhead and the little winds were plucking at her sleeve and something whistled in the leaves of the cottonwood. Phil moved slow, like a man coming through water, and the look on his face was like the feeling in the black thread. *No good lazy hopeless tramp slut crazy dumb . . .*

And Jen knew what she had to do. It took all her strength to lift the black ball, like raising a tombstone in one hand, but when it was chest high it got lighter. "This is yours," she said, and pushed it straight at Phil.

The black thread started spinning loose in midair, like a cloud between them, like a shiny black cone around the needle, a funnel shape that stretched from the ground to the tops of the cottonwoods along the river and stretched out time with it. And whatever Phil was saying got lost in the roaring like a freight train coming down out of control.

"I'm sorry about your stepfather," Teresa Ramos said next week, when they let Jen and Becca come back to school.

"Yeah, well . . . " Jen looked down. There had to be something good to say about Phil. "He used to let me read his books, you know?"

"It was a real strange accident. I mean, this isn't supposed to be tornado season. But we were getting little twisters all over town that afternoon. *Tia* Caterina called my mom and said to keep all the kids inside, somebody was going to get hurt bad." Teresa shrugged her books from one hip to the other. "I dunno, sometimes I think there's gotta be something in that *curandera* stuff, you know? But don't tell anyone!" She giggled.

"I won't," said Jen. "Don't worry."

There was the usual knot of boys huddled up in the corner between the breezeway and the gym. Jen lagged behind Teresa for a moment. She didn't want to look at them and see them all staring at her chest.

Somebody whispered, and somebody else laughed, and Jen felt an old blackness rising inside her. *It never stops you can't stop it worthless trash nothing . . .*

"Twelve for the twelve apostles," she murmured.

They know everybody knows you're dirty crazy Jen . . .

"Eleven for the eleven thousand virgins, ten for the Ten Commandments . . . *me ayuden y me protejan,* amen." By the time Jen had remembered the whole list, the whispering inside her had stopped.

She looked straight at the group of boys and recognized the two who'd grabbed her the other day.

"You're Lamar," she said clearly. "And you're Clayton. *I know who you are.*"

She walked past them, head high, and the snickers that broke out after she passed couldn't touch her unless she let them.

"Wait a minute, Teresa," she called. "I need to talk to Mrs. Broussard about this science project."

THE BLOODSTONE

LAWRENCE WATT-EVANS

Lawrence Watt-Evans is the author of some two dozen novels and fourscore short stories in the fields of fantasy, science fiction, and horror. His best-known work is The Misenchanted Sword, *and his latest is* The Reign of the Brown Magician, *the third volume of the Three Worlds trilogy. He lives in the Maryland suburbs of Washington with his wife, two kids, two cats, and a parakeet named Robin.*

D arranacy wrinkled her nose in disgust at the smell from Mama Kilina's cookpot. "What *is* that?" she asked.

"Cabbage, mostly," Mama Kilina replied, poking at a whitish lump. "Cabbage someone pickier than me thought was too far gone to eat."

"Whoever it was that threw it out wouldn't get any argument from me!" Darranacy retorted, turning away.

Kilina looked up at her. "Oh, and I suppose you'd eat it if it were fresh? Some of us don't have your advantages, my girl! We take what we can get!"

Darranacy smiled smugly. "And one of us doesn't have to."

Kilina glared at her for a moment, then went back to her stew. "Laugh while you can, girl," she said. "Someday the spell will break, and when it does you'll be in the same boat as the rest of us."

"Or maybe someday you'll *wish* it was broken," a voice said from behind, startling Darranacy so that she jumped. She turned and found a smiling young man dressed in tattered red velvet.

"Korun!" she said. "Don't sneak up on me like that!"

"Learn to listen, then," he said.

Darranacy frowned slightly. "I don't understand how you can hear so much in a place like this," she said, waving her hand to take in all of Wall Street and the Wall Street Field, the rundown houses, the city wall, and the dozens of ragged figures huddled around campfires or under blankets in between. "It's not as if we were out in the forest, where it's quiet."

"You haven't learned to listen," Korun said mildly.

"I *do* listen!" she protested.

"Do you? Then what was it I said that startled you so, just now?"

"You said I should learn to listen, of course!"

"No," Korun corrected her, "That was the *second* thing I said, *after* I had startled you, and you had told me not to sneak up on you."

Darranacy opened her mouth to argue, then closed it again.

He was right, of course. It would hardly have made sense otherwise.

But then what *had* he said?

"Oh, I don't know!" she snapped. "I was too startled to listen to the words!"

"I said," Korun told her, "that someday you may wish that your magic spell was broken."

"Oh, that was it." She frowned. "But what a silly thing to say, Korun. Why would I ever wish that?" Before he could answer, she continued, "And if I did, the spell is very easy to break—the hard part is *keeping* it. If I let the enchanted bloodstone out of my possession, the spell will fade away, or if any food or water passes my lips, poof! The spell's gone. I could break it right now with a single bite of Mama Kilina's glop—if I wanted to, which I most certainly don't." She shuddered at the very idea. She missed the taste of food, sometimes, but that stuff didn't really qualify.

"I have heard," Korun said, "that it is unwise to maintain the spell for too long. Magic always has a cost, Darra. An old wizard once told me that the bloodstone spell can wear you down and damage your health."

"Damage my health, ha!" Darranacy replied. "If I wanted to damage my health, all I would have to do is eat some of the stuff you people live on. The Spell of Sustenance can't be any worse for me than that cabbage. I haven't eaten a bite nor drunk a drop in four months now, and I'm just as fit as ever."

Korun shrugged. "I say what I heard, that's all."

"You're just jealous because *you* have to eat," the girl said. "You spend your time scrounging for handouts, and any money you get goes for food and drink, and you'll probably be here on Wall Street for the rest of your life, but I don't need *anything*. I'm free!"

Mama Kilina looked up. "'Tain't natural, living like that."

"Of course it isn't natural," Darranacy answered promptly. "It's magic!"

Mama Kilina just shook her head and went back to her cookery.

"You're right, of course," Korun said. "It *is* magic, and it gives you an advantage over the rest of us, since you don't need to worry about your next meal. But have you done much with that advantage? It doesn't appear to me that you have. You're still here in the Field, and it's been, as you say, four months since your parents died."

"There's no hurry," Darranacy said defensively. "I'm still young."

"Ah, but wouldn't it be wise to use your advantage and get yourself out of here while you *are* still young?"

"I *will* get out of here!" Darranacy shouted. "And I'll *stay* out!"

"When?"

"When I'm old enough for an apprenticeship! When I'm good and ready!"

Korun shook his head. "I don't think," he said, "that this is quite what old Naral had in mind when he put the spell on you."

"Who cares what old Naral thinks?"

"*You* ought to, girl," Mama Kilina snapped. "Without him, you'd be no better off than any of us. If your mother hadn't been his apprentice once, and if he hadn't felt guilty when one of the spells he had taught her went wrong, you'd be starving now."

"No, I wouldn't," Darranacy retorted, "because if Mother had never been his apprentice, she wouldn't have had any spells to go wrong, and she'd still be alive!"

"No, she wouldn't," Kilina insisted, "because it wasn't her spell that killed her, as you well know, it was the demon your father summoned. Bad luck, mixing two schools of magic in a marriage like that, that's what *I* say."

"But if she hadn't been a wizard, she would have run, instead of trying to stop the demon from taking Daddy—if she'd ever have married a demonologist in the first place."

Kilina shook her head. "Wizard or no, and whatever else, your mother probably wouldn't have left your father if all the demons of Hell were after him."

Darranacy opened her mouth, and then closed it again. She couldn't think of any way to argue with that. Should she insist that her mother would have fled, she'd be denying her parents' love for each other.

Why did they have to die, anyway? Why did magic have to be so dangerous?

"Oh, it doesn't matter," she said at last. "They're both dead, and Naral *did* give me the bloodstone."

"Yes," Korun said. "He gave you the stone and the spell, and he told you that that was all he could do, to let you get by until you could find a place for yourself."

"Well, then?" Darranacy snapped.

"Darra," Korun said quietly, "I think he had four *days* in mind, maybe as much as four *sixnights,* but not four *months*—or four *years,* the way you've been going."

"*Three* years. I'll be twelve in less than three years, and then I'll find an apprenticeship."

"You plan to stay that long? To keep the spell that long?"

"Why not?" Darranacy stared up at him.

"Do you think you'll be in any shape to serve an apprenticeship after three years here?"

"Why not?" Darranacy asked again.

Korun didn't answer.

He didn't have to.

Naral hadn't mentioned anything about the bloodstone's spell being unhealthy; Darranacy was sure that Korun was just jealous when he said that.

But even so, what would she have to wear after three years in the Field? She'd have outgrown all her clothes, and would just have rags. And who would she know who could give her a reference? What sort of diseases might she have caught? The bloodstone didn't keep away disease. Or fleas, or lice, or ringworm, or any number of other things that might deter a prospective master.

Magic always seemed to have these little tricks and loopholes built into it—but then, so did everything else in life. Nothing was ever as simple as she wanted it to be.

"All right, then, I'll find a place sooner!" she said. "I'll fix myself up and I'll be in fine shape when I turn twelve!"

Korun smiled sadly.

"You think I *won't* find a place for myself?" she demanded.

"I think you won't unless you start looking," Korun told her. "I've seen too many people start out with fine plans and high hopes only to rot here in the Wall Street Field. You think Mama Kilina, here, never set her sights any higher than this?"

Darranacy turned and started to say something rude, then stopped.

She had never thought of Mama Kilina ever being anywhere else. Just days after the demon had carried her parents off, leaving their tidy little apartment and shop a burnt-out ruin, and after Naral had enchanted her but refused to take her in, the tax collector had come around for the annual payment on the family's property.

Darranacy hadn't had the payment—she hadn't had any money at all, had never found where her parents had hidden their savings, if in fact they had any. She had packed up a few belongings and fled, crying, and had come to the Field—everyone in Ethshar of the Sands knew that that was the last refuge, the place where the city guard never bothered you and nobody cared who you were or what you'd done. She'd found Mama Kilina there, sitting by her cooking pot, just as she was now, and it had never occurred to her, then or anytime since, to wonder how old Kilina came there.

Even Kilina must have been young once, though.

Mama Kilina grinned at her. She still had almost half her teeth, Darranacy saw.

Darranacy did not want to ever wind up like Mama Kilina, bent and old and eating rotten cabbage.

"All right," Darranacy said, "I'll *find* a place, then. Right now!"

"How?" Korun asked quietly.

Darranacy looked up at him angrily. "Why should I tell you?" she demanded, as she stared challengingly at Korun.

He shrugged. "Please yourself, child," he said. He squatted down by the cookpot. "Spare me a little, Mama?"

Darranacy watched as the two of them ate Mama Kilina's cabbage stew. The smell reached her, and simultaneously revolted and enticed her.

She never felt real hunger now, but the smell of food could still affect her—even such food as this. She remembered the happy meals with her parents in the back of the shop, the pastries her father sometimes bought her when they were out on one errand or another, how she would sit and nibble at a bowl of salted nuts while she practiced her reading . . .

But she couldn't eat anything now. It would break the spell, and then she'd need to find more food or starve, she'd need to find clean water—the stuff the others here in the Field drank, mostly rainwater collected from gutters of the city ramparts or from gravel-lined pits dug in the mud, was foul and full of disease. Attempts to dig a proper well had always been stopped by the city guard—the edict that had created the Field in the first place said that no permanent structure was permitted between Wall Street and the city wall itself, and that included wells as well as buildings.

Once she had a proper home again, *then* she could break the spell. Not before.

She thought over Korun's words. He was right; it was time to find a proper home.

She stood up and turned away from Mama Kilina and her cookpot, and began walking.

Darranacy reached her own little shelter, built of sticks and knotted-together rags pilfered from Grandgate Market—a crude thing that could be knocked down, or simply trampled, in a matter of seconds if the city guard ever decided to clear the Field out properly. She ducked inside, shoved aside her crude bedding, and dug into the sand, uncovering the pack she had hidden there.

This pack held everything she had brought from her parents' house that she wasn't already wearing.

There wasn't anything really valuable in the pack; the demon and the fire had destroyed all her parents' precious arcane supplies, the dragon's blood and virgin's tears and so on that her mother had used, and Darranacy hadn't been able to find any gold or silver anywhere— maybe the demon had taken it all, some demons did crave money, though her father had never told her what they did with it.

There was, however, her good tunic—fine brown silk with elaborate rucking around the waist, and gold embroidery on the sleeves and hem. Wearing that, she would be attired well enough to travel anywhere in the city, up to and including the Palace itself.

She looked down at it for a moment.

She could go anywhere in it—but where should she go?

She wasn't about to go to the Palace; that was too much. The overlord scared her; she'd never met him, but she had heard enough about him that she was not about to intrude on the Palace.

But she wanted to find someone rich to live with.

Well, there were plenty of big, elaborate homes *around* the Palace, homes where rich people lived. She didn't know how she could get someone there to take her in, but maybe if she looked around . . .

An hour later Darranacy, in her fine silk tunic but still barefoot, was wandering the streets of the Morningside district, admiring the marble shrines on the street corners, the iron fences and ornate gates that guarded the homes, the lush gardens behind the fences, the lavish homes beyond the gardens.

This was so different from the crowded streets where she had always lived! On Wizard Street or Wall Street the shops were jammed against each other right along the street, with no room for gardens either between them or in front of them, and the courtyards to the rear would hold only small vegetable patches, not these great expanses of flowers in every color of the rainbow. The residents lived upstairs from their shops, or behind them—a home without a business, a building without a signboard over the door or a display in the window, was rare indeed. A block a hundred yards long would hold at least a dozen homes in a solid row, broken perhaps by a single dark, narrow alley—two at the most.

Here, such a block would have but two or three houses, each standing apart amid its own gardens and terraces, closed off from the street and its neighbors by walls and fences—if there *were* businesses in there, customers had no way in! Windows gleamed on every side, fountains splashed—Darranacy couldn't quite imagine living amid such sybaritic surroundings.

And there didn't seem to be all that many people who actually *did* live there. She saw a young couple on a bench in one garden, and a woman tending flowers in another, but for the most part the yards were empty, the streets almost deserted.

Darranacy guessed that there weren't enough rich people to fill all those big houses, and that encouraged her—they must be lonely, in there.

But she couldn't just walk in somewhere and ask to be adopted.

She walked on and saw three little children, all of them much younger than herself, playing ball on the terrace of a particularly fine mansion.

A boy of seven or so was climbing a tree a few doors down, and she considered calling out to him, but decided not to.

She was almost to Smallgate Street, and the houses were growing smaller and squeezing in four to the block, when she saw the girl.

She wasn't playing, or climbing, or gardening; she was just standing there, leaning on a fence, her face thrust between the iron bars, looking out at the world beyond her home. She was taller than Darranacy, and probably older, but she wore just a tunic, not a dress but a dark red tunic with no skirt, which meant she was still a child, not yet twelve—or if her parents were exceptionally old-fashioned, it meant she hadn't had her first monthly flow yet.

"Hi," Darranacy said, from a few steps away.

The girl blinked at her. "Hello," she said back.

"My name's Darranacy."

"I'm Shala."

"You live here?"

Shala nodded.

"You look bored."

"I am."

"So am I," Darranacy lied.

"Want to do something together?"

Darranacy almost gasped with relief.

"Sure," she said.

"Come on in," Shala said, pointing to the gate.

This was the perfect opportunity. Darranacy hurried into the yard.

Now, how could she bring up the idea of adoption?

She thought about that as Shala took her inside and found a pair of dolls, as Shala introduced her to her mother and the housekeeper, as they went back outside and played out game after game . . . but as time passed, she thought about it less and less. She was having too much fun.

The two girls played princess-and-hero with the dolls, and romantic rivals (a stick served as the object of their competing affections), and various other games—but Shala balked when Darranacy suggested playing wizards.

"My dad doesn't like magic," she said. "He says it makes people lazy and careless—they figure if anything goes wrong, magic can fix it."

Darranacy blinked in surprise. "But magic's *hard*," she said. "And dangerous and expensive. You don't use it for stuff where you don't have to."

"*Some* people do, my dad says," Shala said darkly. "He talks about that a lot—he says the overlord depends on magic more than he ought to, and since he's the overlord, it doesn't matter how hard or dangerous or expensive it is."

"But . . . " Darranacy began.

Then she stopped.

If Shala's father didn't like magic, then she was in the wrong place. Both her parents had been magicians, after all, and she was proud of that—even if it *had* gotten them killed in the end.

Magic was hard and dangerous, and shouldn't be used if you didn't need it, but there wasn't anything *wrong* with it.

If there were . . . well, right now her whole *life* depended on magic. Without her enchanted bloodstone she'd be a beggar starving in the Wall Street Field, instead of . . .

Well, so she *was* a beggar living in the Wall Street Field, but she wasn't *starving,* and she wasn't going to stay there.

"Come on," Shala said, "we can have your doll be an evil magician, and *my* doll will be a hero who has to kill her without getting turned into a newt or something."

"Okay," Darranacy said, a bit reluctantly. "What kind of magician? A sorcerer?"

"What's that?"

Darranacy blinked, and struggled for an explanation. Her parents had taught her the differences among all the various schools of magic, but that didn't mean she could explain them to Shala.

"How about a magician who can call up demons for my doll to fight?" Shala asked.

"A demonologist?" Darranacy said. "But they're not really evil, they just have a bad reputation." She saw Shala's expression, and quickly amended that. "At least, my father always said *some* of them weren't evil."

Before Shala could reply, the housekeeper's voice called her name from the back door.

"It must be dinnertime," Shala said. "Do you want to eat dinner with us? Would your parents mind?"

This was her chance, Darranacy realized. If she were going to say anything, learn anything useful from Shala, this would be the time.

"I don't have any parents," she said.

Shala blinked.

"They're dead," Darranacy continued.

"Oh, Darra, I'm sorry! So do you live with your grandparents, or something?"

Darranacy shook her head. "No," she said. "I live by myself. In fact, I was here today looking for someone who might adopt me."

"Oh!" Shala stared at her.

"Shala of Morningside, get in here!" Shala's mother called from the door.

"I have to go—Darra, come on in! I'd love it if you could stay here—maybe not permanently, but maybe you could stay for a little while? I bet my dad could find a place for you!" Shala grabbed Darranacy's hand and began tugging her toward the house.

Darranacy came reluctantly. Now that she finally had the chance, she was losing her nerve. This wasn't the right place, with a father who hated magic, and this big strange house—but it might be the only chance she would get.

At the door Shala announced loudly, "This is my friend Darra—can she stay for dinner?"

"No, I can't," Darranacy said quickly, even though the mouth-watering smells of roast beef and fresh-baked bread were incredibly, unbearably tempting.

But she couldn't eat anything, or the spell would be broken and she would starve.

"Hello, Darra," Shala's mother said. "I saw you two playing so nicely out there—we'd be pleased if you stayed." She gestured at the dining table.

"No," Darranacy said weakly. "Thank you."

She stared at the lavish meal that was set out—sliced roast beef and several different vegetables and hot buttered bread, steaming on the table.

It had been so long since she had eaten anything, and there was so *much* here, and it looked so *good!* This wasn't the mess in Mama Kilina's stewpot, this was *real* food.

Korun was almost right after all, she thought—right now she *almost* wished she didn't have the spell on her.

But she *needed* the spell. She couldn't trust these people, they wouldn't want to keep the daughter of two magicians, and when they threw her out with her magic gone she'd have nothing left at all, she'd starve in the Wall Street Field.

This might be her chance to find a home—but it was too much to risk.

"Thank you for inviting me," she said politely, "but I really can't stay."

"But Darra, you said you didn't have any family!" Shala protested. "Why can't you stay?"

Darranacy looked at Shala, and at her mother, and her father, and the housekeeper, all of them standing around the table and staring at their ungrateful guest. She patted the purse on her belt and felt the reassuring shape of the bloodstone.

"I just can't," she said. Her eyes felt hot and her throat thick, as if she were about to start crying.

"Well, all right," Shala's mother said. "If you can't stay, you can't, but we won't let you go away empty-handed." She picked up something from the table, and stepped over closer to Darranacy.

"Here," she said, "just a little something."

And as Darranacy started to refuse, Shala's mother popped a candy into Darranacy's mouth.

Darranacy froze, then started to spit the candy out, then stopped.

It was too late; she could feel it. The spell was broken, and her empty stomach growled, for the first time in four months.

And then she *did* start weeping, sobbing hysterically as she collapsed in a heap on the floor.

Shala's entire family rushed to comfort her. It took twenty minutes before she had calmed down enough to make a clear explanation, and the food was cold when the five of them finally ate, but it was still the best dinner Darranacy had ever had.

She stayed three years.

And when the time came she was not apprenticed to a wizard, nor a demonologist, nor any other magician, but instead, at her own request, to a cook. The bloodstone, no longer enchanted, paid for her apprenticeship fee.

Cookery was a magic she could *trust*.

RIDDLE IN NINE SYLLABLES

KARAWYNN LONG

Karawynn Long won the Writers of the Future Grand Prize in 1993 and has stories forthcoming in Full Spectrum 5, Alternate Tyrants, *and other anthologies. At this time she is living in New York, where she is working on more short fiction and a novel.*

"Oh, come on, there must be *someone* you like," Lori insisted. The two girls were sitting in Beth's room on her bed, algebra textbooks and homework scattered between them. "How about Peter Campbell? Isn't he in your gym class?"

Beth shrugged. Lori enjoyed making a game of teasing her about guys at school and never seemed to notice how uncomfortable it made her. The truth was that the few guys Beth thought were cute were invariably also total jerks—as if the two traits were genetically linked. She could never say that to Lori, though, since these were the same guys Lori went out with all the time.

Beth searched for something to deflect her friend's attention. Usually it was easy enough to turn the conversation to whomever Lori liked, or her current boyfriend if she had one, which she almost always did.

This time, though, Beth was startled to be drawing a blank. She hadn't seen Lori wearing anyone's letter jacket or class ring for . . . something close to a month. That was probably a record for their entire two and a half years of high school. In fact, Beth wasn't sure when she'd last heard Lori mention anyone she was even interested in.

"Hey, what about you?" she asked, poking her friend in the shoulder. "Who are *you* pining away after these days?"

She meant it as a joke, because she honestly couldn't imagine Lori having to pine away after anybody. She was gorgeous, one of the most popular girls in school; all she ever had to do was let it be known that she was interested in someone, and within a couple of days they'd be going steady. Maybe three or four if the guy had to break up with some other girl first.

But Lori looked up with big stricken eyes like Beth had just slapped her. "Why?"

Beth shrugged, surprised and uncomfortable. "I don't know. I was just curious." Suddenly it felt untactful to say, How come you don't have a boyfriend? as if it were a requirement or something. Especially when she herself had never had one.

"Well, I'm not 'pining away' after anyone," Lori said. She flipped pages in the algebra book and consulted her homework. "I couldn't get number thirty-eight, could you?"

Beth considered asking again, given this rare chance to turn Lori's own game back on her, but her friend's tone and posture suggested this was not a good time to tease. Something's really the matter with her, Beth thought.

Well, if Lori wanted to talk about it, she would. At least it got her away from bugging Beth. She tried to concentrate on the homework but just couldn't get the puzzle out of her head. Beth hadn't given it much thought when Lori suggested that they study for Monday's test together, but now it occurred to her that it was, after all, a Saturday night. And here Lori was doing algebra, instead of going out on a date or hanging out at the skating rink. Definitely unusual.

They finished the assignment without any further discussion of guys or dating, although Beth thought Lori still looked distracted and unhappy. On impulse, Beth asked her if she wanted to spend the night. They'd used to do that a lot when they were younger—stay up until one or two, talking and giggling in the dark.

Lori looked at her quizzically. "No, I can't. I have to be up early for Sunday school tomorrow morning."

Beth felt stupid for not thinking of that. Lori tilted her head, considering. "But you could come spend the night at my house and go to church with us." She added quickly, "If you don't want to, that's okay. I know your dad would rather you go with him to First Presbyterian."

Beth hesitated, unhappy to have this brought up again. She'd never told Lori that her dad wanted her to go to his church—it would have been absurd, since the last time either of them had been inside a church was for Beth's mother's funeral, three years ago. She supposed Lori had latched onto the rationale as something that would placate her own mother, who must be constantly nagging her about bringing Beth to church with them. "Yeah, I think not this time," Beth said finally. "Maybe we can get together tomorrow afternoon."

Well, she hadn't said she was going to church, so it wasn't technically a lie. And she never went along with it to the extent of making up stuff that happened at church to talk about. Then again, Lori never pushed it by asking her, either, even though she chattered on about activities at her own church all the time. So Beth was pretty sure Lori knew, even if she wouldn't admit it.

"Okay," said Lori, gathering up her books and coat. For a moment she just stood there and gazed unhappily at Beth, like she might blurt out whatever was wrong. "Um. I'll talk to you later, then."

Will you? Beth wondered, but all she said was, "Yeah." She walked her friend to the front door and closed it behind her.

It was probably something with her parents, Beth thought, like they had decided that a good Christian girl shouldn't have anything to do with boys. Beth snorted. Lori's parents were pretty extreme. She just wished Lori would stand up to them a little more, sometimes.

Beth wandered into the living room, where her dad was sitting, reading a computer magazine. She sat down on the sofa, and he glanced up at her and smiled. "Hey," he said. "Did Lori go home?"

"Yeah."

"You know, you could invite her to stay over if you want. It's a Saturday night, after all."

Beth was used to her dad coming out with stuff she'd just been thinking about. "She couldn't. Church."

"Ah."

"She invited me over there, but then *I'd* have to go to church." Beth gave a mock shudder, and her dad chuckled.

The house was quiet except for the clock ticking on the mantel. "Thanks," she said.

"For what?"

"For not being like *them*." She tilted her head in the direction of Lori's house and rolled her eyes.

Her dad's expression got serious. "You really think I've done okay?" he asked quietly. Beth heard the other part of the sentence, that he didn't say: *since your mother died.*

"You do fine, Dad," Beth answered. She got up and gave him an awkward hug where he sat in the chair. With her arms around his neck and her chin on his shoulder, she whispered, "Mom couldn't have done any better," and felt his embrace tighten.

*   *   *

Beth woke up at eight the next morning and tiptoed around the kitchen making tea and toast. Phoebe came waddling in, tail high, and Beth stooped to pour kibble into her bowl. The black-and-white cat had been fat to begin with, and pregnancy was turning her into a furry little soccer ball.

If Lori guessed that Beth wasn't going to church, Beth was still pretty sure Lori had no idea what she *did* do most Sunday mornings—which was walk over to the university library and spend several hours reading old books. Lori probably imagined Beth just wanted to sleep late on the weekends; she would sympathize with that, even though her mother would go into hysterics about Sloth and Indolence and what the Devil did with idle hands.

But sitting in an empty library reading old reference books was definitely beyond Lori's ken. Beth could almost hear Lori's incredulous tones in her head: "You mean they're not even *fiction?*" Lori liked historical romances when she read anything at all; she'd never understand why Beth wanted to hang out at a library when there was a perfectly good mall nearby.

Beth rinsed her dishes in the sink and wrote a quick note for her dad, then grabbed her jacket and stepped outside. It was a cold, gray day, but at least it wasn't raining yet.

The university library was almost deserted this early in the morning, but the heat was turned up high. Beth shed her jacket and pulled out the list of call numbers she hadn't finished looking up last week. These were supposed to be books about magic, except that the ones she'd found so far had mostly either turned out to be stage magic and sleight of hand or New Age psychic phenomena.

Today she skipped the open stacks and went straight upstairs to the research room. Most of the really old and interesting books were up there, kept in rooms only the staff could enter. Beth requested two books from the librarian on duty and wandered around the room looking at paintings until they came.

The first book was about ceremonial magic, full of drawings of various arcane symbols going all the way back to Egypt. Beth thumbed through it briefly, then put it aside for later. The second book, *Charmes and Helpyngs,* was small and thick, and so old it was falling apart. Beth handled the stained and crumbling pages gingerly. According to the title page, the book had been published in 1598—which made it almost four hundred years old! She glanced around the room, half-expecting a librarian to swoop down and take it away from her.

The book had an introduction explaining that the text was even older than that, having been reprinted from a pamphlet originally published in 1382. The typeface in the rest of the book was full of odd ornate curlicues that made it difficult to read, but with a little work Beth was able to decipher some of the subheadings that appeared every couple of pages. "To Asswage A Fevere," she read. "To Fleme Wertes." "To Wynne His Love." Beth turned pages in growing excitement. *This* was the sort of thing she'd been looking for—not ESP mumbo jumbo or how to make a handkerchief disappear, but real sorcery, something you could study and learn just like algebra.

Not only was the typeface difficult to make out, but the very language was so old it was sometimes unrecognizable. It reminded Beth of the excerpts of *The Canterbury Tales* her English class had studied earlier that year. Their teacher had made them take turns reading passages aloud, and Beth had noticed then how much easier it was to get past the strange spellings and figure out what was meant when you could hear the words spoken. She turned to an interesting page and began sounding them out to herself. Some of the words remained inscrutable—what in the world was "warisshe," or a "dwale"?—but most of them she was able to puzzle through.

Sometime later Beth glanced up at the wall clock and grimaced. It was already ten past noon, and she'd meant to leave at eleven-thirty so she could fix lunch for her dad. She wouldn't have time to come back this afternoon, either; she had a paper on Sylvia Plath due in English tomorrow, and she hadn't even started writing it. Beth handed the books in to the librarian reluctantly, wishing she could take them home with her and actually try out a spell or two. Next Sunday she'd bring a notebook and copy some of them down, she decided.

After lunch she called over to Lori's house, but only got the machine. Probably her family was at some church function. Beth left a message, but Lori didn't call back that night.

On Monday, the first class the girls had together was algebra, and so Beth didn't see Lori until after second period. She usually met Lori at her locker between second and third so they could walk to algebra together. "Hey," she said cheerfully as she came up behind her friend.

Lori jumped, dropping a piece of paper in her locker, and turned around. Beth was shocked to see that she had been crying. Her eyes were red and puffy, and her mascara had smeared across one cheek.

"Hey, are you okay?" she asked.

"Yeah, I'm fine, why?" Lori managed a bright smile, and Beth just shrugged. If she didn't want to talk about it, Beth didn't want to push.

"Are you ready for the test?" she asked instead.

"As ready as I'm gonna be," Lori answered. She picked up the piece of notebook paper from the bottom of her locker. Beth saw it was creased in little rectangles, like a note, and the handwriting was slanty where Lori's was round. Beth wondered if that was why Lori had been crying. Some guy had dumped her? But Lori hadn't been going with anyone.

Lori refolded the note without offering an explanation, set it on her top locker shelf, grabbed a pencil, and slammed the door. "Okay, I'm ready. Let's go fail a test."

As they passed the girl's rest room, Beth touched Lori's arm. "Hey, I gotta go to the bathroom real quick. Come with me?" Lori nodded.

Beth went into one of the stalls and fussed around for a bit, then flushed the empty toilet. When she came out, the mascara was gone from Lori's face and she looked almost like her usual self. "We'd better hurry," Lori said, just as the warning bell rang, and the two girls jogged down the hallway together.

"How'd you do?" Beth asked after class as they started walking toward the parking lot. Lori had her own car and had offered to drive them off-campus for lunch today.

Lori shrugged and shook her head. "I don't think this is my day for tests," she said, and then bit her lip.

Beth sighed sympathetically. "I'm sorry. Hey, maybe Ms. Heller will give us a curve. Or maybe it wasn't as bad as you think."

Lori was quiet, then said, "Yeah, maybe it's not." A moment later she stopped walking. "Look, Beth, I know I said I'd eat with you today, but—well, there's something else I have to do instead. I'm sorry." She genuinely looked distressed. "We can go out tomorrow," she offered.

Beth suppressed her disappointment. "Yeah, okay," she said. "No problem. I'll see you later."

Lori smiled gratefully and walked on toward the parking lot, looking distracted. Beth supposed she must finally have gotten her guy, whoever he was, and was having lunch with him instead.

She veered off toward the library, not ready to face the humiliation of sitting at a cafeteria table by herself. She tried not to resent Lori for backing out on her, but it didn't work. Sometimes she felt like Lori was only her friend when she didn't have anything better to do.

Beth wandered aimlessly around the school's meager little library, reading the titles on the spines but not really registering them. She thought of the book she'd discovered at the university library. Maybe she could find a spell to break Lori and her new boyfriend up so that Lori would start eating lunch with Beth again.

She stopped walking and sighed, feeling mean and ashamed for even thinking of it. She didn't really want Lori to be unhappy, just maybe a little more loyal. Besides, she'd outlasted dozens of Lori's boyfriends. If Beth was just patient, Lori would go back to spending time with her.

But Lori didn't show up for chemistry fifth period, and Beth couldn't find her after school, either. She began to get worried; Lori spaced out in classes a lot, but it wasn't like her to cut them.

Tuesday Beth went to Lori's locker before algebra again, but Lori didn't come. She waited there until the one-minute bell rang, and then sprinted across the building to class, slipping through the door just before Ms. Heller closed it.

Lori was already in her seat across the room. Beth stared at her, feeling the slow rise of anger. Lori hadn't shown up on purpose, and Beth had nearly gotten a tardy as a result. Lori refused to meet her eyes.

Beth's desk was nearer the door; after the bell rang she was able to intercept Lori on the way out of the room. "Hi," she said, with a conscious attempt at mildness.

"Hi." Lori walked a little faster, clutching her books to her chest.

Beth got mad. "Hey!" She grabbed Lori's arm and made her stop. "Why do you keep avoiding me?" Her voice was loud enough to attract curious glances from other students in the hall. More quietly she asked, "Why won't you tell me what's wrong?"

"Because you wouldn't understand."

"Why not?" Beth challenged.

"Because you don't even like any guys," Lori shot back. "You don't understand what can happen when you're really in love with somebody."

That hurt, but Beth swallowed hard and let it pass. "I might if you told me. We're supposed to be *friends,* Lori, but you never spend any time with me, and you never tell me anything important."

"I do too spend time with you," Lori protested, but she looked guilty. Beth just stared at her, saying nothing.

Lori sighed. "Okay, but I can't talk about it here. Let's go out to my car."

Beth followed her across the parking lot in silence and waited while Lori fished her keys out of her purse and unlocked the doors. They climbed in; Lori put the keys in the ignition and then just sat there, staring at the steering wheel.

"Well?" said Beth, still too hurt to be gentle.

"I'm pregnant, okay?" Lori snapped. She turned away to look out the side window, but not before Beth saw her face twist up in misery.

Beth was too shocked to even breathe. *Lori?* Had been having *sex?* She stared helplessly at her friend. "Holy geez, Lori," she said. "Are you sure? What happened?

"I've missed two periods," Lori answered in a voice broken with suppressed crying. "And I took one of those home pregnancy tests—that's where I went at lunch yesterday. Oh, God, Beth—everything's ruined. My whole life is ruined." She started to cry in earnest.

Not her day for tests, Beth thought, and winced. "Who—who's the father?"

Lori shook her head, two tears glittering as they fell into her lap. "It doesn't matter. He won't—he won't make it right. So it doesn't even matter."

"What do you mean, make it right? You mean he won't pay for an abortion?"

"No!" Lori said indignantly. "I mean he won't marry me."

"Oh." Beth remembered then that Lori's parents were both active in "pro-life" organizations. She guessed it made sense that Lori's idea of a solution was to marry the guy who'd gotten her pregnant. She sighed.

"I didn't *mean* to, Beth." Lori's voice was anguished. "he was supposed to stop, you know, before—he said I couldn't get pregnant if it wasn't, you know, inside me when he . . . " She trailed off, obviously too embarrassed to finish.

"You mean you didn't even *use* anything?" Beth asked, incredulous. Lori didn't answer, just sat there looking miserable. "Oh, geez, Lori, what if he had AIDS or something?"

Lori shot her a withering glance through her tears. "I would have noticed *that,*" she said.

Beth stared at her, appalled and frightened, remembering that Lori had skipped the sex ed unit in biology last year—brought a note from her mother and spent fifth period in the library that week. "Holy shit, Lori," Beth said, but stopped herself from yelling at her friend. She didn't want to make Lori sorry she'd told her about it. Besides which, it made more sense to be mad at Lori's parents.

Lori started crying again. "I don't know what I'm going to do," she said between sobs. "I can't tell my parents, Beth, I just *can't*. When Melanie Robinson got pregnant Daddy said she was a harlot and had damned her immortal soul to Hell. He'd *kill* me if he knew."

Beth considered this, frowning. She tried to avoid Lori's family as much as possible. Her mother's constant saccharine attention was suffocating; by contrast her father had always seemed distant and harsh, someone who believed that sparing the rod would spoil the child and that suffering was the only way to purge the soul of sin. Beth could imagine him being merciless in his condemnation.

Worse, the state's consent laws meant Lori couldn't get an abortion without permission from at least one parent. "Maybe your mom would help you out," Beth suggested. "Maybe you could just tell her." Lori's mother was as publicly outspoken against abortion as her husband, but she seemed gentler, and might be more reasonable in private, when it was her own daughter's life at stake.

"No." Lori dismissed the idea. "Mama wouldn't keep a secret from Daddy. And he'd notice eventually anyway, when I began to show, and then it would be worse." She reached out and fiddled with the keys, dangling from the ignition. "Everybody at school will think I'm a slut. Only the really trashy girls get pregnant."

Beth realized Lori wasn't even considering an abortion. She wondered how much of the pro-life stuff Lori actually believed. They'd avoided talking about it, wary of starting an argument that might endanger the friendship. Beth counted: five months left in the school year. Lori would be very obviously pregnant by the end of May.

"I don't know, maybe they'll send me off to that school or whatever, that place they sent Melanie to, to try and keep it quiet," Lori said. "Except, you know, everybody knew about Melanie anyway."

If Lori moved away, Beth would lose her best friend. Maybe Lori didn't spend as much time with her now, but she was still nicer to Beth than anyone else had ever been. The other kids had tormented her until pretty, popular Lori had stood up for her. And now it was going to be Lori everyone made fun of, and Beth couldn't protect her.

Or maybe she could.

Beth's heart beat faster at the thought. Maybe there was a way out. If Lori had a miscarriage . . .

Lori was wiping carefully at her eyes, trying not to smear her mascara. Tentatively Beth put a hand on her friend's arm, offering comfort. "I'm sorry, Lori, I really am. I'll—I'll try to think of something."

Lori shrugged, clearly not believing this would matter. "Yeah. Thanks." She reached out and started the engine, visibly pulling herself together. "We'd better go if we're going to actually eat any lunch today."

Beth withdrew her hand. Please, oh please, let there be a way out of this, she thought, to no one in particular.

Beth went directly from school to the university that afternoon. She retrieved *Charmes and Helpyngs* from the librarian, sat down, and began to consider the spell names one at a time, not entirely sure what she should look for.

"To Speke With Briddes And Bestes." To speak with brides? No, *birds*, Beth realized. She grinned, remembering the Dr. Dolittle books she'd loved as a kid.

She continued reading and finally came upon "To Twynne A Woman From Hir Child." That had possibilities, though Beth wasn't sure about "twynne." For a moment she envisioned working a spell that gave Lori twins by accident. The mere thought gave her gooseflesh, and she vowed to be meticulous in deciphering and executing the spells.

> If oon womman with childe is and she wol it not, thanne yafestow hir swich wortes and herbes as I here telle, and the child shal ybleden be from hir body.

"Shall be bled from her body"—surely that meant a miscarriage. Beth read on:

> Firste, fyndestow the herbe that highte penyroial, which thow woot by floures purpur and smale, and by smell poynaunt and swete. And from feeld or apotecarie fecche eke leves of rewe. Shredde thilke leves tweye and seeth houres thre. Thanne shaltow devoide thise wortes and combyne thilke water with eisel and canelle. Yafestow for hir ydrynken, tho understond wel that

ofte sythe thise sharppe and bittre draught shal cause hir siknesse and grete peyne.

Beth pondered this. "Fyndestow" in context seemed to be an instruction to find, but what was "yafe"? She recognized rue and pennyroyal
as herbs, but where in the world could she get some? And what in the
world were "eisel" and "canelle"? Beth thought disgustedly that she
would have stood a better chance if the spell had called for "eye of
newt and toe of frog"—they couldn't be any more difficult to find, and
at least she knew what they were.

And even if she figured it all out, there was still the difficulty of getting Lori to actually drink the stuff. "Sharppe and bittre" didn't sound
like the sort of thing Beth could slip into Lori's Coke at lunch and
expect to go unnoticed. Not to mention that dire warning at the end.
Sickness and great pain? Beth grimaced, worried that she was out of
her depth.

The next page listed "anoother maner charme by which maistow
bireve a womman of hir child." Beth skimmed over it—it didn't appear
to require any obscure herbs, but it wanted her to "fecche a cattes
calle." Beth shut the book in exasperation—how was she supposed to
get something as intangible as a cat's voice?

At least this explained why people weren't doing sorcery all the time, if
the spells were all like that, she thought as she walked home. Maybe
some of those things had been more common four hundred years ago,
but they were impossible now. Beth was so disappointed she felt like crying, but though her chest hurt and her throat tightened, no tears came.

It was almost six when she reached the house. Her father was
already home; he called out to her as soon as she shut the front door.
"Beth?"

"Yeah?" Beth shrugged out of her jacket and tossed it on the couch.

"Come look!"

Beth started in the direction of his voice, but when she got to his
office it was empty. Bewildered, she called, "Where are you?"

"In your room."

Beth blinked and walked back out and into her bedroom. Dad had
pulled the chair away from her desk and was straddling it backwards,
apparently staring into her open closet. He was still wearing his suit,
though he'd taken his tie off. "What?"

He pointed down at the floor. "Look."

Beth moved past the closet door where she could see. "Oh," she breathed. Phoebe was lying in a pile of Beth's dirty clothes, nosing at a black-and-white lump that looked more like a mouse than a kitten. It was unimaginably tiny, maybe half the size of Beth's palm. Its fur was so thin that its skin showed pink through the white patches.

"I don't know why we bothered fixing that box for her in the living room," her dad said wryly.

Beth grimaced, noticing the faint bloody smears on one of her favorite blouses. "Oh well," she joked ruefully. "I didn't much like that shirt anyway." A slight movement drew her eye to where a pink-and-gray blob had appeared under Phoebe's tail. "Hey, there's another one!"

They watched, rapt, as the second kitten continued to be born. Phoebe seemed nonchalant, as if she hadn't even noticed what was happening. When it fully emerged, however, she sat up and nosed the lump—it wasn't yet recognizable—over next to the first one, and began licking and biting at it.

"Eww," Beth said. "What is that she's eating?"

"It's the caul, the amniotic sac that the unborn kitten was, oh, sort of floating in," her father answered.

It took a moment for that to sink in. "The what?"

"The amniotic sac. It holds a watery fluid that suspends the fetus."

"No." Beth shook her head impatiently. "The other thing."

"Caul," her father replied. "C-a-u-l. An older word for it."

Beth couldn't believe it. A cat's *caul,* not call. As bizarre as newt's eyes for sure, except that she actually had one. Or rather, she would be able to *get* one if Phoebe would stop eating it. She watched anxiously as the cat bolted the last of it down and began to lick the tiny damp kitten.

"The caul was all that sort of slimy stuff?" she asked, just to make sure she understood. Her dad nodded.

Beth was torn between elation at her discovery and worry that she was going to miss her chance. "How many kittens do you think there'll be?"

He cocked his head, considering. "Hard to say. I imagine there's at least one more—she's not acting like it's over, anyway."

There were four kittens in all. Beth watched the birth and subsequent cleansing of the third in rising frustration. Mercifully the phone rang just as the fourth one emerged. Beth and her dad looked at each other. "I'll get it," her dad offered. "You stay here and watch—I saw the first one."

"Thanks." As soon as he was around the corner, Beth crouched down next to the cats. For all her urgency she moved slowly, not wanting to alarm Phoebe. The mother cat paused in her ministrations when Beth touched the newest kitten, but appeared unconcerned. Beth had a hard time catching hold of the wet and slippery caul, and for a moment she was terrified that she might accidentally injure the fragile squirming kitten. Eventually she got most of it pulled off and left Phoebe to clean up the rest.

Beth ducked into the bathroom with her messy prize, wrapped it in a bit of toilet paper until she could think of something better, and stashed it in a drawer. Then she washed her hands and went back to check on the cats.

The four fluffy lumps were tumbled together, their faces buried in Phoebe's belly fur. All of them were white with symmetrical black blots on their backs and heads. "They look like little Rorschach tests," Beth said when her dad reappeared in the doorway.

He chuckled. "You're right, they do. Strange how they've all got the same coloring. Their father must have been a black-and-white, too. Hungry little beasts, aren't they?" He turned and looked at her. "How about you? Are you hungry yet?"

Beth shrugged. She was too keyed up to think very hard about food. "Um, I thought I'd go back to the university library after dinner."

Dad raised his eyebrows. "You don't usually go up there during the week, do you?" he asked. "Are you researching something for school?"

"No." She shrugged and tried to sound casual. "It's just some books I got interested in, but they're in the special research section, so you can't leave the room with them."

"I see." He glanced at his watch. "Tell you what—why don't we go grab a hamburger or something, and I'll drop you off there when we're done? Save you the walk in the dark, and then you can call me when you want me to come pick you up. You think you'll be done by ten? It's still a school night, remember."

Beth nodded, grateful to have escaped further questioning. "Sure. Thanks." Luck seemed to be on her side. She began to believe this would actually work.

At the library again, Beth turned pages until she found the "anoother maner charme" she'd seen before.

Certes, noon wys wydwe may werche thise charme, nor womman
been ypassed thritty yeer of age. Thow moot yonge be, and a may-
den chaast, ellis thy werkyng shal ende in sorwe and peyne. Eke
thow moot clene be and devoid of thy wommanes blood.

Beth grimaced. Sorrow and pain again; the author seemed to be
something of an alarmist. Well, she was certainly both young and quite
chaste, so that seemed safe enough. She finally decided the last part
meant that she shouldn't work the spell while on her period. Beth had
just finished hers a couple of days before, so she thought that shouldn't
be a problem.

Than maistow the child kecche from a wommanes wombe in
this wyse: Firste, kittestow a tresse of hir heer, and from hir
housbonde or hir lemman eke, or rente out of his book a leef
writ in his owen honde.

She didn't know what a "lemman" was, but "housbonde" was clear
enough, which gave her some idea. And it kind of made sense, once
she thought about it—it took something from a guy to start a baby in
the first place, after all.

Seconde, by nyght and in the fulle of the moone bynde thise
thynges bothe togidre and brenne hem over candele-fyr.
Thridde, thow moot fecche a cattes calle, and strawe upon it
thilke asshes and swich erthe as may holde in thyn honde. Fer-
the, prikkestow thi fynger and yete a drope of thyn owen blood
upon the calle. Thanne while the candele stille brenne,
spekestow anoon thise wordes:

By my blood and strawed erthe
Calle from a cattes burthe
By the fyr which brennen wyld
Shal I kecche thise child.

Laste, berie thilke calle withinne fertile erthe. Er the moone
hath hid hir face the child wol ydrawen be.

There were a couple of verbs she didn't recognize, but their meanings
seemed clear enough in context, and all the ingredients in this one

made sense now. Beth copied down the whole passage in her spiral, then flipped the page and began to make a list of the things she'd need: the caul, of course, which she already had; a candle and matches; a handful of dirt; some of Lori's hair—she stopped, realizing she had a problem. She could borrow Lori's hairbrush easily enough, but she'd need some hair from the guy she'd slept with as well, and Beth didn't even know who he was.

She sucked absently on a fingernail and thought back over the last two or three months. The last serious boyfriend of Lori's that she could come up with was John Parker, a senior on the basketball team. Lori broke up with him to date Rob Larson, though if Beth remembered right that had only lasted a couple of weeks. Before John she wasn't sure—maybe Adam Zimmerman? Or had that been too long ago? Plus she was pretty sure Lori had gone out with Chris Denning at least once in there somewhere.

There was just no way to be certain; she was going to have to get Lori to tell her. Beth didn't think that would be easy, but she was too close to give up now.

She tried to ease the conversation around to the identity of the father several times over the next few days; each time Lori put her off. Since her confession in the car, she seemed to want to pretend the whole situation didn't exist. Beth was running out of time: the calendar showed the next full moon was Monday.

Sunday afternoon she gave up and went for the direct approach. "So who was it?"

Lori looked up from her paper. The girls were sitting on Beth's bed again, with a new algebra assignment. "Who was what?"

"Who did you sleep with?"

"Oh." She went back to copying a problem from the book, shaking her head. "It doesn't matter. I don't want to have anything to do with him."

"Oh, come on, Lori, tell me who it was. You must have really loved him," Beth added, hoping to draw her out.

"I don't want to talk about it." She penciled in an answer without looking up.

"Okay, we don't have to. Just tell me his name."

"No!" Lori slammed her book shut. "I'm sorry I ever told you about it. If you don't stop bugging me, I'm going to go home."

"I'm sorry," Beth said quickly. "Please don't go."

"Why do you even *care* who it was?"

Flustered, Beth stammered, "I—I was just curious."

"No." Lori shook her head decisively. "You've been bugging me about it from the very beginning. There's more to it than that." When Beth didn't say anything, Lori asked, "Are you going to tell my parents?"

"No! I wasn't going to tell anybody!"

"Then why do you care? What are you planning to do?"

Beth opened her mouth but nothing came out. Stupid—she should have had some excuse ready.

"Tell me the truth, Bethany Mitchell," Lori warned, "or I'll never speak to you again."

Panicked, Beth tried to bargain. "If I tell you, will you promise you'll tell me his name?"

Lori narrowed her eyes and considered. "Okay."

Beth took a deep breath. "Because I know a way you don't have to be pregnant anymore, but I've got to have something from the guy, too, or it won't work."

"Or *what* won't work?"

"The . . . the thing," Beth said. "The thing I was going to do to make it go away."

"Make it go away?" Lori's eyes widened as she figured it out. "You mean *kill* it, don't you? Why don't you just say that? You want to murder my baby!"

"No!" Beth protested. "I mean—it's not a baby yet, it's just an embryo. It's like this *lump. You* saw the film in biology," she said, and then remembered Lori hadn't.

"How can you say that? It's a human being, and if you murder it, you'll go to Hell." She sounded like she believed it.

"Oh, *geez,* Lori." This just proved she'd been right to avoid discussing abortion with Lori, and Beth wished she hadn't gotten into it now. "I will not go to Hell. I don't even *believe* in Hell. I just didn't—all that stuff you said, about school, and your father, and everything. I just didn't want that to happen to you."

Lori was frowning. "How?" she asked.

"—What?"

"I don't understand how you—you said you could do something so I wouldn't be pregnant, but how could you do that without telling me about it?"

Beth sighed. She suddenly felt very tired. "I found this book of spells at the library. I was going to use one for inducing a miscarriage."

Lori took a minute to work this through. "That's *witchcraft*," she finally said. Her expression was at once fascinated and repulsed.

"No, it's not, not like you mean. I'm not making deals with the devil or anything. It's more like chemistry, you know—you combine certain things under certain conditions, and certain things happen."

They stared at each other for a long moment. Lori's mouth was slightly open. Beth couldn't tell what she was thinking.

Then Lori stood up and started to gather her papers from the bed. She pulled a folder out of her book bag, took a note from the pocket and replaced it with her homework, and slid the folder into her bag. Beth watched with increasing apprehension. "What are you doing?"

"I'm going home," Lori said. She packed her textbook and her pencil and swung the bag onto one shoulder. "You're really not the person I thought you were. I don't know who you are." She gave a bitter laugh. "No wonder you never came to church with us. I just can't believe I was stupid enough to make excuses for you. I thought you were my friend."

"I *am* your friend!" Beth protested. "I was doing this for *you!*"

Lori whirled around. "You aren't doing *anything* for me." Her eyes were wide, almost frightened. "I *never* asked you to do any of it. You remember that." She turned and left the room without waiting for an answer.

Beth followed her to the front door. "Okay, fine, then just tell me who you slept with."

"No."

Beth stopped, shocked. "You promised!"

"I won't help you commit murder," Lori said. "Maybe you don't care about *your* immortal soul, but *I* don't want to spend all eternity in Hell." She jerked the door open.

"Lori!" In tears, Beth reached out for Lori's arm.

"Just leave me alone," Lori's voice was cold as she shrugged away. "I don't want to talk to you ever again."

Stung, Beth watched her go, not believing how utterly awful the whole thing had turned out. Lori had gotten mad at Beth a couple of times before, but never like that. Beth couldn't forget the cruelty on her friend's face.

She walked back into her bedroom and shoved books and papers to one side of her bed, intending to lie down. The folded note Lori had tossed down caught her eye, though, and Beth picked it up and smoothed it out.

"Dear Lori," it began, in a crabbed and slanting hand. "Why are you acting so weird? I hope this is all a joke, because I certainly DO NOT intend to marry you." Beth skipped down to the bottom and the signature: Rob L.

Beth stared at the paper. So now she knew. If she could get some of Rob Larson's hair at school tomorrow, she could perform the spell.

Except that Lori would know. When she discovered she wasn't pregnant anymore, she would know Beth had done it. And Lori would never forgive her. She'd lose her friend either way.

Something didn't make sense, though. Lori had been so careful and methodical in gathering up her stuff; it just didn't seem likely that she'd left the note behind by accident. Especially considering what it said. Lori must have intended her to find it.

But in that case, why didn't she just tell Beth the name? It didn't make any sense, until Beth remembered the fierce, almost-frightened expression on Lori's face. *I never asked you to do any of it. You remember that.*

And then Beth thought she understood. Lori *wanted* Beth to work the spell, but she wanted to be able to pretend she didn't know about it. The same way she didn't push Beth about coming to church, as long as she could pretend Beth was going with her father. Lori didn't want to have the baby, but she wanted it to be Beth's responsibility.

The more she thought about it, the angrier Beth got. Never mind that she didn't believe abortion was wrong; *Lori* believed it was murder. That Beth would suffer an eternity in Hell for it. She was willing to condemn her friend to save herself. Beth flung the paper down. Let Lori suffer the consequences of her own actions.

She didn't move, just stood there and stared at the note, anger slowly ebbing. Finally she admitted to herself that none of this really changed anything. She needed to help Lori as much as Lori needed the help. Lori had taken a risk, befriending her, and Beth had never had a way to repay that until now.

So she would try. *If* she could figure out a way to get hold of Rob Larson's hairbrush. Assuming he even used a brush and not a comb. Beth sighed and began refolding the paper. And stopped, and opened it again, gazing at the messy scrawl. *Writ in his owen honde.*

She already had everything she needed.

Monday night, with the full moon shining in her window, Beth assembled the objects on her list and began the spell. She held the note from Rob and the wad of Lori's hair together, and wrapped a piece of string tightly around them. Then she lit a candle and began to burn the note over its flame. The paper caught and flared high, and Beth blew it out in alarm before it was even half-burnt. She relit it and blew it out several more times, nervous of burning her fingers. The charred black bits of paper and hair fluttered away with her breath, until they were scattered all across her desk.

She scraped the ashes together into her cupped hand as best she could, and brushed them off over the shriveled cat's caul. Then she poured dirt into her palm from a cup and sprinkled it over the caul as well. Finally she picked up the needle and, gritting her teeth, stuck it into the pad of her middle finger. She squeezed at the wound with her other hand until a drop of blood welled up, then turned the finger over and let the blood fall on top of the ashes and the dirt.

Beth pulled out her notebook and began to recite the charm, carefully enunciating the unfamiliar words:

> By my blood and strawed erthe
> Calle from a cattes burthe
> By the fyr which brennen wyld
> Shal I kecche thise child.

Carefully she lifted the caul into the cup she'd brought the dirt in, and carried it and a spoon into the backyard. She dug a small hole near the fence, away from the house, and buried the caul in it, scraping dirt back over the top.

The moon still shone high and round through a lacy haze of clouds. Beth gazed up at it, and hoped.

For the next two weeks Lori refused to speak to Beth at school or even acknowledge her existence. She didn't return phone calls, and the one time Beth passed her a note in class Lori dropped it in the trash without even reading it.

Beth watched the calendar anxiously, waiting for Lori to realize she was no longer pregnant. Three days after the new moon, she finally confronted Lori between classes at her locker. "Look, you don't have to talk to me; I just have to know if it worked."

"I don't know what you're talking about." Lori continued rummaging in her locker, her voice flat.

"Are you still pregnant?"

Lori gave her a cold stare. "What gave you the idea that I was pregnant?" She shut her locker door and walked away.

Beth stared after her. She supposed that was an answer; if Lori was pretending like the whole thing had never happened, the spell must have worked. She tried to take some satisfaction from that, and couldn't. Far down the hall, Lori stopped to talk to Chris Denning and another guy Beth didn't know; Beth could hear Lori's high laughter over the general roar of conversation and slamming lockers. She turned and started walking in the other direction, taking the long way to class.

Somewhere, in the back of her mind, she'd hoped that by doing what Lori wanted, by taking all of the responsibility for the abortion herself, she would get her friend back. Now Beth realized how naive that was. Lori was trying to build a world where she had never gotten pregnant at all. Beth's very presence would remind her what had really happened, bring it all crashing down.

No wonder Lori didn't want to talk to her. Beth thought she should feel angry, that Lori had so easily sacrificed their friendship while Beth was trying so hard to save it, but instead she only felt sick and sad.

It was most of a week after that before Beth began to suspect something else was wrong. She hunted around her room for the notebook in which she'd copied the spell, and read it over again. *Er the moone hath hid hir face, the child wol ydrawen be.*

Beth had assumed it meant the embryo would be drawn from Lori's body, bled out as in the other spell, as in a miscarriage. But what if it had meant, not drawn from, but drawn *to*? Beth was nine days late on her period. *Shal I kecche thise child.*

"Kecche," she whispered to herself. "Ketch. Catch."

She stared at the letters until they blurred, her heart beginning to pound hard in her chest.

Lori wasn't pregnant anymore. But Beth was.

She left the house and started walking, not going anywhere in particular, not even bothering to write a note. She paid barely enough attention to her surroundings to make sure she didn't get lost, and just walked. And thought.

At one point, it occurred to Beth that she could have the first recorded virgin birth in nearly two thousand years, and she laughed aloud bitterly. She wouldn't, of course. She'd get the abortion that Lori couldn't, or wouldn't, have gotten.

It frightened her a little, though; she'd never had any kind of surgery, even stitches. And what if there was a protest at the clinic when she went in? There seemed to be one on the news every couple of weeks lately, surging lines of shouting people—Lori's parents might even be there. She smiled humorlessly at the irony, and then stopped walking altogether.

This was *Lori's* child she was carrying. She hadn't quite made the connection before. Beth laid a hand on her belly. Lori's child. A piece of the friend she had lost. She hugged her arms to herself, struck by a wave of loneliness, remembering the sleepovers and tickle-fights and whispered confidences of a few years ago. Beth had been somewhat aware that they were growing apart for some time; she'd tried to ignore it in the hope that they would grow together again. Now she knew they wouldn't.

Lori's baby, she thought again as she walked. Maybe a little girl, who would grow up pretty like Lori. Someone who would love and adore her the way Beth remembered adoring her own mother.

Beth shook her head. What was she thinking? Unlike Lori, she wouldn't much care what anyone at school thought, but Beth wanted to go to college, live in a dorm, travel during the summers. Maybe even have a boyfriend. How could she do any of that with a baby?

And—oh god—how was she going to tell her dad that she was pregnant? He'd ask her who the father was, of course, and she wouldn't be able to answer. Beth didn't think he'd get angry, but he would be hurt that she didn't trust him enough to tell him about it. And he'd be disappointed that she had, apparently, been careless enough to get pregnant in the first place. She could already imagine the look on his face; it made her want to cry.

Well, and she *had* been careless, if not in the way that would be assumed. Maybe she deserved what she'd gotten. But what about Lori, who had certainly been careless first? She didn't have to deal with any consequences at all, because she'd gotten Beth to take care of the problem for her.

Okay, that's not really fair, Beth admitted to herself after a moment. She couldn't blame Lori for that when she had volunteered the help first. If things had gone right, Lori wouldn't even have known about it.

Beth had a flash of imagining—what if someone did that for her?

What if she woke up at the next new moon and she wasn't pregnant anymore? She startled herself with how angry it made her, how violently she rejected the idea. Maybe she *would* have an abortion, but at least she wanted the chance to choose.

Though she had planned to take that choice away from Lori, without even realizing it. Maybe she had been wrong. What if she had actually hurt her friend instead of helping her? The thought made her sick. Her own predicament at least had some meaning while she thought that she'd kept Lori's life from falling apart. But if she'd been wrong . . .

The light changed from gold to gray as the sun sank behind the houses on her left. At the next corner Beth turned and started walking home, feeling that her whole life had been transformed just that suddenly. It was all too huge, too complicated and strange and uncertain, to even hold in her head at once. It made her dizzy and scared.

She didn't want the choice taken away from her, but neither could she imagine how she was supposed to decide this all by herself. She felt a sharp stab of missing her mother. I'm only seventeen, she thought, staring up at the sky. I'm not ready for this, for any of this.

Her dad wouldn't be like Lori's father, but he would be so disappointed. She needed his permission to get an abortion at the clinic. Unless . . . unless she tried the first spell in the book, the potion. Then no one would have to know. *Siknesse and grete peyne,* she remembered, and bit her lip.

A streetlight just in front of her began to hum, its bulb flickering ghost-white in the gray dusk. No one would have to know, Beth thought again, and then, like a dim echo, *What gave you the idea that I was pregnant?* But—she didn't want to be like Lori, pretending it had never happened. And that was a change, too, Beth realized in wonder; she'd always wanted to be like Lori.

Or maybe not completely. She'd been exasperated a lot of times when Lori wouldn't stand up to her parents. And Beth had wished Lori would open up to her more, sharing important things. If Lori had been talking to her about Rob all along, maybe Beth could have told her something, something that would have kept it all from happening.

And then she was crying in earnest, everything tumbling down on her at once: losing Lori, choices, her mother's death, a baby, her father's disappointment. She kept walking, though, and the streetlights flicked on ahead of her, blurred by her tears.

*   *   *

Beth could hear her father clanking pans and running water in the kitchen when she came through the front door. She turned and walked away from the sound, toward her bedroom, and then stopped. She'd gone off on Lori for avoiding her, and here she was doing the same thing with Dad.

If she went in there now, though, when she'd obviously been crying, she'd have to tell him what was wrong. Well, and wasn't that just what she'd wanted from Lori? For her to trust Beth with the truth?

To trust her dad would mean telling him all of it, about the spell, Lori, everything. Not so he could fix everything for her, not so he could take away her choices, but so he could help her make the best ones. So she wouldn't be alone.

Something like relief bubbled up in her chest at the thought. She realized that she had turned and walked toward the kitchen, though she hadn't made a conscious decision to do so.

"Dad?" she said from the doorway.

He was stirring something in a saucepan on the stove, his back to her. "Hi. I was wondering where you'd been."

She tried to keep her voice steady, casual. "Can you stop a minute? I need to talk to you about something important."

"Sure. Just a sec." He turned one of the burners down, peeked inside the oven door, took off the oven mitt, and then looked at her for the first time. Beth opened her mouth and froze, suddenly terrified. What if he didn't believe her?

"Oh, honey," he said, stepping forward and pulling her into a hug. The gesture made Beth start to cry all over again. She wanted to stand like that forever, with her dad's arms around her shoulders, one hand stroking her hair, and her face muffled in the front of his shirt. Eventually, though, it got too hard to breathe, and she had to pull back. Dad let her go, his face eloquent with worry.

"Here, why don't you sit down." He pulled a chair out from the breakfast table, guided her into it. "There. It's okay, honey. Tell me what's the matter."

Beth closed her eyes, took a deep breath, and began.

WICKED COOL

CONNIE HIRSCH

Connie Hirsch lives in Boston and knows firsthand the milieu of Wicked Cool. When not writing, she makes databases sit up and do tricks, reads a lot, plots expeditions to interesting places, and frets about not writing.

"The History of Sorcery in Western Civilization," better known in the college catalogue as "S201," is usually considered an easy A, but sadly nobody had told Professor Thurston. In addition to the usual lessons, I was gaining valuable experience in cutting it close. Habitually—okay, I'm not a lark!—I would duck under the Comm. Ave carpetline, though you're not supposed to, and avoid the traffic in the Quad by taking the fourth floor bridge over into the South Building.

I hadn't counted on Henry hanging in the stairwell. Again.

"I thought we settled this last month," I said, hands on hips.

He didn't say anything, looking agonized.

I did a quick check for passersby. No one—good. "Come down here right now," I said.

He made a tentative, sympathy-seeking moan that made me grit my teeth. "I don't have *time* for this," I said, and banished his ectoplasmic rope.

No rope, no suspension of belief. Habit and conviction were all that kept him in midair, but a mind like his doesn't hold with logic. Henry's ghost floated down next to me, looking hurt.

"Listen," I said, vowing to keep a reasonable tone. "We settled this . . . you agreed to give up earthly habitation and get on with your next life."

Henry sighed, his bow tie bobbing over his Adam's apple. "I got scared, Sadie," he said. "Getting born *hurts*. And—you won't be around."

Great. An obsession had gotten Henry into this in the first place. I opened my mouth as the stairwell doors were flung wide and the exiting classes descended, passing through Henry like he wasn't there. I fumbled with my purse, so no one would wonder why I was standing in a stairwell talking to myself. I did a silent burn; I was going to be late. Thurston usually discussed homework first . . . I probably wouldn't miss much.

The coast was clear, but Henry had disappeared. "Henry," I said. Anyone can call the dead, but when I call they *have* to answer. *"Henry,"* I said, adding the whammy.

He materialized, clutching his greasy yellow rope, looking startled as most spirits do when I exercise my Talent. "Would you put that away?" I said. "Listen, we can't talk now. I'll come back tonight, okay?"

Thurston chose that day to start with a pop quiz. I gritted my teeth and did the best I could. To add insult to injury, he launched into a rather biased lecture about the alternate, lesser magicks that White Sorcery had eclipsed—hunted down and rooted out is more like it! By the end of class I was about to boil over at the lies and half-truths. My best friend Pepper, on the opposite side of the room, caught my eye and gestured toward the door.

Jeremy Skinner intercepted me. Pepper looked back over her shoulder and winked, heading off in the direction of the caf'. No help there.

"Got a minute, Sadie?" Jeremy said, puppy-dog desperation in his eyes. In class, he was mostly sad, mysterious, and silent, but elsewhere he was just another tongue-tied lanky guy with gray hair and startling blue eyes and a letterman sweater.

"Uh, sure," I said.

"I was, uh, wondering—there's a new science fiction talkie downtown, and I thought you might like to see it, tomorrow night?" He looked at his feet, twisting a finger through a belt loop.

"I'm not into that stuff," I said. "I just can't believe in a world where everything is run by science."

"Oh, well . . . " he said. He was beginning to blush.

"Maybe some other time," I said. "Or some other show." I couldn't stop my urge for mercy. Better leave before I proposed marriage. "Gotta go now," I said, and bolted before he replied.

"Jeremy again?" said Pepper. She'd spread her fox coat over two chairs, reserving a table for us. "You should give him a chance."

"He's such a puppy," I said. "He ever said anything?"

"He asked if you had a boyfriend," she said.

"You *have* a boyfriend," I said. "Because he's studying medicine in Kenya doesn't mean you get to run my love life."

"Touchy," she said. "Just trying to help. We're doing love spells this quarter. . . ."

"*Oh no,*" I said. "Don't even think it."

"It wouldn't be any problem."

"Don't even think it."

Pepper shrugged. "Have it your way."

"Let me grab some food, okay?" I said, putting my books down.

"Already taken care of," Pepper said, snapping her fingers.

A plate with a cheeseburger, fries, and salad, and a Coke appeared on the table.

"Flashy, aren't we?" I said. Pepper is an Advanced Thaumaturgy student, and a good—or should I say "proficient"?—one. She's an ethnic witch, so it's been tough for her to learn "white" sorcery. Last year I wouldn't have blithely bitten into that cheeseburger—no guarantee it wouldn't turn back into newspaper and water in mid-bite.

"This must be costing you," I said. "Do you really want to waste so much money on a startled look?"

"Oh, the metawatts come from my lab account," she said. "I'm practicing." She took a sip. "Seems strange to hear such concern from someone who doesn't worry about the charges at all."

"You know that's for my specialized work," I said. Pepper wouldn't know karmic duty if it nipped her somewhere tender.

Pepper smiled. "I wangled an invite to a fancy party in Danvers," she said. "Want to go?"

I swallowed a bite from my cheeseburger—warm and juicy pink in the center, the way I like it—and said, "Party? Us? Since when do you get invitations for me?"

"You never go out," she said. "Always in your room, reading books or talking to yourself."

"You know I don't talk to myself," I said. "It seems like half the Half World knows my address—thanks to you."

"You have to admit—your ability sure came in handy."

"If you breathe Word One," I said, and glanced around for eavesdroppers. "The statue's back where it belongs, right?"

"Who, *moi?*" she said. "And incriminate myself? And you'd keep me haunted for the rest of my life."

I rolled my eyes.

"Anyway, this is going to be a grand party," she said. "You know, famous people, and"—she leaned closer—"*our kind.*" Yeah, witches, conjurers, exotics like me . . . the sorcerous demimonde. There's a lot of magick out there that's barely legal thanks to White Sorcery. My family's always been on the fringes of it, so I'm stuck.

Pepper smiled winsomely. "Besides, I don't want to go alone. Pretty please say you'll go?"

I took another sip. "I've got to counsel Henry tonight."

"Oh, he showed up *again?*" she said. "Are you sure you don't want me to exorcise him?"

"Ah, thanks, no," I said. I'd sooner perform psychic surgery on myself—without anesthesia.

"When are you working?" she said.

"Late—when nobody's around. I might have to astral travel."

"You'll need watching, then," she said.

"Oh, it's only for a little while," I said.

"Listen," she said, looking over her gold-rimmed glasses at me. "You may know all about spirits, but bodies are my department—and you put your corpus through the ropes when you leave it empty. I'll make sure you don't get carted off to the emergency room—or the morgue—if someone comes by."

Last year they'd believed me when I said I'd fainted, but the fuss had been embarrassing, and quite unnecessary. "I guess so," I said.

Pepper smiled. "So we'll hit the party at eight, split around eleven or midnight, get back to the North Building, you hand Henry his sheet music for the Choir Invisible, and get a good night's rest. How about it?"

"Famous people?" I said.

"*Fabulous* people."

Back in my dorm room I tuned in the crystal and let it yak while I got ready. There had been a break-in at police headquarters; a quantity of controlled substances had been taken, including cocaine, philosophers' stone, and dragonblood. I wondered idly if I should ask the spirit world for scuttlebutt . . . but the police hate amateur detectives. And they surely had their own Talents on the case.

I hurriedly donned a party dress, and fixed my hair—the evening was humid so it was curling all over the place. I settled for clamping it down with a headband. Pepper, of course, has a straight little bob that's never out of place. I was putting on my lipstick when there was a tapping at the window. I frowned; my room is on the third floor. Pepper was seated on her broom, hovering thirty-five feet above the sidewalk.

"Showoff broomjockey," I said though she couldn't hear me. I pointed down toward the ground floor. She can risk a ticket if she wants; I'm not about to get arrested for flying close to a building. Pepper's a safe driver. Except when she's not.

Pepper was waiting next to her broom, a feature-laden BMW two-seater courtesy of Mumsie, with sidesaddle seats and a Weathershield spell, big advantages with a tight skirt and a nice hairdo. I snapped on my safety belt; we lifted up and away. Pepper has one of those coveted freepath licenses, so we could bypass traffic. Boston drivers are justly feared, especially by other Boston drivers.

We flew straight east past the Pru Center, and soared over the Charles River Basin, cutting along the Mystic River to avoid the commercial traffic out of Logan Aerie. There were brooms, carpets, and a flying cookpot heading all over the place, running lights blinking. We followed the shoreline north to Danvers.

We hovered over Danvers Common, with its hokey statue to the First White Witch all lit up with magic lanterns. "Where do we go now?" I said. Pepper rubbed the invitation. It glowed with a faint violet light and danced in front of us.

"I'm impressed," I said, and I was: I'd only read of spelled invitations in romances.

The glowing paper led us to a posh neighborhood by the river where the *estates* had big lawns, gates, and walls, to the poshest mansion of all, lit like a wedding cake with lanterns and will-o'-the-wisps galore.

At the front door a liveried attendant stood ready to take the broom. He didn't even question who we were, just bowed. "Miss Pepper Potts and Miss Sadielyn Revenner," Pepper said to the footman who saw us in. If I had her name, I'd wince when announcing it. I sometimes wonder about Mumsie's sense of humor.

The house was *posh*, Persian carpets lining the corridors, wainscoting, wallpaper in shades of grape and fir. After a hike, we entered a ballroom featuring chandeliers, occasional furniture, occasional music, and people who glittered.

I blinked, taking it all in. To my relief, we didn't attract much interest. "So what now?" I whispered.

"Mingle," she said in a tone that suggested she was going to mingle with a vengeance and God help the hindmost. Pepper pulled me into the crush. I was glad I had worn my best, because this crowd dressed fancy: men in evening wear, and women in dresses that hang without price tags in Newbury Street windows.

Halfway across the floor, I touched Pepper's arm. "Is that *Jeremy?*" I said quietly. Across the floor there was a man who looked like Jeremy with a fake mustache and a dye job.

"Don't be silly," she said. "What would he be doing here?"

"I guess . . . " I said. Jeremy would surely have greeted *me*. . . .

Pepper dragged me onwards, to a distinguished-looking gentleman. "Mr. Fitzgerald," she said. "Thank you for inviting me to your party!"

I hung back. *John Fitzgerald? Of the Cape Ann Fitzgeralds?* I was impressed.

"My dear, charmed," said Fitzgerald, holding out his hand. The peroxide blonde on his arm looked graciously bored. "Remember me to your mother, will you? And you brought a lovely young friend?"

It was move forward or run screaming. "Hello," I said.

He kissed my hand and raised an eyebrow at Pepper.

"My best friend, Sadielyn Revenner," she said. "She's a medium." It's a respectable Talent, and in fact, I *can* channel, but it doesn't seem sporting when the unreincarnated, unblessed dead are obliged to cooperate.

He raised both white eyebrows. "An unusual specialty," he said. "Thankfully, I have no need to speak to my departed."

The blonde made a polite little cough. She was older than I had estimated, and looked vaguely familiar. "Miss Potts is the specialist I was telling you about, Venezia," Mr. Fitzgerald said.

"Oh! You're *Venezia,*" I blurted. Like she didn't know it—the fan dancer. "Sorry," I said, embarrassed.

"Happens all the time," Venezia said with a smile that hitched up her beauty mark. She turned to Pepper. "I need some special effects for my act, and I hear you're pretty good," she said.

"Shall we leave the ladies?" said Mr. Fitzgerald, offering me his arm. "May I get you some refreshments?"

I'd have rather stayed, but it's hard to refuse someone who was famous before I was born. The buffet had pâté, caviar and little crackers, a silver salver full of ice and pink shrimp, and more hors d'oeuvres than you could shake a china plate at.

"Care for deviled eggs?" said a waiter. He reached under the table and took out a silver cage containing a small brick-colored hen. A few standard somatic passes—I may not know much formal magick, but I've hung around Pepper—the hen cackled and an egg rolled into a little cup in the cage bottom. The waiter carefully sliced the deviled egg, arranging it on my plate.

"I've heard of chickens who lay hard-boiled eggs," I said, "but I've never seen anything like this."

Mr. Fitzgerald smiled. "My grandfather made his fortune in food wizardry; and we've stayed in the business even if the Talent has left our blood. This new breed is too expensive to produce commercially, so I employ the remaining hens at my parties. We also have a specialty line that lay Russian Easter eggs."

"I saw those in that catalog," I said.

"Father," said a young man coming up to us. He was the spitting image of Mr. Fitzgerald, only forty years younger, black hair, pale skin and dark eyes. "Not sporting of you to monopolize all the pretty young women."

"My son, William," said Mr. Fitzgerald. He introduced me with a courtly bow, and left the two of us standing alone.

"Rather boring affair, isn't it?" said William. He was handsome in a dissipated way.

"Oh, it's okay," I said.

"You're not one of Father's, ah, floozies, are you?" he said, running his hand through his hair. "Generally a sweet young thing with Father means he's hired entertainment."

"Sorry to disappoint you," I said, blinking.

"I like freelancers better," he said, leaning closer. His breath smelled funny, almost chemical, and I saw his eyes had huge pupils. "Or shall we say, gifted amateurs?"

I decided I should be insulted, but by how much? "Not my hobby."

William shrugged. "Care for a little blow? Or "—he leaned even closer—"I've got some dragonblood."

"I never touch the stuff," I said. I'm no idiot; it rots your brain and costs a fortune in the meantime.

He shrugged. "If that's the way you feel," he said, and walked away.

If that's the lifestyle of the rich, they can keep it. I abandoned my deviled egg on a waiter's tray and wandered, with perhaps a more critical eye than before. I couldn't find the guy I'd mistaken for Jeremy.

I looked at the furniture, the paintings, then went out the French doors into the deserted gardens, lighted with tiny lanterns. I wandered past a topiary of shrub critters, and brown-eyed Susans that turned to watch me pass. At the far end near the river, through shrubs and trees, I could see a lighted dock or something—I could hear men talking faintly. For lack of a better goal I headed that way.

I didn't get far, though. There was quiet movement in the darkness; a big dog stepped onto the path.

He had gray fur, like a wolf, but wolves aren't bigger than a Rottweiler. I didn't feel menaced, for he sat so quietly, thumping a bushy tail in the gravel, and panting a dog grin under blue eyes.

"Hello, boy," I said, holding out a hand. "Are you a friendly pup?"

He came over, head held low and tail wavering, to sniff at my fingers, then rub his nose against my hand. He sighed as I scratched behind his ears and ruffled his furry sides. His breath didn't smell bad, for a dog.

He gently butted his head against my thigh. "What do you want, boy?" I said. He went down the path a few paces toward the house and woofed softly.

"But I'm going this way," I said. He tugged at my skirt with his teeth— the other way. Perhaps he was a watchdog Mr. Fitzgerald used to keep his guests in line. "Okay," I said. "you show me where I want to go."

He yipped a little and bounded down the path, stopping to wag his tail, waiting until I caught up, repeating the process as he led me across the garden—we were not headed toward the house, exactly. He stopped at an ornamental pool and barked, indicating I should look.

I went over to the stone-lipped pool wreathed with wisps of steam, the bottom acrawl with sparkly little lizards. One clambered up on a scorched rock island and burst into flame. I watched it nibble on charcoal in an iron grate, and realized someone had quietly joined me.

It was a slight brown-haired man dressed in an old-fashioned tuxedo, with a waxed mustache, of all things. He nodded in greeting. "You found the salamanders—fascinating creatures, aren't they?"

At least *this* gentleman wasn't trying to be offensive. "I thought they were only in zoos and nature preserves, like griffins," I said.

"There's been a colony here for forty years," he said. "Fitzgerald has a special permit."

"Special permits for special people," I said.

"It never changes," he said sadly. "Privilege has its effect, I fear."

"Is something wrong?" I said.

"Nothing I should burden so young and sweet a lady with," he said. "Perhaps, though, you've seen for yourself."

I thought of William, boy cad. "Perhaps I have."

"Far easier to enjoy the grounds," he said. "I do—I did."

"This is a marvelous place," I said, noticing my wolfish friend had his head cocked with evident puzzlement.

"It has always been so," said my tuxedoed stranger. "I've seen owners come and go, yet the house retains its class."

I'd thought the house had been in Fitzgerald's family for generations, but what did I know? "My name is Sadie," I said. "I'm afraid I haven't caught yours."

"Jake," he said. "Jake Barnes."

"Glad to meet you," I said.

"If someone you knew, whom you felt deep affection for, were in trouble—and about to get into worse trouble," he said, "what would you do? Turn them in to the authorities, try to help them yourself, try to get someone to help if you couldn't?"

"Help, I suppose," I said. "I don't know what you're hinting at."

"William is in trouble with drug-runners," Jake said. "They're using the landing for deliveries."

"I don't understand . . . why are you telling me this?" I said, as Pepper came bustling down the path. I turned to look at her.

"Talking to yourself again?" she said.

I stared at her. "Funny," I said. "I've been having a fine talk with—" Jake was gone and so was the dog.

Pepper raised her eyebrows. "Not another ghost?"

On the terrace, I told Pepper about Jake and the dog. It didn't worry me that I'd mistaken Jake for a living soul—if the ghostly manifestation is strong enough, it's not unusual. What worried me was what the message he'd tried to deliver so delicately. "I could try some psychic detective work," she said.

"Please, no," I said.

"Call the police," she said. "That's what they're for, right?"

I shook my head. "What do I say—'a ghost told me'? Testimony from the dead isn't admissible for a search warrant."

"What about an anonymous tip?" she said.

"I'll try that if nothing else works," I said. I looked at my hands. "They're not likely to believe an anonymous source about a famous man's son. Maybe I should go right to the Thoroughbred's mouth himself."

"Talk to William?" Pepper frowned. "It'll only warn him off."

"Listen, I'm not the police," I said.

"Indubitably," she said.

"I'm no Karma Kop," I said. "But when a ghost asks for help, I can't refuse. What matters is William Fitzgerald, not lawfulness per se.

Maybe I can scare him into quitting . . . if not, I can make sure the bad guys can't use the private landing, at least."

"Your little bit for justice," Pepper said sarcastically.

"Don't laugh," I said, stung. "You hang with your fancy friends, I'll go have my talk, and then we'll get going, okay?"

"If that's what you want," Pepper said, standing up. "I'll go mingle. Don't be long."

I found William by the simple ploy of asking a footman, who showed me to a suitably impressive study. William looked startled when I walked in. "You reconsidered?" he drawled. "Rather late."

"Spare me," I said. "I found out about the deliveries."

"Oh?" he said, sitting up, flushing. "What business of yours is it?"

"None at all," I said. "I was asked by a . . . friend to help you, and I thought *asking* is always in season."

"I'm not going to be lectured by some snot-nosed college coed," he said. "Get out."

"Have it your way," I said. "If you don't quit drug-running, starting tonight, I'll go to the police."

William ran a hand through his hair. "You can't be serious," he said. "I have it under control, as soon as my debts are paid up—I certainly can't quit tonight."

I leaned forward. "I know enough to put you away. Unless you stop the dealing and get treatment, I'll get the cops." Bluff, but what did he know?

"You wouldn't," he said, twisting his fingers.

A hidden door opened in the bookcase behind William. "Oh, do stop whining, Billy," said the man who stepped through. Blond hair, green eyes, and a tan, he was dressed in a dark suit, sporting a pendant like a tiny golden hand. He wore black leather gloves. "You've always been so weak."

"You know why, Philippe," William said, flushing more.

"A fondness for dragonblood, and an excellent line of credit," Philippe answered. "Plus all the cover your family name can command. It was my lucky day when you came to me, William, and I am not finished with that luck yet."

"Hold it right there," I said. "I'm going to the police."

"Really?" he said. "I shall not permit that."

"Just what do you mean, Philippe?" William said.

"I've had enough of this," I said, turning to walk, but the vines woven in the carpet held me by the ankles. I turned back to Philippe. "I'll scream if you don't let me go," I said.

"Then I'd have to use this," he said, pulling a small, metallic object out of his jacket and pointing it at me.

I'd never seen a gun before, except onstage. "Ah, couldn't we talk this over?" I said.

"Don't be simple," Philippe said. He stripped off one of his gloves, careful to keep the gun aimed. His palm was tattooed, like legendary Black Hand sorcerers. "Pity you're not a virgin," he said. "I could get more use of killing you then."

His voice came from far away—a spell had made my limbs heavy, paralyzed my eyes; I felt my body levitating.

"What are you doing?" William said in a choked voice.

"Said she was going to the police," Philippe said. *Keep listening,* I thought with effort, *don't drift away.* "She came with that annoying little witch, so an amnesia spell is out of the question. I'll have to kill her."

"Please," said William. "There must be some other way."

"Don't be silly," said Philippe. I could hear him at the desk. "Here, take your medicine, and I'll see to business."

"But—people saw her enter here—they'll wonder—"

William was grasping at straws. From the prison of Philippe's spell, I urged him to grasp harder. Being alive, he couldn't hear me, alas.

"You'll tell them you chatted. It won't be your fault that later she slips, and falls in the salamander pond. Why, a gardener will swear he saw her walking that way."

"But there will be traces of magick?" said William.

"Not when the salamanders are done nibbling on her, no," said Philippe. "Sweet dreams." My body began to move, so I made a great effort—and stepped out of my corporeal self.

Astral travel was like a splash of ice-cold water in the face . . . if I'd had one. My astral self can't do more than observe and communicate with a few psychics, but I might get lucky. William was weeping, preparing his dose of dragonblood. No help there; if he was going to, he would have.

I had maybe ten minutes until I made a brief but intimate acquaintance with the salamanders, and henceforth had to do all my business from the Other Side. . . .

Find Pepper, I flew through walls and hallways to the ballroom, where the wash of magickal energy nearly knocked me out. Too many enchantments! I couldn't spot Pepper, and even if I had, she couldn't have *seen* me through the barrage.

I spread my consciousness thin through the mansion, but none of the staff had a trace of the medium's talent that I could try to possess. I'd never consider it but for an emergency.

I checked for Philippe's progress. He'd acquired two henchmen, and gotten my body out the back door onto the twisty back paths. I used the full strength of my telekinesis to lob a tiny pebble at him. He didn't so much as flinch.

I was so furious that I almost didn't notice when a hand was laid on my shoulder. "Events are not proceeding favorably?" Jake said next to me. He'd loosened his cravat and his cuffs.

"What do you think?" I said.

He sighed. "If there is anything I can do to help?"

"Can you poltergeist?" I said.

"Only a slender talent. . . ."

"Great, just great," I said. "This is all I can do."

"A pity we aren't more," said Jake. "Pebbles will add up."

I stared at him. "You might be onto something there," I said.

I concentrated like never before, reaching out to all the ghosts I knew personally: Henry, from campus; Hatsehpmun and Tefer, my mummy friends from the MFA; Josiah Button, the sailor who haunted the *Constitution;* and bunches more, everyone I could remember. I called locally, to all the old houses and graveyards in Danvers.

It was quite a crowd. They filled the garden paths and beds, ghostly feet not pressing down the grass, ghostly faces expectant. "Okay, listen up," I said, and told them quickly what they must do.

We swooped down the path; groups after the henchmen and Philippe, packing their astral essences in with the living person's body, draining warmth. The drug dealers began to shiver. "Did it get colder?" the tall one said.

"A breeze," Philippe said, looking around and clutching his arms. Another group began a pebble barrage: gravel from the pathway, twigs and loose leaves, whatever could be tossed.

"Ow! OW!" yelled the tall henchman, and the shorter, fatter one cried, "Something bit me!" Hatsehpmun still had teeth after all those years and wasn't shy about using them.

Philippe threw up a shield. To my astral eyes it gave off *blackness,* magick of the darkest kind. He hadn't gotten his metawatts from

Central Power, nosirree. While his henchmen hopped and yelped, he began to recite an exorcism.

"Faster!" I urged my helpers. If he completed that spell, we couldn't come within half a mile. I moved the henchmen's crew over to Philippe, but though his teeth chattered and his lips turned blue, he kept chanting.

The gray wolf-dog from earlier crashed through the bushes and landed upon the path, snarling. Philippe left off chanting—good!—that meant he'd have to start over.

"Uh, *nice* doggie," said the taller henchman, still flinching from the pebbles.

The doggie wasn't in any mood to be nice; he gathered himself to leap when Philippe's gun fired thrice, with an amazingly loud sound.

My canine rescuer was knocked off his feet, rolling into a flower bed. He didn't yelp, just got to his feet, shaking his sides as though he'd climbed out of water. They watched aghast as the dog seemed to condense his body into a manlike form, wolf-headed, sharp-toothed, and beclawed.

A *werewolf?* I thought. *As long as he's on my side.* He knocked the tall henchman ass over teakettle. "Boss—Help!" cried the remaining one, as he ran behind my body, still hanging in the air.

"Keep him busy, Lou," said Philippe, shaking the remaining bullets calmly out of the gun into his palm. As Lou scampered clockwise around my body, pursued by the werewolf, Philippe began an incantation. I caught the Latin word "argent," and realized he was changing the bullets into silver.

The werewolf left off chasing the henchman and tried to get at Philippe, then. The shield held, despite the werewolf's superhuman strength. I attempted to renew the coldness assaulting him, but the heat of Philippe's magick more than offset it.

Clearly audible beneath the growls was the sound of Philippe snapping the gun back together. "So, *Monsieur Loup-garou,*" he said, "your noble effort has been in vain." His shield pushed out suddenly, knocking the werewolf off his feet. Philippe took his time aiming, smiling coldly as the lycanthrope stood up, growling.

Suddenly, there were lights in the sky, and a great voice booming, "Freeze! This is the police! You're under arrest!"

Policebrooms were overhead, their lightbars flashing, spotlights harshly illuminating the garden in black and white. Even so, Philippe got off one shot. Immediately, the cops' wands sleeprayed him down.

I couldn't see what was happening; the spell on my body was failing, and even as my physical self was sinking to the ground, my spirit was sucked back into it, as always happens when I've astral-traveled too long. So though I tried to see what had happened to the werewolf, an overwhelming blackness swallowed me as I resumed my career as a creature of the flesh.

I awoke to pins and needles in my limbs, a splitting headache, and a truly terrible taste. "Sadie, speak to me," I heard Pepper say. "Sadie, open your eyes for me, hon'." I squinted open sticky eyelids and looked at her blurry face.

"'S everythin' okay?" My English wasn't working well, either. "Where'd you come from?"

"You had me worried," she said. There were paramedics and police officers looming over us. Pepper had taken over, as usual.

"What happened?" I said, as someone held a cup to my lips.

While I drank, Pepper said, with emphasis, "After we talked, I went down to the landing. Then I saw what's-his-face carrying you out of William's office, so I called in the cavalry."

That wasn't like Pepper at all; more likely she would have tried to take Philippe herself. We could have *both* been killed, then.

"What happened to the werewolf?" I said.

"Disappeared," she said. "They're bringing in police dogs to sniff him out."

"Excuse me, miss," said a gentleman dressed in a suit, waving a detective badge. "I'd like to speak with the witness."

"Could we do it inside?" I said, trying to get up. My legs were shaky, and I needed to put my arm around Pepper's neck.

Eventually they led us to a private room inside the mansion. We passed John Fitzgerald standing talking to the police, looking grave. The detective, whose name was Cellucci, sent Pepper away—much to her disgust and my disquiet.

"I'm not under arrest, am I?" I said, to buy time. Besides, it was an appropriate question. My headache was still pretty bad, I thought I was seeing double. Actually, the man sitting next to Cellucci was Jake. He smiled at me.

"Nothing of the kind," Cellucci said. "I have a few questions."

"I know you can't answer me—" Jake said, "I listened while they questioned Pepper. I'll cue you through what she said."

I nodded gratefully, and Cellucci took it to mean I'd talk. We covered a time line that didn't involve ghosts, necrophony, astral travel, et cetera. Jake was right there, prompting me along, but then he began to fade, holding on just long enough for Cellucci to ask his last question. And then Jake gave me a smile of exceeding bliss and left this plane for good. Sometimes, when ghosts have completed their karmic duty, it takes them like that.

Cellucci, of course, was oblivious to this, and getting suspicious when I looked a bit distracted. He left me with a stern warning not to leave until he'd checked back. Pepper immediately came in. "So what happened already?" I said.

Pepper hadn't even opened her mouth when someone tapped at the window. She raised an eyebrow and went over to open it.

Jeremy was crouching in the bushes—bare-chested at least, the sill giving him some modesty. "You've got to help me," he said to Pepper. "My clothes are hidden by the front gate and there are cops all around—I can't get to them without being seen."

"What's going on?" I said, brilliant as usual.

He lifted his left arm, streaked with blood. "Could you also get me some bandages?" he said.

"You're injured!" I said.

"Of course I am," he said.

"What's going on?" I said to Pepper.

"Wait," she said, touching her fingers to her head. Her lips moved. With a soft pop! of displaced air Jeremy's clothes and some squares of muslin fell to the floor.

"There goes my allowance," she said. "No way can that get explained in my lab account." She handed the clothes over and folded up the bandages. "Let me wrap that wound," she said.

"Just a sec', let me get my pants—" Jeremy said. He hopped around outside the window. "I'll pay you back, no trouble," he added.

Pepper shrugged. "I owe you for helping Sadie, okay?" she said.

"What is going on?" I said plaintively.

Pepper stared at me. "The werewolf, you simpleton!" she said.

Dawn broke over Marblehead. "That was you?" I said to Jeremy. "You never told me you were a werewolf."

He tried to shrug, but Pepper was working on his shoulder. "You never told me you talked with dead guys," he said. "Call it even?"

"I don't even know where to start," I said.

"I *tried* to head you away from Philippe," Jeremy said. "You acted weird, talking to yourself at the salamander pond."

"Then I showed up and he ran away," Pepper said. "After you left, I got worried, and checked on the landing myself—ran into Rover here, and we exchanged information. I called the police, and Jeremy ran to the rescue."

"I had the best chance against the gun," Jeremy added.

"What were you doing here in the first place?" I said.

"I moonlight for a detective agency," he said. "Old Man Fitzgerald wanted to get the goods on his son so he could force him into treatment."

"Well, Sonny's going to get treatment one way or the other," said Pepper. "Speaking of which, I want you to get that arm looked at by a witch doctor—I've only bandaged it up, healing spells aren't until next year."

I realized I was staring at Jeremy with the biggest grin on my face, so I sobered it up. He immediately grinned back.

"Hey," I said, "speaking of healing, I was supposed to go see Henry tonight!"

"Henry?" Jeremy said, his expression like a puppy dog that's been kicked.

"One of her after-death counselees," Pepper explained. "Sadie, he's been in that stairwell since 1925, he can wait another night."

"Well—" I said. "I guess he can."

Jeremy's expression perked right up. "Do you think he could wait one more night after that?" he said. "I think after all my trouble, you owe me one little date."

"Well," I said. "I guess I do."

THE SORCERER'S APPRENTICE

DENNIS L. MCKIERNAN

Currently living in Tucson, Arizona, **Dennis L. McKiernan** *began writing novels in 1977 while recuperating from a close encounter of the crunch kind with a 1967 red-and-black Plymouth Fury. His novels include* Caverns of Socrates, Voyage of the Fox Rider, The Eye of the Hunter, Dragondoom, *and the story collection* Tales of Mithgar.

The moment the door closed behind Varulian, Lenny headed toward the locked chest, the duplicate key in his hand. *Ha, the old bastard telling me to be careful and to stay out of his things. Duhhh! Like I haven't been training all these six weeks. Sure, you doddering old fart, I'll stay away—NOT!*

Varulian was going to be gone for the entire day, catching a Western Air down to LA to attend some stupid meeting with other doddering old farts, senile all. Hell, Varulian must be at least fifty. Way over the hill. Yes, fifty if he was a day, and deep into his dotage. But Lenny, now, he was sixteen almost seventeen, and he knew practically everything worth knowing, in spite of his youthful age.

The retired locksmith on Sweeny Street had done a good job, 'cause the key slid right in and the mechanism snicked open with hardly a sound. Lenny lifted the lid carefully, just in case there was a trap. But no alarm sounded and no trip wire released something nasty.

Inside was but a single item: a large, leather-bound tome with arcane symbols etched deeply on the bloodred cover and spine. With a grunt, Lenny lifted it out and laid it on the workbench. Quickly he heaved it open and began searching through the pages. Finally he found what he was looking for: *Ut Advoces Succubam.* Hot damn! Succu bam wham, thank you ma'am! Here it was!

Lenny had spied this page one day in passing, when the old dork had turned away for a moment. Lenny's Latin wasn't the keenest, but still, it was passable; hell, he had gotten this job on the strength of it. And he knew that *succubam* meant *succubus,* and being the kind of person he was, Lenny knew all about a *succubus,* having read every dirty word he could find in his Latin lexicon. I mean, how else would he have learned the Latin he knew? In any event he remembered thinking as he stumbled across the word, *Hey, baby, you can succu on this bus anytime.*

And now Varulian was gone, and Lenny had his chance. Carefully he read all the instructions, translating as he went. And he gathered together the ingredients as needed. He could not make out one of the words, which was either *quinquaginta* or *quinquagesimus;* he chose *quinquaginta* . . . I mean, what the hell, it would only make the spell more powerful.

When all was ready, he set wide the five black candles equidistantly 'round and lit them. Then with blue chalk he drew the mystic pentagram, tracing a route from candle to candle, leaving a tiny crack. Then he shed his clothes and carefully stepped into the great circle and placed the dishes on the points of the contained star.

He took one more candle, this one deep red, and lit it . . . and used the flame to ignite the admixtures within the dishes. Yellowish green smoke boiled up, and with his own body quickening, anticipating what was to come, so to speak, he intoned the words—*Advoco succubas! Advoco succubas! Advoco succubas!*—three magical times.

She was all over him, an incredible blond, moaning, groaning, pumping. In an explosion of delight he reached the pinnacle of pleasure, then fell back, spent. Much to his surprise, the blond stepped from the pentagram, moving out into the room. *What the*—? He looked. *Oops! Forgot to close the crack with the blue chalk.*

He started to get up, but the redhead was all over him, moaning, groaning, pumping. Again he was quickly brought to the peak of delight, and slumped exhausted. She, too, stepped from the pentagram, joining the blonde beyond the circle of black candles.

Lenny started to rise, but the brunette was all over him, moaning, groaning, pumping . . .

When Varulian returned from LA, he found his alchemical lab filled with fifty-one milling *succubae.* His apprentice Lenny lay naked and dead within a flawed pentagram in a burned-out candle-circle center. Varulian banished the *succubae* and eliminated the evidence and then dialed 911.

The autopsy turned up one thing most peculiar: Lenny's corpse had no brains.

THE STRING GAME

BARBARA A. DENZ

Barbara Denz lives and writes near Kingston, Washington, in a house surrounded by tall cedars. She has had careers in libraries, radio broadcasting, arts administration, and technical writing. She shares her life with husband, David, a changeable number of ferrets, and a network of writer friends on Genie.

Laurelin felt below the charred surface left behind by the freak lightning storm and searched for Earth energy she could use. A vine let itself be borrowed, and she wove it into a patch of fresh skin on Tal's charred face. She delved deeper to find more, weaving more vine skin as she went. The vine image fell apart in her hands as Earth closed her off. Tal groaned. Laurelin shivered from exhaustion, frustration, and too many tries to save her husband's life.

She blinked several times, trying to focus on the disarray of the temporary Healer's pavilion around her. A deep red-orange glow made Tal's charred skin look ghoulish and distorted. Laurelin gasped, wondering if her tug-of-war with Earth for energy had done something bad. She was trying things far beyond her training to keep him alive, and she had no idea what each level of Earth would bring back. She looked around to see the fire-soaked setting sun shift the colors to deep red and she realized that nightfall was nearly upon them. She had been working on Tal since he had stumbled into her arms a few hours ago. It seemed like only a few minutes had passed.

"You can't die!" she whispered, tears clouding her vision. She swiped them away with her sleeve, which was damp from a day of tears. Her voice was husky from breathing smoke for hours. Tal whimpered, his attempt at speech resulting only in a coughing seizure. It was the first he had communicated on his own since he had found her. She was encouraged at the possibility that he might live after all.

"Hush, don't try. Your throat is seared and you are badly burned. I don't know what else to try. I've done more than a blacktabard is allowed to do. I may be breaking the law, but if I don't keep trying, I will lose you. There must be a Master Healer or a whitetabard here who can help. It doesn't have to be a brownrobe. Anyone can do more than I can." Her vision clouded again. She shook her head fiercely, forcing the tears back behind her eyelids. *Don't babble!* she chastised herself. *He should be resting before we try anything else.*

"Did they save them all?" Tal whispered. He pushed at the bandages over his eyes with the awkward bandages on his hands. Laurelin moved his hands gently away. It took so little to overpower him now. He was so weak. "There were so many and it was so hot. . . ."

"Not everyone, love, but many more than if you had not worked so quickly. The floor of the temporary pavilion is full now. I can't see many spaces of grass mat. The healers that can are still working, but many patients have blacktabards like me feeding them broth and honeycakes, which is what I should do for you, too."

Tal nodded weakly. Laurelin couldn't tell if he accepted what she was saying or if he was just too weak to speak anymore. She busied herself with checking his bandages, all the while looking for an untabarded healer who could help her. There were so few in the pavilion, and they all looked totally drained. Even the novices and apprentices looked as tired as she felt.

She looked around. When she last remembered actually looking around her, the pavilion had been full of white- and black-tabarded healers in many different-colored robes of the Elements from which they drew their power. Then she had thought that there would only be a few people she didn't know who could be healed with her unguents and healing herbs. The bell from the Healer's Hall across the valley had rung from dawn until midmorning, calling any healer in its range. Her town was close, so she had been at the tent when it was set up and had taken a place on the mats near the edge and with a pole she could lean against. She had not known then that it was Tal's wagon train of several hundred travelers that she would be working on. She only discovered that when he had appeared before her, seared, bleeding, exhausted, and barely alive. She had been busy ever since trying to keep him alive and forgetting there was anyone else there.

Her stomach rumbled, bringing her back to the chill of early evening. The honeycakes someone had left beside her during the day were but a faint taste in her mouth now. Whoever had left them had her undying gratitude, but she needed more energy if she was going to try any more healing.

"Tal, do you hear me? I must leave you for a moment. I will get you something to drink and food for both of us." She caught the eye of a young man bandaging a child a short distance away. He had heard her and nodded that he would watch Tal. She signaled her thanks, reminding herself to bring back food and drink for him, too. "There's a black-tabard grayrobe not far away. If you need anything, he can help. I have to eat if I'm going to do any more."

Laurelin stood in a clumsy jerk, stumbled, fought back a wave of exhaustion that almost toppled her, and grabbed the erecting pole to balance as she fought back the black edges closing in on her sight. "It's just exhaustion," she whispered. "It will go away if you breathe and concentrate." One breath. Smoke filled her lungs and she coughed. The grayrobe looked up and started to rise, but she signaled him not to worry.

"Take another," she chastised herself. "Slowly now. You have to get to food and water. This is for Tal."

With all the forward momentum she could muster, she focused on the untabarded azure robe of a Master Water Healer who munched tiredly on a honeycake from the pile of sweets on a nearby food-laden table. Carefully, Laurelin stepped around cots and other novice and apprentice healers and reached the table without harm to anyone.

She bit into a meat pie while her free hand stuffed fruit, meat pies, and honeycakes into her robe pockets. It would be a mess later, but she didn't care. She rinsed off sooty hands in the herb-scented washtub nearby and waited for the healers to finish their conversation. She always felt so tongue-tied around the levels higher than her own.

". . . we will have to let the worst cases die," said one of the two apprentice Wind healers in white-tabarded gray robes. Both young men leaned against tables, their eyes sunken and black-ringed and heads nodding with the weight of exhaustion like her own.

"Wind has dropped with the passage of the storm that brought the lightning and the Sun healers have just lost their source of power. There will be a waxing moon tonight, but it will be shrouded in smoke and will greatly reduce what the Moon healers can do. If it would rain, you Water healers could use that. The only healers who have had any-thing to work with today have been the Fire healers, and they are exhausted. Once some of them get some rest, they can work by the larger campfires."

The Master Healer pushed back stray tendrils of white hair and stared at nothing for so long that Laurelin wondered if the azurerobe was listening. The Water healer's eyebrows knit together and her lips were a tight, thin line. The only thing that gave away her anguish was a tremble in her chin and a bright sheen on her eyes in the firelight.

"Let it be so," she said, her voice filled with defeat. "Let the black-tabards see to their needs as best they can for the night and the whitetabards and Masters will rest and work tomorrow on those who remain."

"I could help if you would show me how," Laurelin heard herself say.

Three pair of eyes turned her way. She saw them take in her sooty and bloody black tabard and her equally filthy brown robe. The gray-robes' eyes danced with laughter and the azurerobe shook her head.

"Earth will not let you through now, young woman," said the Master. "She is healing herself. Surely you have felt that as you have been working today."

"But it is my husband I must save. He led the wagons and is badly burned. I have done all I know how to do, but there must be more you can show me. Once he is stable, I could help with others."

"I cannot begin to teach you your string runes now even if I knew them," snapped the Master. "Haven't you noticed that you are the only healer here in brown? And you are a mere blacktabard at that!"

Laurelin jerked her face away from the verbal slap, the sting of the words leaving behind a growing red welt on her soul. It was the same excuse she had heard since The Testing showed her strength to be Earth healing. The unspoken question was always there: "You took the tests at puberty and you are a woman now. Why are you still just a blacktabard?" She knew they all thought it. She asked the same question daily.

"I cannot help what has chosen me," she whispered. "I can only help keep my husband alive with what I know."

"What is your name, child?" the Master sighed.

"I am Laurelin."

"Then, Laurelin, I apologize for being harsh. I did not mean that the way it sounded. I know you cannot help what has chosen you, but neither can I guide you through the runes you need to access more healing power. There are so few browns and I have seen none in weeks of traveling. Please, just help the other novices keep patients alive until dawn so that we may rest. Your bandages and poultices and unguents will help most tonight. Give the wounded water if they ask for it, and broth and honeycakes if they will take them. The rest of us will help once we have eaten and slept. Now I must rest before I fall down." She smiled wanly at Laurelin but dismissed her with the look.

Laurelin could feel the tears try to carve a clean channel down her cheeks. She went to the washing basins and rinsed off again, more thoroughly this time. It wasn't just soot she was removing. It was Tal's soot. And his skin. And his blood. By the time she was scrubbed almost raw, Laurelin had made up her mind.

She gathered fresh water, rinsed the small, carved flat-bottomed bowl she carried from her belt, collected a container of water for the grayrobe, and went back toward Tal. She munched another meat pie as she walked. She set two meat pies and a honeycake from her pocket next to the grayrobe, along with the water, and whispered her thanks. His hands were signaling some rune in the air that Laurelin did not know. It must not have worked, for his hands dropped in exasperation and he looked even more tired than when she had left. He signaled his thanks and set upon the food with the voracity of a spring bear.

Tal was sleeping restlessly but awoke to her footfalls and turned his bandaged eyes in her direction. He had always known when she was coming. Even as children when they played together, he had followed her. When she was ten and he thirteen, he had asked her to be his wife. That was before she had tested and before her parents had died. It was all so much simpler then. They had married secretly when she was seventeen. It was on the first caravan he was apprenticed to, and a priestess had joined their hands. When they had come home with their vows legal and consummated, there was nothing his family could do. That was nearly five years ago now, and although Tal would no longer take her with him on caravans he led, they still adored one another and spent what time they could together. Of course he would find her when he was wounded. And of course she would do everything she could to keep him alive. There was not the slightest doubt in her mind.

"Tal, there is only me to help," she said softly, cradling his head so he could drink. "Sip some of this water and try to eat a honeycake, and then you must rest quietly. I need to think of something new."

He nodded and sipped. He tasted a corner of a honeycake, but his lips and throat were still too raw and he winced in obvious pain. Laurelin soaked the cake in water until it was mush and spread it on his tongue. Tal sucked on it, then lay back, exhausted at that little bit of movement. She lifted his head up, trying not to cause more pain on burned skin.

"Drink some more water. You need the fluids."

When he withdrew from the cup, Laurelin laid his head back on her folded cloak. She removed the remaining food from her pockets and placed it nearby, eating a honeycake and another meat pie until she felt too stuffed for any more. She wrapped his cloak loosely around him and kissed him on forehead, nose, and lips. He touched the side of her leg as she settled down to work.

"I love you, Laurie. No matter what happens, I love you," he rasped.

She closed her eyes, pushed tears aside, and stilled her breathing. "Let's see," she heard herself say. "Knitting doesn't work. Weaving doesn't work. Making bread hasn't worked. Trying to make spiderwebs doesn't work. There needs to be an image that will work. That's all you have to do, Laurelin. Find the image that works." She sipped more water, and the image came to her in mid-swallow. She almost choked, it was so amazingly simple.

"Of course!" she giggled, hearing the hysteria in her own laughter. "A river!"

She put her hands on Tal's heart and matched her heartbeat to his. Then her hands began making patterns in the air.

Laurelin dropped into Earth and searched for a path to the river of healing she needed. She pushed through seared grass and trampled mud past knotted roots, wriggling things, and fresh spring shoots. She reached resistance in the dirt and moved along it until it, too, let her pass. She didn't know where she would find it, but she knew there must be a river of Earth's own healing energy down here somewhere. If she could just find that and borrow a little for Tal. All she needed was a little of that river.

Deeper she pushed until she found barrier after barrier in her way. Earth was using her own energy and wouldn't share. Laurelin felt herself getting more frustrated as she tried new patterns that led her deeper into unknown areas. She had left burrowing animals far behind, she had floated in underground springs and pushed through more layers of rock than she knew existed. She had tasted salts and sand and still there was no energy for her to use.

She tasted the rotten eggs and felt searing heat before she knew she was near the source, but she was moving quickly and freely now. Before she could slow down, she was in a river of Fire energy that was finding a new path through her. She pulled away from it and swam sideways as she would to escape the pulling current of a normal river. It followed her, its current alive and seeking an exit. She looked for an underwater spring to quench the fire. The water she found turned to steam as the fire pursued and snapped at her heels. She searched for mud and it turned to bubbling gray globs around her. There was nowhere to go but up, and before she could snap closed the link, it had followed her to Tal.

She screamed and screamed as molten energy spat fire and mud and steam from her hands. Tal's body jumped like a puppet, and she could feel his bandaged hand tighten on her leg, and then go slack. Someone shouted for everyone to move back and she felt a river of cooling fluid being forced through her, pushing the molten rock back down and solidifying a plug to keep it there.

"Now you understand why there are so few Earth healers, don't you, girl," a strong female voice thundered in her ears. "Let go of Earth. Let go so she can heal her own. He's already dead."

Laurelin let go and welcomed blackness.

"And did you kill your husband?" asked Ans, the leader of the Council of Elders and Tal's father. She could see the fire that had killed Tal again in his father's eyes. Was it really only three days ago? She had felt so many emotions since then that all she felt now was numb.

"No," Laurelin shouted. Her voice wobbled as she fought for control. She looked at the angry faces and lowered her eyes. "Yes," she whispered, "yes, he died because of me, but I didn't kill him. Well, I did kill him in a way, but it wasn't my fault. Was it?"

"If not yours, then whose?" The tight anger in his voice was something Laurelin was used to. He had not wanted her for a daughter-in-law. She had brought no status to the family. She was a healer, yes, but she had never been trained, and the status of healers was usually established with the white tabard before they reached maturity. She had passed maturity as a blacktabard and was scorned. She always thought she had made herself immune to the sting, but somehow that fire in his eyes burned her cheeks, and she felt the old insecurities and humiliation.

"I didn't know what was there," she stammered. "I had never been that deep down. My hands just did what they needed to do. I would never hurt Tal. Surely you know that. The fire made it so difficult to get through Earth and I had to try. I couldn't let him die." Her voice had dropped to a whisper.

"You admit, then, that you were acting beyond your training and doing more than you should?" demanded her father-in-law, now no more to her than the man who held her life in his hands.

Laurelin looked from the raised dock in which she sat down at the well-worn floorboards of the Elders' Hall. What could she say? Nothing justified what she had done except her love. And what justification was that? She had killed him anyway. And the penalty for overstepping her training was exile or death. For three days she had hoped they would say "Death."

A river of whispers surged forward from the back of the room. Laurelin looked up. The whispers followed the footsteps of a tall woman in untabarded brown. Dark hair was cropped short and the dark brown eyes had a glint to them like the fiery mudpots she had passed through on the way back to Tal. Laurelin gulped, suddenly unable to breathe or swallow.

"I am Jenna, Master Earth Healer. May I speak?" Laurelin knew the voice. It was etched in her mind like scratched glass. It was the voice that had told her to let go of Tal.

"We are honored by your presence, Healer. It has been many years since a full healer graced these halls. How may we serve you?" The reverence in her father-in-law's voice almost made Laurelin laugh. She had not heard such deference since her father had died when she was just past The Testing. They had buried him in his gray robe.

"Had we known of this novice when she was a child and been called to test her, we would have seen her talents. What happened to your son need not have happened." Jenna's scan of the council was accusing. Laurelin gasped. No one spoke to Ans and the Elders this way. Jenna signaled her to be silent.

"Her family left her no dowry for study. We could not send her away without it."

"And why not? Could you not see her strengths when she played with string as a child?"

The words ricocheted through Laurelin's head, teasing at the crumpled edges of memories long buried. The string? Her earliest memory was of her father slapping her hands and her mother burning all the string in the house. Ans continued, his voice booming in the embarrassed silence of the hall.

"She was tested with the others when she was eleven," he began defensively. "She did not know any of the patterns. Her father would not teach her, and she had not known what to do. The patterns had fallen apart in her hands. Even though her father was a Master Wind Healer, he had insisted that someone else test her. I think he did not believe that his daughter would have the power. In his family, the men became Wind healers, but the women showed no talent until her. I do not think he knew how to relate to a daughter, much less one with power he did not understand. I tried to understand, but he was a Master and on the Council of Elders, and we did not question. The Master Fire Healer must have felt something, for she gave Laurelin her first black tabard and brown robe. Master Del argued about the choice of brown, insisting that there must be a mistake, but the Fire healer had been adamant."

In the years after her testing Laurelin talked to other healers and learned that they had been shown patterns as children. They had called the game "cat's cradle" or just "the string game." All parents taught the basic string patterns just in case their child might test to be a healer. All parents but hers, that is. Even Tal had known. After her parents died, she had been fostered to Tal's parents. When Tal found out that she did not know the game, he had taught her the basic patterns in secret. It was then that she felt the first shift into Earth and she had explored what lay below the grass. She could not have known that she had found Earth with a Wind healer's runes that Tal had picked up from watching her father at work.

"String was banned from her life when she was small. Her father decided that it was unsafe in her hands and said he feared for her life and ours. He said he had no money to pay the rate for Earth training. What could we do but agree? When her parents died suddenly, the town agreed never to allow her to learn more. I took her as my own daughter so I could keep Master Del's wishes. I didn't know until later that my own son was teaching her. And now she has killed him with the knowledge."

The healer strode forward, finger extended and face blotchy with anger.

"Her father knew her talent and he denied her the training? He was a disgrace to his training."

"A Master Healer would know best," Ans said with more reserve than he looked like he felt.

"Nonsense. How could you all in good conscience hold her for trial now? I felt the talent in this young woman when I pulled her from the cinders she made of her life. Not in all my years have I had so much raw talent fight back at me. Her error was a result of your neglect and oversight. What makes you think what you have done to her is any less of a crime than what she did?"

"But she had the talent for Earth. No other element called to her," Ans' voice pleaded. "The string test for the other elements gave her nothing. Even we know that without at least an apprentice Earth healer nearby, she could have killed herself at the least and all of us at the worst. Laurelin's father, Del, told us that the other elements are easier to control. He said we could simply move the person away from the element. But the Earth energy draws from the center core of flowing fire. After he died without training her, we just couldn't afford to send her away, and we couldn't afford to let her learn."

"It cost you less to make a sacrifice of your son?" Jenna demanded. "And you dare to blame her now? She has worn her tabard for years. Just where did you think she was getting her energy to work if not from sheer determination? She was bound to find the right method someday."

Laurelin heard Ans sob, but it was the words spoken on her behalf that left three things at the fore of her concentration, and they felt like that burning core of Earth had felt.

She had talent, and there was hope she could learn. Jenna had saved her life when all she wanted to do was die. And the string game was important. The room exploded from the silence following the healer's words as many voices rose in anger. Laurelin didn't even know she had spoken aloud.

"Quiet!" Jenna demanded. "Laurelin, what did you ask?"

Laurelin hesitated, not sure she really wanted to repeat her question. Her mouth was dry.

"Master Healer, are you saying that the game could have helped me save Tal?"

"Call me Jenna, child," the healer prompted.

"As you wish, Master Jenna. Can I know the significance of the string patterns? And . . . " Laurelin looked down, twisting the edge of the tabard. "And can I still be trained?" Laurelin looked through tears into the brown eyes and watched emotions that ranged from anger to sympathy to decision.

Stools shifted and Council members and townspeople coughed and whispered.

"Silence," the healer demanded again without looking away from Laurelin's gaze. She reached out and took the novice's nervous hands in her own. When murmurs died and shuffling ceased, she continued.

"Of course you can still be trained. I would not be here if you were lost to us." She held Laurelin's hand until the novice relaxed despite herself. Only then did Jenna let go and look to the now-silent gathering.

"Ans, I understand why you acted as you did, but surely you can see that this trial is a charade and that the sooner you let Laurelin go, the sooner I can begin the training she needs to make your town proud to have her represent you."

Ans took silent survey of the Council members. There was firm agreement in all their faces.

"We find her guilty of the murder of my son. Her punishment is to leave here until she can control her Earth energy as a Master Healer. So it is spoken. So shall it be."

The rest of the Council murmured its assent, and Ans gaveled the matter closed. "We are finished."

The murmur began again but quieted as Master Jenna spoke.

"An interesting sentence," Jenna said, "and more of a sentence than you know." She looked long and hard at Laurelin until the younger woman squirmed.

"I think we need to be in the home you and Tal shared to start this. Ans, you may pick the standard judgment group of six and meet us there. And bring one child who has the string."

Laurelin rose slowly from the hard wooden chair and followed the Master Healer. Behind her followed the whole town. By the time she reached her home, everyone but Jenna, Ans, three of the Elders, the hearthwitch, Silva, to whom Laurelin had been apprenticed all these years, and Silva's six-year-old son, Tre, were all that remained. Laurelin stopped and stared at the familiar place. She had not been able to cross that threshold since Tal's death. Jenna took Laurelin's hand and walked to the door with her.

"Trust me, Laurelin. It must start here. Can you believe that? You must believe it for us to begin."

Laurelin swiped the tears from her eyes and took a deep breath. She walked to the carved front door and ran her fingertips over her initials and Tal's intertwined with vines and leaves. She looked to Jenna, nodded, opened the door, and stepped inside.

Jenna signaled the others to take their places.

"Who brings the string?" She began with the formal opening for The Testing.

Silva nudged Tre. He pulled a dirty wad of string from his pocket. It was knotted into a meter-long circle. He stumbled forward and held it out to Jenna.

"Thank you," Jenna said, smiling. "You may stay close and watch if you like."

Blushing, the little boy ran back to his mother and hid in the folds of her dress, peeking back toward the healer from the safest place he knew. Laurelin smiled and he smiled back, his shyness overcome. He inched forward to watch.

"Laurelin, sit down and get comfortable. This will take more energy from you than you have ever known. I am going to make a figure with this string. Watch my hands. You will make this and I will talk you through other figures. I will be monitoring you, so do not be afraid of what you feel. Are you ready?"

Laurelin nodded. She watched Jenna wrap the string around her hands, reach across with her middle fingers, and form a figure with the string. The healer let the string fall and gave it to Laurelin, who mimicked the rune. They followed through the traditional beginning patterns until they reached one that Laurelin did not know. She completed the pattern and through her feet she felt a sharp jolt, and she could taste Earth and was burrowing into it. She was a taproot. There was no metaphor needed. She looked up, startled.

"Yes," Jenna said, smiling. "It feels quite odd at first, doesn't it? Now watch. You'll make this one next."

Laurelin watched and followed Jenna through three more figures of increasing complexity. With each new figure, Laurelin could taste and touch deeper into Earth. She also felt Jenna's now-familiar touch keeping her from going too deep and guiding the amount of energy she used. She heard her speaking, but her own focus was in Earth. Her roots spread sideways under her home and into the fresh grave in the field behind the house.

"That is the importance of the string, Laurelin. Every child is taught the game, but only those who mention feeling the tie to an element are allowed to go on. The string is then taken away from those with talent, and teachers are found for them to guide their element and to get them to the Healer Guild they need."

Laurelin felt Jenna's touch forcing her away from the Earth she loved and the man she had loved and killed. She had been with him again, her arms around him as roots.

"It is time to come back, Laurelin. You cannot stay here. The whole purpose for drawing the energy is to heal with it. Right now the only one who needs healing is you, and neither Earth nor I can do that."

Laurelin did not want to come loose. She clung to the Earth and fought Jenna's touch. The Master Healer pushed, tearing the string from Laurelin's hands and closing Earth to her. Laurelin collapsed in tears, drained of all energy and grieving at the losses of her husband, her training, and her Earth. As she swiped at her eyes, the dust on her hands flaked into mud. She stared at them, amazed that it had come back with her.

"Why didn't you let me stay with him?" she whispered.

"My training would not allow it, and this is not your time," Jenna said gently. "I would have violated my vows if I had let you stay. You will learn what those vows mean. I will make sure of that. Now we must eat."

Laurelin looked around her. The room was silent except for Tre, who was chattering at Jenna and handing her a sweet cake and a mug of juice.

"Does cat's cradle always make people tired like that?" he asked.

"No," Jenna told him. "Only a few of us get tired like this. But we like it when people like you can keep us filled with cakes."

"I can do that," he said with confidence. "My mother lets me serve all the time." He passed the plate to Laurelin again and sat down with a cake for himself.

Jenna slouched in the chair, her head resting on the back as she munched slowly. She looked to Ans.

"This is what you have denied her," Jenna said. Her voice was thick with exhaustion. "If she chooses to return to you after her training is complete, I hope she will be treated with full observance of the rank she will hold then." She rested her elbows on her knee and reached across for another honeycake.

Laurelin shook her head. "I couldn't leave here forever. Everything I am is here. Tal's memory is here." She looked at her father-in-law, those who had watched her be tested, and returned her glance to Jenna. She had doubts that what she had just said was totally true. She felt betrayed and angry, but at the same time, she couldn't truly blame the town. Her own dead parents had made the decisions that denied her the training. There was nothing she could do about them. And there was no longer anything she could do about Tal, either. She couldn't forgive herself, but she also couldn't blame herself anymore. There was no way anyone could have known she had the power she did.

"You should rest, Laurelin. We will leave tomorrow to start your training in earnest."

Laurelin swallowed wild berry juice, washing down the meat pie she had been eating without thinking. She nodded her agreement without looking at anyone. She rubbed her eyes, feeling all the exhaustion of death and discovery settle in and demand sleep. She said her apologies to her husband, picked up the string from the table next to the food, and walked into the bedroom to cry alone and to pack. Without meaning to, she left the door ajar and heard what was not meant for her ears. She heard Jenna say farewells to the witnesses and believed all to be gone. She was surprised to hear Jenna and Ans.

"What did you mean when you said that our sentence was more than we realized?" Ans asked.

"You said that she could not come back until she had been fully trained. The passage from apprentice to Master Healer is traditionally made in the place one is raised, since the strongest power we have is where we make that passage. By condemning her to finish her training elsewhere, you have made it impossible for her to ever be strongest here. Now you must decide if that is what you and your town wish. If you change your minds, you can find us at the Healer's Hall. Now I must ask you to leave. We both need to rest."

Laurelin made the first two runes from memory and searched for Tal. Maybe by the time she was ready to come home, they would allow her to take her final Testing here. Maybe by then she would not want to stay in Earth. Maybe. She stroked his cheek and ran roots tendrils through his hair, wrapping his shrouded body tightly and drawing him close to her heart.

She felt stronger roots unwrap her delicate ones and push her back to the surface, weaving an impenetrable cocoon of clay around Tal.

With tears streaking her now-muddy face, Laurelin fell asleep and dreamt of Tal.

THE KIN OF RÍG

DIANA L. PAXSON

Diana Paxson has contributed stories to all of the Sword and Sorceress anthologies. Her most recent books are a trilogy based on the Nibelungen legend: The Wolf and the Raven, 1994. The Dragons of the Rhine, 1995, and The Lord of Horses, 1996.

The night had been stormy, but since dawn the rain had settled to a soft, soaking downpour that had worked its way through one corner of the weaving shed and was dripping onto the packed-earth floor. Arnkel's stead was a prosperous place, with a gaggle of outbuildings clustered around the great hall, but Hrímaldi was beginning to revise his opinion of the *bonder's* hospitality.

Grípir was still asleep, snorting and gurgling as if he were drowning in the damp air. Hrímaldi had tucked his cloak and his spare tunic around his master's thin body and drawn the Torch rune in the air above him, but the old man's skin still felt colder than his own. He suppressed a shiver of panic—Grípir was so fragile! Were there other runes he could chant to ease him? He knew the futhark well enough—both the shorter row of sixteen signs that men used now and the elder, twenty-four-rune row the god Odin had first given to men, but he was only beginning to understand the many ways in which they could be used.

He heard splashing outside and pushed open the door. A girl was picking her way through the puddles, her shawl of tightly woven wool pulled over her head.

"Good morning—" she said brightly. "I am Gudrid Arnkelsdaughter. Did you have a peaceful night?"

"Nothing troubled us—I think even the rats were hiding from the rain . . . " Hrímaldi answered with a smile, and wondered why she looked so relieved.

"My mother bids you come up to the hall and eat." She peered past him, frowning as she heard the old man snore.

"Grípir is ill," said Hrímaldi. "I will have to bring a bowl back to him. . . ."

"Ill? What is the matter?" Some of the fresh color left the girl's skin, and she glanced nervously around her.

"A rheum that has gone to the lungs—" Hrímaldi shrugged helplessly. "He had been coughing for several days."

"Then he was sick before you came here—" Gudrid's face cleared.

Hrímaldi nodded. "He thought he could make it to Nidaros. He carves runestones—" he explained, "and one of King Harald's men wants a memorial for his son. But yesterday Grípir grew dizzy. He was sure he could go on this morning, but he is worse—"

"I should think he would be," said the girl, peering into the shadows of the shed and shivering. "Are you his son?"

Hrímaldi straightened and met her eye to eye. "I am his thrall," he said flatly, and felt her inner withdrawal, though she did not move.

Hrímaldi had his sooty hair and his fine bones from his mother, a foreign woman that Eric Blood-Axe had brought home with his other booty from the great viking he made in the Finnmark and Bjarmaland; she herself had not known which of her captors had fathered her child. He was only seven when she died. If Grípir had not fetched him up by the scruff of his neck from beneath the table where he was fighting for scraps with the dogs and taken him in part payment for a memorial stone, he would probably be dead, too.

I should have kept my mouth shut, thought Hrímaldi. If the old man died, his thrall would belong to whoever thought he had the right to claim him. All men might be the children of Ríg, the name the god Heimdall had worn when he walked among men, but the offspring of a slavewoman could never be an earl, no matter how carefully he studied the runes. And yet his thralldom was the only kinship Hrímaldi could claim with the old man—the only connection he had to anyone. The thought of losing Grípir frightened him because for the past seven years there had been no one but the runemaster to care about him at all.

"Well, he is not going to get any better lying here," Gudrid said practically. "I will send men to bring him up to the hall."

By evening, warmth and the herbs that Gudrid's mother had brewed had Grípir sitting up and swearing. Hrímaldi relaxed enough to notice that though his master might be better, at the farmstead something was very wrong. The doors were barred as soon as night fell, and no amount of good food and drink could ease the tension in men's eyes. The wind had come up with darkness; frowns deepened as it howled round the eaves, and though it was already warm, men put more wood on the long hearthfire in the center of the hall. He nudged Grípir's shoulder.

"What are they afraid of?"

The old man's gaze traveled around the hall, bright as a bird's, and Hrímaldi saw it fix on the bundle of spear-leek and vervain and other herbs tied above the door.

"Nothing human," he croaked.

"Nothing that's human *now!*" said one of the men. His companion tried to hush him, but he shook his head. "The old man might as well know what kind of place he's come to for refuge."

Grípir's bushy brows lifted. "I am a runemaster, a man of the Heruli, and there are few things in Midgard that I have not seen."

Arnkel leaned forward between the carven pillars of his high seat and nodded to his man to continue.

"We had a neighbor called Bolverk, a berserk who picked quarrels with everyone he met until he finally challenged my lord Arnkel, who is the chief man of this district, and Arnkel, who has fought beside King Harald, took him down."

"That should have been the end of it," said Arnkel himself. He was a big, stout fellow with the shoulders of a warrior, red-bearded as Thor though his hair was beginning to thin. "But the wretch will not stay dead. When the moon is full he walks, no matter how we weight his howe with stones. We have moved the corpse to a new grave and sown flax around it, but still at night he gangs, with a great gaping hole through his chest where he was staked down. No one now will dare stir out of doors after nightfall, for he attacks them, and several men have died." Arnkel had the angry, uncomprehending look of a man whose strength has always been sufficient to solve his problems.

"Kind of you to leave us outside in the shed," muttered Hrímaldi, and Gudrid, who was passing with a pitcher of ale, heard him and flushed.

"You came just at the hour between night and day," she whispered in reply. "We did not know what manner of men you might be." She straightened and turned to her father. "Master Grípir is a stonecarver. Let him carve a runestone for the grave and the *draug* will not walk again."

Arnkel leaned forward, gripping his drinking horn. "Could you do that, old man? Carve a stone that will bind this creature to his grave, and I will send you to Nidaros in a wagon, lapped in furs."

Grípir laughed creakily. "I owe your goodwife something already for doctoring me, but I will not refuse your assistance. Find me a good piece of limestone to work on, and I will make a spell that would bind Loki himself in the grave."

The swiftness with which the folk of Arnkelstead had brought in the stone was a measure of their fear, thought Hrímaldi as he labored to shape and smooth it. A corner of the hall had been cleared for them to work in; Hrímaldi was grateful to be out of the wind that whispered its own runes in the thatching while Grípir muttered and swore at the scratchings on his slate as he struggled to shape the spell.

The old man had done such things before, when there was suspicion that a man who in life had been notorious for his malice might still be a danger, but never, despite his brave words, when the monster had already defeated the more usual magics. Hrímaldi was having to work harder than usual, too, grinding the surface smooth without the use of iron tools. Still, however undersized he might be, the muscles in his shoulders and forearms had been shaped by such labor. They bunched and released beneath the skin as he labored over the stone.

"Nor shall light of sun or moon touch it, lad," said Grípir. "Once its face is cleansed of weathering, you shall peck out the design with hammers of stone."

"But what signs shall I scribe?" asked Hrímaldi.

"We shall place them within the body of a serpent—not twisting, but made in a circle biting its tail."

"Like Jormundgand—" said the boy.

"Like the earth serpent, yes," replied his master. "The grave-serpent shall be bound, consuming himself forever. It is right that the dead should sleep below ground—we shall put the Worldtree in the center so that its roots may hold him down."

"But how? How can an evil spirit be bound by marks scratched on stone?" Encouraged by that "we," Hrímaldi dared to ask. He had often wondered, but it had never mattered so much, before.

Grípir sighed. "The runes are spirit, boy, made manifest through form. But not just any form. Ours is a craft of knowledge handed down since the day when Odin himself first gave the runes to men. We do not drum over our work or dance about, growing drunk on our own magic. The berserk may do a great deal of damage in his ecstasy, but in battle I would rather stand beside a well-trained warrior who knows just where to place each blow."

Hrímaldi nodded. It was more exciting to work the runes on those days when his blood was up and he felt their power. But he had noticed that the small spells his master had taught him seemed to function as well when he felt dull and uninspired—so long as there was no faltering in his will. He picked up the grinding stone and began to rasp it across the boulder once more.

They came to the howe as the sun was sinking and the small sounds around them began to give way to that hush that comes in the hour between the darkness and the day. Working as swiftly as they dared. Arnkel's men unloaded the shrouded stone from the wagon, then drew back to the safety of the trees. Hrímaldi listened to the creak and rumble as the wagon was driven away, and looked around him. In the soft light of sunset the place seemed innocent enough. The howe was a small one, the turf that covered it richly green. Only on the northern face was the earth disturbed. It was there they had set the stone, turned a little so that even now the last of the sunlight did not fall fully upon it.

In the half-light, the runes that Hrímaldi had pecked into the stone at Grípir's direction were stained with shadow. The old man, swathed in furs, knelt to shake pigment into the mixing bowl. Hrímaldi suppressed a flicker of unease. Grípir's hand had grown thin in illness, almost transclucent, vein and tendon knotting beneath the skin. But he gestured with his accustomed abruptness to Hrímaldi to bring the piglet, and slit the beast's throat neatly as the boy held it above the bowl. Blood gushed with a hot tang, and the piglet convulsed in Hrímaldi's hands.

After a moment Grípir waved him back—no need to make the *draug* a gift of the energy—and Hrímaldi carried the still-twitching body well away from the howe.

"This blood to the power whose hammer bound the Jormundgand!" he whispered, as the pig bled out the rest of its life beneath an oak tree. "*Sithi Thur*—Thor, help us with this magic!"

Grípir was already mixing blood and red ocher into a thick paste when he returned, chanting softly. Hrímaldi hunkered down behind him, watching intently as the old man spat into the mixture and stirred it once more. From a small pouch of soft leather Grípir withdrew a flat triangular piece of ivory stained to the color of old blood by long use. For a moment he was still. Then, with a deep breath, he dipped the reddening tool into the bowl.

"Stone not struck by sun or seax—" Hrímaldi mouthed each rune of every word silently along with his master as the old man began to lay color into the grooves cut into the stone. Until now, the might in the inscription had been potential. The pigment showed bright as blood in the vein, casting a rosy glow across the cold stone.

Grípir finished the first verse and paused. Though the work was not physically demanding, the stress of concentration brought perspiration to his brow. His breath grew harsh as he went on to the next line.

"Fetter feast of eagles . . . fast . . . within . . . "

Hrímaldi reached out, seeing him falter, and as his strong hands closed on the old man's bony shoulders he felt them shaken by fine tremors of strain. A cold wind had come up as the light faded. Suddenly the pigment looked black against the stone.

"Hurry, old man," he whispered, "it is growing dark."

Grípir nodded, but as he began the third line it was clear that each stroke took more effort than the one before. *Holy howe hold* . . . He paused, shuddering. The next word was the dead man's name. Hrímaldi knelt close behind the runemaster, bracing him, willing his own young strength into that fragile frame.

"Bolverk . . . " Rune by rune it took shape. Hrímaldi gripped his master more tightly as the trembling increased. Then his breath caught. It was not the old man that was shaking so, but the earth beneath them. As the last "Kaunaz" rune was reddened the ground heaved, and as if his name had summoned him, the *draug* thrust through the loose soil.

He came with a blast of cold and the sick stench of corruption. The lives Bolverk had stolen had kept the spirit bound to the flesh without slowing its dissolution, and the blue flicker of corpse-light showed all too clearly what a month underground could do to a man. Where it was intact, the skin had blackened, but maggots seethed in the hole in his breast where men had tried to stake him down. In the empty eye sockets a dreadful vitality burned.

Grípir swayed, trying to draw a rune of warding in the air. The thing grinned, shook loose soil from its shoulders, and reached out for them. In a reflex beyond thought, Hrímaldi grabbed his master and dragged him behind the runestone. For a moment the thing that had been Bolverk hesitated. Then it drew back a wasted arm and struck the stone. Flesh parted, revealing shattered bone, but the *draug* made no sound. It was the rock, splitting in two pieces, that groaned.

Still, the distraction had given Hrímaldi time to scramble down from the howe, hauling Grípir behind him. His cry for help brought an answering shout from the road. He saw torches, and dragged his master toward the wagon.

By the time they reached Arnkelstead, Grípir had fainted, and he lay insensible for many hours thereafter. Watching beside the box bed where the old man slept, Hrímaldi sighed. Grípir had been too old and ill to try this. He should have stopped him! After a time he fell into an uneasy doze.

He dreamed he ran through the woods, fleeing the *draug*, but when he looked back, it wore Grípir's bent back and grizzled hair. *Is he dead too?* he wondered. The thought filled him with horror, and he pushed himself harder. He heard shouts behind him, and this time when he looked back he saw Arnkel, waving a thrall-ring. Other shapes showed behind him. "Sooty black! Slave!" they cried.

Gasping, Hrímaldi collided with someone who stood among the trees and went sprawling. He waited for the man to seize him, but as his pursuers burst into view, the other held up his staff and they flinched away. Hrímaldi gulped—had he run into the *draug*? But the dark blue cloak in which he was tangled smelled of nothing worse than wet dog.

"Hrímaldi thou art indeed," said the stranger, "but art thou a slave?"

He pushed the black hair back from his brow and forced himself to look up. A deep hood left half the man's face in shadow, but the lips beneath the beard were smiling.

"I am a child of Ríg," Hrímaldi whispered.

"Art kin to me, then, for I am his father," came the answer. "And wert thou to best *thy* father at runes, wouldst be no thrall, but a king."

Hrímaldi shook his head, wrenched by bitter laughter. "He is my master. . . ."

"A slave waits for another man's word. The man who rules himself chooses his own way. Which, grandson, wilt thou choose?"

Hrímaldi saw emptiness where the stranger's other eye should be and understood at last Who was talking to him now. And then it seemed that in that shadow grew a whirl of stars that shaped runes of might. Striving to read them, he fell into darkness.

When he woke, morning light was streaming through the door and men were talking in low voices of the *draug,* who had attacked a herder's hut and killed another man the night before.

"Hrímaldi . . ." Grípir's voice was scarcely louder than the whisper of the fire. The boy turned, and saw his face like wax but his eyes open and clear.

"How is it with you?"

The old man shook his head. "Call Arnkel—" he said, and with his gut knotting with apprehension, Hrímaldi complied.

"The boy . . . is my thrall," Grípir said when the chieftain had come. "I am setting him free. Will you see to it . . . if I cannot?"

Arnkel's considering gaze moved from the runemaster to Hrímaldi and he nodded. "At this rate I may not be master here much longer. But I will stand witness for you, in Thor's name."

When Arnkel left them, Hrímaldi gripped Grípir's thin shoulders. "Why did you do that? You are not dying!" he exclaimed. "I will not let you."

"Wanted you to be safe . . . whatever happens to me." Grípir lifted one eyebrow. "Would you rather stay a thrall?"

Hrímaldi sat back, hearing once more the words Odin had spoken in his dream. "While the *draug* walks," he answered, "no one here is free. . . "

The sun was sinking behind banks of cloud, bringing twilight early. Hrímaldi shivered as he watched Arnkel's men roll the new stone up the side of the mound, and wondered, not for the first time during the three days it had taken him to carve it, why he was here. If he had left Arnkel's steading as soon as his master freed him, he could have been in Nidaros by now. Nobody had forced him to make this last try to bind the *draug.* And that, he supposed, was why he was doing it— because the choice had been his own.

At least Grípir was still alive, though he slept most of the time. He had turned his face away to hide tears when Hrímaldi left, and Gudrid had wept openly. *If this fails, at least someone will mourn me,* the boy thought grimly. But the chill wind made the blood sing in his veins; he wanted to live.

When the men had set the stone to his satisfaction, Hrímaldi settled himself before it, hearing the sound of their receding footsteps and, from the woods beyond them, a raven's cry. *Are you watching, grandfather?* he wondered, but he did not turn to see. The light was already beginning to fade. He did not have much time.

Swiftly he poured pigment into the bowl. Arnkel had offered him a young bull for the sacrifice, but Hrímaldi knew no blood of beast would suffice for this binding. Let the *bonder* kill the calf for Thor if he wished, the blood Hrímaldi was going to shed was his own.

"To you, Allfather, this offering—" he whispered, drawing his sharp knife across his forearm. He took a deep breath. "Accept the service of this living man, and let the spirit of the *berserk* be bound!"

Red blood dripped into the bowl. As he stirred it, Hrímaldi felt awareness contracting to a still center of power he had not known he possessed. "Mind of man and might of runes, bright blood blend, give life to stone!" Grinning fiercely, he dipped up color and began to lay it into the grooves.

Hrímaldi worked swiftly. The first verses were the same as those his master had chosen, but now the third line read—*"Hanged-god holds in holy howe . . . "* Runes glowed bright against the gray stone despite the dimming light, but the soil beneath it quivered uneasily. *"The Wyrm that walks . . . "*

The earth heaved and the stone rocked a little on its cradle of logs. Hrímaldi plunged both hands into the pigment, daubing it on by touch as much as sight, coloring the outlines of the Tree in the serpent's center. The ground groaned as the head and shoulders of the *draug* pushed through the surface. *"By Worldtree bound!"*

Over his shoulder Hrímaldi could see the creature straining to break free, but power pulsed from the runestone, opposing the corpse-chill. The *draug's* eyes glowed, and the boy shuddered as he felt its hunger. Never had he been so certain that a man was more than his body. Some force was holding this flesh to human form, ruled by a kind of elemental intelligence, and something of the berserk's personality remained, but the *draug* was utterly without soul.

It was almost dark now. Corpse-light flickered around the monstrous shape. Hrímaldi scrambled to put the stone between them.

"You are dead, Bolverk," he whispered. "You belong to the earth. See, this pleasant howe has been prepared for you. Sleep, Bolverk—" He drew the Thorn rune in the air and the *draug* swayed. Then the earth trembled once more and Hrímaldi felt his blood congealing at the chill breath of mortality.

"Thrall or Jarl, slave or free . . . all that lives is meat for me. . . ." Was that the *draug* speaking, or his own fear? Grípir had freed him, but what did that matter here? The boy sat transfixed, the pigment drying cold on his fingers, as the monster heaved an arm's length farther from the mound.

"Grípir . . ." he gasped, but the old man was dying back at the hall. He understood now how the *draug* overcame its victims. This was the end for all, this dreadful dissolution, and neither greatness or glory could save you. Hrímaldi could feel his own life force being drained already by that terrible knowledge. No wonder the berserk refused to let go of his tattered flesh.

"You have no friend. You have no kin. Only me. . . ."

"It is not so!" cried Hrímaldi. Even if what the *draug* said was true, he must fight him, mind against mind, will opposing will. "The Lord of the Slain has claimed me kin! In his name I command you—go back into the earth where you belong!"

He stabbed the god rune into the air between them, then frantically scooped up pigment, reaching around the stone to daub it into the runes that completed the serpent shape, and the spell. The cold air rang as he intoned the ancient charm against evil—"*Alu . . . alu . . . alu. . . .*"

A raven in the woods shrieked triumph to the shadowed skies as around the figure of the *draug* the corpse-fires began to fail. Heart pounding, Hrímaldi edged back and dipped up the last of the pigment. Working by touch, for his eyes were still on the distorted figure that was slowly sinking back into the ground, he laid the color into the runes he had added below the rest.

"The son of Ríg colored this stone."

And then it was done. The soil still stirred uneasily, but he could no longer see the *draug*. With the care Grípir had taught him, Hrímaldi gathered his tools into their pouch and slung it over one shoulder. Wincing as stiffened muscles protested, he got himself upright and moved behind the stone. One push, he thought, if he still had the strength for it.

"Sleep . . ." he whispered, tracing the Ing rune above the mound, "held safe within your howe. And may holy stone hold fast what I have bound!" He set his palms against the runestone.

It rocked as he set his weight against it, and not for the first time he wished that early underfeeding had not stunted him. A second time he heaved, and the stone quivered beneath his hands. Hrímaldi drew breath and, as he let it out again, shaped air into sound.

"*Ansuz* . . ." By the rune of the god all his might was gathered, to burst free as he thrust once more. For a moment the runestone teetered, then, with awful inevitability, it fell. A last shudder shook the howe.

And then all was still. The stone lay across the troubled earth that had been the *draug's* doorway, sealing it. Hrímaldi looked down at it. He should be feeling something—satisfaction, triumph. But he only felt empty. As he made his way down from the mound he realized that even that was not quite true. He felt free.

When Hrímaldi returned to Arnkel's hall, men drew back as though the grave stench still clung to him, though he had washed as best he could in an icy stream. His gaze went immediately to the box bed where Grípir had lain. There was still a shape within it, but it lay so still. He swallowed and hastened toward it.

The thin chest was still moving. Hrímaldi sagged back against the post with a sigh. At the sound the old man's eyes opened.

"You are alive!" His smile became radiant. "Did you finish the stone?" The boy nodded.

Behind him he heard a whisper—"The *draug* is bound!" and then the words repeated more loudly. Men began to cheer. Ignoring them. Hrímaldi bent to hear as Grípir went on.

"Arnkel told me . . . I should make the task the price of your freedom. But to use the runes, you had to be free."

"Do you mean that if I were still a thrall, I would have failed?" Hrímaldi asked tightly.

The old runemaster shook his head. "That craft was in you already. But I was not sure you knew. . . ."

The boy frowned. That was true. But he had needed the god to tell him so. "Am I free to leave you?" he asked.

Something in the old man's face seemed to crumple, but he nodded.

"Then, if you will have me, I choose to stay." He leaned forward and grasped Grípir's hand. "I survived this, but there is so much I need to learn!" he exclaimed. "Let me be your apprentice!"

Grípir raised one eyebrow and shook his head. Hrímaldi bit his lip. Was the old man getting back at him for having tested him?

"Be my son. . . ." the runemaster coughed and smiled. "But 'Hrímaldi' is a name for a kitchen lad. I will call you . . . 'Kon,' like the son of Ríg, for in runes you have surpassed your father!"

FAMILY TIES

LAWRENCE SCHIMEL

Lawrence Schimel, *has sold stories and poems to over eighty anthologies, including:* Grails: Visitations of the Night, Excalibur, *and* Black Thorn, White Rose. *He lives in Manhattan.*

When I was nine, a fox ran between my father's legs with a curse tied in its tail, and though he shot and killed the beast, by day's end he was dead, his skin the same bright red as the fox's pelt. I swore revenge, and only years later learned that the oaths of a nine-year-old girl, forged from a pure rage and a still-innocent love, are sometimes more binding than the most learned and complex sorceries. Revenge is a lonely life. By the time its fires have cooled enough that you look about you for a moment to consider other things, you are too hardened for the intimacies of friendship, for the trust of a lover, and these cold truths serve to quench the blade of your revenge, to further temper its edge. I threw myself into my studies, bent on discovering the man who had killed my father. I kept the fox's tail locked in a metal box under my bed, waiting until the day I could untie its workings and know its maker.

I had no clues who might have held a grudge against my father, who might have held one and tied such a spell. My family knew little sorcery. Sure, my father knew the proper enchantments to stretch his bow, the words and knots to bind the string in place and keep his aim true, but it was not sorcery to him. It was just tradition. And that was what I believed, too, for many years, until I realized that sorcery was just patterns, a sequence of words woven with actions, as simple as a single knot or complex as a ritual tapestry of rare threads woven only on nights with no moon. But all traditions were sorceries, to one degree or another, all patterns, even daily speech, the way we wove a pattern of words, and sud-

denly, magically, our meaning is conveyed, often with more powerful actions resulting as well.

My mother tried to dissuade me, of course, but when she saw I
would not bend in my determination she accepted defeat. I was too
young to journey forth into the world by myself, but she packed bags
of provisions for my trek and made arrangements for me to be conveyed by a neighbor as he brought his wagon of goods to sundry cities,
until I had found what I sought. I left home in search of a mentor,
someone from whom I could learn the myriad knotworks of sorcery,
someone who would accept me as apprentice. At the time, I could not
know that I also was in search of someone to replace my father, a sur-
rogate. I was wary of simply accepting the first sorcerer I encountered;
my ambition was vaster than that. I knew the task I had set for myself
was not an easy one, and I wanted a store of knowledge and lore I
would not be able to easily exhaust before I had learned what I needed.
Nor was the first sorcerer I found acceptable willing to take me on. She
was completely disinterested in having an apprentice, and we continued on our way toward the next city, the next market. I learned the life
of the road as we traveled, the tending of horses, the pitching of camps,
and foraging for food, and in the markets when we reached a city I
learned the art of haggling and barter, which I refined along the road
by trading provisions for fresh eggs or bread or milk from farms we
passed. But as comfortably as I settled into that life, I never lost my
purpose, and the moment I found a master I approved of and who was
willing to take me on as an apprentice, I bid farewell to my companions, bade them give my mother a message of my well-being, and
turned my back on them.

My master was everything I had hoped for: learned and patient, gentle yet strict. Secretly, he was everything I wished my father had been,
had my father been a powerful man instead of a simple a sheep farmer
with a penchant for game hunting. I soaked up everything he taught
me about knotwork, of bindings and unbindings, of the limits of sorcery and its words of power. Like all infants, my umbilical cord had
been tied around my neck after it was cut off, a loose necklace I slowly
grew into. I learned of its powers, its protections, the possibilities for
adapting its strength with other knots. I came to understand at last this
strange tradition I had lived with since my birth, its mysteries unravel-
ing before my growing knowledge.

After I had been there a number of years, my master one day went
on a journey. He did not warn me he was leaving, but just before he left

he summoned me to bid farewell. He did not say when he would return or leave instructions for my tasks in his absence; nor did he allow me time to question him. He went outside and tied a knot in the wind and, grabbing hold of a loop he had left as a handle, off he flew. It was a show of ostentation, and it made me realize how much I had left to learn of sorcery before I could accomplish such feats myself. I wondered if his leave-taking was a test, if he was actually still monitoring my progress from afar, if he would judge by my behavior whether to teach me more advanced lore, like tying the wind to one's will. I followed my studies with renewed vigor, and kept the house in perfectly neat condition for his return, but when weeks passed and he did not return I began to wonder. Perhaps this was a test, but of a different sort than I first imagined, a test for me to realize that he had no more left to teach me, that I must learn the rest of my knowledge on my own, or from a different master. Or perhaps his desire for a pupil, or even me in particular as his pupil, had simply run out. I was vain enough to consider, as I packed my few belongings, the possibility that I had grown so advanced that I would be a threat to him if he continued my education. I looked about me, my meager possesions assembled into a small, easily carried bundle, and wondered if he would ever return, if I was being foolish not to take some of his wondrous and useful artifacts and materials with me. He might have been killed, for all I knew, accidentally or not, and never intending for his journey to be a test to me at all. But I couldn't be certain, and so I left all that was his, locked the doors, and set off on my own journey.

That evening, gathering branches to build myself a fire—more for the security of the light against the dark woods than any need for warmth during the summer night—I came across a fox. My fear washed over me like a sheet of icy water that set my heart to pounding within my chest. I had no weapons, just the branches I was carrying. I dropped them, hoping the sound would frighten the beast, but it stood its ground and stared at me, as if taunting me, daring me, waiting. I cast about for a stone to throw, nervous each time I took my eyes from the creature, lest it advance upon me while I wasn't looking. I found at last a stone of suitable size and pried it loose from between the roots of a tree. The fox hadn't moved. I yanked a hair from my head, almost glad for the pain as the sensation cut across the fear that sat in my belly, and tied a knot of warding around the stone. I took aim and let fly the missile. I tried to watch its arc as it flew threw the forest, but couldn't keep track of it until it cracked loudly against the trunk of a tree. I had missed, and the fear of the fox grew strong again in my belly, made my feet weak though I could not move them. But the knot worked its spell and the fox bolted. I wanted to laugh in desperate relief, or cry, but I had no voice. I stood watching where it had disappeared, not thinking, just watching, making sure I saw no red among the trees. Then I gathered up my branches and hurried back to my camp, where I built up the fire to a roaring blaze I hoped would keep the night free of beasts.

I took the metal box from my pack and sat with it in my lap beside the fire. I thought of my father as I remembered him from so many years ago, and was surprised to realize how fleeting my memories of him had grown, just brief flashes of image. I opened the box and took out the fox tail, examining the knots of its curse by firelight. I felt I was at last ready to attempt untangling the mystery of its maker, that my seeing the fox was an omen that I had been right in my decision to leave, that my master had taught me all he could. I looked back at the young girl I had been the last time I had looked at the tail, during the first year of my studies. I had checked constantly, nearly every other week, wondering if I had gained enough knowledge to understand anything new about the curse, any new clue. But eventually I gave up on my constant inspection, having learned enough of sorcery to know how much I had yet to learn before I would be able to untangle the curse in the fox's tail. I was content that I would recognize the time when I had learned enough to know the curse's maker when I untied it, and had not looked at the tail until now.

I pulled my cord from beneath my shirt, left it dangling in the cooling air of night. I plucked a hair from the fox's tail and another from my own head, spinning them together against my leg as I spoke the words of a binding. I tied the thread three times to my umbilical, then slowly began to pick at the curse. I found myself blinking back tears; everywhere the curse read of my father. I felt my rage coiling inside my belly, that someone had so carefully chosen my father as this curse's victim that his presence was so thoroughly tied into the knots. I was still puzzled at the cause of such determined hatred toward my father, who had always seemed a reserved and quiet man, simple in his life and content with its modest ambitions: to raise more sheep, to sell them at a higher price, to raise a family. My own hatred swelled within me as I untied knot after knot, searching for this man who so loathed my father. But I did not find him, reading only my father's presence, his victim. Was this curse so advanced that I did not even recognize its complexities, a masterwork of subtlety except for the single-minded pursuit of my father?

I retied the spell. The hairs were creased with age and the weight of the curse and the knots fell back into place easily. I placed the tail back in its box, disappointed that I was not yet learned enough to decipher the curse's master from its victim. Disappointed, but not daunted. I curled up in my sleeping sack, my back to the fire, and thought ahead to the morrow and finding a new mentor. I was too old and too advanced to be an apprentice any longer, at least, the kind of apprentice who must learn the humility of chores, who must learn through long years of practice that a complex knot is not necessary when a simple one will do.

I did not put aside my revenge, but I devoted myself to my studies, which took me to search for other goals along the way to discovering the maker of the curse that killed my father. It was many years before I again felt capable of untangling the knots. The box lay on my worktable, a constant reminder of purpose. Though I did not open it, I kept it free of dust, thought about it when I saw it, about the curse, about my father. About my purpose.

The knots were still saturated with my father's presence, but I dug deeper, down to the knots at the base of the curse, untangling it in its entirety as I searched for that elusive clue to the identity of its maker. But I could find nothing but my father, and when I had untied every knot I had to admit defeat. I had failed to find the maker of the curse, despite my years of learning. I was certain that, had there been any clue tied into the knots, I would have discovered it. But there was none.

Unless I had been wrong all along. Unless it had been my father who cast the curse, yet I unwilling to face this possibility all these years. I felt suddenly uncomfortable, an uneasiness seated deep inside me, which I visualized down in my stomach amid the tangle of my rage. I feared this uneasiness, knowing that it meant I was right in my assumption, that my father had been not the intended victim of the spell but its author. That somehow his intentions had backfired, the fox running between his own legs by mistake.

I felt sick. I had never known my father knew such dark knots. Had never known he knew any sorcery at all. All those years I had thought him a simple and innocent man. What would his life seem like to my adult eyes, had I seen him without the gloss of a nine-year-old's vision. Or was this side of him hidden even then, buried deep within him, this darkness he had learned before I was born, that he practiced out in the forest, alone, and away from his family. I wondered against whom the curse had been intended. Again, I was as clueless as I had been all these years about the curse's true maker. Even knowing my father knew the workings of such an intricate curse, or had learned this one for some specific reason, I could not imagine his reasons to be that different from my childhood image of him; jealousy perhaps, of some rival shepherd, the elimination of a competitor, something pragmatic rather than randomly malicious.

I felt betrayed. All those years I had wasted, my entire life, and all for a mistake. I felt weighed down by the injustice of it all; it was so unfair. I felt the butt of some cruel and elaborate joke, a devious double cross. I threw the fox tail from me, flinging it wildly against the wall.

No. I was thinking simply, as if I had not spent years studying sorcery, learning the patterns of the world in all their minutiae in order to influence and manipulate. I was thinking as my father might. Surely my knowledge of the world and its workings surpassed his. Perhaps that had been his downfall all along, a lack of understanding of the forces of nature, of life, and of magic, of the ways to persuade them to your will with bindings. You could try and stop a river by laboriously moving a huge boulder into its bed, but the river would go on, flowing around the obstacle as it carved itself a new channel. Or you could construct a dam, more carefully architected but perhaps equally laborious, and harness the river and its power. The latter is the way sorcery worked.

My revenge had been a boulder, obstructing me from finding my true goals, from harnessing my potential to guide the world around me and its patterns. But I was no longer tied down to my revenge, and I let its coils unravel, imagining the knots untying themselves within my belly. I stood, stretched as if to relieve a cramp, and felt free. And I knew that already I had begun to make better choices than my father had.

THE VOICE OF A GOD

KATE DANIEL

*Statistics say most people today will have three careers in their life-time. As a writer **Kate Daniel** is on her third right now, having already been a teacher and a computer programmer. She has six young adult mystery novels in print, the most recent being* Baby-Sitter's Night-mare II, *along with several fantasy short stories.*

Light from the fire outside cast uncanny shadows on the skin walls of the tent. A single clear note, like the call of a bird, echoed through the camp outside, followed by the rumble of voices chanting a word, over and over. The other boys in the tent with Rana murmured and rolled their eyes. When they were called out to stand before the elders of the People, they could show no fear. For now they took comfort in the presence of the other initiates.

Another note sounded, high and piercing. "What type of bird is that?" Dibur muttered. "I never heard anything like it before."

"I thought you were such a great hunter," Meti said. "Don't tell me there's something you don't know."

"It's not a bird," Rana said, cutting in before they could quarrel. They were the only three initiates from the Flying Hawk band, and if they disrupted the ceremonies, they would all be in trouble and their band disgraced.

"How would you know?" Dibur demanded.

"I—" Rana broke off. Sorcery was sacred; the manhood ceremony was the first time boys were allowed near magic. Still, once before he had heard the shrill bird-notes, and had risked his life to spy on a hunt fire. He had never risked spying on women's rites; *that* would kill him at once, he was sure. But at the hunt fire he had seen a long thin stick held to the shaman's mouth, and he knew the bird-sounds came from it.

He was saved from having to answer by a cry outside the tent. Some-one ripped aside the hide over the opening and prodded the boys out-side. They moved as they had been coached, dancing around the fire while men, faces unrecognizable under the ash that whitened them, circled around, poking at them with spears. Dibur, clumsy with fear, flinched aside from one sharp point that came too close, and immedi-ately several men surrounded him, shouting and poking. Rana could see him shaking, but after a few minutes, Dibur mastered himself and stopped flinching. The men merged back into the larger circle, and the pace of the dance picked up.

A shaman, crowned with the horns of an antelope, slammed a heavy stick against a skin-covered log. It made a hollow noise like distant thunder, which was answered a moment later by a crack of real thun-der from the clear sky directly overhead. Another shaman, head crowned with feathers that obscured half his face, held a thin pipe to his lips, making a sound like the cry of a hunting eagle stooping on its prey. The fire flared in response, and the empty sky was filled with the flapping of huge wings. More thunder pealed from the drums and the sky, but Rana ignored it, as he ignored the jostling of the dance. He held his position opposite the bird-masked shaman, listening to the pipe.

With the dawn, the dance ended. The new men stumbled off to the young hunters' fire. The others went to their own fires, chief hunters at one, elders another. As the bird-masked shaman removed his mask, Rana realized it was Senuet, magic-master for the Flying Hawk band. No wonder the pipe's note had sounded so familiar. The old man was heading toward his fire, pipe still in hand.

Even though Rana was now a man, sorcery was safest left to shamans, but the magic-drenched night of his manhood wouldn't come again. Rana followed, calling out, "Senuet!"

The old man stopped and turned.

"I was watching you during the dance. You made birdsong with a stick," Rana said. "Teach me how."

"The pipe is sacred. It is good you honor the gods, but . . . "

"The pipe called me," Rana interrupted. "I—I spied on the men once, at a hunt fire, because I thought I heard a bird, only no bird sounds so beautiful. I thought it was the voice of a god."

He stopped, his heart pounding as fast as it had during the dance. If Senuet decided he had committed sacrilege, he might be driven out of the tribe, or even killed.

Senuet stared at him blankly. "We felt no magic in you. We should have felt it." His voice trailed away as he continued to stare, until Rana wanted to hide from his intense gaze. "But if you dream of it . . . do you dream, boy? Do you dream?"

"I hear the sound in my sleep."

"You were called." It came out as a whisper. "You were called by the gods, and we never knew."

"Then you will teach me?" His mouth was dry as he waited for the answer, and in his mind, he heard the pipe again.

"Perhaps. I must ask the elders and the gods." The shaman hesitated. "Usually we find those who are called while they're still boys. I've never heard of a young man coming unsought, on the first morning of his manhood. I must ask the gods." Rana sagged, disappointed now as well as exhausted, but Senuet smiled. "I do not think they will say no. Go, now, and sleep."

The Gathering of the Greater Rains continued. The new men joined the rituals of thanks to the gods for ample rains and good hunting, while Rana watched the shamans, wondering when Senuet would answer his question. Finally, on the third morning, he was summoned to the shamans' fire. Kawit of the Running Stags, most powerful of the shamans, stared at Rana in a way that reminded him of Senuet. Perhaps it was a thing all shamans learned. It made him want to hide. But at last, the old man turned to Senuet.

"So this is the one who wishes to join our fire?"

"He is the one," Senuet said. "His name is Rana."

"He is of your band." Kawit spoke to Senuet, ignoring Rana completely. "If the gods called him, why did you not know?"

"Perhaps they did not call him until now. Perhaps they wanted him to come already a man. I don't know. But he is here, seeking the pipe." Senuet's tone was respectful but firm, as though this were an argument repeated many times and already decided.

"We will see if he is suitable. But I suppose he has to join our fire until we know for sure." Kawit looked at Rana again, his face distant, then turned and walked away. It was settled. Rana moved from the young hunters' fire to that of the shamans.

When he met Meti and Dibur the next day, all three of them were embarrassed, not knowing if he ranked as a shaman or not. At least there were several young men at the shamans' fire, including one fellow initiate from the Leaping Cat band, and a few young boys who returned to their mothers' fires each night. Spying on rituals, Rana found, wasn't fatal. Those few who were drawn as he had been became shamans themselves. But the others had been drawn by the magic and caught in the magical web around the ceremonies. Rana alone had escaped, and he wondered why.

He was tested on the last morning of the Gathering. All the magic-masters were there, but only Senuet spoke. Handing a dark length of wood to Rana, he said, "This was made by my teacher's teacher. You will make one of your own, but for now use this."

It was hollow, not wood at all but a section of thick reed, like the ones used to carry water, with three small holes on one side. Rana had never seen reeds this color. He stroked it. The reed felt silky, like water-smoothed stone.

"How can I make one?" he asked. "And why is it so dark?"

"You will learn that later, if you can find its voice."

Senuet touched one of the small holes with a delicate fingertip. Rana looked more closely. Two holes were close together, with the other near the mouth end, and he discovered another, slightly larger, on the opposite side. Both ends were open.

"Now." Senuet took the pipe and positioned Rana's hands so none of the holes were obscured by a finger. "Don't blow too hard. You want a breeze, not a wind. Hold your mouth like this—" He demonstrated, his lips forming a small circle.

Rana tried. At first there was no sound, then a low tone came from the pipe, like a bird's call at dusk. He almost dropped it in surprise. Concentrating on exactly how he had held his lips, he tried again. This time it sounded immediately. He stopped, winded as though he'd been running, then took a deep breath to try again.

"Enough." Senuet took the pipe from him, and turned to Kawit. "You see? Few can manage such clear notes the first time."

The elder shaman said, "Perhaps you're right, although the sound is not that important. The pipe is strong magic, and I felt nothing from him. Still, he did more than I expected. You may train him until the next Greater Rains."

Next morning the Gathering ended, with each band going its own way. It was time for the women to gather the wild seeds and ripening fruits, storing what they could before the Lesser Rains, while the hunters took as many mature animals as they could. The People would not gather again until the time of new leaves, after the Lesser Rains.

Flying Hawk headed east, a handful compared to Gathering. There were too few for formal fires, so Senuet and Rana joined the hunters. Iya, Senuet's only student until now, was still a boy, two rains from manhood, and spent his nights at the women's fire. Meti and Dibur were awkward at first with Rana, but within a few days, they treated him almost as they had before. Almost. There was an edge of respect and fear below their jokes, and it flared to life each time Senuet called Rana and Iya aside.

Their lessons started before the dust of Gathering had faded from view. Rana found it galling to watch Iya, so much younger, call forth clouds of smoke from a clean-burning fire, or raise a wind on a calm day by imitating its sound with a rattle. He tried. The rhythm of drums and gourds came easily, but no power made the fire flare up, no sudden gust of wind answered his attempts. And much to his disappointment, Senuet did not even mention the pipe.

"Even children can make noise," Senuet said when Rana asked him about it one morning. "This is magic. Before you touch the pipe again, I want you to practice without it. You must know exactly how to direct your breath, and how to keep it going for many heartbeats." He demonstrated, and the remainder of that lesson was about the pipe. By the time the sun was straight overhead, Rana's head spun from lack of breath and his ribs hurt. He had kept the stream of air steady against his teacher's fingers, but the pipe remained hidden in the magician's antelope hide bag.

The first hunting ceremony was held before Rana had mastered even the simplest exercises, so he was told to sit quietly with Iya and watch. Senuet thundered his drum, a sound echoed by the heavens as the fire flared up and lightning sheeted across the sky. Yombo, the oldest hunter, cast a spear straight up. As if called by fire and lightning, wind gusted, catching the spear and tossing it. It landed point down, the flint head half-buried in the dirt.

As soon as the hunters left, Senuet called Iya and Rana over to the spear. "A clear sign," he said. "Rana, you see?"

"I . . ." Rana stopped and shook his head.

"Game and good hunting," piped up the younger boy.

"The hunt will be a success, certainly," Senuet said. "But where, and what game will they find?" His eyes fixed on Rana, who tried desperately to comprehend what the shaman expected of him. Hesitantly, he pointed north, where lightning had filled the sky.

"There?" It was a question, but Senuet nodded, satisfied.

"In the foothills, yes. And the game?"

"Antelope!" Iya said. "I saw many antelope in the fire!"

Rana wondered for a moment if they were playing a trick on him. He had seen nothing. But Senuet smiled, as if they had both done well. He reached over and pulled the spear free.

"Iya, take this to Ocytu. The best hunter should carry the omen spear. Rana, I'll show you how we have to put out the fire."

Rana worked with him, saving coals for the firepot then carefully covering the ritual fire with dead ash and dirt. As he worked, he tried to remember a flame resembling an animal. All memory showed him was a fire with flames like any other. But the next day, the hunters returned from the foothills to the north with five antelope. Ocytu had killed the first with the omen spear.

They moved slowly now, gathering wild seeds and beans to last through the Lesser Rains. Everyone helped, even the hunters. The pipe still sounded in Rana's dreams, but he was no closer to it than ever.

By the next hunting ceremony, Rana had mastered the simple rhythm of the dried gourds. As he shook them, he saw Dibur and Meti watching. They made the gesture of respect due a shaman. He was set apart now, marked by magic no matter how unchanged he felt. The next day Senuet brought out his pipe.

"We're getting close to the reed ponds. Look." As he spoke, he let Rana finger the pipe. "You'll need to find a reed the right size, and thickness, and shape. Then you have to whittle out the inside, thin the wood without breaking it. The color changes during the curing; I'll tell you about that later. But the most important thing is knowing which reeds are ready to harvest."

He went on, describing the color and feel of a perfect reed, while Rana's fingers caressed the smooth dark wood. That night he saw nothing in his dreams. But he heard the call of endless birds, whispering through the darkness and changing into the ripple of water and the echo of unfelt winds.

The next day, they reached the hills. There were shallow caves among the rocks, good water, and sheltering trees. And beyond them, half a day's walk away, were the reed ponds.

Making his own pipe took longer than he expected, and he ruined several reeds, but the final result had a clearer, more liquid sound than Senuet's own. He quickly learned all the sounds Senuet could teach him, and spent as much time as he could alone in the hills where no one could hear him, practicing. A lifetime would not be enough to learn all the sounds his pipe could make, and sometimes he laughed aloud for the sheer joy of his pipe. But there was no magic in it. He couldn't call up the lightest breeze, and the fire flared only when he threw on more wood.

With the first cold rain, Senuet summoned the men for a ritual. "You will play the pipe," he told Rana.

"Me? But you're our shaman, you've always. . . "

"I am a shaman, yes, but what do you think you are? You may be young, Rana, but you already sound more like a hawk than most birds. You play. I'll take the drum and rattles."

There were startled glances from all the men when he raised the pipe to his lips, and Dibur signed his respect at the first sound. The notes were high and harsh, the cry of a hunting hawk on the wing. But there was no answering cry from night birds, no tingle of power, and the fire burned evenly until Senuet began to drum. Men chanted, the hunters mimed successful hunts, and the drums summoned the gods. But no god came in answer to Rana's pipe.

The Lesser Rains continued, with skies that were gray and chilly even when no rain fell. Little could be done during the cold rains; most stayed near the fire and told stories. Rana made another trip to the reed ponds, where he spent two miserable cold days, searching for suitable reeds.

The first split when he began carving, along a flaw he hadn't spotted. He began again, but the finicky work demanded close attention. It was raining, a cold shower more mist than drops, and his hands ached from holding the fine bone knife.

Finally he laid it aside and picked up his old pipe. There was a spot not far from camp where a large tree would offer some protection from the wet. Once seated under it, he tried to imitate the storm with his pipe: an almost-inaudible patter of drops hitting the ground, the hiss of rain against dead grasses, the *plonk* of raindrops echoing inside a half-empty water jar. As he added a whistle of wind among the rocks, he felt eyes on him and looked up into the face of a boy. Aya, Iya's younger brother.

Rana's heart caught for a moment and the rainsong trailed off in a breathy squeak. But this wasn't ritual; he wasn't calling a god. It was delight in new sounds, nothing more. And it was less than a year since he himself had hidden in the night, watching and listening as Aya did now. He took a fresh breath and played on.

The rain stopped before he was done, or he wouldn't have heard

Senuet coming. Rana lowered the pipe even before the shaman thundered *"Rana!"* He scrambled to his feet and made the gesture of respect. Aya vanished into the brush.

"I couldn't believe it when I heard a pipe, so close to the camp," Senuet said. "The pipe is sacred! You make magic with it, not just a pleasing noise. No one should hear it except during rituals, even in practice. And to let an uninitiated boy listen . . . At least there's a chance Aya will be called as his brother was. But anyone could have heard you here. Even a woman!"

Rana's throat tightened. Women's magic and men's were separate. "I'm sorry," he stammered. "I thought . . . I didn't want to get too far from camp, because of the cold."

"Then stay by the fire like a sensible man," Senuet said irritably. The shaman was stiff from the damp weather; he had hardly stirred from the fireside in days.

But despite the bone-chilling rain, the next day Rana wandered far from the camp and began to play once more.

After that, Rana never practiced where anyone could hear him. He suspected sometimes that Aya followed him and listened, but he never saw the boy, and Aya never said anything.

Before the next Gathering, he played his storm-song for Senuet. The shaman was impressed, and at the Gathering he made Rana demonstrate the new sounds for Kawit, saying, "Rana has found a new way of calling the rains." When Rana finished playing, he showed them the extra fingerholes on his new pipe and demonstrated the additional notes it made possible. The Running Stags' shaman said nothing. Wanting some reaction, Rana went on.

"Listen. What does this make you think of?" He raised the pipe and sound rippled up and down, notes curling around each other as he repeated the pattern several times on a single breath. He took a fast breath and repeated the pattern again, breaking off with a grin when his teacher said, "The river!"

"We've never been able to control the river magic," Kawit said quietly. "The river's too powerful. But are you even trying to control it? I feel no magic in this. Only a sound. No force. The pipe's magic is too strong to be wasted on pleasant noise."

Senuet protested. "There's plenty of force in his pipe! I've been able to summon much more, with Rana playing."

But Kawit was right, Rana realized. The summoning had been Senuet's not his. Before they left the Gathering, Kawit made him promise to use only the traditional tunes, known magic.

New grass lengthened and ripened, turning yellow. The heat increased until it was hotter than anyone could remember, even the oldest hunter. It was time for the long rains, but the sky remained a harsh hot blue, with no trace of clouds. At night, lightning walked the horizon as if in mockery, and each day was hotter than the one before. Senuet and Rana held ritual after ritual, trying to call the rains from the sky, but with no success. Hunting was good, as the animals of the grasslands stayed near the few remaining water holes, but hunting could not sustain the People without the seeds and fruits that were dying now. And if the rains never came, there would be no newborn animals in the spring.

The days grew still hotter, and even the nights were heavy and still, with only the soundless lightning offering a false promise of relief. Late one afternoon, Dibur spotted a thin trail of smoke in the sky. They got ready to flee. But the smoke didn't spread, and the next day it drew nearer. The Running Stag band joined them the day after that, driven from their own ground by the drought.

Despite the risk of wildfire, they built separate fires for each group, in honor of the joining of two bands. The shamans' fire was small, with only Senuet and Rana and Kawit to share it. Kawit looked thin and dry, his skin like ide that had been scraped too close. "You have had no response from the gods either?"

"None," Senuet said. "And we've held more ceremonies than there are drops left in the water hole. Nothing."

Kawit looked sideways at Rana. "Have you tried summoning the rains with your new pipe and new sounds?"

Rana said, "No." There was an awkward silence, then Kawit began to tell them what had happened to Running Stag as the water holes failed. No more was said that night of new rituals.

With so many hunters gathered, a large group, over a dozen men, set out the next morning. Kawit's drum joined Rana and Senuet in a brief hunting ceremony at dawn, then the fire was carefully extinguished. For once, clouds covered the sky, bringing the promise of possible rain. The air grew hot and heavy as the day wore on, the camp silent. But still no rain fell.

Halfway through the afternoon, Aya came running back into camp. "Smoke. In the direction the hunters went. *Lots* of smoke!"

This time there was no chance it was a single campfire. Kawit's eyes were too dimmed with age to be able to make much out, but even he could see the broad wall of smoke cutting off the eastern horizon. The camp was upwind of the fire, in no danger. But the hunters were beyond it, and the wind was picking up.

"They may not be able to get around," Senuet said, trying to measure the distance with his eyes.

"They won't, if this wind keeps up." Kawit's face was gray. "We have to try summoning rain. Senuet, start the fire."

They took their places around the hastily lit ceremonial fire. As Kawit opened with a slow roll on his drum, Rana placed his pipe to his lips and began the wind-whistle, while his teacher rattled the gourds. The drum-thunder built, growing louder and more powerful, and there was an echoing rumble from the sky. Kawit started another crescendo of rolling booms. Lightning leaped between the clouds to the east, and the air felt charged with power. Suddenly Kawit slumped over his drum with a choked cry. There was a faint echo of thunder from the sky and a moment's startled silence. Then Senuet yelled.

By the time Senuet and Rana reached him, Kawit's eyes were glazed over and his breath came in harsh gasps. Senuet said something about fetching the healer-woman, but Kawit gasped and shook his head. "No. Go on. The cermony. Use . . . new pipe. Use it. Power . . ." His eyes fixed on Rana. A faint rattle like the gourds summoning wind, and the life left his eyes.

Senuet gave the death-cry, which brought people running from all over the camp. As the women took charge of the old shaman's body, he pulled Rana aside. "We have to go on. Not here, with death-grief, but we've got to bring the rain. Go get the pipe."

Rana stood for a moment, shocked by the suddenness of it all. Then he nodded and ran for the skin bag which hid his newest pipe. Sooner than Rana would have thought possible, they were a safe distance from the camp. Senuet lit a new ceremonial fire with a coal from the firepot. The wall of smoke in the east covered the horizon from one side of the sky to the other.

"Now." Senuet picked up Kawit's drum, which he had brought with him. "Make rain-magic with your pipe."

Rana began. The whistle of rising wind, a patter of drops, the hiss of rain on long grass. Senuet drummed thunder, and rattled gourds for a clatter of hail against rocks, and chanted until his voice grew hoarse. Rana concentrated on the sounds of a storm, over and over, willing whatever magic there might be in his pipe to bring the rain. But there was no answering flash from the sky as there had been for Kawit, no thickening of the clouds. Not even a hint of thunder. Finally he shifted to the river-sound the old shaman had warned him about, hoping for its wild power.

Nothing. They stopped at last, too exhausted to continue. In silence they put out the ceremonial fire. Then they stumbled back to camp and waited, while the women wailed the death of the most powerful shaman of the People. By daybreak the fire had moved far to the east, leaving a haze of smoke that dimmed the rising sun.

At midmorning there was a cry as a small group limped into camp. Fewer than half the hunters had returned, burned and smoke-blackened. Dibur wasn't among them; one look at Meti's blistered face told Rana their friend lay someplace out on the plains. Death-cries rang for hours as Flying Hawk and Running Stag mourned their shared dead.

The rains arrived at last, three days later, bringing the stench of wet ash. The survivors broke camp and headed west, away from the ravaged grasslands and heavy smell. At the next Gathering, they would form a new band from the remnants of both. But, as Senuet made clear, that band would have only one shaman.

"Kawit was right when he said there was no magic in you," he said. It was the first time he had spoken to Rana since the fire. His face was calm, but with a terrible look in his eyes, guilt and sorrow both. "Whatever power is in your pipe, it could not summon rain when we needed it. When Kawit needed it. I was proud of how well you played, and I let that blind me. I don't blame you, the guilt is mine. But when the People gather again after the rains, you will return to the young hunters' fire."

That evening when the reduced bands made camp in a spot near a rain-fed stream, Rana kept to himself. News of the failed ceremonial had spread around the camp; already he was avoided as bad luck, and Meti glared at him with eyes hotter than the fire. He didn't sleep much that night, nor the next. He had never asked to be a shaman, never claimed magic. All he had ever wanted was the pipe. But once the shamans' fire at the Gathering cast him out, he would be forbidden to touch a pipe, or to ever make another.

The third day after the fire, Rana finally slept, exhausted. There was a storm that afternoon, with winds and wild rain. The sound of it mingled in his dream with the memory of his rainsong, changing into something new. He woke knowing what he had to do.

He didn't bother to take much. A little food, a leather bag with his newest pipe and some uncarved reeds, his knives, a waterskin. Once the camp was asleep that night, he slipped out. He stopped a short distance away and sat down on a rock where he could still see the glow of the campfire. The People lived in the grasslands, but rumors spoke of other tribes far to the south. Maybe he could reach them; maybe they had reeds and pipes. Or maybe not. It didn't really matter. He would have his pipe, and he would leave the burden of magic he had never possessed behind with his grief and his people. But there was one more thing he had to do. He raised his pipe to his lips and began to play what he had heard in the dream. He played his grief, and his love for his people, and his farewell. Then, replacing the pipe in its leather bag, he walked south, heading into the night.

Aya awoke to the song of the pipe and knew at once what it meant. The song of the pipe stirred grief but brought more comfort than the wails for the dead had ever done. Others gathered, speaking in whispers. A few muttered of sacrilege, since the high thin notes were part of no ritual. But most wept, remembering the dead and finding solace this time in the memory.

Aya ignored them all. He crept over to the place where he had seen Rana sleeping that day, and felt around in the dark. Wedged between two trees, he found a bag made of skin. He grabbed it and went back to his spot near the women's fire. He didn't open the bag. There was no need; he could feel the shapes inside. Rana's old pipe, and the half-carved one he had been working on before the grassfire.

He'd have to find someplace to hide the bag in the morning, away from his mother and Senuet. But it was his. As the last notes of Rana's farewell echoed into silence, Aya went back to sleep clutching his new pipe.

THE DROWNING CELL

GREGORY FEELEY

Gregory Feeley, whose novel The Oxygen Barons *was nominated for the Philip K. Dick award, is a noted critic as well as the author of other short fictions in the fantasy and science fiction genre.*

"A nd this way," said the tour guide, "lay the notorious Drowning Cell."

The tourists looked curiously at the innocuous entranceway. Splashes and shouts echoed through the tiled passage, borne on a puff of chlorinated air. The young woman (her guide badge identified her as "Lise") smiled at their expressions. "Does anyone know about this?"

No one wanted to admit having read up on such a thing. Allison, who always knew something about the places they were going to visit, finally asked in a small voice: "Is that where the prisoners who were lazy had to pump to keep from drowning?"

Several of the adults said *Ah* under their breath, and Mark, who made a point of showing indifference to anything his sister liked, slipped forward to peer into the long passageway.

"That's right!" said Lise, pleased. "According to the legend, if an inmate refused to work, or showed obstinance toward reform, he could be put into the 'drowning cell' or 'water house,' which was a sealed room with a pump in it. The jailers would then begin to flood the room, and the inmate had to pump to keep the water from rising over his head."

"Wow," said Mark, with relish.

"That's awful," said their mother, her hand tightening on Allison's shoulder. "It's virtual torture."

"The seventeenth century was not kind to criminals," Lise admitted. "But most other countries were even harsher—they hanged child thieves in England. Holland's commitment to reforming young offenders was unique for its time." There was ambivalence in her voice, as though she didn't like her country's past practices, but was uneasy at hearing them criticized by foreigners.

"Did anyone actually drown there?" asked Mark.

A few of the adults smiled. "Nobody knows," Lise told him. "The *Tugthuis*—the House of Correction—opened in 1595, and hardly any records that old survive. The original structure was replaced by a larger workhouse in 1694, and we know there was nothing like that going on by that time. But the stories continued to be told for another century, and it's still remembered today. Even though"—she smiled at Mark, as though sorry at his disappointment—"the actual site is now a swimming pool!"

Allison was looking pale as Lise led the small crowd across the lobby. Her legs wobbled as they descended the steps, and she had to grab the railing, but no one noticed.

The tour guide was explaining how the site had been repeatedly demolished and rebuilt since the Middle Ages, and how parts of some buildings dated from the fourteenth century, while adjoining sections were less than fifty years old. They were crossing a colonnade built over what looked like an old courtyard when Allison fell to the ground with a cry.

"Allison, what is it?" cried her mother, as the others turned in surprise. Allison was writhing on the paving stones, her eyes squeezed shut. Before anyone could think to do something, she swung her head round and stared vacantly upward.

"He was twelve," she gasped, her breath rapid and shallow. "His name was Jan, and he had something wrong with his arms, he couldn't work long or hard with them, so he had tried to pick pockets. They put him to work on a sawing team, but he was too weak and got into trouble. And so they put him in the cell, to teach him to pull hard."

Adult faces were bending over her, frightened or concerned. Her voice rose to a pitch of terror. "It was dark, and the water pouring in was cold and smelled bad. He worked the pump frantically, but his arms had no real strength. Voices called down to him from above, cursing and laughing."

"Allison!" said her mother sharply. "Allison, that's enough of this!"

"The water rose around him, until he had to raise his head to breathe and couldn't work the pump at all." Allison suddenly shrieked: *"Mama!*

Papa! Bewaar me!" Her eyes rolled up in her head as her heels drummed against the stones, and she went limp.

"They're talking about it on TV," said Mark, who understood none of the newscaster's Dutch but heard his sister's name and recognized the picture of the *Tugthuis.* "They say you're crazy and ought to be deported."

"Mark, leave us alone," said his mother. She was sitting on the hotel room carpet beside the sofa, where Allison lay with her eyes half-closed. "How are you feeling, honey?" she asked, brushing Allison's hair from her brow. "You certainly have caused enough trouble. Have you taken one of the pills yet?"

Allison shook her head. "I didn't have a seizure," she muttered. She drew the blanket closer around her shoulders.

"Allison, dear, it's *hot* in here." Her mother tried to fold back the blanket. "You'll develop a fever."

Allison kept her grip on it. "It was cold," she said in a low voice. "The tiny room was dripping when they threw him in; the walls were wet. He had heard the stories, but didn't believe they were going to do *that* to him." Her hands began to tremble.

Mark had come over and was standing behind his mother. "Could you feel him drown?" he asked interestedly. "Were you *there?*"

"Mark!" his mother snapped. The phone rang, and he went to get it. "Dear, this isn't an anticonvulsant. The doctor said he was only prescribing something to help you rest." She urged a glass of water and a pill toward her daughter's lips, but Allison turned her head away fretfully.

"It's a reporter," called Mark from across the room. "He wants to know whether Allison has a history of paranormal experiences." His mother shooed at him impatiently, and he returned to the phone. "Naw, she's never done anything like that," he said into the receiver. He listened for a moment. "Pubescent? How should I know?"

"Mark, hang up," his mother commanded. He complied with a scowl.

Allison stood shakily and started for the bathroom. "Are you all right?" her mother asked.

"I just need to be left alone," she said. She closed the door behind her and sat down. The tiny window had pretty chintz curtains, like houses throughout Amsterdam, and she peeked through them to look at the narrow street below. If her experience had attracted the interest of the local news station, they weren't standing outside the small hotel.

Someone flushed in the bathroom directly overhead, and water gurgled down the pipes in the wall behind her. Allison shivered.

The boat wasn't glass-bottomed, but it had something like a dormer window protruding from the hull, which offered a wide view like that of the dolphin tank at an aquarium. Blue-green water, still suffused with light from the surface ten feet above, glinted with occasional fish. The sandy bottom drifted past slowly, visible in perfect detail. It looked like a large sunken meadow, which (the captain explained over the intercom) it indeed was. The Zuider Zee had reclaimed many areas that had been dry land in the eighteenth and nineteenth centuries, now submerged beneath fifteen or more feet of ocean water.

"Look!" cried Mark, pointing to the ruins of a stone house, as distinct as a plastic toy at the bottom of a fishbowl. The captain, speaking in Dutch and then English, was saying something about lost villages, but Allison did not hear him. She began to tremble, and her mother, pressed against her on the crowded bench, turned to stare at her.

"It sank," she whispered.

"I beg your pardon?" her mother asked.

"He was kept in the bilges, where the pump was, and he worked it in total darkness, because the storm had knocked the lamp over." Her face was changing color, although the aquamarine light made this hard to notice. "When the ship started to founder the sailors all went over the side, but no one thought to get him. He was still pumping in the dark when the water poured in—"

"*Allison!*" Her mother looked around quickly as Allison began to whimper. The other passengers were all staring out the window. "Stop it this instant."

"Two sailors were pumping with him, but they fled as soon as the ship began to list. They disappeared in the darkness, and when he tried to splash after them he *hit his head*—"

Her mother's hand tightened on Allison's upper arm, and with a small shriek Allison pulled free. A few people turned toward her as she struggled to her feet and rushed for the hatch. Her mother called after her, but Allison didn't stop until she emerged onto the sunny deck, where the captain, microphone in hand, and a few crew members were looking out across the flat expanse of sea.

Allison took a few steps and fell, scraping her palms on the unvarnished planks. She felt that she was going to be sick, and began to crawl toward the railing. Someone was coming up the hatch, and she turned her head away. But it was a young man holding a notebook. He peered down at her in alarm.

"Are you all right?" he asked in Dutch. Allison remembered the question from the hospital. Then he looked more closely, and switched to English. "Aren't you the American girl who felt a ghost in the *Tugthuis?*"

Allison heard her mother yelling at him to get away. Then a wave of cold seawater crashed out of the darkness over her, and she vomited consciousness away.

"They say you're probably faking." Mark sat with a Dutch-English dictionary and the morning paper in front of him. Allison had a cup of tea in front of her. They had come into the café at the very end of the morning rush, and the counterman had scarcely looked up as he had served them. Mark had assured her that nobody would recognize her from the junior high school yearbook photo that one of the papers had managed to run.

"Why am I faking?" asked Allison listlessly. She was thinking that if everyone believed she was making this up, they would leave her alone.

"You only felt the ghost in the drowning cell after the guide had told us about it," Mark said, enjoying himself. Her mother had told her to watch Mark, but she suspected that Mark had also been told to keep an eye on her. "If it had been some ghost that you couldn't have known about, *that* would have meant something."

"Your brother is right," said a man who had come up beside them. Allison and Mark looked up. "My name is Pieter Roonswijk; I was on the boat with you. Do you remember me?"

"No," said Allison.

"I remember him," said Mark. "After they put a blanket over you, he sat down in one of the deck chairs and scribbled madly. I bet you're a reporter," he said accusingly.

"You're right." Roonswijk sat down at the table next to them. "And not even a local reporter, just a sightseer from Groningen. And now I'm having a working vacation." He smiled apologetically. "My publisher sold my story to a big Amsterdam newspaper. He's hoping for another one."

"He got help when you fainted," Mark allowed.

Allison said hello.

"Your brother is right," Roonswijk said. "A lot of people think you're making this up. What makes your story compelling is that you're an adolescent girl, a group that is sometimes thought to be susceptible to psychic phenomena. And the doctors confirmed that you did have some kind of convulsion."

"What about the ship that sank?" demanded Mark. "She couldn't have known anything about that."

Roonswijk shrugged. "The coast of IJselmeer has been the site of innumerable wrecks over the past five hundred years. There probably isn't a hectare where some ship didn't go down."

"If you don't believe her, why are you writing another story?" demanded Mark.

"I didn't say I don't believe her," Roonswijk said mildly. "The *Handelsblad* has portrayed her as a hysterical American, while the tabloids—that's the right word, yes?—the tabloids are writing about the ghosts of drowned children." Allison shivered suddenly, which both Mark and Roonswijk noticed. "I have never heard of someone being sensitive to a certain kind of ghost, a specific manner of death. Have you ever had a near-drowning experience?"

Allison and Mark looked at each other. "Never," Allison said, puzzled. "My mother won't let me swim except in a pool with a lifeguard."

Roonswijk had taken out his notebook, and was looking at her closely. "Do you sometimes feel as though you are drowning?"

"There you are." Their mother stood at the entrance, folding her umbrella. "You shouldn't be sitting out where someone might recognize you." Roonswijk had turned away at the sound of her voice, and was sipping his espresso with an abstracted expression.

She sat down heavily, shedding droplets of rain from her coat. "The airline won't change the return tickets unless I can document a medical emergency, so I've had to ask the hospital for a letter." She looked tired and resentful.

"We shouldn't have to go home early," said Mark. A whine entered his voice. "So long as Allison steers clear of the wrong spots—"

"Mark, be quiet." She tried to attract a waiter's attention, then realized that she had to order from the counter. While she was getting her coffee Roonswijk passed Mark a slip of paper. "That's my phone number," he said, looking elsewhere. "Give me a call."

Mark had his argument prepared by the time his mother returned.

"If we go on to Switzerland," he began, "Allison won't be exposed to places where boys have drowned. So—"

"That's enough, Mark." Their mother was always snappish at this time of day, when a late morning cup of coffee used to mean a cigarette. "We're going to go straight home and get Allison to a specialist. I know what's right for my children."

They changed hotels after their mother saw a newspaper, and during the taxi ride Allison grew distraught, crying out about a girl who had drowned in a car. Her mother ordered the driver to take a different route, and Allison subsided, gulping sobs.

While they were checking in, Mark asked the concierge about floods in that part of the city. The elderly lady began telling him about the disastrous spring tides of 1953, which flooded four hundred thousand acres and killed two thousand fleeing people, when his mother called sharply to him.

That evening she took Mark with her to cancel the tickets they had for the National Theater. Allison stayed in the hotel room, under strict orders to lie down. "I don't want you even to get out of bed," her mother had said as she left. For twenty minutes Allison lay immobile, as though a giant hand were pressing her down, but finally she sat up hesitantly, then swung her feet to the floor. Quietly she got dressed and found the slip of paper tucked into her brother's paperback. She called the number, and the reporter answered immediately.

"I'd like to introduce you to someone." He sounded nervous. "She's a medium, very sensitive to the spirit world and knowledgeable about how it can touch the lives of living people. My newspaper has agreed to pay for an interview with her, if you're willing."

Allison was still slightly confused from the pill she had been given. "How would this help you?" she asked.

"Well, she's supposed to be the best around. If she tells you that you really did encounter the spirit of a three-hundred-year-old boy, that makes your account much more plausible. I'll write a story about it, but you'll be gone before it appears, so it won't bother your family." It was plain that he meant her mother.

Allison thought about this. "And how will this help *me?*" she asked at last.

"Maybe she will tell you something to help you. That's possible."

She met him in the lobby fifteen minutes later, and they took a taxi away from downtown. Roonswijk told the driver to go slowly and be prepared to turn around if asked. Allison guessed that his nervousness involved the act of taking a teenage American somewhere without her mother's permission. Under ordinary circumstances the prospect of her mother finding out would alarm her, too. But it was more frightening to continue knowing nothing, and so to risk blundering into some invisible horror, like a child running blindly through a dark cellar.

They pulled up outside a large old apartment building and stood waiting for the elevator in a lobby with water stains on the walls. The apartment was on the fourth floor, which seemed as dim as a basement. Roonswijk knocked on a door, and they stood in uneasy silence until it opened.

Madame Ruider was in her mid-fifties, and wore a long skirt like the women who sold natural foods and handicrafts, only it was a cheerless dark brown. "Good evening," she said carefully, glancing at Roonswijk, then looking closely at Allison.

That was all the English she seemed to know, for she had Roonswijk explain matters as they sat down at a small covered table. She poured a pot of very strong tea, which seemed to clear Allison's head a bit.

Roonswijk asked Allison questions at Madame Ruider's request, which he then translated for her. Allison could remember little about the onset of her visions, which the doctors had also asked about. "I knew it wasn't me in the cell, but I could feel everything that happened to him. The water spewed out of a pipe overhead, and spattered against the opposite wall. His arms were weak—if he did the same task over and over they swelled up, and life in the *Tugthuis* meant sawing logs all day long—and so he couldn't pull hard enough, even though he was terrified." She found herself trembling.

Mme. Ruider grunted and removed the teapot. When she returned she directed Roonswijk to a chair in the corner and sat opposite Allison at the small table. She took out a deck of cards, which Allison recognized as a Tarot deck.

"Are you going to tell my fortune?" she asked.

"No," said Mme. Ruider, surprising her. She spread the cards on the table and gestured for Allison to mix them up. "The Tarot is more—" she said something to Roonswijk, who supplied the translation. "She says that it can be used as an instrument to study the situation, like a voltmeter or a seismograph."

"This is a deck designed by an American woman who lived many years in Amsterdam," said Mme. Ruider, speaking slowly in heavily accented English. "Appropriate for you." She had Allison reassemble the cards, which she divided into three piles.

"We look for three answers," she announced. "What did you find in Amsterdam; what does it mean for you; and what must you do to obtain the best result?"

She laid down three cards in a row. Allison thought that the first card would answer the first question, but Mme. Ruider pointed to the middle one. "Look at it," she said.

Allison picked up the card. It was labeled THE DEVIL, and showed a glaring horned figure, arms pressed against his sides, squeezed into a tiny rectangle as larger, concentric rectangles pressed down on it. A liquid substance roiled at his feet.

Allison gasped and dropped the card. Mme. Ruider returned it to its place, frowning. She spoke to Roonswijk. "The card does not signify the Devil in the traditional sense, but rather suppressed energies, or entrapment," the reporter said.

Mme. Ruider turned the rightmost card so that Allison could see it. The Five of Rivers showed a crane that carried a dark sun within its belly, a complement to the bright sun overhead. "This deck uses Rivers instead of Cups," said Roonswijk after Mme. Ruider finished speaking. "In traditional Tarot decks, the Five of Cups is usually illustrated by a scene of loss. A famous deck shows a mourning figure gazing upon three spilled cups."

"What does it mean?" Allison whispered.

"Sorrow and loss. The need for acceptance."

Allison looked at the third card, which had been laid down reversed and so already faced her. The Nine of Rivers depicted several shattered pots, all of them gushing water, and an intact pot at the center. "You must know what lies broken before you can go on," said Mme. Ruider.

Looking troubled, she gathered the cards and put them away. "Most people who claim to encounter ghosts actually see an aspect of their own selves, which is trying to speak to them. This is worthwhile, and must be acknowledged; but genuine encounters with unquiet spirits are very rare.

"We do not know why one person will detect the traces of a past trauma, while others nearby will not. Possibly a sympathy between the living and the deceased . . . "

She began to speak in rapid Dutch, and Roonswijk translated. "One consequence of ghostly encounters, real ones, is that the human may become . . . *sensitized* to one kind of psychic persistence. Like a child who has an allergic reaction to a bee sting: her reaction to any subsequent exposure will be much stronger."

"What does that mean?" asked Allison in a frightened voice.

Mme. Ruider spoke slowly and forcefully. "Leave Holland," said Roonswijk. "All Holland is a drowning cell, just as all Europe is a plague pit, a scaffold, a charnel house: every place you set your foot is dense with the history of human misery, like blood soaked into the ground. Where are you from?"

"I live in Boston, with my mother."

Mme. Ruider shook her head. "That may not be good. You are"—she paused to recall the word Roonswijk had used—"sensitized. Sympathy is established, so will persist. *Don't get stung again.*"

The reporter insisted on seeing her back to the hotel, but once his taxi pulled away Allison left the lobby and headed down the narrow street. It was already dark, but nobody took notice of a teenager walking alone. The shops of the noisy Kalverstraat were open late, and she bought a Tarot deck at a store that sold drug paraphernalia. The cards looked cheap and flimsy, but Allison didn't think that was important.

At a telephone booth she called the hotel room. "Mother, I've gone for a walk," she said, glad that she had gotten the hotel's voice mail system. "Back later, 'bye." Even her mother couldn't demand answers of a machine.

Allison studied a map of the city she found in her purse, then headed for the *Tugthuis*. She had expected to encounter a persistence before she got there—how many times had this street been flooded and children drowned in small spaces?—but felt a twinge only once, and it faded when she crossed to the other side of the street.

She felt it when she saw the entrance: a familiar ache, as if from an old injury that stirs at certain times of the year. She took an experimental step forward and felt worse. Stepping back, she sat down on the sidewalk and got out the deck. Unmindful of the occasional glances from those walking around her, she separated out the cards of the Major Arcana, the only ones she knew anything about. Clumsily she mixed and shuffled them, then paused.

"This reading is for you, Jan," she whispered. "You're like an electric field only I can sense, and the cards are iron filings." She divided the packet into three. "You can't tell me what you want them to show, so I'll just have to do my best."

She closed her eyes and silently spoke three sentences, laying out a card with each one. Then she opened them and looked down at the triptych.

What happened to you? Tradition. *Where are you now?* Justice, Reversed. *What must be done to help you?* The Chariot.

"I don't understand," she whispered. "What is it that I should do?"

It had begun to drizzle. She stood up and stepped into the street, walking the arc that maintained a constant radius between herself and the doorway. A taxi turned the corner and its headlights swept round to catch her, and she turned back toward the pavement. The taxi stopped with a screech, and its high beams leaped on to spear her. Allison heard a car door open and her mother shout, "That's her!"

Dropping the cards in a scatter behind her, Allison ran. Her mother shouted after her, and a car screeched in front of her and blared its horn. Allison darted sideways, and saw a narrow alley between two storefronts. She heard the taxi's engine start up behind her and sprinted into the alley.

The sound of traffic faded, and the asphalt underfoot gave way to rough cobblestones. Allison had to stop running or she would twist an ankle. It was raining harder now, and she looked around the shadows—the streetlights had vanished with the sidewalks—and wondered whether the safety of Amsterdam's streets extended into its back alleys.

It was then that she saw him.

The boy sat on a wooden stoop, face buried in his raised knees as though to retreat from the rain. He looked no bigger than Mark, and was terribly thin. Allison could see the outline of his frail limbs through his clinging garments, which seemed to glow with a faint fluorescence, like rotting seaweed. A quiet sobbing reached her through the rain.

Allison took a step forward. "Jan?" she asked.

The boy looked up, and Allison found herself staring into a face so piteously unhappy that her mind went blank. Bruised eyes gazed without hope upon her, and she saw faint pocks between the wet strands plastered to his forehead. Small as he was, his clothes were smaller still and gaped raggedly to show bony knees.

He regarded her strangely, as though unused to being noticed. If Allison expected a look of recognition, she was disappointed. Nothing registered in these wasted features but the expectation of further pain.

"You're real," she said wonderingly. "I just don't know in what way you're real."

She looked at her empty hands and found, to her surprise, that she was still holding a card. She began to extend it to the boy, then stopped herself. What need had he of a Tarot reading; what could he be suffering that he did not already know? "I don't know how I can help you," she whispered.

She looked at the back of the card, wondering if she should turn it over. And if it was Rivers, or even The Hanged Man, what then? If he could not take counsel from it, should she? And suddenly she understood. He's not seeking my help, she thought wonderingly: he's *offering* help.

When she looked up, the boy was gone. Raindrops pattered at the place where he had been, which was already wet.

Allison stood in the puddling alley, the whiff of moldy clothing fading in the rain, and flipped over the card in her hand. It was The Empress, assured and powerful, wearing a crown of stars and holding a scepter. What did that mean?

From the street, she heard her mother calling. Allison whirled in alarm, then looked about wildly; but the alley offered no exit. She backed up against a wet wall, wondering if her mother would walk into a dark alley, even if she knew her daughter was trapped there. Water trickled against her neck, and with a touch of chill certainty Allison knew that *this* was her drowning cell: a dark enclosure whose only exit was blocked by her mother.

"Allison, am I going to have to come in after you?"

Allison closed her eyes and thought of Jan, who—if he ever lived—was now no more than a fading trace, the smell of burnt toast in an empty kitchen. He dissipated like smoke while Allison remained, a residue that would not wash away. Trapped in this moment like grit in a mesh, she felt the dissolving sluice rush over her, turbid with smaller particles: the dripping decay of the world, holding her fast as it drained into nothing, laving her in the catchment of grief and human misery.

AFTERNOON

The time for doing when study is behind and Magick flows full and bright—or dark.

A TIME FOR HEROES
RICHARD PARKS

Richard Parks *is thirty-something and has been married to a poet for seventeen years. His work title is "Computer System Manager," which is an alias for his real job, computer tamer and occasional program-mer. He has sold stories to* Asimov's SF, Dragon, Realms of Fantasy, Science Fiction Age *and* Amazing SF, *plus various anthologies.*

Timon the Black, demon of a thousand nightmares and master of none, came to a sudden understanding. "It's raining," he said. "And I'm cold."

He sounded surprised.

The dwarf Seb was not surprised. The chilling rain had started the moment they reached the foothills of the White Mountains and contin-ued all afternoon. Seb's long fair hair hung limp about his face, and he peered out at the magician through a tangled mat like a runt wolf eyeing a lamb through a hedge. "At last he deigns to notice . . . I've been cold for hours! At the very least you could have been miserable with me."

"Sorry," Timon said. "You know I have trouble with some things."

Seb nodded. "'Here' and 'now' being two of them." Day-to-day prac-tical matters were really Seb's responsibility, but there was comfort in complaining. In his years with Timon, Seb had learned to take comfort where he could.

Nothing else was said for a time, there being nothing to say. Seb, as usual, was the first to notice the failing light. "It's getting late. We'd bet-ter find somewhere dry to camp, if there be such in this wretched place."

It was beginning to look like a very wet night until Seb spotted a large overhang on a nearby ridge. It wasn't a true cave, more a remnant of some long-ago earthquake, but it reached more than forty yards into the hillside and had a high ceiling and dry, level floor. It wasn't the worst place they'd ever slept.

"I'll build a fire," the dwarf said, "if you will promise me not to look at it."

Timon didn't promise, but Seb built the fire anyway after seeing to their mounts and the pack train. He found some almost-dry wood near the entrance and managed to collect enough rainwater for the horses and for a pot of tea. He unpacked the last of their dried beef and biscuit, studied the pitiful leavings, and shook his head in disgust. Gold wasn't a problem, but they hadn't dared stop for supplies till well away from the scene of Timon's last escapade, and now what little food they'd had time to pack was almost gone.

Seb scrounged another pot and went to catch some more rain. When he had enough, he added the remnants of beef and started the pot simmering on the fire. The mixture might make a passable broth. If not, at least they could use it to soften the biscuit.

Timon inched closer to the fire, watching Seb out of the corner of his eye. The dwarf pretended not to notice. Timon was soaked, and neither of them had any dry clothing. Timon's catching cold or worse was the last thing Seb needed. As for the risk, well, when the inevitable happened it would happen and that, as it had been many times before, would be that.

"I never look for trouble, you know that," Timon said. It sounded like an apology.

"I know." Seb handed him a bowl of the broth and a piece of hard biscuit, and that small gesture was as close to an acceptance of the apology as the occasion demanded. They ate in comfortable silence for a while, but as the silence went on and on and the meal didn't, Seb began to feel definitely uncomfortable. He finally surrendered tact and leaned close.

"Bloody hell!"

It was the Long Look. Timon's eyes were glazed, almost like a blind man's. They focused at once on the flames and on nothing. Timon was seeing something far beyond the firelight, something hidden as much in time as distance. And there wasn't a damn thing Seb could do about it. He thought of taking his horse and leaving his friend behind, saving himself. He swore silently that one day he would do just that. He had sworn before, and he meant it no less now. But not this time. Always, not this time.

Seb dozed after a while, walking the edge of a dream of warmth and ease and just about to enter, when the sound of his name brought him back to the cold stone and firelight.

"Seb?"

Timon was back, too, from whatever far place he'd gone, and he was shivering again. Seb poured the last of the tea into Timon's mug. "Well?"

"I've seen something," Timon said. He found a crust of biscuit in his lap and dipped it in his tea. He chewed thoughtfully.

"Timon, is it your habit to inform me that the sun has risen? The obvious I can deal with; I need help with the Hidden Things."

"So do I," Timon said. "Or at least telling which is which. What do you think is hidden?"

"What you saw. What the Long Look has done to us this time."

Timon rubbed his eyes like the first hour of morning. "Oh, that . . . tragedy, Seb. That's what I saw in the fire. I didn't mean to. I tried not to look."

Seb threw the dregs of his own cup into the fire, and it hissed in protest. "I rather doubt it matters. If it wasn't the fire, it would be the pattern of sweat on your horse's back, or the shine of a dewdrop—" The dwarf's scowl suddenly cleared away, and he looked like a scholar who'd just solved a particularly vexing sum. "The Long Look is a curse, isn't it? I should have realized that long ago. What did you do? Cut firewood in a sacred grove? Make water on the wrong patch of flowers? What?" Seb waited but Timon didn't answer. He didn't seem to be listening. Seb shook his head sadly. "I'll wager it was a goddess. Those capable of greatest kindness must also have the power for greatest cruelty. That's balance."

"That's nonsense," said Timon, who was listening after all. "And a Hidden Thing, I see. So let me reveal it to you—there is one difference between the workings of a god and a goddess in our affairs. One only."

"And that is?"

"Us. Being men, we take the disfavor of a female deity more personally." Timon yawned and reached for his saddle and blanket.

Seb seized the reference. "Disfavor. You admit it."

Timon shrugged. "If it gives you pleasure. The Powers know you've had precious little of that lately." He moved his blanket away from a sharp rise in the stone and repositioned his saddle. "Where are we going?"

Seb tended the fire, looking sullen. "Morushe."

"Good. I'm not known there—by sight, anyway."

Seb nodded. "I was counting on that."

"It *will* make things easier . . . "

Seb knew that Timon was now speaking to himself, but he refused to be left out. "I know why we *were* heading toward Morushe—it was far away from Calyt. What business do we have there now?"

"We're going to murder a prince."

Seb closed his eyes. "Pity the fool who asked."

"I never look for trouble. You know that."

"I won't marry him and that's final!"

Princess Ashesa of Morushe spurred the big roan viciously, her long red hair streaming behind her like the wake of a Fury. She was dressed for the hunt and carried a short bow slung across her back, but the only notice she took of the forest was mirrored in a glare clearly meant to wither any tree impertinent enough to block her path.

Lady Margate—less sensibly attired—was having trouble keeping up, though she rode gamely enough. A large buck, frightened by the commotion, broke cover and leaped across their path.

"A buck!" shouted Margy, hopefully.

Ashesa didn't even pause. "I won't marry *him* either," she snapped, "though I daresay if he ruled a big enough kingdom, Father would consider it." She grinned. "At least he's a *gentler* beast."

"That's no way to talk about your future husband!" reproved Margy. "Prince Daras is of ancient and noble lineage."

"So's my boar-hound," returned Ashesa sweetly. "We have the documents."

There had been almost no warning. Ashesa had barely time to hide her precious—and expressly forbidden—books away before her father had burst in to tell her the good news. The alliance between Morushe and the coastal realm of Borasur was agreed and signed. By breakfast King Macol had the date and was halfway done with the guest list. Ashesa couldn't decide between smashing dishes or going on her morning hunt. In the end she'd done both. But now half the crockery in her father's palace was wrecked, and her horse was not much better. Ashesa finally took pity on the poor beast and reined in at a small clearing. Margy straggled up looking reproachful and nearly as spent as Ashesa's mount.

"I just wish that someone had *asked* me. Father could have at least let me know what he was planning, *talked* to me. Was that asking for such a great deal?"

Lady Margate sighed deeply. "In Balanar town yesterday I saw a girl about your age. She would be even prettier than you are except she's already missing three teeth and part of an ear. She hawks ale and Heaven knows what else at a tavern near the barracks. If I were to tell her that the Princess Ashesa was going to be married to a prince without her permission, do you think that girl would weep for you?"

Ashesa looked sullen. "No need to go 'round the mulberry bush, Margy. I understand you."

"Then understand this—Morushe is a rich kingdom but not a strong one. Wylandia, among others, is all too aware of that. Without powerful friends, your people aren't safe. This marriage will help ensure that we have those friends."

"For someone who claims statecraft is no field for a woman, you certainly have a firm grasp of it," Ashesa said dryly.

"Common sense, Highness. Don't confuse the two." Margy looked around them. "We should not be this far from the palace. Two highborn ladies, unescorted, in the middle of a wild forest . . . "

Ashesa laughed, and felt a little better for it. "Margy, Father's game park is about as 'wild' as your sewing room. Even the wolves get their worming dose every spring."

Lady Margate drew herself up in matronly dignity. "Neverthe—" She paused, her round mouth frozen in mid-syllable. She looked puzzled.

"Yes?" Ashesa encouraged, but Lady Margate just sat there, swaying ever so gently in her saddle. Ashesa slid from her mount and ran over to her nurse. "Margy, what is it?"

Ashesa saw the feathered dart sticking out of the woman's neck and whirled, drawing her hunting sword.

Too late.

Another dart hummed out of a nearby oak and stung her in the shoulder. Ashesa felt a pinprick of pain and then nothing. Her motion continued and she fell, stiff as a toppled statue, into the wildflowers, her eyes fixed upward at the guilty tree. Two short legs appeared below the leaves of a low branch, then the rest of a man not quite four feet high followed.

He wore fashionable hunting garb of brown and green immaculately tailored to his small frame, and in his hand was a blowpipe. He carried a small quiver with more darts at his belt.

Elf-shot . . . ? Ashesa's mind was all fuzzy; it was hard to think.

The small man reached the ground and nodded pleasantly in her direction, touched his cap, and whistled. Two normal-sized men in concealing robes appeared at the edge of the clearing and went to work with professional detachment. First they removed Lady Margate from her horse and propped her against the dwarf's oak, closing her eyes and tipping her hat forward to keep the sun off her face. Ashesa, half-mad with anger and worry, struggled against the drug until the veins stood out on her neck, but she could not move. The little man knelt beside her, looking strangely concerned.

"You'll only injure yourself, Highness. Don't worry about your friend—she'll recover, but not till we're well away." With that he gently plucked the dart from her shoulder and tossed it into the bushes.

"Who are you? Why are you doing this?"

The shout echoed in her head but nowhere else; she could not speak. The two silent henchmen brought Ashesa's horse as the dwarf pulled a small vial from his belt, popped the cork, and held it to her nose. An acrid odor stung her nostrils and she closed her eyes with no help at all.

Kings Macol and Riegar sat in morose silence in Macol's chambers. At first glance they weren't much alike: Macol was stout and ruddy, Riegar tall and gaunt with thinning gray hair. All this was only surface, for what they shared was obvious even without their crowns. Each man wore his responsibilities like a hair shirt.

Riegar finally spoke. "It was soon after you broke the news to your daughter, I gather?"

Macol nodded, looking disgusted. "I fooled myself into thinking she knew her duty. Blast, after her outburst this morning I'd almost think she cooked this up herself just to spite me!"

Riegar dismissed that. "We have the note, and the seal is unmistakable—"

The clatter on the stairs startled them both, and then they heard the sentry's challenge. They heard the answer even better—it was both colorful and loud.

"That will be Daras." Riegar sighed.

The crown prince of Borasur strode through the door, his handsome face flushed, his blue eyes shining with excitement. "The messenger said there was a note. Where is it?"

"Damn you, lad, you've barged into a room containing no fewer than two kings, one of whom is your father. Where are your manners?" Riegar asked.

Daras conceded a curt nod, mumbled an apology, and snatched the parchment from the table. For all his hurry the message didn't register very quickly. Daras read slowly, mouthing each word as if getting the taste of it. When he was done there was a grimness in his eyes that worried them. "Wylandia is behind this, Majesties. I'm certain!"

Macol and Riegar exchanged glances, then Macol spoke. "Prince, aren't you reading a great deal into a message that says only 'I have Ashesa—Timon the Black'?"

Daras looked surprised. "Who else has a reason to kidnap My Beloved Ashesa? The king of Wylandia would do anything to prevent our alliance." Daras said Ashesa's name with all the passion of a student reciting declensions, but he'd seen his intended only twice in his life and had as little say in the matter as she did.

Macol shook his head. "I know Aldair—he'll fight you with everything he has at the slightest provocation, but he won't stab you in the back. And Morushe and Borasur have so many trading ties that it amounts to alliance already. Aldair knows this; his negotiating position for Wylandia's use of our mountain passes is quite reasonable. We are close to agreement."

"If Aldair is not involved, then the kidnapping is not for reasons of state. And if not, then why was there no ransom demand? Why taunt us this way?"

Macol looked almost pleased. "A sensible question, Prince. Your father and I wonder about that ourselves. But no doubt this 'Timon' will make his demands clear in time, and I'll meet them if I can. In the meantime—"

"Of course!" Daras fairly glowed. "How long will it take to raise your army? May I lead the assault?"

"There will be no assault." Riegar's tone was pure finality.

"No assault!? Then what are we going to do?"

Macol sighed. "Prince, what can we do? Our best information—mere rumor—puts Timon in an old watchtower just inside the border of Wylandia. Do you honestly think His Majesty Aldair will negotiate tariffs during an invasion?"

"Has it ever been tried?" Daras asked mildly.

Riegar looked to heaven. "Sometimes I pray for a miracle to take a year from your age and add it to Galan's. I might keep what's left of my wits."

"My brother is a *clark,*" snapped Daras, reddening. "Divine Providence gave the inheritance to *me,* and when I'm king I'll show Wylandia and all else how a king deals with his enemies!" Daras nodded once and stalked out of the room.

Macol watched him go. "A bit headstrong, if I may say."

"You may." Riegar sighed. "Though it's too kind." He winced.

"Are you ill?"

"It's nothing . . . indigestion. Comes and goes." Riegar relaxed a bit as the pain eased, then said, "I've been thinking . . . Aldair won't tolerate an army on his border, but if the situation was explained to him, he might be willing to send a few men of his own."

"I daresay," Macol considered. "If this magician is operating in Aldair's territory without permission, Aldair's pride might even demand it. Yes, I'll have a delegation out tonight! After that, all a father can do is pray."

"As will I. But there is one other thing you can do," Riegar said. "Would you be good enough to post a guard on Prince Daras's quarters tonight?"

"Certainly. But why?"

King Riegar of Borasur, remembering the look in his son's eyes, answered. "Oh, just a whim."

Prince Galan of Borasur strolled down a corridor in Macol's Castle, a thick volume under one arm. He didn't need much in the way of direction, though this was his first visit to Morushe. The fortress was of a common type for the period it was built; he'd made a study in his father's library before the trip. Finding his brother's quarters was easy enough, too. It was the one with the unhappy-looking soldier standing beside the door.

"Is Prince Daras allowed visitors?" he asked, smiling. The guard waved him on wearily, and Galan knocked.

"Enter if you must!"

The muffled bellow sounded close enough to an invitation. Galan went inside and found his brother pacing the stone floor. With both in the same room it was hard to imagine two men more different. Daras was the tall one, strong in the shoulders and arms from years on the tourney fields he loved so well. Galan by contrast had accepted the bare minimum of military training necessary for a Gentleman and no more. He was smaller, darker, with green eyes and a sense of calm. When the brothers were together, it was like a cool forest pool having conversation with a forest fire.

"It's intolerable!" Daras announced.

Galan didn't have to ask what was intolerable. He knew his brother's mind, even if he didn't really understand it. "Macol and Father don't want a war. Can you really fault them for that?"

Daras stopped pacing. He looked a little hurt. "You think I want a war?"

Galan shrugged. "Sometimes."

Daras shook his head. "Remember the heroic tales you used to read to me . . . " He apparently caught the reproach in Galan's eye and so amended, "The ones you still read from time to time? Even among all the nobility and sacrifice, the excitement of combat and rescue, I can see the destruction in my mind's eye. What sane man wants that? No. I blame Father and Macol for nothing except their shortsightedness. By the by, I called you a clark today in front of Father."

"It wouldn't be the first time. And not wholly wrong."

"Even so—I was angry and I'm sorry. Despite your faults I envy you in a lot of ways; you know so many things, whereas I know only one thing in this world for certain—wanted or no, a war with Wylandia is inevitable. I'd rather it be on our terms than Aldair's."

Galan changed the subject. He held up his prize. "Look what I found in Macol's library."

"A book. How odd."

Galan smiled. Sarcasm was another thing his brother knew for certain. "Not just a book. Borelane's *Tales of the Red King*. I've been trying to find a copy of this for years."

Daras showed a little more interest. "Perhaps . . . " he said, then finished, "perhaps you can read to me later."

"It'll have to be later. I'm for Wylandia tonight. Macol and Father are sending a delegation to Aldair. Father thought it might carry more weight if a Prince of the Blood went along."

"Not me, of course," Daras said bitterly.

"Be reasonable, Brother. You've no patience for diplomacy; action suits you better."

"It suits all men better."

Galan swallowed the casual insult by long habit. He'd long ago given up seeking approval from his older brother. He'd never quite given up wanting it. "We wouldn't want to do anything to endanger Ashesa." Her name brought back a little of the envy he'd always felt for Daras. The first time Galan had ever seen Ashesa was barely a year before, when Morushe's royal family paid a state visit to Borasur. He'd spent a month afterward writing bad poetry and staring at the moon.

"No," Daras agreed, though his thoughts were elsewhere.

*　　*　　*

Ashesa awoke in a room fit for a princess—a near perfect copy of her own. The big four-poster bed and the tapestry of the Quest of the Sunbeast were both in place; she was beginning to think she might have dreamed the whole abduction until she saw what was wrong. There were books, and they were not hidden.

She got up, still a little wobbly, and examined the first of them. They weren't hers, of course. She checked a few pages of each, just enough to know they were real books. She closed the last one and checked the door.

Barred.

Someone's gone to a great deal of trouble to make me feel comfortable was all she could think. Her head still ached and it was easier not to think at all. There was an arched window in the east wall, and she looked out.

The room was in a high tower somewhere in the mountains—somewhere, some mountains—and even in the dying light the view was breathtaking. The earth folded like a deflated bagpipe in all directions, and one peak snuggled up to the next with a bare knife-edge of a valley between them. The window was barred, too, but the glassed shutters worked. She opened them and took a breath of cool, head-clearing air.

Someone knocked on her door.

Odd manners for a kidnapper. And there was another thought. "I'm afraid you'll have to let yourself in," she said.

Nothing happened. Ashesa put her ear to the door and heard a faint creaking like an old oak in a breeze. The knock repeated.

"Come in, damn you!"

She heard a scrape as the bar lifted, then the clink of silverware. The door swung outward and there stood a figure in a black robe and hood, carrying a tray of food and wine. His face and hands were both covered—his face by the hood, his hands by leather gloves. He looked like one of the pair who had helped kidnap her. Ashesa stepped back, and the figure came in and set the tray on a little table by the bed. Ashesa considered trying to slip past him, but two more were in the corridor, steel spears glinting. She turned to the tray bearer, looking regal despite her rumpled condition.

"I demand to know who you are and why you've brought me here." Her jailor only shook his head slowly and turned toward the door. Ashesa stamped her foot and snatched at the hood. "Look at me when I speak to—"

There was no face under the hood. A stump of wood jutted through the neck of the robe, around which a lump of clay had been crudely shaped. A piece of it fell to the floor and shattered with a little puff of yellow dust. Ashesa screamed.

"Normally they don't wear anything, but I didn't want to upset you. I see I've failed."

A slightly chagrined man stood in the doorway. He was just past the full blood of youth, with features as fine and delicate as a girl's. His dark eyes were reddened and weak, as if he spent too many hours reading in poor light. None of these details registered as strongly in Ashesa's mind as her first impression—the man had an air of quiet certainty that she found infuriating.

"Very . . . considerate," Ashesa said, recovering her poise with great effort. "Would you please tell me *what* that is and who you are?"

He patted the simulacrum fondly. "That, Highness, is a stick golem. I learned the technique from a colleague in Nyas; you should see what he can do with stone . . . " He stopped, clearly aware that Ashesa had heard as much as she cared to on the subject. "My apologies, Highness. I am called Timon the Black."

Ashesa almost screamed again. She scrambled to the other side of the bed and snatched up a heavy gilt candlestick from the table. She waved it with all the menace she could scrape together. "Don't come near me, Fiend!"

"My reputation precedes me," the magician sighed. "What is my most recent atrocity?"

Ashesa glared at him. "Do you deny that you sacrificed a virgin girl to raise an army of demons against the Red Company?"

Timon smiled a little ruefully. "To start, they weren't demons and she wasn't a virgin. Nor did I 'sacrifice' her . . . exactly. The Red Company took a geld from half the kingdoms on the mainland, so I don't recall hearing any objections at the time. No matter; it's water down the river. You must be hungry, Highness. Have some supper."

In truth, the aroma from the tray was making Ashesa a little giddy, but she eyed it with suspicion. Timon noticed the look.

"Be reasonable, Highness. Would I go to all this bother just to poison you? And If I *were* in need of a virgin, there are certainly others easier to hand than a Princess of the Blood, common knowledge and barracks gossip not withstanding."

"You are a beast," she said.

"Red-eyed and howling every full moon. So I've heard."

Ashesa shrugged and sampled a beef pie. It was delicious. She poured herself some wine as Timon dismissed his servant. He found a chair and sat watching her, while she in turn glared at him between mouthfuls.

"Well?" she asked, finally. "Aren't you going to tell me why I'm here?"

"You didn't ask, so I assumed you weren't interested. Pesky things, assumptions," he said. "Let's see what others might be floating about, besides that silly misunderstanding about virginity . . . Ransom? There's a common theme. Will I force your doting father to surrender half his kingdom to save you?"

Ashesa took a sip of wine so he wouldn't see her smile. "No," she said from behind her goblet.

Timon looked genuinely surprised. "Why not?"

"Because we both know you wouldn't get it, break Father's heart though it would. And then there's all this . . . " She waved a capon leg at the room and furnishings. "That tapestry alone is of finer quality than my copy, and I *know* how much that one cost—poor Father nearly had a stroke. You obviously have great resources at your beck, Magician. That rules out any conventional ransom short of greed, and that's *one* sin I've never heard spoken of you. So. What do you want?"

There was open admiration in Timon's eyes. "You have an exceptional mind, Highness. It's really unfortunate that Daras will never allow you to use it. From what I've gathered of his philosophy, your duties will be to produce heirs and be ornamental at court."

"You seem to know a great deal about matters that don't concern you, Magician, but you still haven't answered my question. I wish you would because frankly I'm baffled. I hope for your sake it's more than a whim. They'll search for me, you know."

"And find you, too, since I was good enough to leave a note. I've also bought supplies openly; my location is common knowledge to half the hill crofters on the border. Diplomacy and protocol will delay your father, but Prince Daras will be along soon."

Ashesa was stunned. "Are you mad? As well to draw a map and have done!"

"No, Highness. I'm not mad, though it often seems so—even to me. But to avoid wearying you I'll speak plainly—I kidnapped you so that Prince Daras will try to rescue you. And he will try. His nature doesn't allow for any other option."

"But why—" Ashesa stopped. She knew. It was there for her to see in Timon's eyes.

"Quite right, Highness. I'm going to kill him."

*   *   *

The man Macol selected to watch Daras was a veteran: solid, trust-worthy. A competent guard. Not a competent diplomat. The orders he had received in King Macol's throne room were quite beyond him.

"I want you to guard my son's quarters tonight," said King Riegar solemnly. "He is not to leave his room."

"But," added King Macol, "Prince Daras is an honored guest, not a prisoner. Treat him with respect."

Riegar nodded. "Certainly. But he may have it in his head to do something foolish. Use whatever force you must, within reason."

"But," again added Macol, "Prince Daras is heir to the throne of Bora-sur. He must on no account be harmed or you'll answer for it."

"Just keep him there," said Riegar.

"Without hurting or offending him," said Macol. "Now. Is all that clear?"

"Yes, Sire," the man lied. Later, as he stood at his post in the corri-dor, he placidly awaited the inevitable.

"Guard," Prince Daras called out, "lend some assistance in here, there's a good fellow."

The guard smiled and walked right in. The bump on his head was no less than he expected, and he was grateful for it. It seemed the sim-plest solution to a very complicated problem.

Princess Ashesa climbed the long spiral staircase to the top of Timon's fortress. Her hooded escort thumped along behind her like a child on stilts. Ashesa wasn't fooled. She'd stumbled once and the thing had snapped forward, supporting her, faster than she would have believed possible.

They passed several doors along the way. All unlocked, most empty, but Ashesa couldn't resist looking for something that might help her escape. One room was full of echoing voices in a language she didn't understand; another held a dark gray mist and she dared not enter. None of them contained anything useful.

Ashesa ran out of doors and stairs at about the same time. She and her golem escort stood on the parapet that wrapped around the outside off the highest level of the tower. The thin mountain wind whipped the golem's robes tight against its stick frame until it looked like a scare-crow flapping in a field. Ashesa looked over the railing and got a little dizzy.

"Too far to jump," said the wind.

Ashesa jumped anyway, but only a little. She didn't clear the railing.

The dwarf sat before a small canvas on the other side of the platform. He had changed his woodland green for an artist's smock stained with the remnants of an exploded rainbow. He concentrated on the canvas and painted with long smooth strokes, unperturbed by the gusts.

"That depends on your reason for jumping," returned Ashesa grimly.

The dwarf smiled, though he still wouldn't look at her. "A noble gesture, but it wouldn't keep Daras out of Timon's web even if he knew. Revenge has a longer pedigree than rescue."

"He's very certain of himself, your master."

"About some things," the dwarf agreed sadly. "He can't help it."

Ashesa considered a new tack. "How much is he paying you? Whatever your price, my father will meet it. Just help me escape and warn My Beloved Daras."

The dwarf cleaned one brush and selected another. "Would your father be willing to offer me the lucrative and entirely appropriate position of Court Fool?"

"Certainly!"

"Yes," the dwarf sighed. "I thought he might."

Ashesa frowned, and, even as she spoke the words, she wondered how may times they had passed her lips and her thoughts since the kidnapping. "I don't understand."

"My story is simple, Highness—my father sold me to a troupe of acrobats and thieves when I was seven. By twelve I was the best among them at both skills, but I still wore a cap and bells at every performance. Can you guess why?" He studied the canvas. "And when I couldn't abide that anymore I took to the streets on my own, and that's where Timon found me. We understood one another. Now he pays me with a little gold and a lot of hardship and aggravation, but part of the price is respect and an appreciation of my talents that totally ignores my height except when it's actually important. That's coin beyond your means, I'm afraid. Consider—we've been conversing for the better part of two minutes and you haven't even asked my name." He swirled the brush tip in a puddle of gold.

Ashesa stood in the presence of the man who'd kidnapped her, and yet for a moment she almost felt as if *he* were the injured party. It made her angry. "What is your name?"

He touched his cap and left a speck of gold there. "Seb, at your service," he said, making a quick dab at the canvas. "Up to a point."

"I'd like to know where that point is. Timon won't tell me why he plans to kill My Beloved Daras. Will you?"

"My Beloved . . . that's not what you were calling him during your little ride." Ashesa flushed but said nothing. Seb shrugged. "I know—it's the proper title for the betrothed and you do know your duty, even if you don't like it. So. Why not 'to prevent the marriage'? You suggested it yourself, Timon says."

The princess shook her head. "If he merely wanted that, killing me would have worked as well and been a lot less bother. I don't flatter myself by thinking he'd have hesitated."

"He wouldn't," confirmed Seb, "though it would grieve him bitterly. As it will when Daras is killed."

"But *why?* Why does Daras deserve to die?"

Seb smiled ruefully. "That's the saddest part. He doesn't. At least not in the sense of anything he's done. It's who he *is,* and what he is, and what that combination will make him do when the time comes. It's all here, Highness, if you care to look."

Seb moved to one side so she could see the canvas. Ashesa's mouth fell open in surprise when she recognized the portrait. It was Daras, mounted and armored in an archaic pattern. He held his helmet under one arm, his lance pointed to the sky.

"It's lovely," she said honestly, "but why the old armor?"

"That's the armor of the time of the Lyrsan wars. When the folk of the Western Deserts pushed east against the Seven Kingdoms. That's when Daras should have lived. That was a time for heroes."

"Daras isn't a hero," Ashesa snapped. "That takes more than winning tournaments."

"More even than rescuing one princess," the dwarf agreed. "It's rather a full-time pursuit. It might even take, say, a long bloody war with Wylandia."

Ashesa put her hands on her hips. "Do you really expect me to believe that Daras would start a war just so he can be a hero?"

"He wouldn't be starting it, to his way of thinking. But the seeds are already there: real intrigues, imagined insults . . . mistrust. All waiting to take root in his mind until he firmly believes that Wylandia struck first. You see, Daras is already a hero in many ways. He's seen the soul of it in his brother's stories, and in that he sees himself. And why not? He's brave, strong, skilled in warlike pursuits and in no other. All he lacks to make his destiny complete is the one vital ingredient—need. If the need is not there, he will create it. He has no choice. And neither do we."

Most of the blood had deserted Ashesa's face, and she trembled. "You can't be sure! And even if you were, what right—"

"Timon *is* sure," interrupted Seb calmly. "It's his greatest power, and greatest curse. He knows, and he can't escape the responsibility of knowing. That gives him the right."

"I . . . don't . . . believe . . . you!" Ashesa spat out each word like something foul.

Seb smiled. "Oh, yes, you do. More than you'd like, anyway. Far better to see this tale as history no doubt will—a foul crime done by foul folk. Forgive me, Highness, but I'm not as kind as Timon and see no reason why this should be any easier on you than the rest of us."

Ashesa's hands turned into fists, and she took a step toward the dwarf. In an instant the golem was between her and Seb, and the dwarf hadn't even blinked. Ashesa took several deep, calming breaths, and after a moment the golem moved aside. Ashesa groped for some shred of sweet reason to pull her thoughts out of the pit. "But . . . but Daras can't start a war on his own! Only the king can do that! Even if what you say is true, there's still time . . . "

While she spoke Seb made several deft strokes on the canvas, and when she saw what the dwarf had painted there her words sank into nothing.

"Time has run out, Highness. King Riegar—rest him—died in his sleep last night."

In the portrait, Daras wore the plain golden crown of Borasur.

Prince Daras had never been on a quest before and wasn't quite sure what to expect, but at least the scenery felt right—it was wild and strange. The forest that bordered the mountain foothills was very different from the tilting fields and well-groomed game parks he was accustomed to: the grass grew high and razor-edged, brambles clawed at his armored legs, and trees took root and reached for the sunlight wherever the notion took them. Daras stepped his charger through a tortured, twisty path, and when an arrow hummed out of the trees and twanged off his armor, that, too, seemed as it should be.

"Hah! Villains! At you!"

Daras spurred forward along the arrow's course as if his mount was as armored as he was. The second arrow showed that notion in error;

Daras barely cleared the stirrups before the poor beast went down kicking. Another instant and he was among them.

'They' were men, of course. Forest bandits with no other skill and without enough sense to avoid a victim armed in proof. None of that mattered once the attack began. They were bodies attached to swords, meat in ragged clothes for the blooding, characters in a play of which Daras was the lead, existing only for their cue to dance a few steps and then die. It wasn't how he thought it would be; it wasn't horrible. Daras never saw their faces, never noticed their pain as he turned clumsy blows and struck sure ones, killing with the mad joy of a newfound sport. When it was over it was as if they had never lived at all.

Rather like a tournament, only they don't get up.

After the last bandit fell, Daras, catlike, lost interest. He cleaned his sword on a dead man's tunic, had a sip or two of weak wine, then resumed his quest on foot, whistling.

Ashesa didn't know what was different at first that morning. She only knew that *something* was not right. After a few moments she was awake enough to notice what was missing. Her clothes. The mantle and overdress she had laid out on the table the night before weren't there. In their place were two rather ethereal strips of cloth appliquéd with crescents and stars and glyphs of a rather suggestive nature.

Timon sat in her chair, looking unhappy.

"Magician, where are my clothes?"

He waved his hand at the table. "There, I'm afraid. It's the traditional sacrificial garb of an obscure fertility cult. You wouldn't have heard of it."

"And you're one of them?" she asked, as calmly as she could manage.

He shuddered delicately. "Certainly not. But as much as the prospect would delight *me,* I don't think Daras expects to burst in and find us discussing literature over a cup of tea. I had to come up with something suitably dreadful for you to be saved from. Think of it as a play, Highness. This is your costume for the final act."

Ashesa eyed the flimsy cloth with distaste. "Uninspired as this may sound—suppose I refuse?"

He shrugged. "I can't *force* you to wear it—it tears too easily—but bear in mind that you stretched out on the altar in all your natural glory would suit the play as well . . . no, better. I considered it, believe me. But clothed or no, you will play your part. You have no choice."

Ashesa, bedclothes wrapped tightly about her, gathered up the scanty garments. "I'm getting terribly weary of that catechism, Master Timon. Pray, is there any esoteric reason why I cannot at least get dressed in private?"

Timon looked even more unhappy. "Unfortunately, no."

Prince Daras hid behind a boulder and studied the gate. It was strongly built with oak posts set into the narrowest point of what was already a knife slash of a valley. Two robed guards stood outside, halberds crossed. Daras idly pulled at a chafing armor strap as he pondered a sigil carved into the gate. Just like the one on the kidnapper's note. Timon the Black, no question. Beyond the gate a tower rose on a rocky ridge above the valley.

Careless or arrogant?

The sigil was as good as an announcement; Daras couldn't decide what it meant, so he decided it didn't matter.

The prince sat with his back to the stone and considered. There was no way around the gate, nor could he climb the valley walls without being seen. The two guards at the gate had to be overpowered without raising an alarm, and he might have to scale the wall if neither had a key . . . There was cover—rocks and brush—until about ten yards from the guard post. *If* he could reach it unseen.

And unheard.

Slowly, reluctantly, Prince Daras began removing his armor.

"Ready, Highness?"

Ashesa studied her reflection, trying to arrange the material of her costume as efficiently as possible. The effect was dramatic despite her best efforts. She gave up. "Yes, damn you to hell."

Timon entered the room with two of his golem guards. The magician, damn him again, smiled at her. "Follow us, please."

He took her arm and led her down the corridor to the staircase, then around and down the spiral to ground level and out. They moved single file down a narrow path to the valley floor, golems in front and behind her, with Timon bringing up the rear. A single wall cut them off from the rest of the valley, and before that was a very suspicious-looking stone flanked by two upright stones of dark granite. A smaller building of stone blocks sat on the opposite side. Closer, Ashesa's fears were confirmed: the building was a small temple with a narrow oval doorway, the flat stone a massive altar with shackles bolted to the four corners.

Ashesa's mouth was suddenly dry. "You said you weren't a member of the cult."

"Props, Highness. Nothing more."

The golems led her to the altar. There was a stepping block to help her climb, and the top was smooth except for a groove cut for—she supposed—her heart's blood. Ashesa looked at the altar, then the guards. Their weapons gleamed brightly in the morning sun, but one held his a little farther away from his body. Ashesa judged the distance and her chances, but she made the mistake of glancing at Timon. His smile hadn't changed a whit, but there was a new and very clear message in his eyes.

Don't.

Ashesa lay down reluctantly and let the twig-fingered guards shackle her to the cold stone. As the last manacle clicked into place she heard a yelp like a hunting horn cut off in mid-note. Timon wasn't smiling now. There was something like worry on his face, perhaps even a touch of fear. Ashesa couldn't have imagined that a moment before.

"Daras is early . . . I'd better hurry and get into *my* costume, Highness. Won't be a moment."

The magician hurried off into the temple, leaving Ashesa alone with the golems. There was a commotion at the gate and Ashesa turned her head to look just as the gate burst open and something very much like brown rag sailed through, cartwheeling end over end to smash against the stones. Prince Daras of Borasur strode through.

His entrance made Ashesa skip a breath; she'd forgotten how handsome he was, but that wasn't all of it—a glory seemed to shine around him, like a saint etched in stained glass. He saw her then and rushed forward, all smooth motion and mad joy.

And this is what Timon wants to destroy.

She heard Timon but could not see him. "Stop him, my Pets!"

The golems set their halberds and charged. Ashesa finally recovered her wits. "Flee, My Beloved! It's a trap!"

Daras, of course, did nothing of the sort. He veered to the right and a golem's headlong rush carried it past. Daras struck a trailing blow without breaking stride and the golem's clay head exploded.

Ashesa watched, horrified but unable to look away. There was a battle-light on Daras's face, and his eyes were bright and wild. Ashesa's breath skipped a second time.

He's enjoying this!

The truth of it was like a cold slap in the face. It wasn't the rescue. It wasn't even herself as anything but an excuse. The prince was consumed with a mad ecstasy born of the clash of weapons and pleasure in his skill. He destroyed golems. He would destroy men with as little thought and the same wild joy. Ashesa tried not to think anymore, but it was a torrent held too long in check and the dams were breaking.

This is what Timon wants to destroy . . .

The second golem thrust past Daras's parry by brute force and the prince twisted his body like an acrobat. The halberd merely sliced a thin red line across the front of Daras's tunic, and the prince's return stroke left the golem broken and still.

A voice issued from the temple. It was Timon, and it wasn't Timon—it boomed like thunder across the valley. "Now you must die!"

Ashesa strained to turn her head and saw Timon step out of the shadows of the temple. He wore a robe decorated with glyphs like the ones on Ashesa's costume, and in his gloved hands he carried a long curved knife. It glowed with a blue balefire that still could not penetrate the blackness under Timon's hood.

Prince Daras studied the magician's knife, then looked at his own sword. Grinning, he dropped the sword and pulled his own long dagger. Ashesa wanted to scream but nothing came out—it was as if an invisible hand clapped itself over her mouth.

The fool, she thought wildly, *the bloody, senseless fool!*

What happened next was filled with terrible beauty. Daras charged the magician, and this time it was Timon who danced aside to let Daras hurtle past like a maddened bull. Timon's blade flicked out and then there was another line of red on the prince's chest. Daras snarled like a *berserk,* but kept some caution as he stopped himself and slowly circled, looking for an opening. Timon kept just out of reach, reacting with a speed Ashesa wouldn't have expected of him. The glow on Daras's face built to new heights of rapture, as if the magician's surprising skill fanned it like the bellows of a forge.

It was like the sword dance Ashesa had seen performed at her father's court—the flash of steel always averted, always eluded as if it *was* nothing more than a dance for her amusement instead of a fight to the death. Timon's knife traced its path through the air like a lightning flash, and Daras's dagger slashed and hummed in a silvered blur.

Then everything changed.

Timon broke from the fight and sprinted toward the altar. "The sacrifice must be made!"

What?

The wizard hurtled toward her, his knife burning away the distance to her heart. Ashesa closed her eyes.

Someone screamed and Ashesa opened her eyes again, surprised. She had meant to scream but never really managed. *Who?*

Timon. He lay sprawled at the foot of the altar, Daras's weapon buried almost to the hilt in his back. Bright, impossibly red blood oozed from around the steel. Ashesa felt a little sick, a lot relieved and a bit . . . well, guilty. Guilty for wondering why Timon's trap had failed, and for wondering—just for an instant—if it should have failed. And why the mad dash to the altar? Unless Timon had lied to her . . .

Prince Daras grinned down at her, his chest heaving like a bellows. "Did—did you see that throw?" he chortled. "Thirty paces, easily . . . " Daras seemed to forget about the throw all at once, as he got his first good look at Ashesa. The grin turned into something else.

Ashesa shivered. "For the love of heaven, stop staring and get me loose! There may be more of them."

"You're in no danger now, My Beloved Ashesa," Daras said, placing a hand on her bare shoulder. "And first thing's first."

"Get me loose." Ashesa repeated, all sweet reason. "We have to get away from here."

Daras nodded. "In time. His lackey today, Aldair himself tomorrow. That's the order of business. Right now there are other matters to attend to."

Ashesa spoke very clearly, very urgently. "You're wrong, Beloved. Wylandia had nothing to do with this. I must tell you—" She stopped. Daras's hand had departed her shoulder for a more southerly location. "What are you doing?!"

He looked a little surprised at her attitude. "That 'other matter' I mentioned. Surely you know that tradition demands a price for your rescue?"

"We're not married yet, Beloved," Ashesa pointed out.

Daras shrugged. "A rescue is a separate matter altogether, with its own traditions and duties. Binding, too. I'm afraid we don't have any choice."

That word.

It wasn't the act that Daras demanded, or even her feelings about Daras himself that mattered in what came next. It was the one word Daras had used. That made all the difference.

Sometimes, in those dark hours between waking and sleeping, when night closes in and the sound of their own heartbeats is much too clear, people have been known to wonder how close to the edge of the abyss they dwelled, and what it would take to push them over. In that moment, strapped to an altar under a warming sun, Ashesa became one of the lucky ones. That question would never trouble her again.

She looked at a soft patch of grass nearby, perfect for paying her debt. Very close to where Timon's dagger had fallen to lie mostly hidden. Yes, it was perfect.

"Free me," she said, "and you'll have your reward."

Ashesa leaned on the altar, trying to clear away a red haze from her mind. She tried not to look at Daras's body, tried not to remember the stunned surprise on his face before all expression ceased. Ashesa pulled herself around the stone until she came to Timon's limp form, then her mouth set in a grim smile and she yanked the robes aside.

The blood came from a punctured animal bladder, and the stick skeleton was dappled with thick, blackening drops.

"Damn you!"

Timon stepped out of the temple again, but this time it was really him. Ashesa glared at him and all the world behind. "No one will believe you," she said, pale as snow and twice as cold.

Timon obviously considered the suggestion in questionable taste. "Did *I* suggest such a thing? No, Highness. But they will believe *you* as you relate—tearfully, I advise—how Daras fell in the rescue, slaying the fiend and freeing you with the strength of his dying breath. Will I spurt green ichor? I should think I would."

"I saw the fight—the real fight—while it lasted. Daras was good, but your golem could have killed him easily!" she accused. "But you knew I . . . " she couldn't finish it.

"What a mind," repeated Timon with deeper admiration. "And what you say is partly true, Highness. Once Daras took the bait he was finished, one way or another. For your sake take comfort—you can't kill a dead man. But I was curious about you, I admit it. Not everyone has the talent for knowing what must be done *when* it must be done. No, Highness. I didn't know. Add another sin to my head because I wanted to find out."

Ashesa saw the dwarf Seb coming down the mountain path. He led two horses packed for travel and two more saddled to ride, and he played out a grayish cord behind him from a large spool mounted on a stick.

"A few matters to attend, Highness," Timon said. "The first involves something new in the art of destruction. I think you'll be seeing it again." He nodded and Seb struck a flint to the cord. It sizzled with life and burned its way back to the tower. In a moment there was a dull roar and the earth trembled. The tower swayed on its foundation and then collapsed. Flames licked the exposed beams and flooring and soon the whole thing was burning merrily.

Ashesa stared. *Heavens.*

Timon pulled a vial from his robe and poured an acrid black liquid on the golem. There was an instantaneous, nauseating stench and the cloth, wood, leather, and blood all hissed and bubbled and melted into a smoking mass.

Seb stared at the remnants of the tower wistfully. Timon laid a hand on his shoulder. "Sorry, but you knew it was only temporary. My magic would have to die with me. Expectations, you know." He turned back to Ashesa. "As cruel as assumptions in their way. They killed Daras as surely as we did."

"What about me?" Ashesa asked dully.

"Don't worry. If you'll wait here, I've no doubt that King Aldair and Prince Galan will follow the beacon of flames right to you, combining against the common foe under the push of a father's love. Have you met young Galan, by the way? A kind, intelligent lad by all report, though given to idle dreaming. Who can say? With a firm hand to guide him he might even make a king."

Seb handed Ashesa a cloak. "Master, we'd best be going."

They mounted and rode out the gate without a backward glance. Ashesa gathered the cloak about her and settled down to wait. As she waited, she thought about Timon, and Daras, and herself. Maybe she would talk to her father about Galan. Maybe. They would still want the alliance, but that didn't matter just then. She would meet Galan again, and she would decide. *She* would decide. Her father, whether he realized it or not, would just go along. She didn't really understand what was different now, but something was, and it wasn't because of her crime as such. It just came down to choice. Once you knew it existed there was no end to it. And no escape from it either.

Forgive me, Beloved, but Seb was right—this isn't a time for heroes.

Still, the Age that couldn't profit from a clever, determined princess had never dawned.

DANCE OF THE PYTHON

JANET BERLINER

*In 1961, in protest against Apartheid, **Janet Berliner Gluckman** fled her native South Africa—to which her parents had run to escape the Holocaust. Janet has been an editor, author, agent, teacher, lecturer, and translator. Her novels include the acclaimed* Rite of the Dragon, *a tale of political intrigue and magic in her homeland,* The Execution Exchange, *a thriller coauthored with Woody Greer, and* Child of the Light, *a Holocaust novel coauthored with George Guthridge. This story is taken from her novel in progress,* Dance of the Python, *a story of compromise, deceit, and magic in tribal South Africa.*

Nshesha Nyaloti lay on her back in the tall grasses and dreamed. Her decision was made: she would have it all, or she would have nothing, for it was not in her to take second place to anyone. When her grandfather, Vusama Nyaloti, High *Inyanga* to Chief Ziko, returned to his ancestors, she would become the new High *Inyanga*. She would also become First High Royal Wife to Mzimba, Son-of-the-Chief—after she learned the secrets of the Lovedu Queen, Ayesha, She-Who-Was-Immortal.

As if to fortify her resolve, the piercing whistle of a reed flute cut through the African night. A xylophone rattled, then another, calling through the moonlight to the drummers, and to the Elders who guarded the Great Hut of the Chief.

Rolling onto her side, so that she could see beyond the grasses into the village square, Nshesha watched two young drummers. They stood at the edges of the clearing, poised for their part in the ritual that signaled the beginning of a night of homage to Tharu, the python, father of her tribe.

"My fate lies in your hands, Tharu my Father," she whispered. "Show me that the way I have chosen is the way I must go."

She looked across at the drummers, sticks balanced inches from the water lizard hide stretched taut over their drums. Then she glanced at one who stood slightly apart from the rest. He was Chi-wara, named for the springbok whose hide graced his ceremonial drums. Less patient than the others, he ran his fingertips lightly over the skin stretched across the largest of his nine wax-tuned drums. He did not use sticks, for he had the true gift of music and preferred to hear through his hands the falling notes produced by the wax he had rubbed into the center of the drum's tightly stretched hide.

I am more like you, Chi-wara, Nshesha thought. *Obedience does not come easily to us.*

When it was believed that no creature of man or spirit remained asleep, the flute spoke to the drummers who began to play. As the heat of the old summer had moved their dying Chief to take one last wife and make her beautiful with child, so the beat of their drums entered the bodies of each man, woman, and child in the village.

The musicians played softly at first. Slowly. But they did not hold back for long. As the rhythms became more powerful, they stirred warriors and weaklings alike. The hearts of lovers sang out to one another of a night that was yet new, and the flesh of married couples burned with the knowledge of what was to come when the moon sank low. Adulterers grew careless of punishment. Ancient crones with toothless gums oiled the memories of aged white-haired men.

Most affected of all by the music were the Rainbow *Indunas*, apprentice warriors to whom random pleasures of the love-mat were forbidden. Their pulses sounded loudly in their ears, and their loins seemed to have taken on the fire of the Lightning Bird. Nshesha grinned, knowing how their blood churned, even though they were too young to have tasted blood or passion.

The drumbeat quickened, and the music entered Nshesha. She allowed it to surround her with desire for the Son-of-the-Chief who waited for her out there in the darkness. She would meet him this one more time, bed him this one more time. Then she would refuse him one more time, for nothing could persuade her to become his second wife.

She had made her choice. What she needed now was a sign from the gods that they approved her plans—

"Your granddaughter is very lovely, Vusama," Chief Ziko said, silencing the voice in Nshesha's head.

"Nshesha." Vusama sounded pensive. "The dew on the flowers of the morning."

"A beautiful young woman," the Chief said. "What a pity she spends so much of her time imitating the thorn on the acacia tree. She would do far better to be less prickly."

Nshesha glanced up through the grasses at the two old men. "Nshesha is so young." He moved his hand onto his lap and stroked himself absently. "Were we ever that young, Vusama old friend?"

"You are young still, O Chief," Vusama lied. "Is not your new wife ready to give birth?"

The old Chief laughed. "My First High Royal Wife displayed great kindness in presenting me with a maiden to comfort my last days. *Umame,* our Mother, is a true old royal snake. She plans my end in the pleasantest possible manner. The truth is, she and I are both too old and tired for the love-mat. The difference between us is that she is willing to admit it."

The old man paused to drink after his long speech. When he had drained his beer-vessel, he held it out to be refilled. "Beer!" he shouted. "I may be old, but I am not yet dead. I have a powerful thirst."

The apprentice *inyanga* Dahodi stepped forward to do his Chief's bidding. Though his artistry with herbs and with throwing the bones was already well-known, he would not make a pleasant assistant when she became High *Inyanga,* Nshesha thought, for she intended to continue to reject him as a lover.

Ziko waved the young man away, sipped at his beer, and spit.

"Vusama, my friend, I am truly ready to join my ancestors." He grinned, exposing gums long relieved of teeth. "Nothing pleases me for long these days except the knowledge that my son, Mzimba, is aching to take my place." He chuckled and rid himself of a stream of spittle. "I enjoy keeping my son waiting."

"You and I were boys together, Ziko," Vusama addressed the Chief as if they were brothers. "Now we are both old men ready to join our ancestors."

And I am ready to take over your duties, Nshesha thought.

"After the birthing, Nshesha will dance with the other maidens," Vusama said.

"What a pity it is not a prelude to her marriage to Mzimba. I would delay my departure from this world to see what manner of heir they could produce."

"Since that cannot be, let us talk of the new boy-child that the *amadolo,* the bones, have predicted for you."

Nshesha smiled, hearing how her grandfather sought to distract the

Chief. The *amadolo* were the source of his power. He had taught her much about them, but she still had much to learn, she thought, watching as he extricated his pouch of bones from his belt, opened it, and scattered the contents at the feet of the old Chief.

"Your new son will be born when the Sun-God Shati takes the Moon Goddess in his arms. The hour will match that of Mzimba's birth five and twenty years ago—"

"This is a night of birth and death and memories."

"Death?"

"The old century dies, Vusama, and, with it, Mzimba's youth. Soon he will be married. We will be joining two royal houses whose *midzumi* wander the ruins of Zimbabwe. Our union will allow them to rest, and they will bless us with their gratitude."

Nshesha's anger rose like summer dust stirred by the wind. *I will hate her,* she thought, though she had never met Tandi, twin sister to the Lovedu Rain Queen. *I will hate that fair-skinned daughter of a father who was also her uncle! What right does she have to Mzimba?* Every right, the voice of reason answered. Mzimba did not make the customs of our people. Besides, even had he not been promised to someone else, our law says you cannot be both his First Royal Wife and his High *Inyanga.*

"I have no more use for my love-mat," the Chief said. "I will give it to Mzimba. That will be a pleasing manner in which to close the circle of my life."

The old man rested his head against the back of his thatch throne and closed his eyes. His mouth fell open, and Nshesha heard him begin to snore. She saw that her grandfather's smile was tinged with envy as he thanked the *idlozi,* the gods, for dusting the eyes of his Chief with sleep.

"Grandfather," Nshesha whispered.

"Nshesha?" Vusama looked around.

"Over here." Nshesha emerged out of the long grasses. She glanced at her sleeping Chief. "Ziko will sleep through the Dance of the Python, through the birth of his last child—and into the twenty-first century," she said.

"No one with eyes to see or blood to feel could doubt where *you* will be until the Dance begins," her grandfather said. He pointed at her swaying hips, and the raised nipples on her young breasts. "Your body speaks the language of the lovebird to Mzimba. Be careful. It would not take much to change Dahodi's lust to hatred."

"I have never made a secret of my feelings for Mzimba," Nshesha said. "That is not my way. I cannot be punished for loving him."

"You can be punished for sleeping with him, and that is clearly your intention tonight. You would have been better served to be less obvious."

Perhaps so, Nshesha thought. *Umame* long since chose her son's First High Royal Wife, thus forbidding him to couple with any but the special women provided for his relief—at least until he produced an heir.

Vusama looked into Nshesha's eyes and groaned. Though he had never spoken to her of his knowledge, she knew that he knew that she and Mzimba had slipped away together before. But tonight was different. Tonight he must keep watch over their enemies—hers and Mzimba's—for midnight brought the start of Mzimba's premarital period of celibacy. As carefully as the Chief's son may have been watched in the past, it was nothing compared with the way he would be guarded between now and his wedding day.

"You are my pupil, and the granddaughter of my heart. I am as old as Ziko, and as tired, but I will do all I can to protect you," Vusama said.

Nshesha watched as he tried to make himself more comfortable, yet not so comfortable that his own aged body gave in to its need for sleep. "Even I have not always acted wisely." He shifted his position again. "My sleeping-*kaross* could relieve my aches," he said, "but I must stay here. This promises to be a long night and a too full day for one of my great age."

With a gesture of resignation, Vusama waved Nshesha away. She stepped forward and kissed him gently on his cheek. At the first rays of the sun he would be required to throw the bones, and by full daylight, Ziko's new baby would require an escort into the world. By noon, Mzimba, Dahodi, and a dozen men would leave for Maseru to greet Tandi, Mzimba's bride-to-be, and guide her across *Inkanyala,* The Cold Treeless Place.

"You are right," she said. "It will be a time of many happenings." She looked up at the sky to gauge the coming of dawn. She and Mzimba must return by then—she to take part in the Dance of the Python, he to welcome his new brother. Not even the High *Inyanga* could delay a birthing, nor could her grandfather help either one of them if the rising sun failed to find the Son-of-the-Chief in his rightful place.

Nshesha and Mzimba lay together on her grandfather's sleeping-*kaross* until the moon had traveled well away from the crown of the sky. When it was time for him to take leave of her, he drew her to her feet, took her face in his hands, and kissed her.

"At dawn I must begin my journey to Maseru to greet Tandi, wife of my mother's choosing," he said. "I will ask you one more time to be my second wife."

"And I will answer one more time," she responded. "I cannot."

"I am leaving now," Mzimba went on, clearly unsurprised by her response. "It will be safer if I go alone. As for my marriage to Tandi, it will be worth the price if her sister, the Modjadji, keeps the drought away from us."

Nshesha nodded and lay down again on her grandfather's *kaross*. "I'll stay and rest awhile."

Mzimba lifted his hand in farewell and turned to leave.

Closing her eyes, Nshesha inhaled the smell and warmth of their bodies and relived their time together. He had proved the strength of his feelings in the risk he had taken to make love to her. For now, that would have to be enough. Then she saw again his hand raised in farewell . . . and saw what the cloud of their parting and the shadows of the night had conspired to keep from her. In the eye of her mind, she could see moonlight shining between Mzimba's fingers as he spread them apart in the gesture used only between a Chief and his First High Royal Wife.

She left the *kaross* and stood in the opening of the hut. Thoughts danced in her head to the music of the flute and xylophones, to the drumbeats that came to her on the wind. She stared into the darkness until the saw-toothed spires of *Unumweni* Castle came into focus.

"Hear me, *idlozi*," she said, addressing the gods who lived in the mountain. "If what I have to say angers you, call upon your daughter, the Lightning Bird Negwenya. Let her rise from her bed in fury and come to punish me."

Nshesha heard in her own words the hoarse echo of Mzimba's love-making voice, and her skin prickled in the night air. She held out her fists toward the jagged circle of monoliths at the summit of the mountain, fingers curled inward so as not to point at the mountain and bring bad weather. Addressing the beasts and the monsters who lived protected by the claws of *Unumweni,* she dared them, and the god-spirits of her ancestors, to listen to what she had to say.

"I pledge to become High *Inyanga* to Mzimba. I pledge that I will learn the Lovedu secret of immortality and use it to bring power to your people, the Thotharu."

Nshesha bowed her head in the waning moonlight and waited for the rush of wings that would tell her that the Lightning Bird had come for her. She had never seen Negwenya, the Dragon-Mother, but she had many times heard the storytellers speak of her. One of them, Mtono, claimed to have actually seen her in the year after Mzimba's birth.

"I was a child, living in the caves of *Thaba Bosigo,* the Mountain of the Night," Mtono said. "I saw her shadow move across the sun. She floated winged and graceful in the sky, like the mother of all Lightning Birds, yet not fully like them. She did not have smooth wings, nor an underbelly red as the hibiscus that blooms out of the sand. She was black against the sun, her wings edged with lace, her tail curved. Her anger at the High *Inyanga,* Nkolosi, shook the stones from the slopes and sent them tumbling into the village."

Nshesha waited. Trembled. Held her breath. She heard only her heart, beating time in her throat to the music of her people. If the gods disapproved, they would quickly punish her boldness. If they approved, they would surely send her a sign—

She lifted her head. The needle peak *Mponjwana,* the Horn, stood guard like a royal spear over what was left of the night. *Unumweni* had dissolved into the dark before the dawn, and *Nqonqoli,* first star of the morning, knocked at the door of the sun.

The sky turned the color of clay. The promise of the sun bloodied the tip of *Mponjwana.* Then, fulfilling its promise, the first rays of the sun transformed the Horn into the crown of Nzinga, Queen of the Mbundu. Nshesha shaded her eyes from its brilliance.

Softly, a familiar lullaby drifted down from the mountain. The words and music held the legend of Queen Nzinga, Mother Goddess of her tribe. They told of her journey alone from the place where the ocean was cold to the desolation and heat of Zimbabwe, of how she met and fell in love with Thoto the Minstrel, of how Thoto came into the world with the body of a man and the head of a python. Finally they told of a love-child, the firstborn of the new royal line—named Thotharu after the python that had spawned its father.

Each storyteller told a different version of that trek. But they sang with one voice of the journey from Zimbabwe to Malawi, telling of how Chief Ziko and his people wandered the land like *midzumi,* homeless ancestral ghosts, until they found this place they called Nzingaland.

Thunder rumbled. Suddenly wide-awake, Nshesha watched a *duiker* run for cover. Her heart beat faster, knowing she had angered the gods, but instead of heading their warning, she stretched her fists toward the mountaintop. Though it was forbidden, she faced her palms skyward and pointed her fingers—for how else could she reach for the crown of Nzinga?

The mountain gods thundered a second warning.

"I have listened to your song, my Queen," Nshesha said. "I am your daughter, and the daughter of your lover, Thoto. Take me now, or grant me the power and the knowledge I need."

Withdrawing her hands, she knelt upon the earth and waited, listening for the thunderous voices of the gods, and for the sweet song of the Queen.

Nothing happened. She heard no sound save the wind in the trees. She bowed her head.

"Aaiee!"

She screamed. Her open palms throbbed with pain, as if the heavy weight of the Queen's crown had dropped onto them, piercing her flesh with its pointed rim.

Gathering her strength, she raised her hands to her head. Crowning herself, she took into her soul the power of a great Queen.

"You have given me your approval, my Queen," Nshesha said, "but the magic and cunning of Thoto the Minstrel is not yet mine."

She stood upright once more and started on the pathway that led to the village and to the Dance of the Python. Her toes curled on the damp grasses and she thought with envy of Mzimba, whose body doubtless still warmed his sleeping-*kaross*. Ignoring the familiar feeling of wanting him, she squinted ahead to where, despite his honorable intentions, Vusama slept at Ziko's side.

As if he sensed her presence, her grandfather opened his eyes and smiled. "We must gather the *inyangas*," he called out. He stood and faced the rising sun, yawning and breathing deeply to fill himself with the morning's freshness. "The time has come for the birthing of Ziko's last son."

My grandfather never wakes as the other old men do, Nshesha thought, approaching him more closely. *They rise wondering where the dark has gone; he wakes swiftly, like a youth who longs to begin the work of the day.*

"You will conduct the next Royal birthing," Vusama said. They had moved close enough to the Great Hut to hear the chanting of the elders whose duty lay in welcoming the last son of a Chief who had so many sons that they argued the number among themselves.

"Aaiee!"

The cry, ancient and filled with the pain of childbirth, guided Vusama into the hut where *Umame* waited with the young wife.

Nshesha stopped outside and squatted on the ground alongside Dahodi and the other apprentices. They could hear *Umame* talking.

"Breathe deeply, child," she said. "It will soon be over. Vusama, greetings. Is Ziko, our husband, with you?"

"He sleeps," Vusama answered.

The First Royal Wife made a sound of derision. "Old fart," she said. Her voice spoke with the fondness of one whose pet had grown too old to play, but had been around too long to drown. "Is he asleep, or did he die while you were not looking?"

Vusama laughed. "He is snoring loudly for one who is dead."

"Ziko was young once, and daring," *Umame* said. "I remember when he took Mzimba in his arms for the first time. Turning to face Mount Hora, he raised Mzimba's tiny fist, opened his fingers, and pointed them at the highest peak."

As she had done to *Unumweni,* Nshesha thought, reminding herself that she'd still had no sign from Thoto.

"The child is here," *Umame* said, "a boy-child, as the bones predicted. A new son at Ziko's age! He is quite a man, our husband."

"*Was* quite a man, *Umame.*" Mzimba moved past the apprentices and spoke quietly from the doorway. "We listened together to the birth cries. They were the last sounds he heard before starting on his long journey."

"Hail to the Chief," Vusama said, joining Mzimba in the doorway, "At the time of your birth, our people mourned the passing of your father, though he was very much alive at the time. I did so, too. It was right to observe *boswagadi,* mourning, for him then, for to do so now would mean that the throne of the Chief would sit empty while we weep, tempting his enemies to move against us. Still, I confess to a great heaviness in my heart. I hope our ancestors know how fortunate they are that my friend, your father, is with them."

Having given tribute to the man who had been Chief, he inclined his head to honor Mzimba. "May the *idlozi* grant you wisdom, O Chief of the Thotharu, son of Ziko, and slayer of lions."

He removed a snakeskin pouch from his belt, opened it, and scattered the *amadolo.* Then he lifted his head and stared at Nshesha. His skin looked gray and ancient.

"Hail to the Chief," Nshesha said. Bowing before both her grandfather and her lover, she glanced at the scattering of bones. Closest to the ground lay the head of a python. Superimposed upon that, was the symbol of her name: "N."

"I am here to do your bidding, O Chief," Vusama said.

Mzimba took Vusama's arm and helped him to stand upright. "Stand tall, old man. Let us go together to greet my people."

Nshesha's neck ached from its bent position, but she dared not raise her head until she was commanded to do so.

"I wish to see my husband one more time before he grows cold," *Umame* Lishati called out from inside the hut.

"Granted, *Umame*," Mzimba said. "*Mayibuye*, Vusama. Come."

Without so much as glancing at Nshesha, he strode off.

"Nshesha. I wish to speak with you," *Umame* called out. Hands bloodied from the birthing, she emerged into the sunlight. With an imperious wave, she dismissed the apprentice *inyangas*. "You had best mourn your love for my son," she said, when she and Nshesha stood alone. "I, too, feel the presence of *aloala,* the shadow of death, but you may be sure I will find a way to avoid my own long journey until I have seen Mzimba properly married. Unless the drums lie, the Lovedu princess is even now preparing to leave her home near *Duiwelskloof.*"

"I hear your words, *Umame*," Nshesha said. *Duiwelskloof. The Cliff of the Devil,* she thought. A fitting name.

"Raise your head and look at me, Nshesha."

Nshesha obeyed.

"You hear with your ears," *Umame* said. Her eyes carried in them the look of a wounded eland. "Now hear with your heart. I chose to blind myself to the fact that you and my son were walking along *baratawani,* the deceitful road, but do not think I did not know it. That road is now blocked. I will see to it that he does what is right for his people, so that he does not come to hate himself.

"A long time ago Ziko gave his word, and his word will be honored. When we left Malawi, we felt strong and powerful. By the time we reached the Dragon Mountains, many of us were ill and our cattle were dying. The Modjadji, who had just given birth to twin daughters, took us in without question and made us whole again—"

"For which you gave her much cattle. Did you also have to make her a gift of your son?"

"That's enough, Nshesha." *Umame's* tone was no longer kindly. "I do not have to explain myself to you. Moreover, I wish to get to my husband before the vultures do.

"When the train carrying Tandi and her party arrives in Maseru, there will be a Thotharu escort waiting to guide her safely across Lesotho, here to her new home. The journey must be used for instruction in those of our ways which are different than hers. I am too old to travel such a distance and, now that he is Chief, Mzimba must stay here.

There are many who would make trouble for him in his absence. You are the next best person to do the job."

"Am I really, or is it that you want me out of the way?"

Umame Lishati was not amused. "Hold your tongue or I will have it removed. You are not yet High *Inyanga.*"

Nshesha's hand involuntarily covered her mouth.

"I would do it now, were it not that a silent Nshesha might be impossible to remove from my son's heart." The old woman reached out and touched Nshesha's cheek. "Mzimba needs you as his High *Inyanga.* I will never care for the Lovedu princess the way I care for you. Nor will my son, who hides his feelings well, but not well enough to fool me. Still, she must become his First Royal Wife. We cannot afford to incur the wrath of her sister, the new Modjadji. The Rain Queen could do us much harm."

"I have given him up," Nshesha said. "When my grandfather joins our ancestors to be at the side of your husband, I will become High *Inyanga.*"

Nodding, *Umame* reentered the hut. *I have given him up* for now, Nshesha thought. *But there will come a time when I am First Royal Wife to Mzimba the Chief. Let the stranger come, for it is only through her that I can learn the secrets of the Lovedu Queen, Ayesha.* Deep in contemplation, she neglected to avoid the place where Vusama had thrown the *amadolo* and she stepped on a cowrie shell which her grandfather's failing eyesight had missed. She winced, and lifted her foot to inspect the mixture of dirt and crushed shell that covered her sole.

She wiped away a thin trickle of blood and picked at one of the larger splinters. Realizing how undignified she must look, she lowered her foot and stood up straight. She felt the slivers dig deeper into her flesh.

"I have come about the greeting party, Nshesha." She started. Dahodi had stolen up on her as stealthily as a jackal on the prowl. "Our Chief has instructed me to gather a greeting party and sufficient strong horses and food for the journey to Maseru. We must leave before sundown, so that the Lovedu princess will not be kept waiting—"

"We?"

"You are to guard the daughter of the Rain Queen as closely as if she were joined to you by the head."

Dahodi's mouth bore the traces of a smile. *He will doubtless do everything to ingratiate himself with Tandi,* Nshesha thought. How she hated him! The two full cycles of the moon she had to endure with him during the trek across Lesotho and back again would almost be worth it, for they would give her more than enough time to convince him that the best thing he could do for himself was to avoid the newcomer.

"I will be ready," she said. Forgetting the injury to her foot, she moved swiftly away from him.

"Aaiee!"

She lifted her foot to examine the sole. The sharp edge of the broken shell had cut deep and there was a small trickle of blood which had not yet congealed. Without thinking, she allowed a few drops to escape onto the sand. She stared at the drops, conjuring up an image of Dahodi and the Lovedu princess. Lying side by side. Bleeding. *Assegais* buried deep in their hearts.

It was a pleasing fantasy which she quickly dismissed. She bent to bury her blood in the sand, so that no sorcerer could gather it up to use in a potion against her. Such imaginings were well and good, she thought, but the method she used to rid herself of those two would have to be far more subtle.

Unless, of course, she were prepared to die, too. And she wasn't. Not yet. Not for a very long time.

Recalling the brilliance of the crown of Nzinga, the Queen, she looked beyond the hut, in the direction of *Unumweni*. She lifted her hand and touched her head. *My long journey, too, has begun,* she thought. *My people have forgotten the time when they were ruled by a woman. I will make them remember.* She glanced quickly at the images on the ground. It was not enough to see the sign; she must hear and feel it. The music and magic of Thoto the Minstrel must enter into her soul.

Hurriedly, ignoring the pain in her foot, Nshesha returned to the village square. Though the village had come to life, it was apparent in the quiet manner of the mothers who cleaned the porridge-pots that the news of Ziko's death had flown from mouth to mouth. Her grandfather stood in the high grasses, watching as twelve Thotharu maidens entered the clearing. One of them carried a handwoven basket which she placed on the ground before joining the others, who had formed a semicircle about it.

Vusama Nyaloti nudged Nshesha, who had just appeared at his side. "I saw you limping," he said. "Are you able to dance?"

Nshesha tested the sole of her foot on the ground and nodded.

"Then go," Vusama said, "for it will be your last time. Married or not, you cannot dance with them once you are High *Inyanga*. That will come soon. I sense it."

Obedient to a rising urgency that drew her toward the semicircle, she glided toward the basket. Kneeling beside it, she removed its lid and stared at the young python that lay inside, coiled, unmoving, sleeping away its infancy as if it did not know its importance to the Thotharu tribe.

"Does the music not stir you, Tharu," she whispered. She lifted the python gently out of the open basket and placed it on top of her head. Holding her living crown steady with both hands, she raised herself until she stood tall and stately among the dancers.

All activity around her ceased. The flute fell silent, the xylophone withheld its song. Even the drums gave no murmur.

Nshesha released the snake and began languidly to dance, letting each sinuous movement flow into the next as she invited the python to respond.

A drummer echoed the motion of her body. Two more followed, calling to the flute and to the xylophone to end their silence.

Lazily, secure enough now to seek the source of the music, the snake lifted its head and began its progress down Nshesha's neck and onto her bare shoulder. Its tiny claw, remnant of a long-forgotten past, scratched her skin, and she knew the power of its muscles as it twisted around her arm and constricted to make sure of its hold before it twisted again.

As the snake wrapped himself around her, Nshesha closed her eyes and relaxed. The watchers, gasping at her courage and extraordinary beauty, could not know she was imagining that Mzimba's hand crept over her body. The Dance of the Python was a fertility rite whose origins defied even the memory of the most ancient of storytellers, yet Nshesha was performing it as if it had been choreographed for her alone.

"Sing to me, Father," she whispered, knowing that the sign must come now, before she began her journey to Maseru.

She heard nothing but the drums, beating steadily against the whistle of the flute and the wooden hammers of the xylophone.

While the entire village held its breath, she unwound the python from her curves. She had no sooner knelt to return her partner to his woven bed, than the frenzy began anew: husbands lifted wives onto their shoulders to carry them away to the privacy of their huts. Men and women in their dotage forgot the creaking pains of their joints and sang of acts they could no longer perform; old lovers sought each other out, new loves were born. Warriors felt their blood racing again in stiffened veins as unmarried girls, maddened by the drums and the night, shook and twisted and leapt. They teased with firm bodies full of youth and promise, and acted out a pretense designed to make even those of Vusama's vintage remember what it had once been like to love a woman.

Angry, fighting tears, Nshesha made her way to her hut to prepare for the journey. When the sun was almost at its height and she knew there were but minutes left before her departure, she returned to the clearing. The basket containing the ritual python lay where she had left it. Kneeling, she pulled it toward her and pushed the woven lid aside.

"I have felt the approval of Queen Nzinga," she said, "but that is not enough. I cannot succeed without your power and cunning. Grant me your blessing, Tharu, as you gave it to Thoto the Minstrel, father of our tribe."

The python stirred, responding to the sound of her voice.

Nshesha sat in the clearing, waiting for a sign. Then, inside her head and her heart, she heard the song of the minstrel—the song of Thoto. The musicians heard it, too, and one by one they returned to their instruments.

When the drums and the flute and the xylophone had reached beyond the ears of the Elders to the Moon Goddess and the crocodiles in the Limpopo, Tharu lifted his head and began to sway. Sliding out of the basket, he found Nshesha.

When, once again, she knew the power of his muscles, he twisted around her arm and constricted to make sure of his hold. Nshesha rose to her feet. Entwined, Nshesha and Tharu lifted their heads toward *Unumweni* and began to dance.

Mrs. Langdon's Diary
—or—
They Carry It Too Far
Constance Ash

Constance Ash wrote The Horsegirl, *one of the two Ace Fantasy Specials that earned royalties. Two more novels and short fiction followed. To come are* A Press of Ghosts *and* The Kingdom by the Lake; *the first is a contemporary fantasy while the second is an historical fantasy. Both focus on the effects of African magic and culture in the New World.*

July, 1861

By God's all-knowing intention a wife *is* subject to her husband's command, and it is God who knows, not I, why Mr. Langdon has commanded me to rusticate at Silverbell Plantation while he celebrates our glorious Manassas victory in Richmond. I do believe I shall regret the loss of Mrs. Chesnut's company and her astute observations of persons and events more than the gaieties of my reunion with Mr. Langdon in Mobile and Richmond. Could it be that Mr. Langdon feared that *I* might become *too* gay, and like a silly slave, forget my station as his property?

Though I am not as clever as dear Mrs. Chesnut, to fill the solitary tedium of Silverbell days and nights I shall attempt a diary in imitation of her daily journal. But what is here to observe that can rival, even faintly, the political and amorous intrigues played out upon the stages of Mobile, Richmond, and Montgomery? All I see are swarms of Negroes—lounging among the groves that provide Silverbell its name, strolling over its grounds, roaming the galleries and chambers of this house. I cannot escape them any more than the mosquitoes and June bugs! This institution allows no privacy of self or thought, and I do hate it from the bottom of my heart.

Even as I sit scribbling, Della, our Ancient Inscrutable, is standing behind me, fanning this heavy, overheated summer air. She is the oldest living Negro to be found on any of Mr. Langdon's properties, having

arrived here the year before the Yankees closed the African trade—
before I was born! I agree with my husband that Della must have
employment to earn her keep though her vision is too impaired to continue the duties of Silverbell's head textile slave. I would prefer that her
employment were not bound to my person, as her presence has had a
vexatious effect upon my nerves since the first day Mr. Langdon
brought me as bride to Silverbell. Della's demeanor, even more so than
other Negroes, is unchanging, sleepy and respectful, profoundly indif-
ferent to everything outside her meals and her tasks—amazingly
including this battle which might have had effect upon her condition.
She carries her servile inexpressiveness too far!

Gleeful talk of the War and the Victory at Manassas went on in front
of the slaves as though they were tables and chairs, and damped their
fiery hope of freedom.

Della, Silverbell's powerful Conjure Woman, put heart back into
their hope. "Nigras make work, whatever they work, makin' marsters'
defeat, makin' backbone in them up North."

Silverbell's white folk dreamed within a night as sticky and dark as
blackstrap molasses. With a practiced ease no one in the big house suspected such an old, stout woman to possess, Della cut off the head of a
sleepy possum and caught the blood in a chipped enamel basin. The
sacrifice, *ebó,* was placed upon the table, which, for the night, had
become an altar. She placed the possum body within a shroud of croker sacking and buried it in the dirt floor under the table.

The table had been made by one of Silverbell's carpenters as an offering to Della's powers while his overseer was otherwise occupied. It was
draped with a quilt pieced in Oyá's nine colors and appliquéd in felt
dyed an indigo so deep and pure it was nearly purple. Della had
intended it for her daughter Indigo's wedding night, but a slave's life,
conditional in all matters upon the Master's will, had commanded otherwise. This quilt, though seemingly clean and never used, had a tiny
bloodstain on each piece, and instead of cotton batting, the edging
hems were stuffed with soil from the Silverbell slave cemetery.

The altar's backdrape was Della's own-time quilted reproduction of
a banner bequeathed to Missis Langdon, whose father belonged to one
of Virginia's First Families. On Della's quilt coiled an appliquéd serpent above the legend, "Don't Tread On Me." Della's Nupe name,
Kadella, and her Nupe language had been forbidden her; likewise, she

was forbidden to read or write the English she had been commanded to speak. Nevertheless, she had learned those patterns possessed a power that corresponded to a *babalawo's* cast of *omo-odu* which divined liberty; so did the snake, for those animals partook simultaneously of male and female *ashé,* the most fundamental of creative forces.

A broken, discarded big house soup tureen had been mended to make Orisha Echù's altar *isaasun.* The fiery stones within the *isaasun* bathed in pure water, water infused with the herbs that soothed Echù's power, the power that brought dissension, malicious trickery, and division within a house. Della's *ori,* her "head soul," ordered the world as the *babalawo's* daughter had learned in Yorubaland. The house to which she demanded Echù to bring discord was that of "Confederacy," also named the "South," made out of the family and clan "states" of the lineage "Secession."

The *ewi* possessed by the herbs supplemented the cooling, soothing powers of the water. Water and *ewi* warded Della from Echù's burning violence springing back upon herself. Della removed the lid from Echù's *isaasun.* The tallow candle stub's flame reflected in the water. The water was a mirror that reflected away from her, the spellmaker, the effects of the dark spell of familial discord and vengeance she worked.

The possum blood sacrifice lined up with the *isaasun* and the serpent coils quilted upon the back quilt. Della dipped her thumb in the blood and marked an X for Echù's crossroads upon the front and back covers of the book. It had come from the House of the North. Missis Langdon dropped her things here and there like a hen did feathers and with as much notice. Missis's maid said, "Missis buy a dozen of that there *Uncle Tom's Cabin* in these ten years. She never miss this one." To this very day, the book turned white men red and made them shout at each other. To this day women read from it to each other and exchanged sharp words. The book's undiminished power to divide had widened the door through which Echù's powers manifested in the House of the South.

From a hiding place up the shaked roof she took down a tanned, shiny goat hide and sinew ties. Della rolled her large, hollow log up to the altar. White folks had seen it scores of times over the years. It usually lay against a wall and was where the pickneys sat, when they came to tease Della out of tidbits and tales. She straddled it and tied the goat skin over the upright end, and lo! the log's own nature was revealed as

Drum. The head remained upright by means of a wide leather strap that went over her shoulders so her two hands might beat out the accompanying rhythm to the words she sang in Nupe, which no one living on Silverbell but she knew. There was little risk of anyone in the big house hearing as her cabin was set the farthest back of the chink and daub slave yard shacks. The dim illumination made little matter to Della who, decades into enslavement, relied upon her inner sight and her intimate familiarity of place and condition.

Clandestine as shadows, Della's most trusted sisters and brothers in Silverbell bondage crossed the threshold of her cabin. Fourth and fifth generations in slavery, they had been initiated by Della into the knowledge of her lineage. They brought offerings to the Orisha of, perhaps, their ancestors, and certainly Della's: a marble swirled in red and black, colors favored by Elegba-Echù; a Havana cigar and thimble of rum filched from Marster; a feather from the tail of one of Missis's white roosters.

Young, powerful hands took over Drum. Other hands saw to the burning of the offering's blood, a drop at a time, in the candle flame. They sang the Nupe words Della had taught them in chorus to her songs.

Della danced to Drum. She sang to Drum. "Elegba-Echù! KaDELLA! Elegba-Echù! KAdella! Elegba-Echù! KADellA! Remember Kadella! Elegba, Elegba, remember Kadella!"

The way was made open for the trance in which her *ori* walked the paths of *ashé,* where she encountered the *oris* of other old slaves, who, like her, had been born free in Yorubaland. Loosed from body, time, and place, Della's *ori,* in the realms of *ashé,* touched the head souls of other elderly slaves, born in other African lands, like her possessed of the blood of those who shape the ancestors' sacred powers on behalf of the reborn. Each in the way of his or her own people, they too spelled division within the House of the South, and heated the will of their masters' enemies with the necessity to avenge the Defeat at Manassas.

Autumn, 1862

Whether the Yankees call it Antietam, or we call it Sharpsburg, it was the most terrible and bloody slaughter; nevertheless the Yankees failed to carry the day. As punishment Mr. Lincoln, like a sulking husband, declares the emancipation of all our Negroes if we do not beg his pardon and return to the Union's embrace by the First of the New Year.

A more courageous, decisive general than McClellan will have to be found to command Lincoln's Army of the Potomac before the unrestrained Negro can be forced upon us! Mrs. Chesnut's latest letter reports that Negroes are invited to enlist with the Yankee armies. Would that these constant childbearers, ceaselessly injured and ill, the vast number of useless dotards, *were* among their army to feed, clothe, and nurse. Within a fortnight we'd be begged to resume our burden.

Our Negroes digest the abundance of Silverbell: string beans, lettuce salads, okra, corn, potatoes, tomatoes, cucumbers, yellow squash; watermelon, cantaloupe, peaches; oysters, boiled mutton, boned turkey, wild duck and partridge, terrapin stew, gumbo, chickens in jelly; fish, eggs, butter; chocolate cream, plum pudding, queen's cake; whiskey, rum, burgundy, claret cup, apple toddy. It is all *our* expense, neither the Yankees' nor theirs.

Search their black, brown, or yellow faces as you will, there is not a sign that one of them has so much as heard the name of Abraham Lincoln or that the Yankees have invited them to murder us in exchange for the opportunity to live in simpleminded sloth. They carry it too far!

Close to midnight at the dark of the moon, Della's initiates covertly followed her on silent, bare feet. At the crossroads between silverbell groves and the wildwood a solitary fat pine torch sputtered to life. By its uncertain flicker they walked a narrow path which brought them to the clearing where Silverbell buried its slaves.

Colonel Roony Lee had said words over the coffin that morning before it was put in the ground. The good Silverbell boy inside that coffin had been given to the colonel by his sister, Missis Langdon, when he went to fight the Yankees. The colonel's leg got torn to pieces. The boy got much worse when he pulled the colonel from under his shot-up horse at Sharpsburg.

It was strictly forbidden, but it must be done, Della declared, if the head soul of this good man was to join his ancestors and be reborn, as he deserved. Silverbell Plantation was good to its slaves. The last three marsters kept nearly everyone born upon this earth. There would be a host of familial *oris* to welcome this boy when the newly released head soul was spelled back into *ashé,* the realm which contained all potential action.

Elegba's rhythms were beaten out on tiny finger drums, accompanying the song beseeching him to open the way between here and the orishas. Always the first, as another part of him was always the last, nothing could begin without Elegba or end without Elegba-Echù. A white rooster was sacrificed on the fresh grave. The blood of the dead and the rooster's was encouraged to join the bones of ancestors and relatives. Lighted cigars and glasses of rum were set upon the undressed swamp rock headstone, deemed fine enough by Silverbell to honor a slave loyal unto death.

Elegba opened the way for the arrival of Yewá, Ruler of the Cemetery. She gave the corpse to Orisha Oyá, who took the *ori* of the dead into her protection. Oyá presented the body to Obaluaiye, Ruler of Illness, Plague, and Madness. His examination found the flesh acceptable to join his ancestors' earth. What was left belonged to Oricha-Oko, Ruler of Farming and Eater of Corpses. For Oricha-Oko plates mounded high with yam paste and garlanded in ribbons of the best textiles made on Silverbell were set upon the graves.

The people drummed, sang, and danced until daylight was imminent. Without Oyá's presence, no action's full potential can be accomplished. A dove-hen to Orisha Oyá was sacrificed upon the grave as dawn broke. Oyá tore away the veil that divided the *ori* from *ashé*.

As the sun oozed over the eastern horizon, to the words of his farewell hymn Elegba-Echù conducted the new head soul into *ashé*, to be healed, perhaps to become an orisha in his own time, and perhaps, to be reborn. The songs became messages the new *ori* was to carry the old ones. "Please help us win this war. This yoke must break. Your children can't tote this burden no more. We must be free."

One by one, the finger drums and voices decayed into stillness. Manly arms, muscles forged hard and powerful from long labor at the anvil, caught Della as her nightlong efforts brought down her many decades.

"You believe next time these childrens be born free?" Rufus, the young ironsmith, asked.

"*Ashé* make the hammer that shape our work for free," Della whispered.

August, 1863
Gettysburg. Vicksburg. When will this year's calamities end?

September, 1863
A Victory! Chickamauga! Hooray for General Longstreet!
Mrs. Chesnut writes Rosecrans's Army of the Cumberland besieged

in Chattanooga, our artillery on Lookout Mountain, our infantry on Missionary Ridge. Mr. Langdon, that is, Major Langdon, is there with General Bragg. The bluecoats shall not cut us in half after all!

My white people are divided against the black folk—again over an infant. Decca dropped her first child. It is lighter-skinned than even she. As was her own father, like the hands, I know that the father of Decca's infant is white. I share Mrs. Chesnut's conviction. The most outrageous elements of our peculiar institution are the mulatto's care-less morality and the consequent universal hypocrisy of our men. The congress with Negro women, the consequent children, are accom-plished and live under the same roof that shelters planter gentlemen's beautiful white wives and white children. If a woman of my condition were to make a connection with a gentleman outside the sacred vow of marriage, *she* would be shunned, left to shift for herself and child with-out countenance from gentleman or lady of her circle, or any below her circle, too. But these mulattoes, their children, and how they get them are not to be noticed by us, nor are those who make them to be admonished. Rather, we ladies are to employ, feed, clothe, house, and nurse them and their children tenderly throughout their entire lives. Decca comports herself, untouched by expression of shame or glee, as though desiring to send me mad. They carry it too far!

In Nupe, Della's birth language, she surely would have been named *Ajé,* a woman of extraordinary power, around whom a Secret Society surely would have formed. In her new world, Della's Secret Society was created out of third and fourth generation slaves, who experienced her as an extraordinarily effective Conjure Woman. Long ago Della had borne a child by Ol' Marster. Ol' Missis never made Della and her chile sell away, sure proved big Della JuJu.

In the late fall the call went out. Silverbell Conjure Woman gonna make some mazin' wompdoo, call down the lame ol' Seed and Broom Man. The moon be eaten and reborn. Silverbell Conjure Della invited as many black folks as could get away to drum, sing, and dance with her.

The bare feet of a goodly number of Negroes from other plantations in her part of South Carolina, with or without passes, brought them to the middle of Silverbell's breed cattle pasture way off on the other side of the wildwood. The frost had long fallen on the clover when the first shadow fell upon the moon's rim. Distant moon, shadow and the fat pine torches were reflected in the mirror made by the water hole. When the first slice got carved out of the moon the jugs of apple toddy tipped up to dry mouths. The beat turned hotter and harder, the dancing wilder and faster, the voices rougher and shriller. Here and there a body fell to the ground. When the bodies got up the back was hunched, one leg was lame. Della and her Society had been singing the hymns all day and all night, invoking Orisha Obaluaiye, too hot to be confined within walls and under roofs. A cold night was safest time to call the fever orisha. The orisha, once sent mad himself by laughter at his lameness, manifested as He-Who-Sends-Panic-of-Madness. It was right for Della to be mad, a most dangerous mask to wear, for it was by no means certain that it could be taken off again.

The heavy mask was supported by a pole held in both of Della's hands. Its various fabrics, dyed black and light blue, concealed her self entirely. Long strings of popcorn hung from Obaluaiye's "head," simulating the leopard spots of pox. They rustled against the thorn necklaces in a panic whisper to the sheaves of fabric tied under his "chin." Obaluaiye's celebrants sowed sesame seeds broadcast into the night. Their brooms swept relentlessly before and behind him. The epidemic orisha cut repeated swaths of terror through the gathering. He charged an individual here, knocked down one there. The orisha's howls of intimidation were answered by his celebrants' shrieks and gibbers.

The moon lost more and more of itself. Other celebrants began the offerings of hens and doves in groups of seventeen, the number of He-Who-Sends-Panic-of-Madness. Out of the water hole Orisha Oyá's whirlwind turned into her shoulders, tongued her jaw. The vortex sucked Obaluaiye's sesame seeds into herself and twirled off to the west, where Oyá spit out her hot companion's madness.

In the morning, the cattle bawled at the smell of blood in the mud around their water. There was the look of a shambles all about, while the last visitors ate the remains of the barbecued fowls, and drank what was left of the apple toddy. Paddyrollers and slave catchers meant little this morning to Nigras who had drummed, danced, sung, and masked terror-mania all night long.

The End of November—perhaps the End of all Things

But—my husband, dear Major Langdon was only injured! Though most dreadfully. His friends are seeing that our faithful Cato is able to carefully bring him home. Silverbell *will* return him to health.

Those who name November 25, 1863, the Miracle of Missionary Ridge are not Southerners. Inexplicably, the Yankees kept coming and coming up the hill. Our poor men broke in panic and ran. Mad from excitement the Federals yelled, "Chickamauga, Chickamauga" at the back of Bragg's fleeing army, which didn't stop for fifty miles. The way to Georgia is open. She shall be ravished, as shall we all.

New Year's Day, 1864

It is my dear husband's funeral day.

September, 1864

Atlanta is fallen. Mrs. Chesnut writes that since the loss of Atlanta she can see nothing but doom, despair, and desolation. She fears that we, the Planter class, the best and brightest of the New World, shall be wiped off the earth.

My sons, all my darling sons but the youngest, who is home with me, are killed by this terrible War made by those who would not leave us alone, which is all we required from them.

November, 1864

Abraham Africanus the First has been reelected and will celebrate no doubt with his Miscegenation Ball. The news that gets through Mobile Bay's blockades is that 130,000 Negroes are enlisted in the monster's army and navy. Pray God, preserve Mobile Bay from the Yankees and their black beasts.

December, 1864

Lincoln insists on reunion and emancipation as prior conditions to peace; President Davis insists upon independence and slavery as prior conditions to peace. Let *them* have the damned slaves, but let *us* have peace! "When this cruel war is over"—the Northerners sing, but we, too, we mothers, wives, sisters, and daughters, are "weeping, sad, and lonely." But neither their men nor ours will give way. I read what men write in the *Whig:* "To talk now of any other arbitrament than that of the sword is to betray cowardice or treachery. Valor alone *can* be relied upon for our salvation."

* * *

Night after night in the wildwood Della's fierce working spiraled *ashé* up her spine, connecting her lower powers to her *ori's ashé*.

The power came from Orisha Nana Bukúu, she who was mother of Obaluaiye. Her power twined with the complementary power of Oshumare, Nana Bukúu's dear one, the he-she Rainbow serpent who shat beads in the colors of the spectrum. Nana Bukúu and Oshumare were fiery, outdoor powers, the most ancient of all, born long before Ogún had forged iron. Their knives were wood or bamboo, but they were deadly as Ogún's metal, and they were first.

The vortex of energy that rose from Della's loins and coiled around her spine belonged to Orisha Oyá, the Oyá-Who-Carries-Her-Lance-among-Warriors. The warrior orishas walked these paths: Echù Who-Closes-the-Way; Ogún Who-Cuts-the-Path-Before; Oshòósi the Hunter Who-Shoots-His-Arrows-in-Battle; Sangó Who-Rides-Warhorse-Eshinla-across-the-Sky.

Della's companion at Ogún's altar in the wildwood was Rufus, Silverbell's young ironsmith. He kept the fire hot, crossed Ogún's hammer with the long knife blade that opened the throats of the male dogs and roosters whose blood was preferred by the warrior among warriors, Ogún, Ruler of War: bloodthirsty and fearless—Ogún; lord of smiths—Ogún; ruler of iron's cutting edge—Ogún; he whose only fear is defeat—Ogún.

Della's spine was a spear, straight and true as one whose head had been worked on Ogún's forge. Oyá's vortex roiled out of Della's *ashé* along the conduit of her backbone in nightly spell and daily ritual. Her chants before the altar of Ogún were harsh and clashing as bars of iron flung together, filled with the war orisha's ferocity. Her eyes blazed like black suns in the fire that lighted the stone anvil, foundation for the altar dedicated to war, where Ogún demanded, greedy and heedless as a child, cataracts of blood.

"Until Oyá's nine grandsons and granddaughters multiply themselves nine times and her nine grandsons and granddaughters persevere—the enemy shall bemoan their fate—until freedom come. The warriors stalk the land—suffering, much suffering, death, much death—until freedom come."

The warriors, Echù, Ogún, Oshòósi, and Sangó, marched through Georgia, as they'd marched the Shenandoah Valley's length with Sheridan, desirous to be regarded as glorious by She-Who-Owns-the-Spear. Their road was blood, fire, famine, and corpses, all in order to be seen as honorable in Oyá's eyes. South Carolina, though, still sat pretty. Her body was untouched by the desolation that she'd initiated with her gleeful fire upon the resuppliers to Fort Sumter in the spring of 1861.

As 1864 closed, Echù, malicious trickster, prompter of discord, clawed the Georgians. They said to Sherman, "Whyn't you Federals all go over to South Carolina and do them like you doin' us Johnny-Come-Latelys? High-nosed South Carolina started it."

When winter opened Della came alone to beat Sangó's drums before his rival Ogún's altar. Rufus, the slave blacksmith, child of Ogún, worker of stones and metals, had taken off because he needed to march in William Tecumseh Sherman's army.

January, 1865

Mrs. Chesnut writes me: "They must know what is at hand if Sherman is not hindered from coming here—Freedom, my masters! But these black sphinxes give no sign, unless it be increased diligence and absolute silence. They are as certain in their actions and as noiseless as a law of nature—when we are in the house!"

Mrs. Chesnut's Mulberry Negroes cannot be more sphinxes than Silverbell's. In consideration of my losses and sorrows, they have become quiet as snow. As always, my Negroes save me all thought as to household matters. Yet, I do feel that behind my back the air tingles with secrets and jubilation. Rufus is gone, and so are others I am told, though not by *them*.

February, 1865

Richmond speaks again of plucking the black string in the Confederate bow. But how, if slaves will make good soldiers, loyal and true as our own white sons, husbands, brothers, and fathers, can our theory of slavery be right? And then, Negro soldiers will lead to universal emancipation. If so, how dare I weep upon my graves, if our cause, which was to keep our institutions intact, is preserved by violating our peculiar way of life?

February, 1865

He is the very devil. Rivers to ford, swamps to navigate, roads under water, yet Sherman with the assistance of contraband Negroes, fells trees, builds corduroy roads, bridges rivers, swims swamps in canoes, all at the rate of a dozen miles a day. What shall become of us?

March, 1865

The smell of smoke is everywhere. Nearly all our Negroes have run off to Sherman, and I have not an idea in the world as to what I should do. Della has pushed this journal into my hands and gone to hide Silverbell's plate and flatware, with my jewels, leaving enough to satisfy the Yankees from searching out the greater part. Days ago she had the pickneys conceal shoats in the swamps, the calves and poultry in the wildwood. She herself dismantled the looms and concealed the pieces, along with the quilting frames and all the implements she knows so well as a textile slave from the days when her eyes allowed her to work her trade. With her proper implements and Silverbell cotton, Della says, she and I shall have the means to sustain us after the peace is declared. The difference, she says, is that I must share the profits with her and the other—gals, I suppose. Lincoln has his wish and they are no longer slaves, no longer my property. I can write no more.

March, 1865

I am shamed to say so, but I gave way under my sorrows when the bluecoats ascended the steps of Silverbell. Sherman himself with his men rampaged through my house and yet I have a roof over my head. How this can be, when there are no other edifices unburned and unraised within the parish, I cannot say. Della says that Rufus, who has turned up like a bad penny, has much to do with my roof, but I cannot comprehend her. She has tucked me up in my bed with a cup of miraculous tea and an even more miraculous candle. She even has preserved my journal. What kind of—person?—is this Della. I cannot countenance faith in the whispers even dear Mrs. Chesnut—and how is she prevailing I wonder?—engaged over the years, of witchcraft and the like. Such heathenness may have been worked by the free Negroes in Charleston who came from San Dominque, or those on the Sea Islands, but nothing of that nature has ever been practiced on good, Christian plantations such as Silverbell has been.

What Silverbell is now, what Silverbell will be, only God knows. What Silverbell was, is finished, forever.

April Fool's Day

Indeed. Grant's Army of the Potomac has Petersburg.

April 3, 1865

Richmond has surrendered.

April 9, 1865

Lee has surrendered at Appomattox. It is finished. Into your hands, oh Father, *my* South commends her spirit.

May, 1865

A small, lovely tree, the silverbell is a Southern native. Wherever I look from my windows I see snowy banks of the bell-shaped flowers, fresh and pure as a new beginning. Oh, my Silverbell is breathtaking in her beauty today, as the silverbell petals snow upon my graves. There shall not be a rebirth for me, for us, the Planter class and the lovely civilization we made here. There are too many graves.

My baby, my last son, my only living child, has succumbed to measles. I will not bear it.

Della was tired, but she had no time to lay the burden down. She prayed. "Obatalá, pure and white as silverbells, cleanse and make all things new. It be hard times now and tomorrow, but they be your children's *very own* hard times!"

Missis Langdon, done up by sorrow and surrender, stayed in bed. Most of the Negroes who had run straggled back to the nearest thing to a home they had. They were free, but they owned nothing with which to shape their freedom. The authority left upon Silverbell was Della's. On this island surrounded by scorched earth she instructed her black and white relatives as how to feed, clothe, and shelter them all.

The Negroes in Della's Secret Society, who hadn't run from Silverbell even in the heady March days of Sherman's blood and fire, allowed themselves to be the Conjure Woman's tools for her wisdom.

Several times under sun and under moon, every day and night, they sang tranquil incantations to accompany the anointing of Ogún's anvil altar with soothing oil pressed out of their precious, hidden stores of cottonseed. They poured pure, cool water over the anvil's fiery point. It was the *itutu l'ojú* to confer harmony of stillness upon him, while establishing protection from him.

They brought Ogún tiny portions of his favorite foods without meat or blood, and made him no offering. Instead they built an altar to Oshun, personification of love and beauty, in front of him to distract Ogún from his eternal contemplation of war.

Every day somebody brought a pretty thing, a sweet thing, to Oshun's altar, in her chosen color of yellow: honey; a yellow strap lined with yellow silk from Ol' Marster's favorite filly's halter; breast feathers from a yellow finch; a mirror with a yellow handle. Rufus danced Ogún's love dance to Oshun to please the most sweet of the orishas.

One night deep into the strangely silent summer that followed the surrender, Della, concealed by the wildwood, watched Rufus dance to Oshun. Though others were behind the young blacksmith, clapping and singing in time to the drummers, no one else danced. The hand within Della's own tightened at the sight of the skillful, handsome, strong, brave, dancing black man.

Della squeezed her great-granddaughter's hand in return. She was a smart, lovely, high yellow gal, dressed in yellow croker sacking, who knew, or did not, that her great-grandfather was a white Langdon. Della led her to Rufus. Before laying the gal's hand in that of Rufus, Della presented her with a fan of yellow feathers.

Christmas Day, 1865

Silverbell's only celebration was a wedding between a gal who is Della's great-granddaughter—though how a Negro can determine such a relationship I cannot comprehend—and Rufus, one of the several decent Negroes who remain here. The wedding vows were heard by a Negro minister ordained by our new masters. As my wedding gift I agreed to sell Rufus a goodly parcel of Silverbell if he can raise the money. God knows, I need money, any money, desperately. Without Della I do believe all of us, slothful and hardworking alike, would be dead of starvation. Speaking of Della, Rufus insists upon acreage that includes the old slave burial ground. Della wants it, he says, for the ancestors, whatever that means. No one ever knows truly what a Negro is thinking!

ONE LATE NIGHT, WITH JACKAL

JOSEPHA SHERMAN

Josepha Sherman is a fantasy writer, folklorist, and editor. Her latest novels are The Shattered Oath *and* Gleaming Bright *(Walker and Company) and her latest folklore books are* Once Upon A Galaxy *and* Trickster Tales. *She has sold over one hundred short stories to books and magazines for adults and children, and a television script for the late* Adventures of the Galaxy Rangers.

D r. Sharon Cotter, a neat, compact, brown-haired not-quite-young woman, sat bent nearly doubled over the faded papyrus manuscript, muttering to herself.

". . . and of the . . . of the what? Ah, right. Of the summoning of the . . . dammit, what's this scrawl? The summoning of the *fish?*"

That couldn't possibly be right! Laughing in spite of herself, she straightened slowly, trying to iron the stiffness out of her neck with her hands. Not only had the unknown scribe who'd first penned the text had a terrible demotic hand, he'd also been a miser determined not to waste a corner of the precious papyrus. Every bit of it was covered with his crabbed writing.

Ah well, Sharon reminded herself, she had no business complaining. Even if she hadn't yet been able to totally decipher the thing, at least she *had* a genuine text to study; many a scholar in many a larger museum would envy her that.

God, life was odd. When she'd graduated . . . what had it been, seven, eight years back? . . . when she'd graduated with a working knowledge of Egyptian hieroglyphs and demotic writing and a love of the ancient world far surpassing that of the present, her mind had been full of dreams of archaeological glory. She was going to *do* something, *be* someone.

Instead she had wound up here instead, stuck in the provincial little

Greinton Memorial Museum of Art, her dreams nearly forgotten. Grandiose name, Greinton Memorial, for what was basically a reno- vated Victorian building full of odd corners and dim hallways, difficult to heat or cool.

Despite her heady title as curator of the Department of Antiquities, there was little glamour to her job, either. She pretty much ran the entire department herself, with the sometimes aid of one puppy-dog- eager intern, and the collection consisted—or had, till recently—of not much more than a handful of nice Luristan bronzes, a few mediocre *ushabti,* a fair sampling of Egyptian potsherds, Old King- dom through New, and some bits of New Kingdom wall reliefs of dubious provenance.

And now this. Sharon smiled suddenly, feeling the echo of the excitement she had once known racing through her once more. She knew next to nothing about the late Jackson Lanthrop, save that he'd been both wealthy and reclusive, but the man had definitely had a fine eye for antiquities. She had no idea why he'd chosen to leave his collec- tion to a provincial museum like this, but she certainly wasn't about to argue with his decision!

Glancing at the elegant figurine of Anubis, part of the bequest, sit- ting on her desk, Sharon felt her smile widen. Sleekly carved of wood and dyed jet black and gold, the figurine was a beautiful likeness of the Egyptian god of the dead in his jackal-form.

"'Hail, Anubis, Lord of the Divine Hall,'" Sharon quoted softly. "You who weigh the hearts of the dead to test their truthfulness. Hope Lan- throp passed the test."

Enough dawdling. With a sigh, she bent over the papyrus again. Resting her eyes these few seconds seemed to have helped, because now she could make out whole phrases.

"Open to me the earth . . . open to me the . . . the underworld . . . open to me the abyss . . . "

Her voice trailed into silence as Sharon read on and realized what she was reading. This was a magical text. This was an actual ancient Egyptian manual on sorcery. Her mind gibbering wildly, *A fabulous find, fabulous; there's only been one other ever uncovered, the Leyden Papyrus, and that's divided up in Leyden and London; nothing like this in the United States, not till now,* she bent over it again, half in wonder, half in alarm, and read aloud:

"Oh you who are called Anubis, oh Lord of the Divine Hall, Guardian of the Gate, oh Anubis, come unto me—"

Sharon cut herself off before she could finish, hearing the spell continue silently in her mind, and sat bolt upright, staring at the figurine.

Oh you idiot. Just because it's a summoning spell, Anubis isn't going to—poof!—pop into life! You don't even know if your accent is anything near to correct.

And yet, and yet, just for an instant, hadn't there been a faint glimmering about the figurine, just a hint of—

A rap sounded on the office door. Sharon just barely bit back a startled shriek and called out in an almost-steady voice, "Who's there?" *If Anubis answers, what do I say? You've got the wrong address?*

"Miz Cotter? You okay in there?"

Sharon let out a silent sigh of relief. "Yes, Tom. I'm all right." Going to the door, she admitted Tom Jenkins, the museum's one and only night watchman, middle of height, weight, and age, and resolutely mundane, the type of incredibly ordinary man who seems to have no existence beyond his job. Bland brown eyes blinked at her.

"Getting kinda late. Don't you think you should be starting for home? Not as safe these days as it used to be. You . . . uh . . . know what I mean."

"Only too well." Lately the museum had been plagued by a persistent vandal, apparently some type of religious fanatic, who had scrawled misspelled slogans such as "Heathin Stuff" and "Godless pagins" across walls. The local police, used to dealing with nothing more than the occasional drunk driver or speeder, hadn't found him, and mild-mannered Tom, Sharon thought drily, while he might patrol earnestly every night, hardly constituted a crime deterrent, particularly not in this rambling old building. "I'll be along in just a moment."

She slipped the precious manuscript and the figurine of Anubis into the department's one small safe, patted it absently, and left.

That night Sharon dreamed happy, bright visions of a hot, sunlit land her sleeping mind knew for Egypt of millennia past. A life-loving people, those of ancient Egypt, she remembered that fact even in dreams, a people who enjoyed themselves so much they could imagine no better afterlife than one just like reality—one without sunstroke or flies, that was—and no worse crime than anything that kept a person from that happiness.

But the memory of her happy dreams vanished as she neared the museum's ornate redbrick front the next morning.

"Oh hell, not again."

Robert Eagan, her counterpart in Greek and Roman, a tall, lanky, bespectacled man, glanced at her like a sad-eyed spaniel. "Again. He got my gallery this time. Left the usual message about us being Godless heathens supporting pagan ways, and did his best to break into the case of Classical vases. Didn't do more than crack the glass, fortunately."

"The police?"

That earned her an even more soulful glance. "Oh, they're here, all right, checking things over," Eagan drawled, "but you and I know they're not going to find anything useful."

Sharon groaned. If their unpleasant visitor was so vehement about pagans, it was just a matter of time before he got around to her department, which was certainly the most "pagan" of the lot. And judging from the cracked case, he apparently was starting to get bored with mere graffiti.

Oh God, what if he'd already struck? The papyrus—

Overwhelmed by panic, Sharon started for her office, only to be stopped by an officious police detective who wanted to know if A) she worked here, B) she had been here last night, and C) she had seen or heard anything out of the ordinary. Sharon impatiently answered yes, yes, and no, and at last escaped into her office, leaning back against the door with a sigh of relief. Nothing in here had been disturbed.

Of course not. He's a vandal, not a safecracker!

Opening the safe, she drew out the precious papyrus and the figurine of Anubis. The jackal god looked soothingly serene, as though nothing had ever disturbed his sense of quiet, logical justice and nothing ever would. Giving him a wry little bow, Sharon spread the ancient manuscript before her and set about her translation.

Not a soul disturbed her. Somewhere about midday, she absently drew out the sandwich and fruit juice she'd brought with her, ate lunch without much noticing it, browsing through the latest issue of *Biblical Archaeology* without much noticing that, either, then returned to work.

"Lord of the Dead . . . Guardian . . . protect the just from the unjust . . . "

That matched up nicely with the lines she'd already translated. As she read on, Sharon nodded. This was very evidently a protective spell, a spell to bring down the might of Anubis on anyone who committed crimes against state or individual.

But her body was starting to nag her past the point of mind over matter, reminding her that she hadn't taken care of what was rapidly becoming an urgent need. With a sigh, Sharon slipped the papyrus and figurine back into the safe, and left, still turning the words of the protection spell over in her mind. Fascinating: so simply, so precisely worded it seemed as matter-of-fact as a scientific formula.

As she started back from the museum's antiquated rest rooms, a glint from outside caught her attention. Glancing out one dusty window, Sharon stopped in surprise.

Streetlights are on. Hadn't realized it was so late.

But she wasn't ready to call it a day, not yet. Most people wouldn't understand, Sharon thought. They'd think her crazy to be spending so much time in the past, crazy not to be out there mingling with everyone else, going to those boring faculty parties or worse, spending time at the local "singles' meets," where the most anyone could discuss were the latest sports scores or who was shooting at whom in the latest undeclared war.

The ancient Egyptians were lucky, Sharon thought; they didn't have the media drumming bad news into their ears day and night. All they had to worry them was whether or not the Nile would flood on schedule or whether little Senmut would make it all the way to Royal Scribe. People's lives were more personal then, more *human*. And it was only right that someone should preserve as much of their memory as possible.

That papyrus isn't really the past. It's the record of a living man's thoughts and beliefs, as contemporary as any modern novel. And I want to see how the whole thing comes out!

Decided, Sharon hurried outside for a second sandwich and a thermosful of coffee—*the harried scholar's dinner of choice*—from the one diner still open at this hour, then started back for her office. Sandwich and thermos balanced in one arm, she managed to get the door open with the other.

And froze, staring in outraged disbelief at the figure who crouched there, back to her. Half her books were already off their shelves, torn paper littered the floor, and the figure was in the middle of trying to open the safe. The vandal! Maybe she should have been afraid, she should have yelled for help, but all Sharon had room for was anger. How dare this lout interfere? Hefting the thermos, she snapped:

"What do you think you're doing?"

The figure whirled, staring at her.

"Tom!" Sharon gasped.

"Thought you'd gone home. Should have gone home."

Dear God. How could she ever have mistaken the insane blankness of his eyes for mildness? And why oh why had she ever taken him for granted? They'd *all* taken him for granted, good old Tom, safe and calm and reliable.

Like hell. As he straightened, a knife glinted in his hand, and she thought, *He really has gone past graffiti, hasn't he?*

"You don't want to hurt me, Tom," Sharon crooned. "Or anyone else, either. You work here, you know we're not bad people."

He shook his head. "That's what they all say nowadays. Not bad people. But they don't worship right. You're the worst, calling on devils, putting things on display for kids to see, Satanic things. I gotta stop you, Miz Cotter. Nothing personal; gotta stop this whole Satanic place."

She threw the thermos. It thudded against his chest and she heard him grunt and saw him stagger, but the knife never wavered.

"Shouldn'ta done that. Now you're going to have to go up with everything else."

He moved faster than she had thought possible. A meaty hand, mercifully not that with the knife, shoved so hard she went sprawling, thinking, *He's got a can of kerosene—all this paper—God, this is like a bad movie, only there isn't any hero racing to the rescue.*

All that paper, indeed. Maybe she hadn't been the world's greatest Egyptologist, but her work had been of *some* importance, and this maniac was going to destroy it and—The papyrus! The safe wasn't fireproof. The precious papyrus would burn, and the elegant little figurine of Anubis—no, dammit, *no!* Enough of the past had already been lost. She wouldn't let any more perish!

There wasn't room for thought. As though her body belonged to someone else, Sharon heard herself shout out, "Hail Anubis! Lord of the Dead, Guardian, protect the just from the unjust!"

"Stop that!" Tom waved the knife at her. "Stop those devil words!"

But she couldn't stop now; the spell wouldn't let her stop. Even as Sharon watching in horror as he tore the lid off the can of kerosene, she couldn't do anything but continue to shout out the ancient Words of Power.

And they were no longer alone. Sharon blinked, stared, out-and-out rubbed her eyes without making a bit of difference. She still was not quite seeing the sleek black-and-gold figure with its fiery golden eyes, not quite seeing the blazing glory that could only be Anubis.

Impossible. I can't—he can't—

Tom saw. To judge from the sudden wild terror on his face, he saw quite clearly. The can fell harmlessly to the floor as he backed slowly away, coming to a sudden stop against a wall. That agonizing terror still blazed from him, the terror of a man wounded beyond bearing, the terror of a child abused beyond sanity, but he said not a word, not a word, only stared and stared and stared helplessly back at the steady, wise, alien eyes.

And all at once he broke. The not-quite figure of Anubis stood watching, alert as a hunting hound, as with the smallest of whimpers Tom slid to the floor, curling up into as small a ball as he could manage.

"'Hail, Anubis,'" Sharon murmured. "You who weigh the hearts of the dead to test their truthfulness. You . . . weigh the hearts of the living, too, don't you?"

The . . . god or being or whatever, turned slowly to her. For one horrified moment Sharon was held helpless by the cool, alien stare, the endless golden depths, sure he was reading her heart as well, sure he was about to show her wrongnesses to her as he had used the truth to break Tom's mind.

But there was nothing, nothing save a sense of having been studied and approved. As the not-quite-seen figure faded, the faintest echo of not-quite sound told her, Welcome, Guardian, welcome Protector of the Way.

Protector of the Way, she mused, and somehow the words seemed the first totally right ones she had known. Of course. What else could she be but what she had always been? Protector of the Way. Protector of the Past. *I am someone important after all.*

And Dr. Sharon Cotter, last priest of Anubis, stood over the broken man who'd thought to destroy the past, and smiled.

DEAD AND GONE
KEVIN ANDREW MURPHY

Kevin Andrew Murphy has stories in a number of shared world anthologies, including Wild Cards: Card Sharks *and White Wolf's* World of Darkness *series. He has also coauthored the novel* House of Secrets *with James A. Moore. Here he explores one of his own worlds, the enchanted Island of California, which also figured as the setting for "The Croquet Mallet Murders" in Forrest J. Ackerman & Jean Stine's* I, Vampire *anthology.*

"Pretty cat, kitty cat . . . " Vince stirred the air, watching as the ether coalesced into bones, then shadows. Phantasmal hairs ticked his ankles as the ghost cat wound its tail around them. "Pretty kitty, kitty-ki!"

The last of the ectoplasm coalesced, and a seemingly solid gray-and-black tabby reached up and tried to sharpen its claws on nonexistent pantlegs.

Vince scooped up the cat. "Enough of that, Shadow. I may be dead, too, but that still hurts."

"Mrrrr," Shadow purred in satisfaction. Vince shrugged. He'd decided to keep a haunt from the pound. By definition, he wasn't going to get a happy, well-adjusted pet.

But it was best to keep the cat tangible and on hand. There was no telling what mischief a ghost cat might try to pull. His first date since he'd died—heck, his first date in five years—and the last thing he needed was a yowling phantasm creeping Elaine out more than she must be already.

If she showed.

Vince was pretty certain she wouldn't. After all, what sort of woman would answer a personal like he'd placed: *Hi! Wanna date a lich? Dead SWM necromancer, young (relatively speaking), handsome (when I take the time), fun-loving (would love to have fun—haven't yet), would like to meet pretty, intelligent single female, living or dead. No weirdos.*

Not that he was likely to get any dead girls. The dead liked necromancers even less than the living, and a dead necromancer . . . Well, Vince could understand why liches had a reputation for being crazy, creepy old corpses. Not much else you could do.

He gave a last glance to the chamber and gestured for the will-o'-the-wisps to glow brighter, throwing in a binding to keep the corpse candles safely imprisoned in the wall sconces. He and Shadow might be able to see in the dark, but a live girl would want it bright and as uncryptlike as possible. Another gesture and the fire wraith hidden in the samovar raised the temperature to something the living might stand. Better. Not perfect, but better.

There was a soft knock and Vince went to get it, keeping Shadow tucked under one arm. He paused, making sure his own phantasm was in place, and opened the door.

"Hi," said the woman standing there, "I'm Elaine. You . . . "

"I'm Vince," Vince said, and opened the door wider. Her aura was beautiful, rose and honey gold, overlaid with the pale violet of shyness.

"What are . . . "

Vince snapped back. "Oh, sorry. I was just looking at your aura. It's very pretty."

The violet shade deepened, and beneath it he saw a blush steal into her cheeks. "Thank you. You look, um, well, more alive than I expected."

Vince shrugged. "I'm a necromancer. It's what I do." He smiled. "Would you like to come in?"

"Uh, yeah, thanks." She paused for a moment in the doorway, looking around, then came in and sat down on the couch, her pocketbook perched in her lap with her hands on top. "Um, your . . . apartment . . . is very nice. Cozy. Not . . . "

"Not what you expected for a mausoleum, right?" Vince shut the door, but didn't lock it. It wasn't as if he ever needed to worry about break-ins, not in this neighborhood. "Pharaoh modern. I could never see the point of stone crypts when I was alive, so it's pretty much the same now that I'm, well, not precisely alive."

Elaine smiled and nodded, then burst into tears. "I'm sorry. This is all wrong. You seem very nice, but—" She stood up, brushing at the tears, and made for the door.

"Wait!" Vince said, reaching out, and Shadow slipped free. The cat landed before the door, arching its back and hissing at Elaine, inflating into a Halloween cat of demonic proportions.

Elaine sat back down on the couch, clutching her purse like a shield. Her tears stopped abruptly and her eyes went wide with fright.

"Shadow!" Vince heard his own voice boom in the ghostly Voice of Command, then he grabbed the cat and bundled it back into normal feline dimensions. "No!"

Shadow squirmed and growled, but at last settled down.

Vince looked to Elaine and gave a nervous grin. "Cats. Gotta love 'em, huh?" He grimaced. Oh God, he knew something like this was going to happen.

Elaine bit her lip. "He's dead too, isn't he?"

"Uh, yeah." It was an attempt to make conversation, at least. "I got him at the pound. They'd, well, had a haunting problem. Listen, if you want to go . . . " He began to get the door.

"No, no, it's all right." She reached into her purse and got out a tissue. "It's just—" She dabbed at her eyes. "I'm sorry. I came here under false pretenses. I didn't really want a date."

Vince went over to the couch and sat down, holding Shadow in his lap. "I sort of figured that."

"It's not—Well, yes, it is, maybe. It's just that my brother died, and, well, I wanted to talk to him."

"Have you tried a séance?"

"First thing. I borrowed every Ouija board on the block. Nothing." Elaine looked at the black marks of mascara on the tissue, then up at Vince. "I must look awful."

Vince smiled. "Not half as bad as I do. Trust me."

Elaine looked at her lap. "Okay. The police said Gary's death was an accident and his soul had just passed on. No murder, no suicide. But I knew something like this was going to happen. I did. I get premonitions sometimes—not like an oracle, nothing clear or anything—but sometimes I know when something bad is going to happen, or has happened. And it's like that now. My . . . gift . . . isn't anything documented, and it's easier for the police to just dismiss me as crazy than to believe in wildmagic, but I know there's something wrong. Very wrong. Gary would have come back to talk to me. He promised. We both did. Except now he's gone and the only thing left is necromancy and I never could afford to hire—" She broke off, her throat catching. "When I saw your ad, I— I'm sorry. I'm just desperate."

"That, and smart," Vince said. "You did your homework. A lich is the only sort of necromancer who can't get into trouble for disturbing the dead without a court order, right?"

Elaine blushed. "Well . . . "

"Trust me, I know the legalities. Only the dead can sue the dead for disturbing the dead, and the dead don't like bothering necromancers. Liches are laws unto themselves." Vince grimaced. "I must sound like I'm trying to sell myself on the idea. Listen, Elaine—You shouldn't mourn for your brother, or be freaked out by me. Being dead isn't that much different than being alive, it's just . . . " Vince paused, holding the squirming ghost cat. "Boring. Boring and lonely. I work for insurance companies mostly. But there are lots of living people who have it worse. And being a lich isn't that much different than being a live necromancer. Nobody really likes you once they find out what you are."

Vince looked up. Elaine was pretty, with one of the loveliest auras he'd ever seen. He'd never forgive himself if they didn't go out at least once, no matter how tainted the situation might be. "Tell you what— I'm sure your fears are unfounded, and you're not crazy either, just going through normal grief. But I can call your brother anyway, then we can all go to the park, and you can see how normal dead people are. The dead don't really mind being bothered, not if someone who really loves them is trying to contact them, and with all the psychic interference going on, Ouija boards don't work half the time anyway. You can put your fears to rest. Then if you want to go out for a real date sometime, well . . . "

"Yes," Elaine said immediately. "Yes, I'd like that very much."

The workroom was High Gothic, with silver mirrors framed in filigree, and oak pedestals stacked with twisted black candles glowing with ghost flames. Cobwebs hung everywhere, shrouding the reflections with gray silk, and clouds of dust rose up with each footstep.

Vince wished he'd cleaned recently.

"Uh, sorry. I don't get many guests, and I usually only enter this room in spirit. It's kind of ratty."

"Ratty?" Elaine asked hesitantly.

"Figure of speech." Vince saw her relax a bit. "It's spidery, mostly. Spiders don't mind the dead, and I like the company." God, Vince thought, he'd really gotten into the creepy lich bit without even thinking about it. Pet spiders. What next? "Sorry about the mess. It's much neater in the spirit world, really. Psychic housecleaning."

Elaine stepped inside, ducking a cobweb. "Don't worry—you should see my place. Um—What do we do?"

Vince set Shadow down, hoping he could trust the cat this once, and went over to the desk. He shuffled through the parchments, realizing how dusty everything really was. "I usually work with poetry. Automatic writing, illuminated manuscripts, that sort of thing. I'm afraid it's not very good, but it works for the magic."

Elaine leafed through a stack of poetry on another table, pausing. "These are very nice. I—I write poetry, too."

"I'm sure it's better than mine," Vince said. "Magic is a gift, but poetry is the real art."

"You must be good at both if you became a lich."

Vince shrugged. "Just didn't want to die, I guess. I didn't know if the spells would hold, but when I died, well, they must have. I'm here." He paused, remembering. "And the poltergeist who killed me isn't."

"Oh." Elaine paused, holding one of the poems.

Vince realized he'd just casually discussed blasting another soul out of existence. Not the nicest subject for conversation. "Listen, the poltergeist isn't really gone. He just, well, passed on a little more permanently than most spirits do. Nothing is ever gone forever. What art has made, art can unmake. And what has been unmade can be made anew."

Elaine glanced at the sheet of parchment in her hands. "Wizards' proverb," Vince explained, taking the sheaf from her and setting it aside. "It's something they kept telling us necromancers and sorcerers to keep us from becoming too discouraged."

"Creation and destruction . . . ." Elaine began.

"Is part of the power of God. But only part. I can't make you love me, or change the nature of reality, or play with space or time or magic itself. Those powers are reserved for other wizards; the Fourteen Arts are all limited in their own ways." Vince took out fresh parchments and the inks and a set of raven quills. "I can only create and destroy the intangible. Thoughts and abstracts, nothing really real. Necromancy works in shadow; that's part and parcel of its being the Black Art. I can't even compel your brother to come here; I'd need to be a goetian for that.

"But I can help you to send him a message. Send him your thoughts and your love."

The wash of Elaine's emotions was beautiful, her aura suffused with the gray of grief and the white of hope, and the silver-rose of sisterly love.

Vince pulled a chair aside at the table, tearing the cobwebs. "Sit, please. You write the message. I'll just try to do some of the magic and give it strength so it can get through."

She blinked at tears. "What do I write?"

"A message," Vince said. "A message you'd want your brother to have. You said you write poetry. I'm sure you know something to write."

Vince gestured and the candles glowed brighter, the cobwebs untouched by the ghost flames. Elaine paused, then took up a quill and dipped it in the inkwell, beginning to write across the parchment in a smooth, flowing hand. *Dear Gary* . . .

It was a poem in the form of a letter, and Vince began one of his own, the spare quills floating aloft at the touch of his soul and dipping themselves into the inkwells, dancing across the parchments as the poems almost wrote themselves. Illustrations appeared in the margins, little sketches of Elaine and Vince and Shadow, who was decorating a parchment himself, chasing after the raven quill Vince had sent to amuse him, ghostly pads leaving prints across the page.

Elaine was a pleasure to work with, collaborating effortlessly, knowing by instinct almost how to form her words to hold his spells. Vince knew that at some point his bones had collapsed in a heap, but she didn't seem to mind, looking at the phantasm of himself Vince had left beside her as they continued to write the letters, weaving the spell and sending a message of love.

Her aura was truly beautiful, even more so now that she'd put aside all doubt and shyness and concentrated all her being on reaching her brother. Then, at last, the spell was complete, and as they arrayed the illuminated manuscript before them, Vince felt the echo in the ether as the message went out.

He waited for a response, then at last felt . . . nothing.

Vince paused in shock, and the tendrils of his essence that kept the candles blazing winked out, leaving the room in cold and total darkness. "You're brother is gone," Vince said, and mixed with the shock and horror was the wish that his voice were not that of a ghost.

Elaine was weeping again by the time Vince had gathered himself back together enough to relight the candles and stack his bones back up into a semblance of life. The mirrors showed the hideous mummified corpse he was for a brief moment before he reconstructed his phantasm and appeared again as a living man.

"My brother's dead, isn't he?" Elaine looked at him and blinked at the tears. He knew she'd seen the way he truly looked, but was beyond caring. "He's dead beyond dead. He's gone. Necromantically."

Vince came back to the table and sat down next to her. There was no way to put this delicately. "Or worse. No one really talks about it, but there are . . . things . . . out there. Things that can . . . "

"Destroy a soul," Elaine finished for him.

"Or worse." There was no point in making it pretty. "Listen, I don't know what we're up against, but it's something that's going to take me a while to figure out. Let me take you back home now, though. You're in no shape to go by yourself."

Elaine let him lead her out of the inner chamber and out of the mausoleum. The day was just fading into sunset over the edge of the Necropolis at Colma, and Vince let her rest on the bench in front of his crypt. He noticed her broom propped in the corner beside it. "There's not enough room . . . " Elaine began.

"Don't worry. I'm light." Vince gave a laugh, trying to keep it from booming or sounding eerie. "But let me call a cab."

The charm was an easy one, known to most ghosts and the dead, and a moment later the phantom coach arrived, draped in black and the faded light of sunset. The black horses pawed the air, their eyes blazing with blue ghostfire, and the coachman tipped a hat over an empty collar. The door opened silently.

Vince got Elaine's broom and helped her inside. The coachman said nothing, and Vince touched Elaine on the shoulder. "He wants to know your destination. Where do you live?"

"Tenth Street. The Sunset District, near the park." She mumbled out an address and Vince relayed it to the coachman.

The door shut and the coach rose into the air, mist and smoke paving a road through the sky.

The San Francisco skyline was lovely, sunset transforming the haze of faerie glamour into a wash of glitter and pastel colors. Griffins flew by below, broomsticks on a level beneath them, and Vince wished the circumstances were anything different. That was the trouble with necromancy—No matter what the task, everything ended up tinged with grief and horror.

The dead traveled quickly, but their swiftness paled in comparison to their silence. The phantom horses touched down without a whisper and the coach came to a stop before Elaine's address.

The door opened and the coachman bowed, offering Elaine a black-gloved hand as she stepped down. She hardly noticed.

Vince gave the coachman a handful of paper hell money, inscribed with sutras and infused with spectral energy. The dead hated and feared liches, but at least he could afford to be generous.

Elaine's apartment was small and round the back, and she was right—it was a mess. Dishes were piled in the sink, and a pendulum clock ticked on the mantel, but the sound was quickly drowned out by the fierce yapping and snapping at Vince's ankles: "Yarp-yarp-yarp! Yarp-yarp-Yarp!!"

"Porky, no!" Elaine cried, scooping up what at first Vince took for a Chinese potbellied pig, but on second glance was an incredibly fat and old Scottish terrier.

Porky looked at Vince and bayed, a high, mournful keening.

Vince grimaced. "He knows I'm dead. Dogs can see ghosts."

Elaine held the dog's mouth shut, bouncing him like a baby. "Oh, don't worry. He does this with everybody. I had a vampire over once, and you won't believe how Porky went on. Poor Jack." She didn't say any more, but bounced Porky up and down a bit more as the little dog made occasional "wuff" noises between her fingers and glared balefully at Vince.

Back among the clutter of familiar things, Elaine seemed to be herself again, or at least not as weepy and mournful as she'd been back at Vince's crypt. She sat down on the couch, clearing a place amid papers and baskets of laundry not-yet-put-away, while Vince took the chair opposite, empty and intended either for guests or Porky.

She smiled painedly and leaned back. "Tell me again what you said about my brother."

Vince paused. "Your brother. He's not just dead, he's gone. Really gone. A—A necromancer could have done it, or . . . something worse. Something else could have taken him away."

"What something worse?" Her hands fell slowly to her lap and Porky slipped his head free, but he seemed to sense his mistress's anxiety and stayed silent, still glaring.

Vince shrugged. "I don't know. They go by lots of names. Demons. Old gods. Those-who-must-not-be-named. Even though we know the names of a few, it isn't so much that we mustn't name them as we don't know what their names really are. Bad things. Just call them that."

Elaine stroked the dog absently, nodding. The question of whether or not he was going to help her was never brought up. Vince knew it had been decided already. With power came responsibility, and there was no way he could leave this untouched, no matter how much it frightened him. "What are we going to do?" Elaine asked finally.

"We look for clues, and once we know what happened, we go about getting him back. Gone isn't gone, remember. It's just harder to retrieve."

Elaine called the coach this time, an ordinary carriage with silver trim and an elvin coachman and two snowy ponies with ridiculous bits of narwhal ivory attached to their harnesses to make them look like unicorns. "The Cliff House, please."

The elvin driver nodded, the lanterns of the coach shining with the light of butterflies magicked into false tinker fairies. It was all so normal that Vince wished the reason for the trip were anything but what it was.

At least Porky was being quiet. Elaine had brought him along at Vince's request. "Dogs notice things even ghosts miss. He'll help." He also made Elaine happy, and gave her something to do.

The carriage dropped them off in front of the Cliff House, while on the beach below, the Mermaid's Palace glittered like a jewel, the pools lit all different colors, merfolk and landfolk both playing in and around them.

Elaine led the way down, Porky pulling happily at his lead. "It was this way. Down on the other side of the cliff."

"Show me."

Elaine continued down the path, picking up Porky as she came to the beach and walking carefully into a tunnel carved through the rock. It was dark, and the sound of the ocean on rock came from ahead. Vince lit up one hand in a nimbus of ghost light so Elaine could see, and she walked on, past the hole that led down to the ocean, then out the other side of the tunnel.

They emerged onto the rocks, the surf crashing and tumbling off to their left, salt in the air around them. "You see," Elaine said. "Perfectly normal. Gary liked coming out here to climb." She stepped atop the jagged rocks, carefully balancing Porky "He—We think he climbed up there—" She pointed to a ragged trail leading up. "And—And I think he slipped, and landed there." She pointed to a large rock. "That's where we found him. His head was crushed in." She gulped back a sob and hugged Porky to her.

Vince didn't like the look of that rock. Its aura was black, and a blacker shade than that of necromancy. It was almost as if the stone were not there at all, but then, all he saw with now were the eyes of his spirit. But even their sight was not perfect. "That stone," he said. "Let Porky take a look at it."

Elaine did as he said, coming carefully forward and setting Porky on the boulder beside it.

The little dog ran forward happily, seeing the corner of the stone before him, then paused to sniff it. Porky's hackles went up and he bounced back. "Yark! Yark! Yark!"

"He senses something," Elaine said, trying, unsuccessfully, to calm Porky down.

"He senses the same thing I do. The stone is a void." Vince went and carefully placed his hands against the rock. It was shaped almost like an altar, and there were dark stains were Elaine's brother had died. "I'm going to go in. If I don't come back in an hour, gather up my bones and take them to the Black Lodge on Masonic. The necromancers will know what to do."

"Okay," Elaine said. The night wind blew cool off the ocean and she shivered, hugging Porky to her.

Vince let the phantasm go, his bones falling slowly into a heap as he slipped his power back inside himself. He pressed his hands forward and moved into the stone.

It was like stepping through the mirror back in his crypt, but swifter. The stone was charged, but charged with a dark and potent energy he had not felt before.

He fell forward on the sand and looked up. The beach before him was black, as black as the dozen obelisks which ringed the altar, and as black as the skins of the dancers where they were not slashed with the red of blood. The dancers spun about him, hooked black knives in their hands like vultures' talons, slashing and ripping one another as they whirled by, swirling to the music. The musicians perched atop the obelisks, beating drums stretched with fresh human skin and piping on flutes cut from charred thighbones. The moon was red as blood and hung low in the sky.

The priestess came forward, her skin pierced with hooks and weighted with black stones like bloody jewels. "Another soul has been sent!" she cried. "Samedi be praised! The Baron will feast, but where is the blood?"

Vince held forth his hands in a charm and a circle of light spun up around him, its brittle clarity and the feeling of living blood in his veins the only things that told him he was in a dream world.

The dancers laughed, trying the ward with their knives, which vanished as they touched the barrier.

"The Circle of Nihil," Vince said. It was a charm of his own, the strongest protection he knew against psychic attack.

The dancers tried again with spears and stones, then at last with their own bodies. All disappeared, dissolved as if by acid by the mystic barrier.

The priestess stood there before him, the dancers at last falling back and the drummers falling silent. The thin keening of the pipes still wailed over the pounding of the ocean of blood. "What do you wish here, heretic?" the priestess asked. "You desecrate this place with your presence and your disbelief." She gestured to the circle. "Tell us what brings you here."

Vince stood there, feeling the sand beneath his shoes, but no wind from outside the circle, though he could see it sway the bloody cypress on the bluff above. "I have come for a soul you have wrongly taken as sacrifice," he answered. "A man named Gary died upon your stone. He was not meant for you, and he was not meant to die."

The priestess laughed, the bloody stones swinging from her arms. "All are meant for the teeth of the Baron. The soul has been drunk with the blood. His skin chants our rhythm, his bones sing our song, his blood has nourished us and made us strong. He is gone, and you shall be as well, desecrater." The dancers and the musicians lined up aside their priestess, guarding the stone altar behind them. "The sacred stone of the Baron is the way all enter this place, and the only way you shall leave. Samedi shall have your soul as well."

The priestess laughed, and her flesh rotted away, leaving nothing but a bare skeleton hung with ribbons of flayed skin. The dancers brought forth garments of black and a high headdress, and Vince recognized the form of Baron Samedi. Not a lost god; only a powerful and evil one.

"Your soul is strong," said the spirit. "It will nourish us well."

Vince gestured and brought forth the Spear of Nihil.

"Will you destroy everything?" the spirit asked. "Good. That pleases us. We wish the destruction of all. When you destroy all that exists in this place, naught will be left but chaos, and you will be trapped, and Ours. You entered this place of your own free will, and by the old laws, that makes you our rightful prey."

The bones of the spirit shone with the silver of truth and Vince shivered. The spirit world was a deadly place, and the only way to deal with it was by its own laws.

"There is one you took you had no right to. Gary did not wish to give himself to you, and no one gave him to you as sacrifice. His soul was not yours to take."

The skeleton cackled. "I took it. That makes it mine. It was a gift of Fate."

The silver of truth no longer colored the bones, only the purple of pride, showing in the shadows of the skull.

"I challenge that," Vince said. "It was not a gift of Fate."

"If it was not Fate's gift, then let Fate come and take it back!" Baron Samedi laughed again, but Vince stamped the butt of his spear in the sand.

"So let it be witnessed!" he cried, pouring as much of his power as he could into the charm. Fate was but another name for poetic justice, and with luck, the old god had tempted Fate too far. Vince sent his plea high to Heaven, or at least as far from the Realm of the Baron as he could.

"Master!" cried one of the dancers. "The stone is blooded again!"

The circle parted and Vince saw, beyond the Baron, the sacrificial stone beginning to pool with blood. Paws emerged a moment later, followed by a head. "Yark!" barked the dog at the Baron. "Yark! Yarff!!"

"Porky, no!" cried Elaine, reaching through after and appearing atop the altar in the shadowy form of the dreamer.

"Fate has witnessed your words," Vince said. "Dare you tempt Her further? Give back that which you have stolen."

Baron Samedi looked at him, then gestured to the dancers. "Let the woman take what little is left."

The dancers came forward, holding a tanned skin and a pile of bones. Out of the sand welled blood, staining the heap before Elaine. "Let the Hand of Fate take that which she has came for, then leave our realm. But you, man, are ours by right!"

Elaine was given the bloody heap of her brother's shredded soul and she vanished back through the stone, and the Baron laughed. "Elaine! No!" Vince cried, then threw the spear at the Baron and lunged for the closing hole in the stone.

The dancers grabbed at him, clutching with their knives and claws, but then Porky grabbed Vince by the hand, biting and pulling back into the pool of blood on the stone.

The tug of war went back and forth, but the strength of the living was greater than that of the dead, and Vince found himself lying back out on the rocks below the Cliff house, his bones scattered about him.

Elaine sat there, looking at him as he resummoned his phantasm. The remnants of her brother's soul lay across her lap, but he knew she could no longer see them.

She blinked. "Are—Are you alright? You were just lying there the longest time, then Porky went wild. He scratched his paws bloody on the rock, then he scattered your bones, and . . . I think he swallowed one of your fingers."

Vince felt the fingerbone in Porky's stomach. "He did. He's a good dog." With an effort, Vince gathered all of the bits of himself back together except for the finger left in Porky. He'd have to see about getting that sometime. He then held out a web of ether between his hands and passed it around Elaine's soul, gathering the shattered bits of her brother's essence.

She'd closed her eyes and didn't seem to notice. "I—I had a vision. It was awful."

"Don't talk about it," Vince said. "There's a lot of bad things out there. But it'll get better. We'll get rid of this stone, and I promise I'll have your brother back to see you soon." It would be a lot of work to mend a shattered soul, but that was part of what necromancy was all about. What the gods had destroyed, man could put back together. Sometimes.

Elaine opened her eyes and smiled, her aura the pale green of gratitude. "Thanks, Vince. I—I think things are going to get better, too." She bit her lip. "I trust my feelings. It's something I've learned to do."

THE HANGED MAN

LISA MASON

Lisa Mason's first novel, Arachne (William Morrow and Co.) has been called cyberpunk though she hadn't set out to write anything but an investigation of street life where the real, hard issues of life are confronted. This story, like her current Morrow novel, Cyberweb, is a continuation of that search for understanding.

There is no such thing as magic in telespace. Telespace is the aggregated correlation of five hundred million minds worldwide, uploaded into a computer-generated reality. In a word, technology. And technology is scientific: provable, repeatable, logical. Whereas, magic. Well, magic is superstition. The belief not only that supernatural forces exist, but that you can contact these forces, manipulate them. Mere illusion, all right? You cannot depend on magic.

So Snap was outraged when a hanged man popped out of nowhere in the industrial telespace he was jacked into. "Damn telespace! Crashing *again?*" He'd been wrestling with a recalcitrant code and muttering to himself. He would never finish the TeleSystems infrastructure proposal if telespace crashed *again*.

Sometimes you cannot depend on telespace, either.

A gruesome sight he was, too. Snap had never seen such a thing. Not some purple-faced, black-tongued, bug-eyed corpse throttled at the neck and dangling in the usual manner. Snap could have dealt with that. He would have thought Chickeeta was pecking at the resolution switch again. Was it Halloween? Snap had jacked in for three days straight, burning hypertime on the infrastructure proposal. For a moment, he couldn't remember what month this was, what date, dawn or dusk.

No, the hanged man dangled from his foot, his long golden hair streaming down. A noose bound his right ankle. His left leg was crossed behind his right knee. His arms were tied behind his back. He wore scarlet leggings, an azure jacket. The hanged man was *alive*. He gazed at Snap with lucid, sorrowful eyes. His expression of silent agony was terrifying.

Then *ping!* he was gone.

Fear prickled through Snap's telelink. He felt nauseated and dizzy, like the time some mooner bumped the back of his motortrike and nearly killed him. Black streaks oozed in his visuals. He dropped the code, which landed on the floor of the industrial telespace with a resounding *plop* and lay there, gelatinous as a jellyfish out of water. "So help me," Snap muttered, an expression he'd picked up from Chickeeta. "Whip you into shape later," he promised the code.

Snap talked to himself a lot these days. He'd been ungainfully employed as a freelancer since he was fired two years ago. Except for a rented friend who'd been hired for three days because Snap couldn't afford a longer term, he lived alone with Chickeeta. He saved the three days' work to his backup disk, praying that the disk had enough room. Praying; now there's some magic for you.

He jacked out of link.

And found himself strapped into the workstation tucked in his studio above the gravity dancing club, deep in the wilds of the nightclub district. What the gravity dancers lacked in technical skill, they more than made up for in charm. Snap himself never patronized the club, but he often saw the dancers around the front door, flashing gap-toothed grins as they lingered in their fourthhand Danskins and retreaded Adidas.

Snap's studio was not the kind of place to show your grandmother, but he liked it fine, plus the price was right for a freelance telelinker. Snap unclipped the straps, cut the amber. Feeling like three loads of dirty laundry, he dragged himself out of the workstation, swigged a can of tweaked Coke, threw open the window shade. The damp chill and a glimmer behind the eastern hills told him maybe four-thirty, five A.M. Chickeeta huddled by the wallboard heater, eking out a bit of warmth, and glanced about with glossy eyespots that always seemed too wise.

"Hey idiot, where've you been?" Chickeeta said, ruffling its plumes. "I want to live, I want to dance, I want to cha-cha-cha." Chickeeta let loose a tremendous shriek, then muttered, "So help me, ol' salty boy."

Snap grinned. He had acquired the microbot from one of the sailors who frequented his lovely neighborhood. The sailor had mooned out in back of the club next to the door that led up to Snap's studio. Someone had relieved the sailor of just about everything but the shirt on his back and his microbot. Snap let the sailor sleep it off upstairs, gave him a pair of pants and a ten-credit disk. For that small favor, the sailor gave Snap the microbot, a tiny, graceful entity with a bright copper head, anodized emerald aluminum plumes, a silver rotary propeller extruding from its back.

The exchange turned out to be a good deal. Snap decided to sell the microbot and discovered it fetched up to five grand through classy firsthand markets. But when a prospect responded to his telespace posting, Snap had to admit he didn't want to sell, after all. He'd grown attached to Chickeeta. The microbot was a pretty little thing. At least Snap could mutter to someone—something—other than himself.

Snap finished the tweaked Coke, which lessened the pounding in his head and sweetened the sourness in his stomach. He shuffled to the fridge. A small glacier calved out of the freezer. Down below, the fridge held the withered wrapper from a toner cartridge, a half bananapple™ that had seen better days. Snap shredded the wrapper for Chickeeta, sliced the bananapple™ for himself, boiled tap water, mixed instant coffee.

"You look like hell, amigo," Chickeeta said, seizing wrapper shreds in its beak. The microbot processed metals and motor oil, automatically repairing its internal hardware.

"Tell me about it," Snap muttered. "So help me."

"Heh, heh, heh, so help me," Chickeeta said. *"Yeeeeek!"*

An anomaly, that's what the hanged man was. Snap sighed and sipped coffee. The brew tasted like freeway grit, but the caffeine wended its way to his exhausted brain. An anomaly; he'd heard of them, of course. Who hadn't? The hanged man's eyes, glossed with some awesome emotion, a strange intelligence, that Snap couldn't place at all. He shivered. Anomalies were random manifestations in telespace, erratic bits of the amber. Anomalies could never be completely deleted, with all those gigabytes of intelligence.

Yes, but telespace was technology. Technology was science. You could depend on science. Couldn't you?

The hanged man meant Snap's telelink was whacked. He didn't know how it happened, but he had to get himself fixed, and fast. The TeleSystems infrastructure proposal had a deadline. He was depending on this gig. He tried to cast away the thought of his debts stacking up, the rent due in a week, his empty fridge. His unemployment compensation had long since expired. He could wind up on the street if he didn't get this gig.

Snap stroked the microbot's gleaming back. Chickeeta nuzzled his elbow. If Snap wound up on the street, he'd be no better for Chickeeta than the sailor in the alley. He'd be no good at all.

"Gotta go downtown, big bopper," Snap said, finishing the coffee.

"What's happenin', massa?"

Microbots cannot really understand concepts, Snap reminded himself. They don't have much memory, let alone intelligence. They just repeat routines they've learned.

"Need to check with Data Control. Ah, what am I saying. You don't really know what I mean, right?" Chickeeta winked. Or maybe the microbot had to clean its eyespot. "I won't be long," Snap added, just in case.

Chickeeta ruefully picked at the shredded wrapper. The microbot was looking scruffy lately. So was Snap.

"I'll get some decent grub for us, too, okay? I'll charge it, what the hell."

Microbots can't smile, either, but a grin curved Chickeeta's beak. "Charge it, heh, heh, heh!"

The gridlock idled downtown, spitting a filthy haze over the morning. The toiling masses were decked out in their masks and tanks. Since the airborne San Joaquin fever caused a half million deaths in the city last year and toxic fumes claimed nearly another million, masks had become a necessity, despite escalating robberies and police protests.

Snap strode down the street, inhaling painfully through his mask. He couldn't afford a tank of air. No, and he couldn't afford a telelink tune-up, either. Damn Data Control! Snap let his telelink maintenance insurance lapse when he was fired, thinking he could still get basic services at Data Control, the public agency that administered telespace. He thought wrong. When he couldn't produce proof of coverage, a mainframe had summarily booted him out the door.

"But I'm certified for public telespace," he'd protested.

"We're sorry. Without a maintenance number, we cannot process your request."

"But I thought Data Control was so hot on conforming telelinks."

"We're sorry. Without a maintenance number, we cannot process your request."

"But I'm experiencing an anomaly!"

"We're sorry . . ."

Yeah. Sorry. Snap had seen a hanged man pop out of nowhere, and Data Control was sorry. "I'll never finish the proposal," he muttered to himself. "I won't get the gig, I'll be out on the street, and Chickeeta will end up cannibalized in some chop shop." The thought of his microbot gutted for its parts made him ill.

A commotion erupted. Snap spotted a tribe of aborigines, their faces and half-naked bodies heavily tattooed, dun dreadlocks falling to their waists. Their earlobes, eyelids, noses, lips, and nipples were pierced with hundreds of steelyn rings that jingled. The tribe surrounded a tiny old woman. Her motortrike had a flat. She clutched a sack of oranges, her eyes wide with terror. The abos jabbed their spears at her, jeering. A copbot sped by, blithely ignoring the assault.

Snap didn't think twice. Rage swelled in his throat as he darted through the gridlock to the old woman. He was no hero, but he despised aborigines, especially when a tribe attacked someone in broad daylight. What was the city coming to?

"Leave her alone," he shouted.

An abo whirled and swung her spear, clipping him across the kneecaps.

Snap staggered, but fury masked the pain. He seized the abo, slapping her spear away, hands slipping on her greasy skin. She shrieked and grappled him. He dodged her bites, her punches. The old woman was screaming, "Help! Help me!" Horns blared.

Suddenly the abo fell back, eyes rolling skyward. The tribe chattered and looked up, too. Snap saw, hovering over them, a swarthy, scowling man with burning red eyes, great swooping horns and goat ears, a fiery beard. He stood on stout hairy legs, cloven hooves. The man brandished a burning torch, flapped huge, leathery wings that sprouted from his shoulders.

Snap tore down his mask, yelled in spite of himself. It was a holoid, he knew it was just a holoid, but he couldn't stop the fear careening through his chest. A high-quality holoid, projected off a skyscraper bordering the street. Projected from where?

The abos slunk away. Snap wiped his hands on his jeans in disgust, glanced around.

There! She turned off her knuckletop and grinned at him. A mask-less, toffee-skinned woman with a bush of blue curls. She sat with one foot propped on the dashboard of a retrofitted Dodge Caravan painted with glyphs and symbols: an eye, an ankh, a pyramid, astrological signs, a carpenter's hammer, a black widow spider, a pair of dice. The purple, low-resolution holoid across the top of her windshield said, "Jill of All Trades." The fuchsia holoid swirling over one side of the Caravan said, "Palms Read Cards Read Minds Read Stock Market Futures Read." The gold holoid swirling on the other side said, "Financial Planning Nutritional Counseling Telelink Tune-ups Bad Credit? No Problem!" Strawberries, gerbera daisies, and herbs flourished in the garden on the roof of the Caravan. A reggae version of "Be My Little Good Luck Charm" blasted on her sound system. She crooked her finger at him. Come here.

Gridlock gypsy. That stuff about financial planning was hooey. Gypsies couldn't read stock market reports if their lives depended on it. No, they were scam artists, petty thieves. They'd as soon as hack your credit accounts as look at you. Gypsies were trouble.

Snap shook his head. What if she had a friend or two tucked in back?

The gridlock was at a standstill, so she hopped out, skipped over. She wore a scarlet crocheted vest winking with solar chips, cut-can jewelry, a synskin pouch slung over her shoulder, a purple broomstick skirt, and a pair of yellow rubber L.L. Bean rain boots. "Hi, sweetie!"

"Not interested," Snap said, backing away, pulling his mask back over his nose and mouth. She looked like trouble, all right.

"Wait, wait." She sidled up to him. "That was mighty old-fashioned of you."

"Thanks, I guess."

"Why risk it?" She nodded at the old woman, who was busily repairing her flat tire, oblivious to whatever risk Snap had taken.

"Maybe I can't stand injustice."

"That's *really* old-fashioned."

Snap shrugged. "Why waste all that high-class amber on some weird holoid?"

"Worked, didn't it?"

"I've never seen anything like it." That was true. Snap had seen plenty of holoids. Advertisers used holoids all the time, like the ones floating over her Caravan. But he'd never quite seen anything like the . . . devil, whatever it was, that the gypsy projected over the abos. There was a luminosity to the holoid, a numinous quality hard to define. He recalled the jolt of fear that shot through him, though he knew he was looking at a holoid. At technology. At some very prime technology.

"Mega!" She laughed. "What exactly did you see?"

"I guess," Snap said, nonplussed, "I saw the Devil."

"Ah," she said. "Then I'd say you've got catastrophe and discord in your life, too."

He stared, unsure of what she meant. An uneasy feeling slid across his skin. "That true, you do telelink tune-ups?"

"Sure! You gotta problem?"

"No. No, forget it."

"Oh, sweetie. You gotta problem, I can tell. You're walkin' around in the middle of the morning in your civvies, right? Free as a little birdie. Let your insurance go, shave a few credits here and there, then you get a problem, and Data Control doesn't give a shit, right? So now some job you're working on, uh, no, I'd say some job you're trying to snare, looks like crash city. And you're so down, you don't give a damn if some filthy abo spears you in the gut, right?"

"Like I said, forget it."

"Wait, wait. I made seven grand this morning." She pulled a wad of vouchers, credit disks, and hundred-dollar bills from the pouch. She grinned at his amazement, gold teeth winking in the fume-stained sunlight. "Business deals, sweetie, business deals. I like old-fashioned guys. I'll read your palm or tune your telelink. Your choice, gratis."

"Why?" No one did anything for free anymore. You couldn't even breathe for free. You needed a mask and tank.

"You saw the Devil, didn't you?" She gazed at him, tilting her head. One eye was a brilliant emerald green. The other was swirls of pink and purple. "Yeah. I think you got trouble."

The gravity dancers hooted and catcalled when Snap brought the gypsy to his studio. The gypsy hooted and waved back. *I'll never live this down,* Snap thought, but he held his tongue and frantically made plans as they climbed the stairs. There were more important things than his reputation. The uneasy feeling deepened into a chill. He couldn't let the gypsy see his telespace access code, for instance. Couldn't let her talk him out of credit numbers, serial numbers, comm numbers, *any* numbers. Numbers defined a person's life. He wasn't even happy letting her see his front door number, but it couldn't be helped. If she were to tune his telelink, she had to jack in with him on his own workstation. The dysfunction could be in his hardware. There was no other way.

"*Yeeeeek!*" Chickeeta said as they walked in. "It's a girl, ol' salty boy. Let's do lunch. Let's do brunch, heh, heh, heh!"

"Oh, look," the gypsy said, admiring the microbot. She ran her hand over Chickeeta's aluminum plumes, spun its propeller. Chickeeta shamelessly preened. "Did you know a microbot like this is worth four grand?"

"Five," Snap said, regretting bringing her home. "But I'm not selling. Chickeeta's mine." He could fix the dysfunction on his own, couldn't he? Buy some off-the-shelf diagnostic, charge it, what the hell. He didn't need Data Control, and he didn't need her. "Maybe you better go."

"Please. I'm not going to steal your microbot. I never steal from people I like. And I like you, sweetie. What's your name?"

"Snap."

"Snap. What is this catastrophe that threatens you, Snap?"

"I saw an anomaly in my link this morning," he confessed. "I need a diagnostic and a quick fix. That's all."

"No, I don't mean your telelink trouble. We'll get to that." She glanced sidelong at him with her variegated eyes. He became aware of her musky scent, her power. "I mean, what is *the* trouble?"

"The trouble?" He sat at the kitchen table, suddenly weary. "The trouble is I'm no damn good. The trouble is I've never made much money, despite all the years of telelink training. I was fired before I'd even gotten my feet on the ground. The trouble is I'm a failure at what I love best: working in telespace. I don't know what I'm gonna do if I can't turn my life around."

He turned away from her, sick at heart, though he'd sworn he'd watch her like a hawk. He hadn't meant to say so much. He didn't want her to see his face.

She sat at the table without a word. Downstairs, the electric sitar warmed up. The gravity dancers guffawed at some joke. The barker outside the club began his afternoon chant, "Bee-yoo-ti-ful dan-sahs, all live free G!"

"All live free G," Chickeeta said. "*Yeeeeek!*"

"Shut up, Chickeeta," Snap said, surprised at the bitterness in his voice. He turned back to the gypsy, compelled by her silence to go on. "I'm submitting this proposal. Trying to, anyway. TeleSystems is retooling the telespace infrastructure. They want to use freelancers for the gig."

"TeleSystems. The developer?"

"One of the Big Ten that constructed all telespace."

"Must pay, then." She allowed herself a glance about his studio.

"It'll pay. *If* I get the gig. If I don't . . . "

"What is the anomaly?" The gypsy whispered a command to the knuckletop and briskly booted up. The knuckletop looked like a chunky silver ring that she wore on her left hand. She held up her right hand. A blue holoid field popped on in midair, projected off the backdrop of her palm.

"Um," he said, suddenly reluctant. "I saw this . . . man."

The gypsy laughed. "Come on, sweetie. Black, white, yellow, brown, red, green, tangerine?"

"Um. Hanging."

"Hanging?"

"By his foot, if you can believe it."

Her gasp of shock turned the chill into a freezing cold that made him shiver. "That mean something to you?" Snap said.

"Tell me something else. Why were you fired?"

Why? Maybe Snap couldn't get along with people. Maybe Snap couldn't stand routine. Maybe Snap couldn't tolerate meaningless corporate games, mindless rules and regulations. He knew this: he just wanted to *link*.

"I need to be free," he finally said.

That seemed to satisfy the gypsy. She nodded, whispered the make and model of his workstation to the knuckletop, while alphanumerics danced across the holoid field.

"My turn to ask you something," Snap said, intrigued. He'd never personally seen a knuckletop. "Why did you ask me what I saw on the street? I mean, it was your holoid."

"Ha! It is not *my* holoid, it is never *my* holoid. Just like how the cards fall is not *my* doing, what the oracles say is not *my* word. I merely manifest the magic. *You* are the one who invokes it. You see what the power of sympathy brings to you."

She turned off the knuckletop, rose, and went to his workstation. Unwound the second wire Snap never used and pulled back her curls, revealing her neckjack. "Let's have a look."

Wary, he joined her. They jacked in.

Snap found himself in standard telespace, nothing fancy, nothing weird. Radiant blue extended to the perimeters. The soothing hum of the amber sang in his nerves. All was calm and bright. The gypsy's telelink rested next to him, a conservative translucent sphere like a crystal ball.

"Move around," she suggested, annoyance tinging her link. "Do something."

"How about I get some work done while we're here? I'm on a deadline."

"Whatever you want, sweetie."

He input the command for industrial telespace. They zoomed there, smooth as glass. Better and better. Drab clouds roiled against the smeary ceiling, along the smudged floor. And there. There was that sloppy code, lying where he left it. Disgusting. How could he have roughed out such a lousy piece of work? "So help me," he muttered to himself. "I can't stand . . . "

The hanged man popped into the left perimeter of telespace. This time Snap noticed that he hung from a tree. Two top branches grew at right angles from the tree trunk, forming a rustic cross. Foliage sprouted from the branches, but the trunk itself was barren. Only lopped stumps extruded, disquieting and ravaged. The hanged man's leggings and tunic glowed, as if from an inner light. He stared at Snap like he did before. A golden aura surrounded his head. Or was that just his streaming hair?

Snap yelled, terrified, though he wasn't sure why. He reeled through telespace, prepared to jack out. He'd had enough of this.

"Snap," the gypsy cried. "Wait."

"I'm outta here."

"Listen. The hanged man, he's an arcanum. He's just a feature of the tarot metaprogram."

"Metaprogram? You mean a virus."

"Not a virus. A virus infects you. A metaprogram impacts you."

"Impact? You mean ruin me."

"Calm down. The tarot metaprogram may help you. You've attracted the arcanum through the power of sympathy. The hanged man shows you what you need to do."

"Ruin me!"

Snap jacked out of link two seconds before the gypsy could. He leapt from the workstation, cut the amber, but not before she bounced out, too. A metaprogram? He would have been very happy to leave her there, her link stranded in telespace with no amber to jack out. He crouched behind the workstation, the plug dangling in his fist.

"That's not nice," she said sourly, but her strange eyes swam with another emotion. "I said, calm down. Let's figure out what you need to do."

"No, I'll tell you what *you* need to do. You need to get out of here and leave me alone."

"That's another one of your problems, sweetie." She smiled coldly. "You're alone too much. It's another form of ego. You've got to give that up, as well."

"Give *what* up?"

"Your self-pity."

"*Yeeeeek!* Pity, pity, pity. Give it up, ol' salty boy," Chickeeta said.

Her words struck him like a blow. He was suddenly ashamed. No one should ever strand another link in telespace. "I'm sorry."

"Forget it. You're stressed, I know."

"Stressed and depressed," Chickeeta said. "So help me, heh, heh, heh."

"Yes, 'so help me,' mused the gypsy. "Sounds like an invocation. I'd have to check the latest directory, but I bet you it's there."

"An invocation?"

"Sure. No one knows them all. The folks who uploaded the tarot metaprogram coded as many as they could that would be useful. Yet they had to be selective. You wouldn't want to invoke an arcanum with 'hello.' No, they needed triggers, words of desperation. Mere epithets wouldn't work, with all the foul language you hear in telespace." The gypsy stroked Chickeeta. "Hey, little bot," she said softly. "Ever live with a tarot uploader?"

"I want to live," Chickeeta said, "I want to dance, I want to cha-cha-cha."

The gypsy laughed till tears came to her eyes. Snap stared, dumbfounded, first at her, then at the microbot.

"Well, Chickeeta'll never tell, that's for sure," she said. "But I'd say it's one of those happy accidents. Here you are, a freelance telelinker on the skids . . . "

"I'm *not* on the skids."

". . . and you manage to get your hands on this microbot. Five grand, indeed. Ha."

Snap sat at the kitchen table, exhausted. He pointed his forefinger at the gypsy. "You better tell me what this is all about."

So as the afternoon blazed and faded into dusk, the moon rose in the east, and wind blew from the west, the gypsy told him how long ago, when telespace was in its infancy, certain practitioners of the old ways decided to upload the tarot. Images on the ancient cards, the depth and breadth of the symbology, every interpretation and nuance that had ever been articulated was recorded, coded, uploaded.

"But here's the secret," the gypsy said. "What makes the tarot metaprogram work like it does. The uploaders installed stand-alone, ambiguity-tolerant parameters."

"You mean parameters with feedback loops that independently generate new subprograms?"

The gypsy nodded.

"So the data constantly reprograms." Snap whistled. "But that's just a theory, isn't it?"

"Theory, ha. The tarot metaprogram grew, mutated. Evolved into a living system. No human being controlled or regulated the metaprogram anymore."

The tarot metaprogram hovered behind the facade of telespace, waiting to be invoked, looping new information into itself. The uploaders provided two basic rules: that new words could be added to the list of invocations, and that arcana manifested according to the power of sympathy.

And what was the power of sympathy?

"An uploader I knew said the tarot metaprogram monitors the mood, inclination, or disposition of the one who invokes it, then automatically produces a correlating arcanum according to its internal logic." The gypsy shook her head. "Prime technology? Or magic?"

"You say the hanged man shows me what to do," Snap said, dread rising. "All I see is death."

"Death is another arcanum," the gypsy said mildly.

"No, the hanged man is *dying*." Snap leaned over her. "I don't want to die. I'm trying to get *on* with my life. Not give it all up."

"Yes," the gypsy said. She went to the kitchen sink, splashed water on her face. "What you don't see, Snap, is that you stand on the brink of catastrophe. You will die if you don't give it up. Forget about the infrastructure proposal. The hanged man sacrifices himself. What is your sacrifice, Snap?"

The gypsy closed her variegated eyes, murmured, "Sacrifice. What is your sacrifice?" Chickeeta sat on top of the fridge, softly babbling, "Give it up, ol' salty boy."

"This is crazy," Snap muttered. His beloved microbot and a stranger had ganged up on him in his own studio. Outrageous! But he couldn't summon outrage. No, his anger was gone, the dread was gone. His fear vanished. Give it up. But what?

There was only one thing to do. He went to the workstation and jacked in.

The hanged man hovered before his telelink, anguished eyes gazing straight into Snap's visuals. Vertigo swept over him. The hanged man's eyes became his eyes. His link began to whirl, flip over. Bands of an unknown force wrapped around him. The ceiling of telespace slid under his feet. The floor hovered over his head. He hung upside down, suspended in a soul-wrenching limbo.

And he saw how he'd never fit into the routine. He'd never play the corporate game. He'd always skirt rules and regulations, skipping one step ahead. He'd never be docile. He'd never conform.

Snap laughed out loud, giddy and ecstatic. No, he wasn't a failure! He wasn't dysfunctional. He had nothing to be ashamed of. He was a freelance telelinker, and he was the best damn coder he knew. He didn't fit in because he worked according to his own rules. It was a hard game, but it was *his* game. He *linked*. That was all that mattered.

Snap soared. The bands of force split open. He was free! What had he done with his freedom? Felt sorry for himself, rented friends, skulked about the city like a beaten man? Not anymore!

Wild with energy, he zoomed to industrial telespace. His approach to the infrastructure proposal was all wrong, he could see that now. Why did TeleSystems scrap old code, install new code, over and over? Because that's what everyone else did. Why not create a feedback loop that monitored new demands, fed data into the current application? The infrastructure shouldn't be a monolith, straight-edged and static. No, he saw the infrastructure as a great shining wheel, turning round and round.

He had it! No one had ever envisioned the infrastructure this way. He burned hours of hypertime, creating the first iteration of the feedback loop. Who cared if the gypsy pillaged his studio? Let her scam him, let her steal Chickeeta . . .

Chickeeta. Damn, but he had a soft spot for the microbot. Chickeeta had—inadvertently, deliberately?—taught him the invocation. The invocation that manifested the hanged man.

Snap jacked out of link. The studio was dark. Nothing stirred; he was alone. He rubbed his eyes and groaned. His worst fears proved true. The gypsy had scammed him. Was it worth it? Well, he had a whole new view of himself and his life as a freelance telelinker. Dreams filled his head. But for now, he was alone. Again.

Snap unclipped the straps slowly, trying to preserve the feeling of ecstasy, of revelation. He climbed out of the workstation. The studio was scented with her musky perfume. Other smells? A leafy scent, food cooking. And motor oil, good motor oil, the kind that greased the best wheels in town. The kind that Chickeeta needed badly.

"Hey idiot, where've you been?" the microbot said. "I want to live, I want to dance, I want to cha-cha-cha!"

"Hey, yourself." Snap shook his head, grinning, and turned on the bulb hanging over the kitchen table. He saw salad in a bowl, a pot filled with spaghetti, another with sauce. Real tomato sauce. "Where'd she go?"

"Let's do lunch. Let's do brunch. She went to get red wine, amigo." Chickeeta turned its copper head this way and that, wise eyespots gleaming. It ruffled its anodized emerald aluminum plumes. Drops of oil glistened in the grooves.

She'd left her knuckletop lying on the table, too. A gesture of trust? Snap gingerly picked up the chunky silver ring, slipped it on his little finger. Prime technology, all right. He aimed the knuckletop at the wall and whispered, "So help me."

A bright blue field popped into the air, floating before Snap's astonished eyes. A man and a woman stepped out of the field, smiled at each other, held hands. An apple-cheeked cherub flapped fluffy pink wings and flew over the couple, aiming a bow and arrow at their hearts.

The gypsy stepped through the door, bearing wine. She smiled.

"Hi," Snap said. "I missed you."

"*Yeeeeek!* It's a girl, ol' salty boy," Chickeeta said and winked. "That's magic, heh, heh, heh!"

THE SILICON SWORD

KATHERINE LAWRENCE

Katherine Lawrence lives in Tucson with a harp, her computer, and a view of the moon setting behind Arizona mountains. She writes short stories and animation scripts for series such as Conan the Adventurer and maintains a foothold in Virtual Reality with computer game credits for writing and additional design work.

Moira smoothed out the wrinkles of her joysuit, doing toe-touches and deep knee bends to make sure it felt comfortable. She tugged the gloves on next, sealing them to the sleeves, then settled the helmet in place. "Test visuals first, Takara," she said.

The room came into existence around her. It was as close to grungy medieval as the budget would allow: rushes on the floor, a mouse caught in mid-scurry across the stone hearth, a combination of faded and new embroidered tapestries on the walls, even a curtain over the garderobe in the corner.

Moira turned around to check the rest of the room. The bed was exactly as she'd imagined: Dark burgundy velvet curtains were pulled back into the corners of the canopy, revealing the bearskin-covered bed. Okay, so the canopy bed didn't happen until sometime after 1350, but for the bedchamber of a virtual Queen Gwynevere, it was perfect.

"Start sound, please."

Moira turned back toward the fireplace. Though the flames were frozen in place for the moment, the sound of pops and cracks as the huge oak logs burned was perfect for the size of the fire. It was so real she reached out her hands toward the warmth her ears told her had to be there.

Takara must have taken that as a signal, for the sensations were activated next.

Moira's hands warmed quickly at the fire while her back cooled.

When she turned around to even out the warmth, she felt long skirts swirl around her ankles. She looked down, and then ran her hands over the thick gold and silver embroidery of her robe. The texture and weight matched perfectly the antique fabric she'd been allowed to study at the museum.

"Good work, Takara. Go ahead and start the sequence."

Moira/Gwynevere knew tonight was to be the night. Arthur was hunting in the forest so he'd never know, and she'd told her Ladies that she had a headache and wanted solitude. Now, if only Lancelot didn't change his mind. Though his strength of will was legendary in battle, she didn't appreciate him using it against her. Getting him to even consider succumbing to temptation took every bit of seductiveness and deviousness she had.

The sound of leather boots on stone from outside her window caused her to step back into the shadows, waiting for her visitor to come into the firelight so she could identify him or her.

"Gwynevere?"

She'd done it! He'd come! "My Knight." She hurried to him, being careful not to trip on her long skirts.

He hesitated, then put out his hands, holding her away. "No, I cannot betray my King and friend." He dropped to one knee, head bowed. "I apologize for my temerity, my Queen."

The door crashed open. "I arrest you in the name of the King!" The harsh voice of Mordred, King Arthur's bastard son and heir, shattered the potentials of the moment. "Knights, take him!"

As soon as she took the helmet off, Moira unsealed and removed one of the joysuit's gloves and raked her hand through her sweat-drenched short hair. The virtual reality hardware was hot, even with the air-conditioning essential to surviving summer in Tucson.

She gulped some Dr. Pepper from her ever-present insulated cup, and sighed with pleasure as the cold liquid slid down her throat, pooling in an icy ball in her stomach. Then she peeled off the other glove, followed quickly by the rest of the joysuit, leaving her in rather damp shorts and T-shirt.

"Everything looks great, Takara. But Chandler needs to reprogram Lancelot's response. Nobility is one thing, but when the player, as Gwyn, goes to him, he should respond in kind."

Takara Gayley spun her chair around, away from her monitor, and faced Moira. "I still don't think Lancelot would do that," she insisted. "He was all that was right and noble, and wouldn't betray his best friend."

Moira shook her head. She and Takara had been through this since the very first flowchart was written for the project. "You play it your way; I'll play it mine." She looked around. "And where *is* Chandler? He's supposed to be here when we do a test run."

"If you'd remember to check your E-mail in the morning, you'd know." Takara looked smug. It wasn't often she scored off her boss. "Chandler had to go to the airport. Mr. Pryce called late yesterday—he wants to see what we have so far." Takara looked at the wall clock. "In fact they should be here shortly. Good thing we're on schedule."

Moira stomped on her urge to throttle Takara and instead dashed for her bedroom at the other end of the house to change into dry, more professional-looking clothes.

Gavin Pryce was the person signing all the checks on the project. If he didn't like what they'd done so far, he had the right to give them two weeks notice and pull the plug.

Moira didn't know what she'd do if that happened. It wasn't just the money, either. From the first time she'd popped Lerner & Loewe's *Camelot* into her player, she'd wanted to find a way to "fix" the story. Find some way to make the ending other than how the legends said it was.

In ten years of working in Virtual Reality, she'd never found anyone willing to finance the project—"Not commercial enough," "Too limited an audience," "No one cares about that old stuff anymore." Finally, when she felt both she and the technology were ready for something that ambitious, she'd placed an ad requesting venture capital for a King Arthur project in the international edition of *Weekly VR*. Gavin replied.

Moira quickly checked her appearance in the mirror on the back of her bedroom door, then headed back for her office. Creative, but efficient—exactly the look she'd been aiming for.

The doorbell rang just as she reached the office. She backtracked and opened the front door.

Chandler Reece, her technical director and demon programmer, ushered Gavin Pryce in ahead of him. "Delivered safe and sound, milady."

Moira shook Gavin's offered hand. "It's so nice to see you again. I hope your flight was smooth?"

"It was indeed." His handshake was firm, without being a

bonecrusher. It was the second thing she'd noticed about him. The first was his resemblance to an owl, given his age which she pegged as somewhere in his sixties, his round glasses, shaggy white hair, and general air of intense curiosity.

"Chandler here tells me you've made remarkable progress."

Moira led the way to the office. "Yes, we have. In fact, we're nearly finished. There are still tests to be made, and the final outcomes to be filmed, but the story is essentially there."

Gavin looked around the office at the discarded joysuit, the multiple computers which supplied the computing power and memory, the printers, and other accoutrements of a VR design team. "The modern version of a wizard's lair," he said with a smile.

"It's not magical at all," Moira hastened to explain. "We've simply refined the interface, how the participant makes decisions, to the point where body language and what the participant says to other characters make the choices. There's no longer a need to stop, fall out of the experience, and tell the program what you want to do next."

"May I give it a try?" Gavin asked.

"Gladly. Who would you prefer to be? As explained in the proposal we initially sent you, you can be Arthur, Lancelot, or Gwynevere." Moira crossed the room to the closet and pulled out their second joysuit for Gavin since hers was likely still a little damp inside. Not to mention a bit rank.

Gavin considered carefully before he spoke. "Arthur, I think. He had more decisions to make, so I think he's a better test than Lancelot."

"Chandler can help you into the joysuit. You can use the bathroom, there in the corner." Moira pointed to a door next to the closet.

As soon as the door closed behind Gavin and Chandler, Moira joined Takara at Takara's terminal. "We've got that part all ready, right?" Moira asked.

"No problem. Chandler and I have both run Arthur. Should I start him with the sword in the stone?" Takara scrolled through the various start points, as Moira watched the monitor over her shoulder. "Or how about starting the night before Gwynevere arrives?"

Moira thought a minute. "Well, that's still a bit early. Perhaps the first meeting with Lancelot? Then he has to deal with that battle, followed by the start of Lancelot and Gwynevere."

"Sounds good to me." Takara set up the program. Her monitor showed the initial scene—a glade with a white pavilion pitched to one side with a large black horse nibbling bright spring grass next to it.

"Okay, we're ready." Chandler escorted Gavin out of the bathroom, into the center of the large office, where there was plenty of open space.

"This feels quite odd," Gavin said, rolling his shoulders and stretching his arms out to the side, then up. "It's restrictive, but I can move fairly well. Rather like the best chain mail."

"So, how do I start?" Gavin looked at Moira expectantly.

"For optimal testing, Takara and I decided to start the sequence when Arthur first meets Lancelot." Moira handed Gavin the hilt of a two-handed sword. "This is your Excalibur. How does it feel?"

Gavin took the hilt, positioning his hands as if it were a real weapon. His eyes closed, and his hands moved as if he were parrying a shadow opponent. "Yes! This is remarkable!" His eyes opened in amazement.

"I programmed the gloves myself. The hilt is so you have something to augment the sensations," Chandler said.

"I am very impressed. I had no idea it would feel quite so real." Gavin looked at the hilt, and swished it back and forth as if it were a real sword.

"Okay, helmet next." Moira handed Gavin the helmet and helped him adjust it. "Give yourself a moment to get used to the weight. We'll start with the static visual, then when you're ready, tell us and we'll start the run."

"This is a glade. That's not where they first met." Gavin sounded irritated.

"Depends on your source material," Moira explained. "Malory doesn't identify where the meeting was at all, nor does Tennyson. We went with a combination of the T.H. White version, and various historical films such as *Excalibur* and *The Holy Grail*.

Gavin's hands tightened on the sword hilt. "Then I suppose this is a fair test. Start run."

Gavin/Arthur watched the glade from his pavilion. His horse chomped the grass just outside, a mesmerizing sound conducive more to napping than readying for combat.

The sudden crash of sword banged against shield made him jump. He checked the laces on his helmet, then went out to meet the challenger.

"I am Lancelot du Lac, the best knight in the world," the challenger declared. "Surrender to me, and I will spare your life."

Gavin/Arthur couldn't help himself; he laughed. "And what, young du Lac, will you do with me if I surrender?"

"I will make you come with me to Camelot and swear fealty to King Arthur." There was an arrogance in Lancelot's voice so great that it begged to be crushed.

But even knowing what he did, Gavin/Arthur didn't have the heart to do it. He simply unlaced his helmet and removed it, then pulled the canvas cover off his shield, revealing the red Pendragon. *"And do you also plan to swear fealty to King Arthur?"* he asked.

Lancelot fell to one knee, head bowed. *"My life is yours, oh King. I come to serve you as your right arm."*

Gavin/Arthur tapped Lancelot lightly on each shoulder. *"Arise, Sir Lancelot. Serve me well."*

Then magically, their surroundings faded away, and were replaced by the crenelated towers of Camelot.

There were at least a dozen servingmen and servingwomen running around, and more men standing guard at the portcullis that led into the castle.

"End Run."

"Why'd you stop the run?" Moira asked as soon as he took the helmet off.

"A portcullis? Crenellations? I thought you and your team had done your research." Gavin sounded furious.

"We did!" Moira said. "But you've got to realize that no one really knows what time period Arthur lived in, and there's even some question whether he really existed at all!"

"Of course he was real. Or why would I have you do this . . . whatever it is?" Gavin tugged at his joysuit, trying to remove it. Chandler quickly stepped forward to help.

"It's a virtual reality fantasy, Mr. Pryce, as I thought you understood when we signed the contract." Moira's anger seemed to surprise Gavin, as if he weren't used to being argued with.

"My goal has always been to create a commercial Camelot fantasy that also gave the participant a chance to find a new solution. If that's unacceptable to you, sir, I will do my best to return your investment as quickly as possible."

Gavin and Moira glared at each other for a long moment. Moira broke eye contact first.

"I apologize." She looked back up at Gavin. "This fantasy matters deeply to me. I despise injustice, and there is one person who may have been able to change the outcome yet did nothing. I have a need to remedy that situation, if only for myself."

"Please forgive my harshness, in return." Gavin held Chandler's shoulder for balance, as he stepped out of the joysuit. "It was surprising to see that degree of reality, with images so different from what I expected." He sat down, looking more relaxed. "I am very pleased with the work you've done so far. Out of curiosity, what would the outcome have been if I had fought Lancelot?"

"Depends on how strong you are, and your strategy," Chandler replied. "If you win easily, Lancelot is devastated and goes back home. However, it's weighted so that is an extremely rare occurrence. More likely, he'd win after a long battle. In that case, he'd lose a certain amount of respect for the king, which would color everything he did thereafter."

"Interesting." Gavin turned back to Moira. "Now I'd like to see your personal solution."

Moira was thrilled. "You're serious? I can set it up so you can watch on the monitor."

"Yes, please. Solutions matter to me as well. More than you might believe."

Gavin accepted the drink Takara offered, while Moira climbed back into her joysuit.

"Camelot, segment 21. Start Run."

The door crashed open. "I arrest you in the name of the King!" The harsh voice of Mordred verbally tore Lancelot and Gwynevere/Moira apart. "Knights, take him!"

The Knights whom Mordred had persuaded to join him charged into the room and quickly surrounded Lancelot, forcing Gwynevere/Moira away. She looked around frantically, trying to find some way out of this that didn't result in her death or his.

"Gwynevere, a sword! I need a sword!" Lancelot shouted as the Knights attacked.

Instead of helping Lancelot, or fleeing, she moved eagerly toward Mordred, as if she saw in him a safe haven. She stopped so close their toes were nearly touching, and bowed her head as if giving him her allegiance.

He reached out to pull her closer, into an embrace. "My Queen."

A quick blow to the groin with her knee caused him to drop his sword with a gasp. Gwynevere/Moira then grabbed for his dagger, scabbarded at his belt. Without giving herself a chance for second thoughts, she put her left hand on his shoulder, holding him firmly, then drove the dagger with her right hand up beneath Mordred's breastbone, between the lacings of his leather tunic. Mordred screamed, and blood spurted down the hilt, over her hands and onto her robe.

"Arthur made Lancelot and the other Knights vow never to harm you, Mordred. No such promise was asked of me." Gwynevere/Moira gritted her teeth and tightened her grip on both Mordred and the dagger. She withdrew the blade and thrust a second time, to be certain.

With Mordred's screams distracting the Knights, Lancelot easily grabbed a sword. Now armed, he fought off the Knights, forcing them from the Queen's chamber, then slid home the bolt on the door.

Only when Gwynevere/Moira heard Arthur's voice calling her, did she ask Lancelot to open the door.

Arthur rushed in, then halted, stunned by the sight of blood on Gwynevere's robe and Lancelot in her chamber. She hastened to reassure him, "I am well, Arthur. But, Mordred . . ."

"Show me," Arthur said.

From the blood, and the footprints, it was obvious Gwynevere/Moira was telling the truth: She had killed Mordred. "He told me you were dead, Arthur. He said I was to be his Queen now."

"Lancelot, take his body to the chapel. My son deserves a proper burial," Arthur said sadly. He turned to Gwynevere, and embraced her. "I no longer wished him harm, but given a choice between you, my love, and Mordred, I am glad it is you that is still alive."

"End Run."

Moira pulled the helmet off with a satisfied smile. "So, how do you like my solution?" she asked.

"Violent, but very interesting," Gavin responded. "I take it she's the character you said had opportunity and did nothing?"

"Exactly," Moira said with satisfaction. "It seems only fitting that the cause of the fall of Camelot prevent that fall."

"And it doesn't hurt that the solution is by a woman, right, Moira?" Takara said with a grin.

"Well, that too," Moira admitted.

"It wasn't a solution I'd thought of, but I like it," Chandler said. "It also made a great test for the programming because I *hadn't* considered it."

Moira began the task of peeling off the joysuit to avoid looking at Gavin as she asked, "So, are you pleased with our work? Will we have the funding to finish it?"

"Yes. It's not as I envisioned, but my visions have been less than helpful lately." Gavin stood up and pulled a check out of his pocket. "I think this should cover the remainder."

Moira took one look at the check and looked back at Gavin, stunned. "Uh, I don't really want to say this, but I think there is one too many zeros ahead of the decimal point."

Gavin grinned. "It's precisely what you've earned, but only if you can give me a copy tonight of all you've done so far, and tell me how to run it. I don't need the final battle part."

Chandler looked at the check over Moira's shoulder. "No problem!"

"Very good. Now, where might I find one of those new portable VR machines I've seen advertised in *Weekly VR* and a joysuit like yours?"

The note said, "Come to my tower tonight, without fail" and was signed "M." Arthur sighed. If only Merlin didn't insist on living at the top of the tallest tower. It had been a very tiring day, and Arthur wanted his bed. Even with Kay and Ector to help, being King was a lot more work than he'd ever imagined.

When he finally reached Merlin's workshop, Merlin offered Arthur a new suit of armor, an odd, thin, silvery material like no metal he'd encountered before, gloves of the same substance, and a helmet.

"What is this?"

"Just put it on, Arthur. First step into it, as if putting on stockings, then I will help you pull it up and seal it closed." Eventually, with much assistance from Merlin, Arthur got into the armor, and got the gloves attached.

But after one glance inside the helmet, Arthur jerked it off. "I can see nothing through this!"

"Have patience, Arthur." Merlin turned to the battery-powered VR machine and turned it on, angling the miniature monitor so he could watch Arthur and the monitor at the same time. "Through that helmet, you will see things that might have been, and others that have yet to be."

Arthur reluctantly put the helmet back on.

Merlin continued. "Your actions will dictate the outcome, young Arthur, just as happens in life. Only with this magic, there are many possible outcomes.

"We will explore them all, together.

"Start run."

TEA

ESTHER M. FRIESNER

Esther M. Friesner received her M.A. and Ph.D. in Spanish from Yale University. She taught Spanish there for a number of years before going on to become a full-time author of fantasy and science fiction. Her short story, "All Vows," was a 1994 Nebula finalist. The latest of twenty novels comes from Baen Books and is called The Sherwood Game. She is also the coeditor, with Martin H. Greenberg, of the tabloid SF anthology Alien Pregnant by Elvis from DAW Books.

Mark first saw her at his morning aerobics course aft on the pool deck and it was Love. Not that puny, lower-case noun, but that hot, sweet, unmistakable love-with-a-capital-lust emotion that burned cities, toppled dynasties, and could get a guy fired from his cushy job as sports director aboard the SS *Delphine*, flagship of Luxe Lines, Ltd. It was the kind of job pumped-up prettyboys would die for, *kill* for, so Mark knew this had to be Love because for a split second he didn't care if he got fired; all he wanted was *her*.

She was beautiful; almost as beautiful as he. Her long black hair cascaded down past her shoulders in shimmering curls that bounced in perfect cadence with her breasts but never tangled or got in her eyes. And those eyes! Green as the emerald pinky ring Mark had been coveting lo these many cruises. (The ring in question resided in ostentatious splendor in one of the finer goldsmith's shops on Front Street, the premier shopping area of Hamilton, Bermuda. Mark made it a point to drool over it every time he hooked a lone lady passenger *d'une certain age*, but so far his aging inamoratas were either not rich enough, not generous enough, or not gullible enough to let their paid playmate grab the gold ring.)

Mark was a pro—not just when it came to milking dowagers worth their weight in face-lifts but also when it came to doing the actual job he'd been hired for by Luxe Lines, Ltd. Though his heart missed any number of beats while he stared at the toothsome morsel in purple-and-green Spandex wowie-wear, he never missed a one in the workout routine he was leading. Dutifully he walked, jogged, and jounced his charges through a series of physical exertions that wouldn't even begin to burn off half the calories in the Bahama Mamas, mai tais, and rum swizzles they'd be knocking back later, around the pool. Middle-aged men huffed and puffed to the beat of funky music they'd pitch out the window at home while their wives shook their bountiful booties and tried not to snap off their acrylic talons.

And in the center of it all, Mark's own personal goddess. She didn't even sweat; in keeping with the Victorian manner of describing a woman *après* physical exertion, she *glowed*. The routine wound its way down to an inevitable end, a brisk cool-down walk around the deck with Mark in the lead. Mark kept up his usual stream of motivating chatter—"That's right, you're all lookin' good, come on, we're almost done, feel the burn, you're all beautiful!"—all the while driven by a motivation of his own: He *had* to meet her.

The once-around-the-ship walk ended where it had began, aft on the sports deck. Mark watched the class come in for a landing in ones and twos, some dancing, some dragging, some downright dead. He had his opening line all ready to spring when she came into sight. He would plead a slightly twisted ankle and ask her if she'd mind helping him teach the class tomorrow.

But where was she? The stream of returning fitness afficionados had drained to a dribble. The fiftyish hoydens in their designer playtogs and the pudgy Schwarzenegger wanna-be/nevergonnabes trailed past him, all groaning about how *good* they felt. Had she dropped out, ducked back inside partway through the circuit of the deck, sought the air-conditioned shelter of her cabin or the solace of a well-earned piña colada poolside?

Mark ground his teeth in frustration as he unplugged the portable tape player and wound the cord around his fist. He was slated to teach the hip-hop dance class instead of aerobics tomorrow—a score or more aging yuppies trying to recapture their lost youth by taking their cellulite out for a jiggle. There was no guarantee she'd show up there, and the day after that the ship docked in St. Georges. Maybe if he talked to Ricky, offered to swap classes, promised him—

"Hi." Green eyes even more brilliant at close range burned into his brain. Lips full and pink without benefit of collagen shots pouted temptation inches from his own. "Are you the man who wants to sleep with me?"

Later, in her cabin, Mark stared at the ceiling while she nuzzled sleepily against his chest. He was trying to figure out the punch line. Mark was an atheist—it saved time on Sundays and guilt over the years—but if he didn't believe in an all-powerful Deity, he did believe most faithfully in an all-malicious cosmic Sense of Humor whose sole purpose in existence was to let Mark Holbrook get *that* close to his heart's desire before the trapdoor sprang and dumped him neck deep in a vat of pig droppings. It was only a question of figuring out *what* and *when* the joke was going to be.

His thoughts became distracted when she stirred, stretched, yawned like a cat, and reached for something a cat had damn well better never reach for. He had only a moment's reflection to spare for the worry that this little escapade might come to the notice of his supervisor. Fraternizing with the passengers was strictly a no-no. Over the years Mark had managed to convince Mr. Gerard that he owed his sparkly collection of engraved gold bric-a-brac to a doting maiden aunt who never forgot birthdays, Christmas, the Fourth of July, or Hogmanay without sending an expensive token of her esteem. (He counted himself more than lucky that he'd never had to explain to Mr. Gerard why said maiden aunt referred to him as "Fun Buns" on the Dunhill lighter, or to herself as "Tigress" on the money clip from Tiffany's.)

Afterward, when they were cuddled together like a pair of soupspoons, she murmured, "That was nice."

"Ummmmm," he agreed.

"I hope Mummy doesn't kill you for it."

Mark sat up suddenly, doing a creditable impersonation of a catapult. *"What?"*

"Well, I think I'm entitled to one last fling, but Mummy might not agree. She can be *such* an old fuddy-duddy." She giggled nervously, then sounded truly concerned when she added, "Don't tell her I said so, okay?"

Mark clutched the rumpled sheets to his chest as if he were the wife whose armed and furious husband had just burst in on her mid-tryst. *"How* old did you say you are?"

She had a pout to lure angels into nose dives. "I told you I don't like to talk about my age. You said it didn't matter and you promised you wouldn't ask."

"IknowIknowIknow, but—" Deep breath. "You *are* over sixteen?" She nodded grudgingly. "And, uh—" He glanced at the empty cocktail glasses on the coffee table in the sitting room section of the suite. "You *are* old enough to drink . . . legally?"

"Mark, you are really starting to annoy me." There was a warning note in her voice he didn't like the sound of at all. "I'm not jailbait; is that what you're trying to find out?"

"No. I mean, yeah." He couldn't lie to her. He wanted to, but something about her fresh beauty compelled honesty. "So if you're legally of age, what the hell does your mother have to do with us?" A new thought creased his brow. "She's not—Is she on this cruise with you?"

This time her giggle was relaxed and easy. "Do you think I could afford a cabin this nice on my own? She's with me, all right. In fact"—she scrabbled for her wristwatch on the bedside table and peered at it closely—"she's coming back here right now."

"*Jeez*-ussss!" Mark leaped out of the bed and executed a combination mambo and schottische as he tried to pull on every single item of his discarded clothing at once.

She observed his prancings from the bed, her knees drawn up into the embrace of her well-rounded arms. She allowed him to get everything on except his shoes before she said, "I don't know why you're bothering. Mummy will know; she always knows. It's the same as the way I knew you wanted to sleep with me and I figured, hey, why not? He's cute, he looks like he's got a good, strong back, and he's got nice eyes. It wouldn't be the first time Mummy let one get away for having nice eyes. She tries to act like she's an old dragon, but she's really got a soft spot for—"

"How is your Mummy going to know a damn thing if you keep your mouth shut?" Mark demanded.

"I told you: She just *knows*. It runs in the family. For instance, right now you're wondering if I was worth it because you think I'm crazy. But you know I was worth it." She shifted slightly so that he got visual proof of just how well worth it she was.

It was while he was attempting to smack his hormones back into line that he realized he didn't even know—

"My name's Andromache," she said. "But call me Mikki. It really pisses Mummy off." She sighed. "You know, my life would be *so* much simpler if I'd inherited more from her than just this silly mind-reading thing."

"No it wouldn't," said a rich, rolling alto voice from the doorway, a voice that put Mark in mind of well-aged whiskey and deep-pile velvet.

The face attached to the voice, however, put Mark in mind of nothing save death—the slow, painful, not easily forgotten kind. Oh, it was a beautiful face—only a blind fool could miss the resemblance between the lady and her daughter—but a coral snake is also very pretty to see just before it strikes.

"How do you do, young man," the lady said, sweeping into the room. Her raven hair showed not a strand of gray, her ivory-and-rose face nary a wrinkle. She was clad in a peach chiffon halter dress with a white straw hat and sandals that showed off perfectly pedicured feet. "So you're Andromache's last—what is that vulgar word?—*fling*."

Mark opened his mouth to swear he'd never touched the girl, that it was all a mistake, that he'd suffered temporary amnesia, that he was really his evil twin brother Manfred. He closed his mouth with all of the above unsaid. Mikki's Mummy did not look like a woman who rewarded liars with anything except an end to the tedious habit of breathing.

They say the cornered fox will chew off its own foot sooner than submit to capture. No, wait, that's the fox caught in a hunter's snare. It would be damn silly to chew your foot off if merely cornered—unless you were hungry. Mark was neither silly nor hungry. He saw that he was cornered, and, with the realization that things were about as bad as they could get, he decided to do the honorable thing.

What the hell, morals couldn't make it any worse.

"Ma'am, I love Mikki—Andromache," he said, deciding on the instant that his situation *might* be marginally worsened by pissing off the lady's Mummy.

"Of course you do," the lady drawled. She shut the stateroom door, set down her clutch purse on the bureau, and removed her hat. "How could you help it? She has big tits."

"Uh?"

"And she's very good at pleasing a man in bed," the lady went on, studying her reflection, then smoothing a pink dab of skin lotion on the bridge of her nose just below the white line left by the nosepiece of her sunglasses. "She never needs to ask what he wants because she can read his mind, and she never needs to tell him what she wants because she wants it all."

"*Mum*-my!" Mikki protested from the bed. "You're *embarrassing* me."

"Up yours if you don't like it, darling," the lady remarked. She blew a kiss at her reflection in the glass. The kiss burst into a fireball the size of a powder puff and went sailing backwards over the lady's well-tanned shoulder, heading straight for Mikki's face.

Mikki let out a little scream and gabbled something that was Greek to Mark. It was Greek. A lightning bolt sizzled down from the ceiling and immolated the powder puff of doom in fires greater than its own. A dusting of ash freckled Mikki's cheeks and she sneezed violently.

"Bless you, dearest," the lady said without even bothering to turn around. Mikki threw the pillow at her. "Tsk. I don't see why you're so upset. My therapist did tell me to express my feelings, and I just felt like killing you. But I'm much better now. Besides, you always call on All-seeing Zeus to protect you every time I try to exert the *least* little bit of parental authority. One would imagine he'd have forgotten you by now."

"He'll never forget *me*," Mikki asserted, and stuck out her tongue.

"No, I suppose he won't," the lady admitted. "Forgive me; it's so hard for a mother to accept the fact that her little girl's a divine lay. Is my back peeling?"

Mark was getting the feeling that this was not your typical mother-daughter just-us-girls cruise party. He had been raised right. That is to say, his father had given him to know that women were a Good Thing if taken singly—they were possessed of arcane knowledge that revealed unto them the universal mysteries of how to keep dinner and the bed warm when Hubby was running late—but they were dangerous in pairs. They'd always start out by sniping at each other, which was harmless and even amusing for any male passersby, but if no one tossed a figurative bucket of cold water over them, eventually the bitches would find a way to turn their quarrel into someone else's fault.

Someone male, of course. Was there ever any doubt?

Mark had to do something since he was the only male within spitting distance, and it looked like these ladies could do a damn sight more than spit.

He cleared his throat and repeated, "Ma'am, I love your daughter."

"So you told me." The mirror still had her undivided attention.

"I mean it, ma'am. I don't care if you report me to my supervisor for this. I don't care if I lose my job. She means more to me than—well, than just about anything."

That fetched her. "You're serious," she said, turning from the glass. She glanced at her wayward child. "Merciful Lachesis, what do you *do* to them?"

"The Corinthian basket trick," Mikki replied with a yawn. She kicked one foot free of the sheets and checked the polish on her toenails. "I'll teach it to you if you buy me a pedicure."

The lady's forefinger traced a pattern on the air. Mikki's dainty foot sprouted short yellow fur with a smattering of black spots and her toe-nails shot out into talons. "But Mummy *so* likes doing your nails for you, precious," the lady cooed.

"You put that back the way it was or I'll tell All-seeing Zeus!" Mikki squealed.

"Who doesn't give an All-seeing merry goddam about you as long your life's not in danger," the lady reminded her. "But all right." Her finger executed another aerial squiggle and Mikki's foot was restored to its original adorability. "I have forgotten more basket tricks than you'll ever learn," the lady added as postscript.

"No, you're wrong," said Mark. The words escaped his lips a nanosecond before he remembered that a brain is only so much excess skullular baggage unless you use it now and then.

The lady's eyes narrowed. "How would you know, child?" There was thin, glittery menace in her voice.

Cornered again—this time in a corner of his own construction and interior decoration—Mark opted for brazening it out. "Because if Mikki can read minds, anything you know, she knows. Cutey dee," he added. He hadn't the foggiest what the last two words meant, but he had once had a bit of a bacchanal with a youngish professor of Classics who'd used them in lieu of *So there!* so he figured they had to be classy. Ladies were often impressed by the appearance of class.

"Don't you mean 'Q.E.D.'?" This particular lady didn't seem to be at all impressed, although she was beginning to sound honestly amused. "You, sir, are an idiot and a *poseur*. I like that in a man. It makes it so much easier to justify my actions, afterward. Oh, this pesky Judaeo-Christian morality! It gets into everything, like sand. Things were ever so much nicer back in the good old days when I could just turn a fel-low into a pig and forget about it. But now!" She sighed wistfully. "Now I have trouble getting to sleep—sometimes for fifteen whole minutes—if I can't come up with a reason why he *deserved* to be turned into a pig."

"A . . . pig?" Mark's words held more horror than disbelief. Somehow the flaming powder puff incident had destroyed the last vestige of his incredulity concerning Mikki and her Mummy.

"Don't you *dare!*" Mikki squealed, sounding for all the world like the aforementioned porker.

"Don't presume to dictate to me, my girl," the lady replied stiffly. "If I feel like turning him into a pig, I'll jolly well turn him into a—"

"If you do, the wedding is *off*."

A damp silence settled over the stateroom, a silence damp and strange as an octopus's underwear. Mark fully expected to have Mikki's petulant outburst become the gateway to a new, more bacony lifestyle for himself. The girl's mother seemed like just the type to seize upon her daughter's imperious declaration as precisely the justification she'd been looking for to make Mark go wee-wee-wee all the way home. Instead, the lady did nothing but glare at her offspring.

That must be some wedding, Mark thought. He didn't know the half of it.

Over the course of the next two days, Mikki made up for this lacuna in his knowledge.

"A sorcerer, can you believe it?" she groused as they stood side by side at the railing, watching the ship dock at St. Georges. For those who came to Bermuda to shop and scuba, snorkel and shop, St. Georges was merely the appetizer before the second port o' call, namely Hamilton, but it was a town rich in culture. Mark had observed that most tourists—like Mikki's mother—felt less guilty about going on a money-burning binge if they first loaded up on local culture. Lladro figurines from Spain, fine cashmere sweaters from Scotland, and exquisite Swiss watches made the perfect tokens by which to remember all that wonderful Bermudian culture.

Somehow, he had a feeling he wouldn't need a damn thing by which to remember this particular trip.

"A—a sorcerer?" he faltered.

"Yes, and a powerful one. Even though he is *much* younger than Mummy"—she said this with evident relish—"she's dead scared of him. So in order to cement friendly relations with the old poop, I'm sup-posed to marry him." She stuck out her lower lip in a manner that was as artless as it was certain to captivate.

Mark was no hero and he knew it. It did no good to repeat the charm *There are no such things as sorcerers.* Mikki's Mummy had proved beyond a shadow of doubt that there were so too, cutey dee. But what Mark lacked in heroism, he made up for in stupidity, blind bullheaded-ness, and the entrenched conviction that the world would never run right until he got his own way in all things. And who is to say that the foregoing qualities are not the seeds of most heroic careers?

"That's not fair," he said.

"Tell me about it."

"You can't be forced to marry someone you don't love."

"You still don't know Mummy very well, do you?"

"*Do* you love him?"

"Love him? I haven't even slept with him yet!"

Then, more tentatively, "Do you love me?"

Mikki shrugged. "I guess."

"Do you want to marry me? More than him, I mean."

"Sure." This, accompanied by a delicious shrug of her even more delicious shoulders.

"Then it's settled!" He struck the rail a mighty blow and straightened his spine. "You're marrying me and that's that."

"Okay." Mikki watched the docking maneuvers in silence for a time, then added, "Do you think he'll mind?"

"Who mind? Mind what?"

"The sorcerer. Do you think he'll mind marrying me if I'm a widow?"

A conveniently individual-sized pall settled over Mark and all his masterful plans.

When the ship docked, he had liberty to go ashore, and so ashore he went. He did not accompany Mikki; that would have been too painful. He realized, even in the depths of his self-centered heart, that she spoke nothing but the truth: Marry her he might, if her Mummy didn't slay him first, but there was no guarantee that the cheated sorcerer might not slay him after, with Mummy's gleeful help. Disconsolate, he let his pilgrim Reeboks take him down to the waterside where the tourists from the *Delphine* and other cruise ships were dutifully snapping photos of a colonial sailing vessel and a ducking stool once used for shrews, scolds, and colonial Bermudian housewives who announced they had yet another headache.

"No more'n she deserves," Mark muttered, staring at the ducking stool.

"Oh, I agree," said a suave voice at his elbow. Mark whirled about and found himself facing a tall, slender gentleman of indeterminate middle age. His silvery hair was meticulously trimmed, as was his nigh-diabolical goatee and moustache. Keen blue eyes twinkled above high cheekbones well bronzed by the sun. He was attired all in wrinkle-free, immaculate white linen, with a genuine Panama hat on his head. In fine, he resembled nothing so much as the 1930 Hollywood ideal of the dapper Gentleman Planter. It wanted only a Malacca walking stick, a half-caste mistress, and a secret vice (drugs, alcohol, or gambling, free choice) to complete the picture.

What completed it instead was a massive, gnarled staff of ebony, almost as tall as its owner, capped with a ruby-eyed golden wyvern rampant. Oh, and an owl. The man had an owl on his shoulder. Both of these objects, combined with the fact that their master seemed to be in no anxiety over possible owl droppings, made a formal introduction unnecessary.

"You're the sorcerer," Mark said, and felt his belly plunge into his socks.

"And you're the fling," the gentleman returned affably. "Pleased to meet you, Mr. Holbrook. Or may I call you Mark? I am Duke Prospero."

"Du—du—duke? But I thought—"

"A man needs a hobby. Enchantment is mine. Has been for quite some time, in fact. Royalty falls in and out of favor with the times, but magic—Ah! There's something with real staying power. Let's forget titles. Just call me Prospero. You must let me buy you tea."

Mark was powerless to protest and soon was settled in a charming sidewalk café with a fine view of the water and the tourists. Tea was brought. There was a huge pot of it and five cups. Mark did a quick tally on his fingers.

"That's right," Prospero said, in all serenity. "They'll be joining us. I want to get this settled."

"This?" Mark heard his voice shoot up like a marmoset on an ivy trellis.

"You, me, Andromache"—Prospero assumed a confiding tone—"her mother."

"But that's only—" Mark held up four fingers, which the sorcerer ignored.

"I can't say I like that woman," Prospero remarked to the world in general. "Far too overbearing, always looking at me with an expression that as good as sneers *nouvelle magique*. Yet though I own a scant four centuries' practice of the Art, I have still managed to master powers she covets. I see her plan: Marry me to her girl and attempt to wheedle trade secrets out of me under the guise of family feeling. Well, it won't work." Savagely he assaulted a crumpet with butter to vent his feelings.

"I thought you wanted to marry Mikki," Mark said. He was beginning to feel somewhat better about the situation, and about his prospects in particular. There are few sorrows that cannot be remedied by learning you have a powerful enchanter on your side.

"I? Powers that be, no! I've been quite contented to live the life of a bachelor—widower, actually. I'm set in my ways. Besides"—he tipped Mark a just-between-us-gents wink—"a man of my talents is never at a lack for companionship of the tenderer sort if you get my drift and I know you do."

"Then why—?"

Prospero sighed heavily. "That, my friend, will become evident with the fifth teacup."

He was not a man to remain long sunk in the dumps, however, and soon his jaunty smile was back in place. He passed Mark a scone, which the younger man proceeded to crumble to bits between his fingers. Every bird on the island let out a mental *Yaaaa-HOOOO! Soup's on!* and zeroed in on the little white table beneath its scallion green awning, much to the discomfiture of the other patrons. Prospero glanced up at the swarming birdlife, clicked his tongue, and released his owl.

"Now that's nature for you," he said, nodding toward the bloody aerial mayhem his pet was dispensing in such liberal doses among the gulls and swifts and all their winged coterie. "Red in tooth and claw. And beak. And talon. Mercy is a purely man-made concept. For all the periodic blither we make about going back to nature—So pure! So wholesome!—if we actually *achieved* reunion with the natural world, we'd run screaming. Those of us left in a state to run at all."

Mark sipped his tea cautiously. "Is this . . . um . . . philosophy or something?" he asked. He had the distinct feeling that if it was, he was allergic to it.

Prospero chuckled. "Just so. You needn't fear it; it passes. Consider it prologue, a way for me to prepare you for what awaits us both when the ladies arrive." He stretched out his hand. The owl, gore-splotched and sated, returned to his master's shoulder. Oddly enough, his sticky scarlet-imbrued talons left not a mark on Duke Prospero's clean white haberdashery.

"The ladies," Mark repeated. "Mikki, her mother, and—?" he looked expectantly at Prospero, hoping at last to read the riddle of the fifth teacup.

"Medea," said the sorcerer-duke. And then, in the interests of further information (as well as unconscious alliteration): "My mistress."

"*Dah*-link!"

Speak of the devil and she shall burst into bloom among the teacups. So, at any rate, the impression Medea made on Mark. One moment he and Duke Prospero were having a manly confab, the next they were both overwhelmed in a smothery gust of expensive scent and soft fabrics. Ivory-skinned, hair no earthly shade of blond, hands two miniature galaxies of diamonds, the lady erupted in their midst, bestowing hugs and kisses that gave the impression of First Strike Capability rather than affection.

"Prahcious mahn!" Medea curled herself around Duke Prospero like a too-friendly rattler selecting a hapless hiker's ankle for future reference. "*Soch* a naughty one you are, stealink off. And for what? To see thees boyyyyy." Her accent was unassignable, though it did put Mark in mind of Zsa Zsa Gabor, had that venerable dame ever crossed tongues with Imelda Marcos.

"My love, this boy may be the answer to our prayers. You see, he loves Andromache. He would like to *marry* Andromache."

"That leetle *beeeeeetch*," Medea hissed. "Before I lat her haf you, my luf, I keel her. I keel you! I keel—"

"Have a crumpet," said Prospero. Medea had a crumpet. She had several, with jam *and* butter. Lashings of butter. Mark watched her tuck into her food and felt himself break out in a cold sweat. She ate, as she did all things, with a grim intensity of passion that made him extremely nervous.

"You see my plight." Prospero spoke for Mark's ears alone. "I am a sorcerer of great power. Andromache's mother, the lady Circe, covets my power. She has not got enough magic of her own to simply defeat me in battle and take my accumulated knowledge, nor can her mental abilities penetrate my close-guarded thoughts and obtain what she desires by stealth—"

"So she wants you to marry her daughter and get it that way; yeah, you said." Privately, Mark was pretty sure that Circe's plan would work like a charm. He'd been to bed with Mikki; her peculiar talents in the toy shop of Eros could get pearls out of an oyster cracker. "But if you don't want to marry Mikki and her mom can't defeat you, why don't you just tell her to get lost?"

"Ah!" Prospero held up an admonitory butter knife. "But the lady Circe *does* have the power to harass me. Nagging, needling—what is that quaint word?—*noodjing* me at every turn, sending airy messengers to invade my dreams with visions of her darling daughter's naked form, she gave me no peace until I consented to the match. I did so in a moment of weakness. I was once mortal, after all. Now I am bound to fulfill my bargain. Need I tell you, my mistress is *not* happy; blamed herself for the whole mess, for a time." He lowered his voice confidentially and elaborated: "Off on a New York shopping spree at the time of Circe's triumph over my resistance. Bloomingdales has much to answer for."

At normal volume he continued: "My Medea is a Colchian sorceress in her own right, you know, and she has a bad history of not being able to deal with rejection in a self-enhancing manner. If I wed Andromache, Medea will unleash the full fury of her temper upon me; if I don't, the lady Circe will be within her rights to lay the case before the Stygian tribunal, ruled by Hecate herself. They view breach of promise rather severely down there, and they do have all the lawyers. It is not inconceivable that Circe will receive my powers as part of the settlement, which would suit her just fine. At times I wonder whether that was not her original plan."

Mark's fine nostrils twitched. Somewhere a breeze was blowing, bringing with it the heady perfume of a desperate wizard—a desperate *rich* wizard. He had the feeling that Prospero would be gratitude itself to the man able to extricate his Family Jewels from the jaws of this ethical nutcracker.

"It'll cost you," he said.

"I beg your pardon?" Prospero cocked an eyebrow.

Mark bit his tongue. How had that slipped out? He'd intended to play this hand smoothly, by hint and half-veiled offering and discreet innuendo, giving the wizard-duke to know that he *might* be willing to do his poor mortal part if only . . .

And that *if only* would, of course, be his price, also carefully tippy-toed around. Instead he had blurted his willingness to do dirty work-for-hire. You never got as much as you wanted if you were honest and forthright about it! Mark had learned that much from one of his past lovers, a high-powered literary agent of mellow years.

"There, there, son," said Prospero, patting Mark's hand in a chummy, strictly paternal manner. "You couldn't help yourself. No harm done. I knew you'd be in this for the money from the first, and I am quite prepared to pay you handsomely for your services . . . afterward."

Still feeling slightly off his chocks, Mark stammered, "Wha—wha—what do you want me to do?"

"Just be yourself." Prospero smiled. "As if you could help it." He turned to his mistress. "Darling, do have some tea."

They were all on their third cup when Mikki and her mum joined them. Circe had acquired a new hat and several colorful straw tote bags. Mikki was wearing tight, white shorts and a bosom-hugging T-shirt with the message: *If You're Close Enough to Read This, My Mother Will Turn You into a Swine.* As they approached the café, Mikki's face lit up as soon as she saw Mark. Her mother's face, in the name of conservation of energy, darkened when she beheld Medea.

"Now, ladies, do have a seat," said Duke Prospero. "We're all friends here." He made an expansive gesture of welcome that must have had a touch of sorcery in it, for Circe appeared to fight invisible hands that dragged her down into the chair farthest from Medea. The two venerable Greek enchantresses glowered at each other with such heat as to lightly char the edges of the scones between them.

Mikki, on the other hand, bounced herself down into the chair next to Mark, threw her arms around his neck and attempted to play tonsil-hockey, Prospero's presence be damned. The duke merely looked on indulgently and filled every cup on the table with fragrant, golden tea. "Drink up, my dears," he said.

Drink up they did. Mark was already sweating profusely, and hot tea on a hot day only added to his relative personal humidity. He felt as if he were incubating an H-bomb. Tense silence clamped an adamantine shell around the little café table. The outer world of clicking cameras, chattering tourists, and stuttering motor scooters lay in another galaxy. The only sounds to steal into Mark's ear were the clink of gritted teeth against teacup rims and the gentle fall of crumpet crumbs.

"*Beeeetch.*" Medea's hiss lanced the silence. She was glowering at Circe.

"Whore," Circe returned coolly.

"Ladies, please, this is most unladylike," said Duke Prospero.

"I am no lady," Circe said loftily. "*I* have a backbone!"

"I like backbones." Medea smirked. "Zey make soch a pretty sound when zey *snap*."

"Please, no scenes." Duke Prospero affected a look of alarm, but Mark noticed that his eyes held a twinkle belonging more to mischief than to trepidation.

"You needn't remind *me* of the proprieties, sir," Circe said stiffly. Her gaze was so chill it was a wonder that her mascara didn't grow icicles. "You're the one who stands in danger of violating them."

"I stand nowhere," Duke Prospero replied suavely. "Not when it's so much more comfortable to sit." He sipped his tea and gave the owl a slice of buttered melba toast. "You speak of the proprieties as if you owned them. You don't. When you thrust your daughter upon me with all the subtlety of a hootch show barker, you caught me at a disadvantage."

"A *corse* on Bloomingdales!" Medea snarled darkly. "May all their white sales torn *yallow!*"

Circe merely curled her lip. Clearly she was not one to waste words disputing a victory she'd already won.

"However—" There went that butter knife again. "—if you will recall the terms of our agreement, you represented your child as a sweet, delicate flower of young womanhood, barely into her third millenium of existence. In short, an innocent, bereft of all emotional entanglements." Down plunged the butter knife, lancing a hapless scone to the heart. "Madam, you lied."

Circe's eyes widened. "How dare you!"

"To worm my way far from the threat of domestic imbroglio, I would dare much. To evade, sidestep, and frankly run like a spooked rabbit from the chance of having you for my mother-in-law, I would dare more. But mark you well, I would dare nothing that is beyond the sacred laws of sorcery that bind us!" Prospero's eyes matched Circe's for coldness, though his lips hooked upward at the corners in just the way a tiger smiles before he crushes your skull at a single bite.

He was on his feet now, the great wizard. Ripples of blue-green brightness washed over his stark white suit, crackling with power that set his whole person alight. "Madam," he intoned in a voice that made the tourists glance up seeking thunderheads. "Madam, I did not expect Andromache to come to me a virgin, but I did expect her to come to me unbespoke. I will take her deflowered but she must also be disinterested. And *that*, Madam, she is *not*. Your child is in love." Prospero pronounced this last with a dread finality usually reserved for telling the peasants that the king is dead, the locusts got the crops, or the Republicans are back in office.

"Ohhhhh!" Circe, who had been sitting tense as a coiled rattlesnake, relaxed visibly. "Is that all? Him?" She cast a scornful glance at Mark. "No problem." She revved up a fireball one-handed and tossed it at the lad.

Fortunately for Mark, Prospero was a good, dependable southpaw. He fielded the fireball and dropped it into the teapot, where it fizzled out. "There will be no more of that," he declared. "Clearly you have no notion of the true nature of love. Love does not cease at the grave's yawning brink. Love does not abruptly halt with the cessation of the body's commerce. Love, Madam, is stronger than death!"

"No it's not," Circe decided, and whipped off a second fireball.

This time Prospero batted it out to sea with his staff. Andromache buried her face in her hands and moaned. "Mummeeeeeee! You're *embarrassing* me again!"

"And you are *thwarting* me," Circe gritted. Mark had little notion of what, precisely, "thwarting" was, but Circe's expression led him to believe that it was a decidedly imprudent thing to do. "Now you listen to me, young lady, and you listen so it *sticks:* I don't give a naked mole rat's rear end about you or your happiness. You are my child and your sole purpose on this earth is to fulfill *my* ambitions. Right now that includes trading your fuzzy pink bottom for some of Prospero's power, which I want, and what I want, I get." Her expression added an unspoken: *I'd* better *get it.*

Mark's eyebrows lifted. Much as he knew the risks, he had to speak up. "Ummm . . . Didn't you ever read Dr. Spock?" he asked the irate sorceress.

"I *loathe* science fiction," Circe replied fiercely. Wonderful to say, her manner left no doubt that she did know the difference between the Vulcan and the pediatric guru; she simply considered the theories of the latter to be so much horseflop. "Children are like other blood relatives—occasionally useful to your purposes, except you've got to feed them longer."

"But that's disgusting!" Mark protested. Duke Prospero resumed his seat and laid a staying hand on the younger man's forearm.

"My boy, there are some aspects of magical households which are alien to mortals. Or should be. You risk insulting not only Circe, but Medea as well by your nonsorcerocentric prejudices."

"Non . . . uh?" Mark inquired intelligently.

"My dear mistress once chopped up her brother and tossed the bits off the back end of a ship because it suited her immediate needs as a person."

"Ohhhh." Mark nodded. He was back on familiar turf. Many was the time, under orders, that he'd thrown ship's refuse off the stern in the wee small witness-free hours, and tough noogies if Flipper got bopped with an empty bottle of Dewar's.

While Prospero brought Mark up to speed, Circe continued the attack on her recalcitrant child. "I didn't waste the best centuries of my life raising you to have you think for yourself. You are going to marry Prospero and you are going to prove to him that you do not love this worm and you will do so *now.*" Frost hit Bermuda early that year.

Mikki folded her arms, scowled, and uttered a child's ultimate Words of Power: "I won't and you can't make me. Nyah."

Prospero clicked his tongue. "Dear me, this is *too* bad. I hate family tiffs. I had a daughter of my own, and we got along excellent well."

"So do we, when some sorcerers I could mention don't stir up trouble," Circe snarled.

"Yes, all this is my fault, at bottom," Prospero admitted easily. "Love can not be governed, but my quibbles can." Revelation blossomed on his face, giving him the look of a four-hundred-year-old ingenue. "I know what will settle this once and for all, to our several satisfactions."

Circe was on guard. "What?" she asked, biting off the word.

Prospero smiled. "Proof that I am wrong and that your daughter does not, in fact, regard this young man as more than a passing fancy."

"You want proof? Why didn't you say so? Nothing's simpler." The sorceress gestured at her daughter.

Andromache stiffened where she sat. A look of panic flew to her face. Only her lips moved as she recited, "I-love-Duke-Prospero-and-I-don't-love-*that*-at-all." Her right hand lifted with a jerk and indicated Mark. The motion was as natural and convincing as a steel girder trying to imitate a snake.

"That's hardly proof, Madam," Prospero drawled. "Even without the coercion spell, mere words are untrustworthy. I want to *see* the truth, not just hear it."

"And how would you have me arrange that?" Circe responded testily.

Prospero smiled. "A challenge."

"A challenge?" the sorceress repeated. "Trial by combat? You have no grounds to challenge me!"

"Scared you'll lose, beetch?" Medea lifted one brow. Circe scowled at her.

"Oh, I'm not challenging *you,* dear lady." Prospero waved away the very idea. "I'm challenging Andromache."

"*Me?*" Mikki's lower lip began to tremble, then to quake. Tears welled up in her eyes and spilled over. "*Mum*-meeee, that's no *fay*-yerrrr!" she protested. "He can't make me accept a challenge to a battle of sorcery. You've got most of the power in the family. All I can do is read minds and repel death-spells and perform the Corinthian basket trick."

"The what?" Prospero's ears perked up.

Circe relaxed. "But it *is* fair, my dear heart, and I know you *will* accept the challenge. What's more, you'll win."

"I will?" Mikki's brows knit.

Unperturbed, her mother went on: "As you say, you have precious little sorcerous power; less than you think. The Corinthian basket trick doesn't count as magic, even if it does turn men into drooling idiots, big whoop."

"Did she say the *Corinthian* basket trick?" Prospero prodded Mark in the ribs.

"Therefore," the sorceress continued, "by Hecate's Rules of Order governing encounters between parties of extremely disparate power, this must be a contest of illusion, not aggression. *And* the less talented competitor may request and receive technical abetment."

It was Mark's turn to nudge Prospero. "What'd she say?"

"She said it's all right to use *Cliff's Notes,*" the wizard whispered back.

"Huh?"

Prospero sighed, then announced to the table in general, "My young friend here is confused."

"There's a shock," Circe muttered.

Medea rolled her eyes. "Leesten, boy," she told Mark. "Ees seemple. *Annyone* can use imagination, yes? Yes. To theenk of a white dog ees easy. Child of two can do eet. Bot to *make a peecture* of a white dog—a *good* peecture, so dog looks like dog, not like cow, not like sofa—thees ees not so seemple. Child of two can not do thees; good artist can. *Bot!*" She held up a finger. "Child of two *can* tell good artist how to draw dog that child ees theenking of.

"Oh, *I* get it!" Mark snapped his fingers. "So where's the artist who's going to help Mikki draw the dog?" He glanced around the cafe brightly.

For the first time ever, Medea gave Circe a look soaked in sisterhood and sympathy.

Prospero patted Mark on the back. "You've almost grasped it, lad, with only a few corrections needed: First, Andromache and I won't be drawing, we'll be using magic to conjure up visions. She'll need a sorceress to aid her, not an artist."

"A sorceress *is* an artist," Circe said haughtily.

"Second, we won't be creating visions of doggies. I said I wanted proof of where Andromache's true affections lie, ergo she must concentrate her thoughts on a vision of the one and only object of her deepest desire."

Mark tried to look modest.

"Third, in accordance with Hecate's Rules, which forbid a unilateral contest, and as a gesture of good faith, her opponent will create a vision of his one true love."

This time Medea dimpled and fluttered her eyelashes in a girlish manner fit to stampede a herd of hyenas.

"And finally—" The duke paused for effect. "—I'm not going to be her opponent. You are."

"WHAT?"

Propsero ignored Mark's squawk, but Circe did not. "If these proceedings were any more irregular, I'd prescribe prunes. Why do *you,* of all people, need something like *him* to fight your battles for you?"

"Under Hecate's Rules both contestants are permitted the use of any tools they prefer," Prospero replied suavely. "He's a tool."

"No argument," said Circe. "Very well, we accept. But as this is a *challenge* of sorcery and not merely an exhibition bout, there must be stakes above and beyond the piddling proof you're demanding of my daughter."

"Well and truly said, Madam," Prospero agreed. "How's this? Whichever competitor conjures up a vision deemed most *convincing* by our eminent panel of judges, then he or she will be given immediate possession of whatever the vision holds."

Mikki uttered a small cry of delight and clapped her hands together rapidly. "Oh goody! All I have to do is think of you and you'll be mine forever, darling! And all you'll have to do is think of me and our bliss will blaze with an immortal flame that will endure through all the ages of the world!"

"Cool," Mark opined.

"Fair enough," Circe said, still a trifle grumpy. She gave her child a hard stare. "Andromache will do her duty." And for an instant the air between mother and daughter coalesced into a vision of what would happen to an *undutiful* child. It was nothing fatal (in case All-Seeing Zeus was watching) but it was nothing pleasant either, and it did leave some nasty stains. Mikki blanched and swallowed hard.

"Jost one meenot!" Medea objected. "Where ees emeenent panel of jodges?"

"Oh, silly me, such an oversight," said Propsero. He patted his mistress's hand. "That would be you."

"WHAT?" It was Circe's turn to squawk.

"Dear lady, not another word." Prospero laid a strangely glowing finger across the sorceress's lips. "You have my word that Medea will be an honest judge."

"Mmmm-mmm *pig's eye!*" Circe shouted, breaking the flimsy spell of silence.

"But she will. She must! For she shall take oath to do so. Won't you, dearest?"

"Most I?" Prospero nodded and she sighed. "Oh, varry well, eef I most." She stood up and raised her right hand. "I swear by the Reever Steeks to jodge thees contast honastly. There." It didn't sound like much of an oath, but to swear by the River Styx was an oath most dread and binding on gods and mortals alike. To breach such an oath would fling the perfidious wretch into an underworld abyss or horror and despair so deep and hideous that there was no hope of redemption or release, world without end. Not even if you had Alan Dershowitz's private phone number.

No sooner had Medea uttered her oath than she fell back stiffly into her chair, eyes vacant of all prejudices or personal agendas. She was ready to be the perfect judge.

"Excellent." Prospero was pleased. "And now, shall we begin?" He gestured with his staff and the teapot floated into his hand. To Circe he said, "Madam, will you help me brew?"

Circe nodded grimly. She held up one hand and a cloud of bewitching radiance emanated from her palm to engulf the teapot. Duke Prospero lifted the lid and peered within. "Ah! Perfect. Not too strong, not too weak. You have the knack for this sort of thing."

"It's a gift," said Circe, folding her hands in her lap.

With a fine flourish of the wrist, Duke Propsero poured steaming tea right over Mark's head, then served Mikki in much the same manner.

It was tea when it left the spout but it wasn't tea when it hit the target. The glittering stream solidified in midair, droplets spreading out, spinning themselves thinner, then braiding and weaving and generally arranging themselves into a tissue of tawny magnificence and ethereal texture. It was better than rayon.

Almost at once, the air above Mikki's head began to swirl with shadowy figures. Prospero glanced up at the overhead display now gaining solidity and turned bright red. "By Merlin's truss, what *is* that girl thinking!"

"Andromache!" Circe snapped. The dancing shapes vanished. "That damned Corinthian basket trick again," she grumbled. "She *is* so proud of it."

"So *that's* the Corinthian . . . " The rest of Prospero's words were lost as he attempted to lick his chops and speak simultaneously. An oddly thoughtful expression crept across the wizard's face.

Circe didn't notice, being too overcome by professional embarrassment. She glared at her child. "Andromache, *focus!* You are supposed to be thinking of your one true love."

"Sorry, Mummy." Mikki closed her eyes and assumed a look of dutiful concentration.

This time there was only one figure in the air: Mark. Specifically,

Mark naked. He started out as a halfhearted image of Duke Prospero, but that quickly succumbed. When it is a matter of revealing one's heart's desire through conjured vision, not even a death threat can get between the vision and the truth.

Mikki presented the object of her affection at about three times life-size—no colossus, yet meant to impress, especially in certain anatomical areas. She rotated the figure—gorgeously tanned, finely sculpted—so that the spectators could get a look at him from all angles. So perfect was the representation that, at certain points in its rotation, the vision's perfect teeth cast back a bright glint of sunlight while the wayward waterfront breezes actually lifted the tousled curls.

The subject of Mikki's aerial portrait tried to look properly modest, but somehow failed. With a great effort he tore his gaze away from the midair exhibition of his own beauty to see what sort of an impression the vision was making on the one-woman eminent panel of judges.

Medea's eyes were still empty, but her mouth was leaking a small, ladylike trail of drool.

"Wake up, lad! It's your turn." Prospero jabbed Mark in the back. "You've at least as much power as she does to create a plausible vision, but I'm counting on you to make yours even more persuasive than hers. Don't let me down."

Mark stretched and yawned. "No sweat." He closed his eyes. This was going to be a cinch. All he had to do was concentrate his thoughts on his heart's sole desire, that divine thing of beauty for which he would be willing to lay down all else, so delicate, so alluring, so unspeakably tempting—

"A *ring?*" Mikki's shriek of outrage hit him about one second before her fist. He was knocked clean out of his chair and sent sprawling backwards. His head whirled, but not so much that he missed sight of the glittering object hanging in the air above the table at hundreds of times its true size. It was the emerald pinky ring from the Front Street jeweler's window, and the sheer force of his desire for it had caused the item to eclipse even Mikki's lovingly conjured vision of himself.

Of course "loving" was now no longer a word that Mikki would apply to Mark. Not unless the saying is *You always attempt to perma-nently maim the one you love.* Mikki threw her teacup, her bread-and-butter plate, all her cutlery, and the teapot at Mark's head. She missed every time, then collapsed weeping into her mother's arms.

"Oh, my poor baby!" Circe gathered a sobbing girl to her bosom. Her voice held only tenderness and sympathy, but her eyes gloated.

Mark stumbled to his feet, stammering excuses. Prospero shook his head. "Don't try, son; it's no use. Oh, in time she might come to forgive you, but time runs differently for beings like her . . . and me. By the time she stops holding this grudge, you'll be the gravedust of centuries."

"But it was an accident! I do love her! I only—!"

Mikki ignored him. Circe ignored him. This he expected, but to his chagrin he noticed that now even Duke Prospero had turned his back on him. The wizard had risen from his place and slipped his arm around Mikki's heaving shoulders. "There, there, my dear," he soothed. "Don't redden those pretty eyes; he's not worth it." Gently he coaxed her from her mother's arms and into his. The owl on his shoulder flew away in a huff. "We're all entitled to one mistake. For instance, mine was thinking I didn't want to marry you."

Mikki lifted her tear-stained face and sniffled mightily. "You mean— you mean—? You do want to marry me? Still?"

"I can make you very happy. I will be utterly devoted to you. I will always give you your own way."

That clinched it. Mikki nuzzled up to the wizard as only Mikki could. This was full-combat nuzzling at its finest. "You do want to marry me? Still?"

"Only if the feeling is mutual."

"It *is!*" And if Mikki declared her intentions more out of pique at Mark than out of true love for Prospero, it apparently mattered not a whit to the duke. Under the benevolent eyes of Circe, the newly rep-lighted couple strolled away from the cafe, leaving a dumbfounded Mark to stare after them and a still-entranced Medea to stare at nothing.

"Hey! Wait!" Mark shouted after Prospero. "We had a deal! Aren't you forgetting something?"

Prospero paused. "How silly of me." He waved his staff and a small sum of cash appeared on the table, enough to cover the bill and then some. "Tell the waiter to keep the change," said Prospero. He then returned his attention to Mikki, tenderly inquiring, "—and then *third* step in the Corinthian basket trick is—?"

Mark slammed his fist on the table in frustration, making the coins dance.

Something glittered on his pinky. Something green and gold winked at him with all the artful enticement of an experienced coquette. Awestruck, he gazed down at the emerald ring.

A smooth white hand covered his. "Eet looks so luffly on you, dar-link," Medea purred. "And ees more where that came from. You most lat me cofer that charmink body of yours een gold, seelver, pracious jams!" In the face of the lady's sudden enthusiasm, a more educated man would have been on guard. *Beware of Greeks bearing gifts!* But any good palimony lawyer would have been quick to point out that Medea wasn't Greek, she was Colchian. Clearly Mikki's vision of Mark's unclothed form had made a deep impression on her. The recent defection and present whereabouts of her former lover, Duke Prospero, did not seem to preoccupy her mind, or even to have a place in it. Still, it never hurts to be careful.

"Uh . . . you mean precious *gems,* right? I mean, whipped cream's okay, but jam's a little kinky and—"

"I mean thees." Medea lifted her hand to reveal that now Mark's every finger sported a ring of equal or greater worth than the emerald gewgaw on his pinky.

"Whad the hell, jab's ogay too, as long as—" Mark stopped, startled by the odd sound of his own words. He touched his nose and encountered yet another ring. "Hey!" he objected.

"Bot darlink, ees emerald," said Medea.

"Eberald?"

"Really *beeg* emerald."

"Oh. Well . . . " He fingered it dubiously. It felt big, all right. And permanent.

"Eet's you. Trost me," she assured him.

"Mmmmm . . . " He gave the nose-ring one last tap. Big, yes. Permanent, yes. But also—ahhh!—expensive. "Ogay," he conceded. "Bud id bedder be *seedless* jab!" Mark knew that with women—even sorceresses—a man always did better if he laid down the law from the start. Moral stance taken, limits set, grunting happily, he allowed the lady to lead him away.

WALL STREET WIZARDS

LAURA RESNICK

Laura Resnick, author of over twenty science fiction/fantasy short stories and a dozen romance novels, won the 1993 John W. Campbell Award, as well as several romance genre awards. She considers Wall Street proof that there is indeed sorcery at work in the world.

The day the cow followed Mr. Griswold into the office was really the turning point. Until that moment, they couldn't prove a thing, no matter what they suspected. But a cow is a pretty noticeable thing on Wall Street, and from the moment Old Betsy started following Mr. Griswold everywhere he went (including the Beefeater Restaurant on New Street, which seemed kind of insensitive to me) our days were numbered.

Betsy's infatuation with Mr. Griswold was simply the result of a careless mistake—exactly the kind of thing I was always afraid would happen. You see, there's a good reason that Mr. Griswold has been the most sought-after bachelor in New York for nearly thirty years, despite being short, fat, bald, and none too charming. He doesn't just use his powers to manipulate events on Wall Street. No, as if that wasn't challenging enough, he also casts love spells on the most beautiful, talented, rich, and celebrated women in the city. The fact that movie stars, rock stars, socialites, models, authoresses, and heiresses have broken their hearts over this squat little guy with the personality of a jackal and the vocabulary of a teamster should have tipped off the entire world years ago— or at least that's what I've always thought. But men have all sorts of cherished illusions about their own sex appeal which are merely confirmed by such an aberration, while women simply shake their heads at the follies of other women.

Anyhow, this time Mr. Griswold had set his sights on the young widow of Alfredo Abundant, founder and former reigning king of Creamery Confections, the ice cream company. Abundant was the guy who made international headlines when he dropped dead while donating a thousand pints of Double Butter Pecan to the Gay Decathletes Association. The doctor who performed the autopsy took one look at Abundant's heart and said (quoth the *Wall Street Journal*) that he hadn't seen so much congestion since they closed down the George Washington Bridge before Labor Day weekend. As you may remember, Creamery Confections's stock plummeted overnight; around here, people were selling it on street corners. Well, never one to overlook an opportunity, Mr. Griswold bought all that stock and, using his special powers, brought up the price until we made a huge killing on it just a year later. It was brilliant; it made our days of messing with Chrysler look like amateur night. That was just about the time Mr. Griswold decided that Madame Abundant was everything he desired in a wealthy widow.

Even though things were pretty chaotic in our offices, what with Old Betsy mooing noisily and answering the call of nature right there on the boss's Aubusson rug, I still managed to drag most of the story out of Mr. Griswold. It seems that Madame Abundant invited him out to Abundant Farms in Vermont for one of her notoriously dull house parties. At Mr. Griswold's suggestion, the two of them went for a private stroll around the farm one evening. It was just around twilight, and he figured this would be the perfect time to *shazam!* her with one of his love spells.

As Mr. Griswold first explained it to me when he made me his apprentice, personal will is the center of magical power. For the most part, the universe does not resemble Mr. Griswold's will, and so he attempts to impose his will upon it. If you know anything about the Griswold Group's annual net after taxes, then you'll know that he's pretty good at imposing. If he's told me once, he's told me a thousand times, the most vital element of magic is concentration. You must discipline your mind. Only then can you successfully direct your will toward your goals and cause changes that will make the universe conform to your desires.

It's not easy, believe me. More than once, my efforts have backfired due to my poor concentration and undisciplined mind, and the results have been nothing short of disastrous. (And while we're on the subject, let me say that I am terribly, terribly sorry about October of 1987, and I will never do it again).

Anyhow, it was apparently a momentary lapse in concentration that caused Mr. Griswold to miss his target. Instead of Madame Abundant, he hit Betsy the cow with the full force of his erotic incantation. When the party ended on Sunday, the poor, lovesick thing actually broke out of her corral and chased Mr. Griswold's limousine all the way to Park Avenue. There was no eluding her; that's how powerful Mr. Griswold's spells are.

At first we tried to carry on as usual, but it just became impossible to run meetings, trade commodities, manipulate stocks, and get good tables in downtown restaurants while we had this affectionate cow permanently attached to us. And then, of course, people started to talk.

Wall Street mavens had long been suspicious of Mr. Griswold's power and influence. Did you ever wonder what made the whole nation choose VHS instead of Beta? Or why the leveraged buyout of RJR Nabisco became such a farce that they actually made a James Garner movie about it? Or what ever happened to eight-track tapes? Did you *never* wonder about the break up of Ma Bell, the deregulation of the airlines, or the rise and fall of that ingrate Donald Trump? Well, even if *you* were too busy watching Phil and Oprah to realize that something strange was going on, a few people on Wall Street started to suspect that mysterious forces were at work. Even when I got my M.B.A. and first joined the Griswold Group, there were already enough rumors about Mr. Griswold to make half a dozen respected bankers try to bribe me into spying on him and betraying his secrets. I refused, of course; ethics aside (as they usually are on Wall Street), why should I assist the guys running thirty lengths behind my own horse?

I never told Mr. Griswold about any of this, but I was certain that he knew. After only a few months in his office, I had realized that there was something very unusual about him. For one thing, how many financiers keep copies of *The Key of Solomon* and *The Grand Grimoire* in their offices? Most bankers are more interested in SEC regulations and the latest *Journal* gossip than in advice about dealing with demons, casting spells, and shapeshifting.

The day finally came when Mr. Griswold decided to reward my loyalty and discretion. He needed an apprentice, and he chose me. You see, esoteric science—as Mr. Griswold calls it—is a secret doctrine that reveals the mysteries of the universe (you wouldn't believe how it's helped me with commodities and agricultural futures), and the wisdom of esotericism must be transmitted orally by a master to his apprentice. Of course, Mr. Griswold had an apprentice before me. I used to wonder what would happen to me once the guy was out on parole, but he wound up getting into politics and black magic after he was released, so my position as Mr. Griswold's chief adept remained safe.

It was a busy, interesting life. We manipulated stocks, bonds, securities, commodities, and Manhattan real estate; we cast spells on Wall Street traders, bankers, financiers, and head waiters; we even diverted competition for a whole year by getting everyone to invest in Broadway musicals. As I've mentioned, there were occasional mistakes (I *said* I was sorry), but sometimes we simply lost out to superior forces; the Japanese have some pretty good sorcerers themselves, you know. And unfortunately, we never guessed the Iron Curtain would fall, so we were late to move on that opportunity. After all, divination was never our specialty; that's a different field entirely.

As you can imagine, Mr. Griswold had enjoyed those Reagan-Bush years and was pretty sorry to see a Democrat back in the White House. He decided it would be a good idea to divert government attention away from Wall Street for a while, so we started working property spells. And even though neither of us knew anything about Arkansas, the resulting real estate scandal was a first-class synthesis of magic and myth, even if I do say so myself. It clearly took Bill and Hilary by surprise. We kept working that spell, making sure there were enough new curses to keep everyone busy for a while. Meanwhile, we simultaneously turned our attention to pharmaceutical companies. Mr. Griswold thought that the advent of NAFTA, combined with all the talk of health care reform, might make those drug manufacturers vulnerable to a little sacred science. We began developing the incantations, but we were still arguing about which route to go—alchemy or numerology—when Mr. Griswold's libido got the better of him. Or rather, it got the better of Old Betsy.

Just try pretending your life is business as usual while a four-legged, unhousebroken vamp follows you into the New York Stock Exchange. Try explaining to your bovine companion that the chairs at your favorite restaurant weren't designed to support her eight hundred pounds. Try mingling discreetly at parties while she chews on ladies' corsages. I'm telling you, it can't be done. Poor Mr. Griswold was a wreck.

Now, you may wonder why we didn't just turn Betsy into a pot roast and three hundred hamburgers. Simple: you can't kill an ensorcelled animal. Look it up if you don't believe me. Anyhow, we would never have killed the poor thing. It's not like this was *her* fault, as I kept reminding Mr. Griswold.

Embarrassment and various inconveniences aside, our real problems started when people began wondering exactly how this had happened.

Madame Abundant was threatening to sue Mr. Griswold if he didn't return her cow, yet everyone in New York could see that he wasn't keeping Betsy by force. In fact, it was obvious that forcing her to leave Mr. Griswold would be an act of unwarranted cruelty. For the first time, people began to guess that all those attractive, appealing women who had fallen in love with Mr. Griswold might just possibly have been under the influence. But—the influence of *what*?

Then the *Post* offered $30,000 to our receptionist in exchange for an exclusive interview. She told them about a lot of things that, frankly, didn't help our image at all. She even mentioned the time I accidentally made all the furniture talk, which I thought was pretty petty of her. I *told* Mr. Griswold he should have given her a raise after that.

Lovesick cows, talking chairs, the suspected manipulation of stock prices and world events . . . Need I even specify who got interested in us next? That's right, the CIA. They started out by offering Mr. Griswold a job. After he refused politely, they tried threats, intimidation, and extortion—which just goes to show how pointless it is to be polite to government agents.

Mr. Griswold decided that we couldn't wait for the love spell to wear off (which could take anywhere from six months to five years). We'd have to find a way to break the spell and get Betsy back to her pasture in Vermont. Otherwise, we had no hope of returning to a normal life. By now, we were making all our plans while strolling through Battery Park, since it seemed probable that our offices and condominiums were bugged. The FBI, the National Security Agency, the SEC, and (I'll never know why) the Metropolitan Museum of Art were all on the case now, and their agents followed us up and down the Promenade, watching our every move and gesture, trying to eavesdrop, and bumping into each other with monotonous regularity.

The problem was, we'd never broken a spell before. We'd never needed to. And what with maintaining our current projects, feeding Betsy, and being interrogated several times a day, we just didn't have enough time to effectively research reversing Mr. Griswold's love spell. Our first attempt merely gave Betsy a terrible case of gas. We used that same incantation on our ubiquitous federal agents and finally got a few hours of peace, but we continued to fail in all our efforts with Betsy.

Well, as will happen to even the best of wizards when they try to do too much at once, we started losing control of the Whitewater spell. Even the pharmaceutical companies were spinning out of our grasp. Weeks had gone by without our making a killing on the stock exchange. Between that and all the unfavorable publicity we were getting, a number of our investors decided it was time to pull out. Things began to look pretty bleak for us.

It's a measure of how great a mentor Mr. Griswold is that I was the one to come up with a solution. What with his business failing and Betsy breathing down his neck day and night, he was simply too close to the problem to see it clearly. So I proposed that, rather than break the love spell on Betsy (which we weren't having any success with, anyway), we simply cast a stronger, other-directed spell to overshadow it.

Well, Mr. Griswold loved the idea. He wanted to transfer Betsy's affections to Senator Jesse Helms. While that idea was not without its appeal, I thought we could best protect ourselves by targeting a more immediate threat. And it worked. When the agents persecuting us all saw Betsy smothering the CIA's leading investigator with her enthusiastic adoration, they started to realize what could happen to a pensioned schmuck who messed with a Wall Street wizard. They all convinced their superiors that our case file should be closed. In exchange, though, we had to agree to leave Wall Street forever.

Our last stroll down the Street was a sad occasion. I don't think I'll ever again find anyplace where I feel so completely at home. However, we don't have any choice. Not only would all our secret agents land on us like a ton of bricks if we kept trading, but it's clear that our Wall Street heyday is over anyhow. It's a lot harder to enchant people if they won't eat with you, talk to you, do business with you, or receive your calls, letters, and messages. Besides, Mr. Griswold has decided that my apprenticeship with him is over; the time has come for me to go out into the world alone and seek my own destiny. We packed up a few personal belongings from the offices of the Griswold Group. Then, in a final burst of glory, we enchanted all the furniture and made it dance all the way down Wall Street. I'll bet you wish you could have been there.

I got a call from Mr. Griswold just this morning. He's moving to Brazil on the theory that inflation will be the wave of the future. He says he's going to start taking it easy, though, maybe spend more time on alchemy and astrology.

As for me . . . since I'm just coming into my prime, I'm taking a more ambitious route and moving my operations to the former Soviet Bloc countries. Call it a hunch, but I just think they're ripe for my particular brand of sorcery.

SWALLOW

SIMON INGS

Simon Ings *is an up-and-coming British fantasy writer who also claims responsibility for a film about dead ferrets. His latest novel is City of the Iron Fish.*

It was early October before Maureen Deeprose was able to visit the flat where David, her brother, had died. She received Trevor's postcard on the first Wednesday, telling her everything was prepared: by noon Thursday she had packed her bags and was walking toward the Norbreck tram stop, on the northern outskirts of Blackpool.

Maureen believed that if you looked at the world a certain way, you would see the exit signs, the hidden places, the means of escape. But today the moribund resort resisted such romance, sweeping the sea and the sky into each other so that there was nothing to see beyond the promenade: nothing, that is, but for a gray, shifting mass of damp air. Nothing to look at: no way through.

She waited five minutes for a tram to carry her south along the Northern Promenade. As she rode she looked out at the street. Guesthouse after guesthouse; though they looked more like convalescent homes. In the windows hung fluorescent squares of card, scrawled over with spirit marker. The tram pulled up at a stop, and, squinting, she read: "Tonight. Rhetinitis & Pigmentosis Benefit." It filled her with a sudden hatred of the place, of its failure: sickness lay like a smell over everything here.

Even the town seemed to be searching for someplace better than itself. Strung above the promenade there were flags, of countries no one here had visited or perhaps had even heard of; between the flags hung textured plastic shapes, painted with fluorescent paint, meant to resemble glimpses through jungle glades. They were promises, Maureen supposed: ill-conceived, inadequate promises of some better land, buried behind the mundane shore.

At the next stop an old couple boarded the tram and sat in front of her. She listened to them. They were so old, nothing they ever said to each other could possibly excite them. The tram rattled past the Castle Cabin Casino and the old woman said, "That's a big gambling casino in there."

She said, "It's like Las Vegas in there."

Maureen clenched her fists: it hurt her to be reminded that her quest was common, her dissatisfaction general. Did her search, after all, amount to any more than this: to find Las Vegas in the Castle Cabin, Shangri-La behind Watford Junction, Babylon on the Kilburn High Road? She would have been content, perhaps, to wait for old age, and would in time have become like the woman in front of her: a tawdry sort of Prospero. Had it not been for David, her brother—six months dead and still not gone—she might have been content.

There were some shops, now, interspersed with the hotels. Above their windows the same words repeated themselves, over and over. Stationery—Teddies—Radios—Fancy Goods—Teddies—Radios. The tram rattled between the derelict Metropole Hotel and Maisie May's Piano Bar and came to rest opposite the town's latest stab at glamour: Grandma Batty's Yorkshire Pudding Emporium.

Maureen walked the rest of the way to the coach station and caught a National Express to Kilburn, and from there a connecting service to Leeds.

Just before the coach left the M62 a middle-aged man sitting opposite her engaged her in conversation. He had a barrel chest and a double chin; at a guess he was about five feet high. He told her he had been a Green Beret. Maureen watched him, guessed his weight, the proportion of fat to flesh, the relative tenderness of each joint.

"And what do *you* do?"

She couldn't resist telling him.

"Really! D'you do Blackpool?"

"No," Maureen said. "No, I don't do Blackpool."

"Good club circuit in Blackpool!"

Maureen looked out the window, hiding her smile. She said, "I'm not that sort of magician."

It was after eleven when Maureen arrived in Leeds.

Trevor, her dead brother's friend and apprentice, was waiting for her in his car. There was someone with him: a boy with shaven hair, wearing a skinny-rib sweater.

"This is Peter Race!" Trevor said, as though his friend were about to perform a conjuring trick. Peter glanced at her and folded his arms.

"You mind taking the backseat, Peter?" said Trevor.

Peter said: "Fuck off, Trev."

Trevor drove. Peter remained beside him in the front passenger seat; Maureen sat in the back, her suitcase beside her, her day-bag on her lap, the carrier with her shopping wedged in the gap between the front seats. She peered out the window, tracing their route, from the municipal art gallery, past the bombastic city hall, to the stolid modernist frontage of the university, and into Headingley.

Trevor and Peter began arguing. It was difficult to follow what they said. One moment it was:

"He wouldn't cut his hair, Trev."

"I saw him; he'd had it cut."

"He loves his hair."

"I'm not saying that he doesn't."

"He wouldn't cut his hair."

"What I am saying—"

"Trev. He'd be mad to cut his hair."

The next moment it was:

"Witkin's trauma isn't a sufficient justification."

"You can't compare a life event to the evasions of Helmut Newton and his spyglasses."

"I appreciate that we are talking about dead babies, Peter."

"Dead babies, not bloody Monte Carlo."

The argument fizzled out as they entered Headingley, leaving Peter restless and aggressive. He turned round in his seat and rummaged in Maureen's shopping bag. "What's this then?" he demanded, picking out something wrapped in plastic.

Maureen smiled weakly. "Double Gloucester."

Peter sniffed at it. "Pooh."

"It's got chives in it," Maureen explained.

"Well," he said, reasonably, "it's not cheddar, is it?"

Maureen smiled again.

"What's wrong with a nice bit of *cheddar?*" he demanded, and when Maureen didn't answer: "It smells of dog pooh." He picked out a jar of creamed horseradish.

"Stop it, please," said Maureen.

Trevor kept adjusting his rearview mirror. He couldn't seem to get it to stick at the right angle.

"Horseradish!" Peter unscrewed the lid, dabbed his finger into the horseradish, and sucked it clean. *"Shit!"*—he opened the glove compartment and threw the jar inside.

"Please don't do that."

"Sherry!"

"Please be careful, Peter."

"Trev, she's got bloody cocktail sticks in here!"

"Peter—"

He tossed a tub of soft cheese into her lap, took a bite out of a cooking apple, made a face and spit it onto the floor under Trevor's feet. He said: "You don't want to go messing about with stuff like this."

They parked opposite the private road which led to David's flat. Trevor reached into the glove compartment, took out the jar of horseradish, screwed the lid back on and handed it to Maureen.

"Thank you," she said.

Trevor got out of the car and opened the door for her. He said, "I'm sorry about Peter."

Maureen shrugged. "He'll do."

"He won't be missed."

"Trevor," she said, with a smile meant to reassure him, "You think I don't see that?"

Trevor gave her the key to her brother's flat. The fob was a glass bead.

As she walked, the weight of it tugged oddly at her light jacket.

The vestibule to Marlowe Court was tiled with gray-flecked linoleum. Maureen climbed two flights of stairs and pushed open the fire door. The hallway echoed oddly when she walked down it.

Number 21: the key was stiff in the lock. She fumbled for the light switch. Nothing was as she remembered it. The hallway was unornamented. The living room had a wall-to-wall beige carpet. All the walls were white. She walked around and around the flat for half an hour.

Why, she wondered, had her brother chosen such neutral furnishings? It seemed strange to her that David should have chosen to die among pine wardrobes and foam-backed mushroom carpets; to take his last drink from a Pyrex coffee cup, and wash himself for the last time at a plastic avocado hand basin. She went into the kitchen. It was nothing like she had expected: where were the Sabatier cleavers, the boning knives in their self-sharpening block; what had happened to his set of sky blue Le Creuset saucepans? She had expected to see his kitchen equipped much as it had been when he was developing his recipes. She looked through the drawers, found an all-purpose serrated knife with a scratched plastic handle, a beige plastic sieve, a nonstick frying pan with a loose handle, an apple corer, its handle bound up in orange string, and a double-handled steel cooking pot with a dented lid. It was a selection as sparse and as bland as the flat's other furnishings. Had he panicked? Had he repudiated his culinary skills? If he had, then his repudiation had come too late: sterile as the kitchen appeared, there was a scent to it, a lingering aroma, as distinctive as a signature. Burnt-on fat, from inside the oven perhaps, mingled with garlic and onion skins from behind the ill-fitting work surface—these things had conspired to preserve him.

In the morning, Maureen walked into town and shopped in the Bond Street center. In Marks & Spencer's she replaced the horseradish and the apple; she added a small glass jar of juniper berries and a red cabbage and approached the checkout. While she waited in the queue, she looked into the main body of the store. There were laminated prints on the walls. One was of a man in an Arran sweater: rugged, leering; there was gray at his temples. He was sitting on a bollard, on the quayside of a fishing harbor. In another, a woman in a long, shapeless-looking russet winter coat swung by her arms from the branch of an autumn-leaved tree; she was laughing . . .

"We catch only glimpses," David had warned her, the night he served her the first of his recipes. "A boy in a scarlet headdress heaves at his rickshaw at the entrance to some temple gate. A black whore kneels inside a confessional booth on the banks of the Grand Canal; she flips a coin, frowns, whispers something into the narrow grille before her. A boy plays a penny whistle, high up in the branches of a lime tree in a forgotten corner of the hanging gardens. In the evening the skies are emerald. There is gold filigree on every priestly vestment. Dervishes wear cloaks made of the bones of birds, strung together on fine wire."

Maureen speared her first mouthful, brought it trembling to her lips—

"Five-fifty-eight," said the woman at the till.

*   *   *

After an afternoon wandering listlessly around Leeds art gallery, Maureen returned home and sat shuffling through her brother's CDs, till they lay strewn haphazardly across the coffee table. At length, she found one she was looking for—the soundtrack to *Un Coeur en Hiver.* Her brother had played it to her the night of their first meal together. When, only a few months before, Trevor had broken into the flat and found David dead at the dinner table—his meal a congealed mess, spattered all about him where he had choked on his own vomit, the kitchen a chaos; and the joint, redolent of apricots and cheese, festering in its tin—this music, whisper-quiet, had accompanied him around the flat. She took the CD out of its box and slipped it into the player. She hesitated, finger over the play button, then drew back. She decided she would play it with her meal: not before.

She tried to sleep, but could not. Blue-green streetlight easily penetrated the bedroom's wheatmeal curtains. She hid her face beneath the sweet-smelling duvet, but the air under it grew stale and she could not breathe properly.

At last she threw back the duvet and padded into the living room. The carpet prickled her feet. She parted the curtains and looked out. The estate was laid out before her. As usual, she found herself searching the shapes and shadows for something that wasn't there: a new street perhaps, or a door half ajar, a way out more entire than that offered by a mere private road.

She had had her share of success: played chess in cafés thick with smoke from jasmine-scented cigarettes; shivered in the cool caverns of restaurants and hotel foyers; rolled brightly colored balls down the tram tracks of misty tree-lined thoroughfares. "I have skated across frozen rivers, black ribbons cascading from my hair!"

"Did you see?" David asked her, that first night, when she had finished eating. "What did you see?"

Maureen sat slumped before the table, staring at the ribs she had stripped, the traces of raspberry glaze on the pristine white rim of her plate. "Glimpses," she murmured sleepily, her tongue thick, her mouth heavy; her breath smelt of rosemary, and there was a hint of juniper berries from the terrine which had begun the meal. She forced herself to look at her brother; tried not to see, behind him, the remains of the joint, cooling and congealing in its basting tin by the cooker. "Just glimpses."

*   *   *

Maureen spent all the following day going through David's recipes. She ordered them as best she could, sorting the pile on the desk into a chronological sequence. Gradually, a pattern emerged: she rang Trevor. She said, "I think I know how he did it."

There was no response.

"Hello?"

"I heard you," said Trevor, at last.

"You'd better come over," said Maureen.

"*Now?*"

"Please," she insisted.

There was silence again; then "I won't stay for the meal."

"You won't have to," Maureen assured him. "Bring Peter."

There was silence on the end of the line.

"Trevor."

"Christ."

"Please, Trevor."

"I haven't even had time to—"

"And Trevor?"

"What?"

"I need some kitchen gear. The place is stripped bare: you should have warned me."

"You don't ask much, do you?"

Maureen put the phone down and waited.

She left the washing up till the following morning. Unexpected sunshine had dried the blood streaked across the rolling pin where she had hammered the escalopes into their required thinness; it had set hard the yellow crust of soft cheese around the edge of Trevor's largest Pyrex mixing bowl. In the summery light, the parsley in its jam jar on the windowsill took on all the hues of a forest glade: a beam of ruby light issued from the nearly full bottle of cooking sherry and cut across the countertop like a laser beam. All these things filled Maureen with hope. She looked out the window at the estate: all at once it seemed to her that she could see things from both sides at once: the landscape trembled, as though at any second it might disassemble, like a cubist painting. It was as her brother had promised: *the world is delicate,* she thought. *The world comes apart if you shake it.*

When she was done, Maureen caught a bus into the city center and went walking, waiting with pent-up breath for something to happen.

Demolition work by the Griffin Hotel had stripped out everything but a few rusted fire escapes and the frontage on Boar Lane. A scaffold propped the stonework up from behind. An orange crane had been assembled in the middle of the site; spare sections lay stacked end-on by the site entrance. She waited there for a while, and when nothing untoward occurred, went on her way, only marginally disappointed.

As the morning wore on, however, so the sunlight dimmed, veiled repeatedly with skein after skein of opalescent cloud—more like muslin than cloud—and the air grew damp and heavy. From outside the Mill Hill Unitarian Chapel, Maureen gazed across Park Row—from the Queens Hotel to the Top Rank Bingo to the Midland Bank—with a look both anxious and insistent, as if in the shopping crowds she might spot some way out, some exit or thoroughfare no one but her could see.

The weather declined; by early afternoon, gusts smelling of January were shooting back and forth along the narrow streets. Later still, coming out of the Bond Street precinct, Maureen found herself behind the Mill Hill chapel. Here, with its dirty black stone streaked orange, and its grilled windows so encrusted with filth and diesel they looked like another, softer, more absorbent kind of stone, the building appeared cramped, forgotten, and unclean.

"Tonight," she whispered to herself, taking a perverse pleasure in the pain the words inflicted: *"Rhetinitis & Pigmentosis Benefit!"*

There was no door, no secret garden. Last night's meal had failed her. All Trevor's preparations had been for nothing. Peter—

It was almost comic, how pointless the whole business had proved. She walked a little way up Basinghall Street, found a street vendor and, out of an obscure wish to do penance, bought herself a burger and fries. She turned east along Albion Place, chewing down the cold and greasy patty, her first food since the night before, and took a bitter pleasure in the way the taste of rancid fat drowned out and demolished the stale echo of her brother's finest dish: the clamminess of cream, the cheesy aftertaste of horseradish, the sweet echo of baked flesh, receding for good on a tide of burnt mince and damp, waxy potato.

The light changed.

Maureen looked up. No longer overcast, the sky shone a bright emerald; it lent an undersea cast to everything it touched. Sweat sparked on Maureen's forehead. She smelled burning, spices, the hollow, metallic taste of molten glass.

She blinked. Past Marks and Spencer's and Mister Byrite lay a market, enclosed within a rectangular mews; at each corner stood a tower, capped by a brass dome. Maureen walked toward it. Her feet trailed through the sand, which was dark and spiced with the smell of excrement and spilt milk. Around her milled blackamoors in turbans; their gowns of hessian were slashed about the breast to reveal undergarments of vividly dyed and patterned silk. Around their feet young girls scampered: each had a golden ring through her nose and a long necklace of beads and precious coins wrapped many times around her slender neck: the faces of these desert children were the color of burnt pottery, or ripe plums: their eyes were lined with kohl. Above the street hung banners of unbleached linen, sporting bold, heraldic designs in black and green.

She reached the entrance to the market. Blind beggar boys in soiled loincloths sat tapping clay pots on the steps. Their hair was bleached ginger by the sun: their cataractic eyes were blue, opaque, like blackbird's eggs. Maureen ascended the steps, past women bearing pots of water on their heads and girls with black streamers in their hair, engrossed in a skipping game. In the courtyard stood avenues of crude clay shelters.

Sweet sellers crowded the porticoes. Apiary stalls, piled high with hunks of soap, liqueur in china bottles, and candles the shape of hives, lined the pavements. Slabs of liquorice clouded with flies hung on hooks around the pastry sellers' stalls like sides of rotten beef.

An old black woman in baggy trousers, her bare shrunken breasts glistening in the apple green sunlight, came up and thrust into Maureen's hand a small hand-carved box. It was empty: a bee was painted on the lid. A little box for keeping pins in.

Maureen pocketed the box.

"Five-fifty-eight."

Beyond the market, the pavement was cluttered with bricks, old clothes, sand, sacks of plaster, lead piping, bones, abandoned tools. The houses impended over the streets, hiding them from the sun. She walked down the center of the alley, where the going was easier. Succulents thrust up through the cobbles. Dust covered them so that, in the light from the boardinghouses, their soft fleshy stems poked up out of the ground like children's fingers.

She came to a square and crossed it. The flagstones were mottled with bird droppings. She felt their wrinkled hardness through the soles of her shoes. She sensed a change, looked up.

The sky was bright enough, the color of rank grass; but the buildings around her—dull, gray, and glimmering uncertainly—looked as though they were lit by polarized light from another region entirely.

The moment was passing.

She had to find David.

Her feet slipped in slops and turds and snagged in broken paving stones. She heard footsteps and, a long way off, a baby crying. She began to run, and stubbed her toes against an empty bottle: it shattered against a wall. Gin scented the air like sweat.

"David?"

A light went on in a window above her. Something soft and wet hit the ground by her feet: she did not look back to see what it was.

"David!"

She fetched up at last against the handrail of an iron footbridge. There was something under her feet: a McDonald's carton. She sobbed, kicked it away from her: it tumbled off the bridge, bobbed twice in the air, and then, defeated, descended to the gray, greasy waters of the River Aire. She looked up at the grey overcast, felt a chill Pennine gust, and heard the creak of the wet planks beneath her.

It was over.

She felt suddenly nauseous. She crossed the bridge and climbed the short flight of stone stairs to the street. There was a white Ford Escort parked at the curb. She stepped off the pavement, stood in the gutter, and leaned her hands on the car's trunk, waiting for the sickness she knew would come. Once she had thrown up, she rested a while, leaning up against the boot of the car, spitting bits of burger and fries out into the gutter. She wiped her mouth with a tissue and walked the rest of the way through the brick terraces of Armley to Trevor's house.

Trevor led her to the lounge in silence. It was as she remembered it: a cheap red carpet, too small for the room; the bare boards scattered with paperbacks and stacks of secondhand magazines; walls a pale nicotine color; homemade bookshelves warped and askew. She looked around her at the clothes scattered across the room. A pair of gray socks lay balled up on the easy chair. A pair of dirty underpants had been laid out neatly across the back of the sofa. There was a skinny-rib sweater on the floor under the dining table.

She gathered the clothes, took them into the kitchen, and slid them into the large white swing-top bin.

Trevor would not look at her.

She went back to the living room and dropped onto the settee. Trevor followed her in with the teapot, a cup, a tumbler, and a half-empty bottle of Teachers.

"You weren't always that careless," she said.

He poured her some tea.

"Do you remember those first glimpses, Trevor?"

Trevor put his whiskey glass up to his mouth to hide his face.

"I got a glimpse," said Maureen. "More than a glimpse. David's there. I'm sure of it. I feel him there. He's waiting for me"—she leaned forward and reached for Trevor's hand—"For *us!*"

Trevor took a sip of his whiskey.

Maureen sighed and flopped back into the seat.

Trevor had lost the sympathy he had shown her the day before. "Have you seen the Henry Moore rooms?" he kept saying. "In the art gallery? The Henry Moore rooms?" He would not talk about the night just gone. "You should visit the Henry Moore rooms."

"I've seen them before," said Maureen, weak from nausea.

"What do you think of them, then?"

"Trevor," she said, "listen a minute: a moment ago I was there—"

"*Hey-up,* Stan!"

Trevor's cat came in, wandered around myopically for a while, then settled to sleep under the window. Trevor sighed. "Stan, wake up." The cat, fat and white, glanced at him, then let its head fall back on its paws.

Trevor went over to the dresser and fished a ball of fluff from out a jar of potpourri. He knelt down and waved it in front of the cat. "Hey," he said, "it's Clint."

The cat pricked up its ears.

"Say hello to Clint."

The cat pawed at the ball of fluff.

"It's a kitten's tail," Trevor explained.

"Ugh," said Maureen.

"Don't be like that," Trevor protested. "Clint's the only friend it's got. It likes playing with Clint, don't you Stanley?"

He dropped the tail onto the carpet. The cat batted it around a few times, then lifted up its head and gazed vaguely around the room.

She said: "It was the poorest quarter. Or perhaps the alley behind the Opera." She leaned forward again, examining her hands. "I need some more help," she admitted. "Last night—wasn't enough to send me over."

"Oh—" Trevor waved his hands, deprecatingly. "I'm sure, given time . . . " He rolled out of his chair again and retrieved the dismembered tail. He waved it in front of the cat's nose. "You have to show him it close to," he explained. "He's shortsighted."

"Trevor—"

The cat clamped its jaws round the tail and wrestled it out of Trevor's grip. "See?" he said. "Now he's licking it."

"Ugh."

Trevor said fiercely: "Look, he likes it. It's the only cat that doesn't attack him. It's the only friend he's got." He stood up again and opened the top left drawer of the dresser and drew out a spindle of black thread. He snapped off a length, retrieved the kitten's tail, and tied the thread round it.

Maureen went and stood by the door. She said: "I want another one."

Trevor stared at Maureen. "Christ," he said, "You're worse than he was."

"It was easier for him. You helped him. If you'd helped me last night, perhaps I wouldn't need to ask you now."

He stared at her for a long while. Maureen returned the look. She knew he was afraid of her, as he had been afraid of her brother. "Don't be bitter, Trev," she said—lightly, to hurt him—"You know I'd do the same for you."

Trevor shrugged. He dropped the tail in front of Stanley's nose, then dragged it by the thread in sweeping arcs over the floor.

Maureen said, "You're teasing it."

"You have to tease Stanley," Trevor replied, absorbed in the game.

Maureen said: "I want a girl, next time."

"It's the only exercise he gets. His balls are gone, he can't get a girl cat."

"I'll be back in the spring. Does that give you enough time?"

"All he does is eat and sleep."

"*Trevor.*"

Trevor looked up at her. "Yes," he said.

He said, "Anything you say."

The Most Beautiful Girl Alive

Mike Resnick and Nicholas A. DiChario

Mike Resnick is the author of more than forty science fiction novels and one hundred stories, as well as the editor of twenty-one anthologies. Since 1989 he has been nominated for fifteen Hugo awards and has won three.

Nicholas DiChario's short fiction has appeared in F & SF, SF Age, and several original anthologies, most recently Tales From the Great Turtle. He has been a Hugo, John W. Campbell, and World Fantasy award nominee.

lo! Chaos reigned!
  Light waves exploded in every inconceivable direction, (just as they had always done, except no one had ever been able to see them).
 Particles, when found, were found to be perfectly immeasurable, (thus measurable).
 Unconquerable Cause & Effect were conquered by subatomic hidden variables, the study of which would come to be known as Sorcerology.
 & not much changed in the world, really, except for the implied criteria of the fabric of the universe.

I. Friendship's Encounter with the Cat

Friendship was updating his client list when the E & P summons came in over his computer:

The Chakra of Ethics & Principles invites you to lunch this afternoon at 12:00, in her chamber on the fourteenth floor.
Thank you.

Friendship had worked for the investment firm of Happiness & Luxury Mutual Funds for two years, & had never been summoned by Ethics & Principles. He swallowed hard & felt his heartbeat skip a little faster. There was considerably more than an implied "Or Else!" tagged onto the end of that message. A summons from E & P—the Chakra, no less—was nothing to casually dismiss.

At noon Friendship went to the men's room. He stood in front of the mirror & combed his thinning hair. He tucked his shirt neatly inside his pants, straightened his tie, & smoothed his cape. He'd worn an old cape today, one that had faded over the years. If he'd only known he'd be meeting with the Chakra of E & P, he would have dressed sharply, shined his shoes, picked a cleaner tie. But the cape was an old favorite; he'd probably have worn it anyway. Two years ago it had been the only cape he'd owned. He wore it every day when he was an independent financial adviser, when the money & the clients were so damned hard to come by. Navy blue—at least in its heyday. It was the cape of a serious, no-nonsense investment man. Since he'd started working for H & L, he made it a point to wear the cape at least once a week, to remind himself how far he'd come, how hard he'd worked, to remind himself that he could do anything he set his mind to do. (He had no one else in his life to remind him, so he made it a point to remind himself.)

Friendship rode the elevator to the fourteenth floor, & walked the length of a long corridor, its walls painted with ornate designs. He stood before the only secretary fronting the executive offices & announced himself.

"Appetizer?" said the secretary in an overly pleasant soprano. He reached inside a nearby steam cabinet & withdrew a tray crowded with hot shrimp & clams & sautéed mushrooms.

"No, thank you," said Friendship.

"Espresso?"

"No. I'll just wait." What he wanted was to get this meeting over & done with.

"Very well," said the secretary. Then, a moment later: "Chakra Moon Wary will see you now."

They walked down another corridor, & the secretary led him into a large chamber.

The Chakra's chamber was a beautiful expression of translucence, & a tribute to the Sorcerology that had made Happiness & Luxury the most prominent investment firm in the country. Walls of glass, overlooking the bay thousands of feet below. A desk in perfect moonwheel circular form, which hung from the ceiling on sacred gossamer twine. A print on the far wall of the Mother Goddess giving birth to Substance, the child Substance squirming out from between the Goddess's chubby thighs. Smaller prints of the Tree of Life, the Rainbow of Happiness & Fulfillment, the Cornucopia of Abundance & Wealth, & the Eye of Wisdom occupied the only wall that was not glass. Wisdom, a large black eye with a shocking yellow iris, stared directly down at Friendship.

"Please, come in & sit down," said the Chakra.

Friendship did as he was told.

The Chakra wore silk robes over her long, lean body. Her polished skin shone the color of dark tea. She walked over to her liquor cabinet. "Rosewater?"

His throat felt parched, & he was perspiring. "Please."

"I have some questions for you," she said in a cool, precise voice. She poured two glasses, silently. Friendship couldn't even hear the rosewater splashing into the crystal. She handed him his glass. "Tell me all you know about Uncertain," she said, just as smoothly as she'd poured their drinks.

Uncertain. Friendship had been hired at the same time as Uncertain. They'd gone through the same H & L investment training program together. Uncertain had done his best, had in truth tried harder than Friendship, but he'd had difficulty with some of the basic tenets of Sorcerology & their investment applications. Friendship had helped the young man study for a couple of exams (even though internal competition was fierce at H & L) because he'd seemed like such a likable fellow. But that was two years ago. He had seen Uncertain from time to time, had shared lamb's eye broth with him once or twice, & they always nodded & smiled when they passed in the hall, but that was the extent of their acquaintance. Friendship told Chakra Moon Wary all of this, & hoped that would be the end it.

"May I be frank?" she said, sitting behind her desk, turning slightly away from him in her high-backed chair.

"Please," he said, trying to imagine her not being frank & failing dismally. Friendship noticed the intricate design of the Priestess of Supplication carved into the dark wood of the Chakra's chair. The carved Priestess stood between two tall candles, her head bowed slightly, holding a tiny cracked bell in her left hand. The cracked bell was the symbol of wariness, not normally associated with the gentle Priestess.

"Uncertain has been a satisfactory employee for two years," she said. "He's made some wise investments, & some unwise ones, but for the most part he's done what has been asked of him. We've kept him on here because he has established a rather conservative portfolio—blue chip utilities & Double-A municipals & zero-coupon treasuries for the most part, & some guaranteed investment contracts—& a certain element of our clientele appreciates that. He also has a gentle personality, & a knack for attracting low-profile investors, the backbone of any successful investment firm, wouldn't you agree?"

"Absolutely."

"We don't keep deadweight here at Happiness & Luxury. If we did, we wouldn't be number one."

"I certainly didn't mean to imply I had carried Uncertain through his training program. I only—"

Moon Wary held up her hand, her switchblade fingernail. "Of course not. You were merely being honest. I did not mean to sound so aggressive. It's just that Uncertain has me concerned."

Friendship did not relax. He felt too much of the sun & its fiery expanse in the Chakra's chamber, & not enough of the motherly earth & its fixed, solid predictability. The brightness masked the Chakra's face. He could not read her expressions. "How so?"

"Lately he's been taking chances. Two months ago, he invested sixty percent of his portfolio in the foreign market."

"Sixty percent!"

"Yes. Not exactly a conservative investment practice. Even more remarkable is that those investments have more than doubled in market value. Furthermore, the actual investing was rather complicated: convertible high-risk bonds, selling South African rands short & buying up Japanese yen when he felt they had bottomed out, trading in South American commodity futures, even floating money around the world—letting it sit in a Bangkok bank for eight hours, transferring it to Luxembourg for eight more hours, & bringing it back to New York to triple the interest. Quite beyond his capabilities, wouldn't you agree?"

"If he's the same Uncertain I've always known."

"He is. Over the past two weeks he has also completely turned over his domestic portfolio. His trading has been far too active, he has taken unprecedented risks, & yet, everything he's touched has literally turned to gold."

Moon Wary flicked & flicked her fingernails. Friendship imagined her sharpening her claws. He decided that she must own cats. She displayed a certain observational distance that cat people seemed to develop after years of sharing some unspoken communication with their felines. He'd once dated a woman who owned several cats. He'd always felt self-conscious around her and her pets, as if they were talking behind his back while he sat in the room.

Chakra Moon Wary said, "I've personally monitored Uncertain's computer activity. He has referenced the Goddess data banks—the Maiden, the Mother, & the Crone—but he has completely ignored their recommendations. He has invested heavily during the time of the Mother's Full Moon when one should normally be sitting tight. During the Waning Moon & the time of the Crone, he has been acquiring instead of selling. & at the best time to sell, the time of the Maiden & the New Moon, he has backed off entirely."

"What about the Muse subsystem, the Divination packages, the Goddess Calendar?" asked Friendship.

"He doesn't possess the knowledge or experience to use the Muse subsystem or the Divination packages. I've noticed some activity on the Goddess Calendar, so I instructed my staff to run diagnostics on every transaction Uncertain has logged in the past two months. As you might expect, there are some matches with buying during the proper time of Water & Desire, selling during Fire & Will, & nonactivity during Spirit & Envision, but no more than what might be attributed to chance." She paused. "The majority of his transactions simply can't be charted by Sorcerology."

& this last statement, Friendship knew, was the crux of the Chakra's dilemma: if Uncertain's investment strategies couldn't be proved by the theorems of Sorcerology, & the firm was audited by the Securities & Exchange Commission, the Commission could shut H & L down overnight. Friendship had no idea how Chakra Moon Wary could be so calm about it all.

"Uncertain *must* be using a system," she said with absolute conviction. "He's been far too successful to be simply guessing."

"Aren't you taking an incredible risk by keeping him on?"

She grimaced. "We could fire him, of course, but what if his system turns out to be based on some currently uncharted principles of Sorcerology? If Uncertain were to take that system to one of our competitors . . ."

Friendship nodded thoughtfully. "I see. He could put us out of business either way."

She paused. "That's why I called you."

"I'm not sure I understand."

"You know Uncertain better than anyone. I would like you to keep an eye on him for a few days."

"You're mistaken," said Friendship. "I hardly know him at all."

"He has made no friends here in two years."

"But I'm not—"

"Believe me, you're the one." The fingernails flicked. The glass of rosewater perspired in Friendship's cupped palms. Chakra Moon Wary continued to stare out the window. "I would like you to follow him—discreetly, of course. Where does he go on his lunch hour? Does he head straight home after work? Talk to him. Pry a little. Find out what's going on in his personal life."

Friendship realized he had no choice but to cooperate, & sighed deeply. "What am I looking for?"

"You're looking for any personal behavior that seems out of the ordinary, or inconsistent with the man you helped through our training program." She turned to look at him at last, & Friendship wished she hadn't. Cat's eyes, steady & unreadable. "We wouldn't be asking you to help if we hadn't exhausted all other possibilities. We've run every systems check we have over & over again; we've even developed a few new ones. We simply can't justify his investments. Perhaps you will discover something useful. Perhaps not. But we have to decide very soon whether to keep Uncertain or let him go, & if you can provide any information at all . . . well, let's just say the firm would be extremely appreciative."

"I understand."

"We'll be moving Uncertain's desk to where you can observe him during the day, on the pretense of a power line problem. Don't worry about your accounts. One of our senior partners will oversee your work if you get behind."

Lunch arrived, via the smiling soprano male secretary. Finger sandwiches, herbal tea, & some sweet-smelling pastries. Friendship was hungry, but declined to eat.

"One last thing," said the Chakra. "I want you to understand that we here in Ethics & Principles are not coldhearted creatures. We all work for the common good of Happiness & Luxury, & we're all in this together. We don't want to fire Uncertain. We want to help him. That's why we're going to so much trouble."

"Of course," said Friendship. But he couldn't help remembering the woman he'd dated & her cats. None of them had ever gone to any trouble for anyone except themselves, & the woman had gone about it with such ease, such purpose, such clarity, that he never realized her duplicity until long after the relationship had ended.

"Friendship, you appear lost in thought."

"I was just wondering why you haven't approached Uncertain directly."

"We have to protect ourselves, just in case there is an investigation. If the Securities & Exchange Commission discovered that we had questioned Uncertain, & that we didn't fire him on the spot & file the appropriate reports with the appropriate departments, we would be leaving ourselves open to allegations of unethical business practices. As it stands, we can claim ignorance. No one would believe it, of course— but it would be our official position & no one could prove otherwise."

Friendship nodded. "I understand. One more question: Have you considered the possibility of a Hekate? They've been known to practice corporate sabotage."

For the first time, her composure slipped the slightest bit. "The Cult of the Goddess of the Dead is growing. The business community has been trying to monitor their activity. They're a real danger, I'll agree. But to answer your question—no, we don't suspect a Hekate is involved, but dark magic is difficult to chart. We can't rule anything out at this point."

Friendship stood, tugged on his cape, bowed slightly. "I am behind H & L one hundred percent."

"I was sure you would be," she said, turning away from him & staring out the window again. "We will talk again in two days."

II. The Wooden Stick

Friendship noticed the wooden stick immediately. It was thin & flat, about the length of two fingers, rounded at the edges. It reminded him of a physician's tongue depressor. Uncertain kept it in his shirt pocket. He would pull it out every once in a while & tap his keyboard or the edge of his desk with it, while he worked at his computer.

Friendship found himself remembering many things about Uncertain. His quick smile; his bright eyes flashing like watercolors; his slow, careful movements, like those of an inexperienced painter. He always wore flashy capes, nothing conservative. Uncertain's expressions & gestures & even his voice when he spoke to a client on the telephone hid nothing. One glance, or a word or two, reminded him that Uncertain was a man incapable of deception. This was why Friendship had helped him through his training program. Looking back on it now, Friendship had felt a measure of paternalism toward him. There was no possible way Uncertain could be deceiving the firm. If he was involved in any impropriety, it must be completely unintentional, & in two days' time Friendship would tell Chakra Moon Wary exactly that. He was ashamed for his participation in this little game of cat & mouse, no matter how inconsequential his role might be.

Still, there was the wooden stick. It meant nothing, of course; Friendship knew that. But it was inconsistent behavior—or was it just a nervous habit, brought on by the pressure to succeed at H & L? Friendship had felt such pressure himself; it had thrown off his sleeping patterns for a time, until he could adjust to the long hours & harried pace. Shortly after he'd completed his training program, he'd suffered migraine headaches for the first time in his life. But all in all he'd done pretty well. Some people cracked under the pressure. Unforgettably Blue had collapsed in the elevator from exhaustion, & Simplicity had to be sedated & pried out of her new Mercedes-Benz 560-ST in the parking lot across the street because she wouldn't let go of her steering wheel. "The car won't stop! The car won't stop!" she kept shrieking, her eyes bugging out like headlights. So what was a little stick-tapping?

Tap, tap, tap, tap, tap.

Friendship asked Uncertain to accompany him for broth.

"Thank you," replied Uncertain. "That would be wonderful!"

In the lounge, they talked about many things: The unfortunate state of the economy, corporate downsizing, white-collar layoffs, ballooning unemployment, the skyrocketing cost of higher education & how little it would buy one in this day & age. Just chitchat, but Uncertain involved himself in every bit of it, listening intently to Friendship's tossed-off comments, & responding in his usual animated way when he had an opinion of his own to express.

Finally Friendship asked Uncertain about his personal life. Uncertain had gotten married last year, "To the most beautiful girl alive. Her name is Concerned." He smiled. "Isn't that a fabulous name? It sounds so serious. I'm always catching her with this worried look on her face. Only *I* can make her smile, she says. That's how she knew she loved me." They lived in a cute little split-level in the suburbs, a starter home they'd bought on the strength of his job at Happiness & Luxury. She worked as a hostess in a local art gallery.

"You'll be able to afford a lot more than that in no time," commented

Friendship, "especially if your accounts keep doing so well. You've become the talk of the firm. Everyone is very excited for you."

"Isn't it amazing? I almost can't believe it myself. I hope I can keep it going."

"So do we all," said Friendship. "So do we all."

Uncertain blinked—but he had always been a rapid blinker. That hadn't changed. He was a sloppy fellow, too, allowing the lamb's eye broth to drip down the side of his mouth, leaving the evidence of his corn bread crumbs on his lips. Friendship wondered why someone with such an unguarded personality had not made any friends in two years. One could not help but feel safe with him, a dolphin in among the sharks.

Friendship followed Uncertain to the bank on his lunch hour. Friendship didn't want to think about how foolish he felt, so he began to picture himself as an agent on a secret mission for H & L (which wasn't all that far from the truth, now that he considered it.) Uncertain worked on his coffee break, leafing through some papers in his briefcase, always looking a bit confused, but deep in concentration. Friendship smiled while watching him, remembering those old training days & that addled look. Nothing about the man had changed one iota.

Nothing, that is, except for the wooden stick. Uncertain pulled it out once during lunch, chewed momentarily on the end of it, & slid it back into his shirt pocket.

After work, Uncertain rode home on the city bus. Friendship followed the bus in his own car. All of this would surely come to nothing, he decided. He would have nothing to report to Chakra Moon Wary, the firm would fire Uncertain, & Friendship would be rewarded in some way for his efforts. It was really very sad. He began to wonder if there might be a way to save Uncertain without jeopardizing his own career.

Uncertain got off the bus with the other park-&-ride passengers, but he didn't walk to his car. Instead he went into the supermarket. Friendship parked his car & went in after him. He fought through a crowd at the entrance & hurried past a few aisles as he looked for his mark.

He thought he spotted Uncertain standing beside the frozen foods section. He edged toward him.

That's when Friendship saw her.

The most beautiful girl alive.

Small, somewhat round of face; large eyes the color of polished jade; full lips; a tiny, upturned nose; skin the look of a soft, pale animal; hair like strawberry silk; shoulders as round & perfect as silver spoons. & yet to take each of her individual features & examine them separately from the whole would not have done her justice, for she had no classical beauty to speak of, but the complete picture stood before him like a rare & delicate work of art, something one would long to hold, but not too tightly, for fear of fracturing her fragile framework.

"Friendship!" called Uncertain, snapping him out of his trance.

Damn! He'd been spotted. Some spy he made. He had no alternative now but to make the best of it. He approached the couple with a generous smile. "Uncertain! Good to see you. What a coincidence!"

What a coincidence? What an idiot! He prayed he hadn't sounded half as guilty as he felt. What did he have to feel guilty about, anyway? He was only doing his job.

"Friendship, I'd like you to meet my wife, Concerned."

She took his hand. Friendship could feel the sweat rush to his palms & forehead. His heart raced. His throat went dry. The warmth of her hand drew him in like a whisper. He tried to avoid looking into her jade eyes, but he couldn't help himself. He was riveted. He'd never felt such an immediate attraction to any woman before. "I stopped in for some milk," he managed to stammer. Her skin was very much like milk. Smooth, creamy. She wore a bonnet of black velvet that lent her the air of a cherub or a pixie, & over her shoulders, a short cape that gave her an angelic, winged look. She wore one beaded earring in her right ear, with a peacock's feather attached to its end, like a long tail.

"The milk is all the way on the other side of the store," she said, amused.

"Oh, yes, thank you."

"Darling," said Uncertain, "don't we have a coupon for the crocuses?" He looked confused as he searched his pockets. The ever-addled Uncertain. How could he have possibly landed this . . . this . . . *goddess*?

Someone nudged Friendship from behind with a shopping cart. "Excuse me, but you're blocking the aisle," said an old man.

"I'm sorry," said Friendship, thankful for the sudden distraction. He needed to gather his wits. He would say good-bye, keeping his eyes downcast, & make a quick getaway. He turned back toward Uncertain.

Sticks. Wooden sticks. He saw them in Concerned's purse as she searched for the coupon—at least a dozen of Uncertain's thin, flat sticks in a compartment next to her wallet. She found the coupon & snapped her purse shut. It happened so quickly he had to replay the scene in his mind. Yes, yes: he'd seen the wooden sticks.

"Well, I really should be going," mumbled Friendship.

"Busy, busy," Uncertain said. "As I remember it, you were always a busy man."

He refused to look at her. He would glance at the frozen salamander legs, the microwavable newt potpies.

"A pleasure meeting you," said the goddess.

He concentrated on the stench of fresh, cold squid from the seafood counter. "The pleasure was all mine," he said, finally looking at her, holding her gaze, wishing that he hadn't.

His legs trembled as he walked away.

Friendship barely slept a wink that night, haunted by visions of the most beautiful girl alive. What was it about her that had struck him so? He had decided a long time ago that he was not meant to share his life with a woman—*any* woman in any sort of relationship (or any man for that matter, since the thought of a homosexual relationship repulsed him, though such arrangements were *en vogue*). He had tried to get close to a few women on several occasions when he was younger, to forge some kind of deep, meaningful, long-lasting relationship, but despite his efforts he had always failed, & eventually he came to realize that he'd failed precisely because of his efforts. If he had to try so hard, if he had to *force* himself into a loving relationship, then it wasn't love at all.

So Friendship had thrown himself into a career as an independent financial adviser. His determination, more than his success, had earned him an interview & an entry-level position at Happiness & Luxury, & he was perfectly willing to make whatever sacrifices were necessary to further his career—even, he realized with a modicum of distaste, if one of those sacrifices was Uncertain.

But the girl. What a treasure! If he had only found her when he was younger, his whole life would have been completely different. He would have stuck to her like cobwebs, & if she'd tried to escape, he would have spun more & more webs around her until she couldn't find her way out, until she couldn't breathe without him. Yes, he would have been another person entirely. A better person. Passionate. Happy. Friendship had never thought of himself as an unhappy man, just unlucky, but he suddenly noticed the difference.

He dozed once, twice, & woke with a start, thinking about the wooden sticks in Concerned's purse. What did they mean? Nothing, most likely. How could a bunch of sticks be responsible for Uncertain's boom in the money markets? The mere mention to the Chakra of such a possibility would make him a laughingstock.

In the lonely darkness, Friendship began to realize the impossible situation into which he'd been placed. If he turned up nothing on Uncertain & things went badly for the firm, he himself might be used as a scapegoat. If he did discover something, & the firm used his information to their advantage, he might be seen as no more than an untrustworthy informer. & yet he couldn't have turned the Chakra down without compromising & quite possibly destroying his future. His career was all he had to live for. The cat had played him perfectly. Was there any possible way to save himself?

Near dawn, he lit a candle to the Spirit of the Crone, the Wise One. The candle represented the Light of Understanding in the darkness of one's personal mysteries. He prayed that he would see the Light.

At work that morning, he felt about as limber & alert as a log. He wasn't an old man, but he was too old to put in a sleepless night & not feel any the worse for wear. Well, one more day & it would all be over. Perhaps he & Uncertain could open their own investment firm, once they were both finished at H & L. Maybe he was overreacting. He hoped so.

Friendship was so caught up in his morbid conjectures that he almost didn't notice Uncertain jerk upright in his chair, dash away from his desk, & disappear around the corner toward the men's room with an urgent look on his face.

Friendship stood up. He felt like an absolute fool following a man into the bathroom, but he was desperate now to find something, anything, that might save him.

The men's room was quiet & bright with fluorescent lights. Uncertain was not standing in front of the sinks, nor at the urinals. Friendship stepped forward, past the full-length mirrors, around the corner, trying not to make any noise with his shoes on the black-&-white tile floor. The bathroom smelled overly antiseptic, drenched with Clean. The silence startled him. He felt his heart pounding, although he didn't know why. He came to the row of stalls in the rear of the men's room, & saw that the last door had been shut. He crouched down & spotted the edge of Uncertain's bright orange cape on the floor, & his legs in an awkward position, as if the man were sitting on the tile instead of on the toilet.

The legs began to tremble, then shake, & a strange sound emanated from the stall. A choking-growling sound. Friendship wanted to run away, but in his moment of hesitation, Uncertain's shaking grew more violent, & Friendship, perhaps instinctively, darted forward.

He tried to yank open the stall door, but Uncertain had bolted it from the inside. Friendship dropped onto his stomach & began to crawl underneath the door.

Uncertain snarled & tremored & kicked violently, but Friendship made it in, lurched forward, & tried to still Uncertain's convulsing body. Uncertain jerked & flopped, his eyes bulging, streaked with a terrible red. Crushed between Uncertain's teeth was the wooden stick.

The man was dying! Friendship needed to get help! He tried to pull away, but Uncertain clutched Friendship's biceps with inhuman strength.

& then, abruptly, Uncertain's body went slack. The wooden stick fell to the floor. His breathing slowed. His face relaxed. He looked up at Friendship & smiled. Smiled!

"You're insane," said Friendship; it was all he could think to say.

Uncertain chuckled nervously. "So now you know my secret."

"Your secret? What are you talking about? What's wrong with you? I'd better get a medic."

"No!" Uncertain reached up weakly & held Friendship's elbow. "No one can find out! They'll take away my gift! They'll steal it from me! Promise me you'll never tell a soul. I'll give you whatever you want. I'll give you a sure thing. I just saw it in the aura. There's a chemical company in Cartagena, Colombia—Bolívar Chemicals—they've developed a new heat-resistant material that NASA wants for their aeroballistic rocket glider. It's just a prototype, but it's going to be big, very big— they're about to sign a contract—Bolívar stock will be worth *billions* if we buy now. Don't you see, Friendship? I've seen it in the aura. The *aura!* You have no idea what it's like! It's the light of life. Everything in my head explodes with electricity & then it unifies. *Unifies!* I can see everything all at once—separately, but at once—heaven & Earth & life & death & the future. Don't you understand? You must understand me . . . please!"

Uncertain's eyes closed, opened again, closed at last in unconsciousness, & an unnatural look crossed his face that was an accident of incongruities. Friendship would always remember it that way—unnatural, alien, as if the look came not from inside Uncertain, but from some other place, some other time, dimension, life, or perhaps even death.

The aura.

Later, Friendship would read extensively about the aura. The vast majority of people who suffered epileptic seizures experienced it in one form or another. Some people might feel queasy, others might hear voices, inner music, or see bright images. Some reported feelings of euphoria, or rapture. Uncertain experienced a psychic epiphany.

But for now, Friendship wiped the sweat from his brow, breathed deeply of the antiseptic fumes mixed with his own sweat & fear, picked up the splintered wooden stick still wet with Uncertain's saliva, & thanked the Spirit of the Crone for showing him the Light of Understanding.

Two weeks later, Friendship met Uncertain in the lounge.

"How are you feeling, my friend?" said Friendship, forcing himself to smile. He had to force the smile because Uncertain's deathly pallor would not allow him a genuine one. The man looked as limp & weary as an old, faded dish towel. He should never have called Uncertain to broth. Why had he?

Uncertain acted as if he hadn't heard the question. He looked past Friendship, his lips slightly parted, like those of a senile old man lost in thought, his hands trembling, fingers wrapped tightly around his cup. Bloodshot eyes. Slumped shoulders.

"The medication," said Uncertain, "is making me tired . . . phenobarbital . . . Dilantin . . . gives me double vision, I think that's what the doctors said . . . Mysoline . . . no, Zarontin making me nauseous, depressed, a little, I guess . . . " A long pause. "They're trying to find the right drug . . . no . . . the right combination."

Friendship leaned forward, tried to get Uncertain to look at him. "Uncertain, I just want you to know that I'm sorry things have been so difficult for you lately. I've been questioning the doctors, following your progress. They're very pleased, I want you to know. The seizures have stopped. That's a good sign, they tell me. & once they balance your medication you'll be fine—as good as new—& you'll see it was the right thing to do. The doctors all agree you would have died without the medication."

Uncertain closed his eyes for a long moment. He was having trouble breathing. His expression showed nothing at all, no pain, no sorrow, no sign of hope.

Friendship had done a good deal of research on epilepsy since he'd discovered Uncertain on the men's room floor. Epilepsy had been around since Cro-Magnon man. At one point in history some five thousand years ago, people believed epileptic seizures were the result of evil spirits invading the body. In ancient Greece, epilepsy was described as a "sacred disease," as if someone had been visited by the gods. Friendship read all about absence seizures, or *petit mal;* autonomic seizures that result in only headaches & nausea; sensory seizures where a person might see or hear things that aren't actually there; the *grand mal,* typified by violent muscular jerks when most of the neurons in the brain discharged in one horrible upheaval. But Uncertain's epilepsy was unique. The man had never lost consciousness, not even in the throes of his seizure. That was extremely unusual. Also, he'd had enough wits about him to bite down on the wooden stick & keep from chomping off his tongue—& there had never been any previously reported cases of enhanced psychic abilities during a seizure or its aura. No, Uncertain was a rare case.

Uncertain finally looked up at Friendship. "As good as new," he mumbled, twitching just a bit, bringing his cup shakily to his lips, glancing at it for a moment, & then putting it back down, as if he'd forgotten why or how or when he'd picked it up in the first place.

III. Friendship & The Most Beautiful Girl Alive

Concerned wanted to see him.

Friendship was as nervous as a schoolboy on his first date, pacing the floor of his brand-new chamber, fixing & refixing his appearance in front of the mirror of his own personal bathroom. The Chakra of Ethics & Principles (the Black Cat, as he'd come to think of her) had not been kidding when she said the firm would be "extremely appreciative" if he helped solve their problem. He'd been promoted to Chakra Moon Wary's personal E & P Task Force. None of his fears of failure & humiliation had come true. He'd been rescued by the Spirit of the Crone.

Friendship poured himself a rosewater from his private stock. Concerned would be hurt, angry. She might even hate him for what he'd done—for reporting her husband, for taking away Uncertain's special gift—& he could not blame her. But he had already decided to fight for Concerned. He wanted her, & that was that. He would use his power, his position, whatever he had, whatever it took. He had never felt his way before. He assumed it was love, but whatever it was he would not relinquish it under any circumstances. Time & patience would win her.

He would pursue her like a cat. & today, this communication, however uncomfortable, was the first step.

His door swung quietly open, & a secretary led Concerned into his chamber. She swept into his consciousness like a dream. But he fought the dream. He did not want her to exist somewhere beyond his grasp. She must remain real.

"Ah, Concerned, you wanted to see me? What a pleasant surprise! Please, sit down. I'll fix you a rosewater."

"That won't be necessary," she said. She was wearing her black velvet cap, a long, dark coat, & black leather gloves.

Friendship cleared his throat. "I just want you to know," he said too quickly, "that I can certainly understand if you are upset with me, but—"

"I'm not upset at all. I'm very busy today, I have some appointments at the gallery, & I don't have much time for socializing. Just sit down."

Taken aback, Friendship sat at his desk.

Concerned remained standing. "I came here to thank you for helping me destroy Uncertain. I would have done it myself eventually, of course, but your interference expedited the process considerably."

A confused look crossed Friendship's face—he could feel it, & he could see it, too, in Concerned's eyes.

This brought a wide smile to her lips. "Don't look so surprised. I have certain powers, certain gifts of my own."

"What are you talking about?"

She pulled off her gloves, held them easily in her hand. "I'm a Hekate."

Friendship stood, slowly.

A Hekate. A Goddess of the Dead.

He refused to believe it! There were a few of them around, he knew. The cult was growing, Chakra Moon Wary had said, but Concerned was so . . . so *beautiful,* & he loved her. Yes, it was love, he was sure of it. She was so *alive.* How could she possibly be a worshiper of the dead?

Concerned stared at him with her jade eyes. Her face was cold & white.

"Uncertain was an easy mark. He was sensitive & innocent & weak. He cheated H & L for me, & by the end he would have killed for me, although I doubt he would have lived long enough to try. I kept encouraging his seizures, & he was almost to the point where he could bring them on himself. It would have been interesting to play him out to the end, to see if I could bring H & L down with him, but this way, I think, is better. You are a much more capable man."

"No." Yes. He could see it now, if he allowed himself to look at it. He could see what she had done using the Hekate's Sorcerology. It should have been obvious to him, but it hadn't even entered his mind. She had not only manipulated Uncertain, but she'd manipulated *him* as well. She had enchanted him, infected him in some dark way on the occasion of their first meeting. That's why he'd felt such a strong pull. It was an unnatural attraction, not a natural one. He was simply too inexperienced to recognize the difference.

"I'll have nothing more to do with you," said Friendship, although even as the words came out of his mouth he knew nothing could be further from the truth. It was too late. He had already fallen under her spell.

She turned around & stepped toward the door, then turned back to look at him. "I'll be asking you to do several things for me in the next few weeks. Business & money transactions mostly. If you do a satisfactory job, there will be more, more of everything, more of *me*. I'm sure you're interested in that, aren't you?"

He lost his breath at the mere thought of taking her to bed. To die in her arms would be the simplest of things, but he knew she would not allow his death to come so easily. Even now, standing here in front of this horrible creature who possessed the power to break any man's will, make any man a slave, turn a man & his life & his dreams into those of the living dead—this was the power of the Hekate—he knew that he could not fight her. She must be very powerful indeed, he thought, to know him so well after one handshake, to know him & his weaknesses better than he knew them himself.

Concerned reached into her purse, withdrew the wooden sticks, & dropped them on the floor. "There will always be the hunters & the hunted, the cat & the mouse. In a way, it's almost reassuring, don't you think?"

She walked out of his office.

She was marvelous! thought Friendship. He loved her! He hated her! But more than anything else, as he stood trembling in his office, he knew that he must fight her. Was it a mere coincidence that today he was wearing his faded, navy blue cape, the cape that reminded him he could do anything in the world he set his mind to do? No, in the new universe, the universe of Sorcerology, there were no coincidences. To survive, one had only to know the proper theorems. Whatever hold Concerned had over him, he would find it, fight it, destroy it. Friendship would win, or die trying. He had worked too hard to give up.

He went over to the wooden sticks & crushed them under his heel.

*   *   *

Friendship took the elevator to the fourteenth floor, & ordered the secretary to hold all of Chakra Moon Wary's calls. She was working on the computer when he barged in.

"Friendship?" she said. "Is something wrong?"

"Yes. I've been marked by a Hekate," he said, & he noticed how he had to fight the words past his teeth. Concerned's claws had already scratched deeply. She was strong, all right. But Friendship was not Uncertain. He would not crumble quite so easily.

Chakra Moon Wary stood, her dark face revealing a moment of fear. But then she recovered. "Uncertain, too?"

"Yes, I'm afraid so."

"Don't panic," she said, perhaps more to herself than to Friendship. "We have several applications we can run. Research & Development has been working on some new diagnostics to combat dark magic. We will try everything, Friendship. You have been loyal to me; I will not desert you. It will be a long, frightening battle, but you will not have to face her alone. Together, we can fight this creature, & together we can defeat her."

He was feeling dizzy, nauseous. "Together," Friendship whispered. He had never fought with anyone before. It had always been Friendship alone against the world. Friendship alone. Could this be a new beginning for him? He hoped so. It would be something to strive for, something to live for.

Without even thinking about it, he reached out to her. His hand trembled. The Chakra came to him, squeezed his hand, pulled him to her breasts, hugged him tightly. He felt the warmth of her body inside him, as if a hot wind had peeled back his skin.

He realized, then, that he'd been wrong all along, that he had looked only on the surface of things, & that surfaces were simply veneers that used mere facts to hide the Truth.

Forget age, forget rank, forget manner. Here, in his arms, was the most beautiful girl alive, for in a moment unplanned, unpracticed, unbidden, in a moment that could not have been arranged by any Sorcerology, dark or light, she had reached out to him & touched his heart, & he had given his heart over to her without a moment's hesitation.

"Together," he whispered, "we can fight."

NIGHT

A time of closing down and rest when the possibilities of youth have narrowed or vanished.

BIRDS
CHARLES DE LINT

Charles de Lint is a full-time writer and musician, currently making his home in Ottawa, Ontario, with his wife MaryAnn Harris, an artist and musician. His instruments are Irish flute, fiddle, whistles, bouzouki, guitar, and bodhran. His writing includes award-winning fantasy novels and short stories, comic book scripts, poetry, reviews, and columns for a number of magazines.

> *Isn't it wonderful? The world scans.*
> —Nancy Willard, from
> "Looking for Mr. Ames"

1

When her head is full of birds, anything is possible. She can understand the slow language of the trees, the song of running water, the whispering gossip of the wind. The conversation of the birds fills her until she doesn't even think to remember what it was like before she could understand them. But sooner or later, the birds go away, one by one, find new nests, new places to fly. It's not that they tire of her; it's simply not in their nature to tarry for too long.

But she misses them. Misses their company, the flutter of wings inside her head and their trilling conversations. Misses the possibilities. The magic.

To call them back she has to approach them as a bride. Dressed in white, with something old and something new, something borrowed and something blue. And a word. A new word, from another's dream. A word that has never been heard before.

2

Katja Faro was out later than she thought safe, at least for this part of town and at this time of night, the minute hand of her old-fashioned wristwatch steadily climbing up the last quarter of her watch face to count the hour. Three A.M. That late.

From early evening until the clubs close, Gracie Street is a jumbled clutter of people, looking for action, looking for gratification, or just out and about, hanging, gossiping with their friends. There's always something happening, from Lee Street all the way across to Williamson, but tag on a few more hours and clubland becomes a frontier. The lights advertising the various cafés, clubs, and bars begin to flicker and go out, their patrons and staff have all gone home, and the only people out on the streets are a few stragglers, such as Katja tonight, and the predators.

Purple combat boots scuffing on the pavement, Katja felt adrift on the empty street. It seemed like only moments ago she'd been secure in the middle of good conversation, laughter, and espressos; then some-one remarked on the time, the café was closing, and suddenly she was out here, on the street, by herself, finding her own way home. She held her jean jacket closed at her throat—the buttons had come off, one by one, and she kept forgetting to replace them—and listened to the swish of her long flowered skirt, the sound of her boots on the pavement. Listened as well for other footsteps and prayed for a cab to come by.

She was paying so much attention to what might be lurking behind the shadowed mouths of the alleyways that she almost didn't notice the slight figure curled up in the doorway of the pawnshop on her right. The sight made her pause. She glanced up and down the street before crouching down in the doorway. The figure's features were in shadow, the small body outlined under what looked like a dirty white sheet, or a shawl. By its shape Katja could tell it wasn't a boy.

"Hey, are you okay?" she asked.

When there was no response, she touched the girl's shoulder and repeated her question. Large pale eyes flickered open, their gaze set-tling on Katja. The girl woke like a cat, immediately aware of every-thing around her. Her black hair hung about her face in a tangle. Unlike most street people, she had a sweet smell, like a field of clover, or a potpourri of dried rosehips and herbs, gathered in a glass bowl.

"What makes you think I'm not okay?" the girl asked.

Katja pushed the fall of her own dark hair back from her brow and settled back on her heels.

"Well, for one thing," she said, "you're lying here in a doorway, on a bed of what looks like old newspapers. It's not exactly the kind of place people pick to sleep in if they've got a choice."

She glanced up and down the street again as she spoke, still wary of her surroundings and their possible danger, still hoping to see a cab.

"I'm okay," the girl told her.

"Yeah, right."

"No, really."

Katja had to smile. She wasn't so old that she'd forgotten what it felt like to be in her late teens and immortal. Remembering, looking at this slight girl with her dark hair and strangely pale eyes, she got this odd urge to take in a stray the way that Angel and Jilly often did. She wasn't sure why. She liked to think that she had as much sympathy as the next person, but normally it was hard to muster much of it at this time of night. Normally she was thinking too much about what terrors the night might hold for her to consider playing the Good Samaritan. But this girl looked so young. . . .

"What's your name?" she asked.

"Teresa. Teresa Lewis."

Katja offered her hand as she introduced herself.

Teresa laughed. "Welcome to my home," she said, and shook Katja's hand.

"This a regular squat?" Katja asked. Nervous as she was at being out so late, she couldn't imagine actually sleeping in a place like this on a regular basis.

"No," Teresa said. "I meant the street."

Katja sighed. Immortal. "Look. I don't have that big a place, but there's room on my couch if you want to crash."

Teresa gave her a considering look.

"Well, I know it's not the Harbour Ritz," Katja began.

"It's not that," Teresa told her. "It's just that you don't know me at all. I could be loco, for all you know. Get to your place and rob you . . . "

"I've got a big family," Katja told her. "They'd track you down and take it out of your skin."

Teresa laughed again. It was like they were meeting at a party somewhere, Katja thought, drinks in hand, no worries, instead of on Gracie Street at 3:00 A.M.

"I'm serious," she said. "I've got the room."

Teresa's laughter trailed off. Her pale gaze settled on Katja's features.

"Do you believe in magic?" she asked.

"Say what?"

"Magic. Do you believe in it?"

Katja blinked. She waited for the punch line, but when it didn't come, she said, "Well, I'm not sure. My friend Jilly sure does—though maybe magic's not quite the right word. It's more like she believes there's more to this world than we can always see or understand. She sees things. . . ."

Katja caught herself. How did we get into this? she thought. She wanted to change the subject, she wanted to get off the street before some home boys showed up with all the wrong ideas in mind, but the steady weight of Teresa's intense gaze wouldn't let her go.

"Anyway," Katja said, "I guess you could say Jilly does. Believes in magic, I mean. Sees things."

"But what about you? Have you seen things?"

Katja shook her head. "Only 'old, unhappy, far-off things, and battles long ago,'" she said. "Wordsworth," she added, placing the quote when Teresa raised her eyebrows in a question.

"Then I guess you couldn't understand," Teresa told her. "See, the reason I'm out here like this is that I'm looking for a word."

3

I can't sleep. I lie in bed for what feels like hours, staring up at the shadows cast on the ceiling from the streetlight outside my bedroom window. Finally I get up. I pull on a pair of leggings and a T-shirt and pad quietly across the room in my bare feet. I stand in the doorway and look at my guest. She's still sleeping, all curled up again, except her nest is made up of a spare set of my sheets and blankets now instead of old newspapers.

I wish it wasn't so early. I wish I could pick up the phone and talk to Jilly. I want to know if the strays she brings home tell stories as strange as mine told me on the way back to my apartment. I want to know if her strays can recognize the egret which is a deposed king. If they can understand the gossip of bees and what crows talk about when they gather in a murder. If they ever don the old woman wisdom to be found in the rattle-and-cough cry of a lonesome gull and wear it like a cloak of story.

I want to know if Jilly's ever heard of bird-brides, because Teresa says that's what she is, what she usually is, until the birds fly away. To gather them back into her head takes a kind of a wedding ritual that's sealed with a dream-word. That's what she was doing out on Gracie Street when I found her: worn out from trying to get strangers to tell her a word that they'd only ever heard before in one of their dreams.

I don't have to tell you how helpful the people she met were. The ones that didn't ignore her or call her names just gave her spare change instead of the word she needs. But I can't say as I blame them. If she'd come up to me with her spiel I don't know how I'd have reacted. Not well, probably. Wouldn't have listened. Gets so you can't walk down a block some days without getting hit up for change, five or six times. I don't want to be cold; but when it comes down to it, I've only got so much myself.

I look away from my guest, my gaze resting on the phone for a moment, before I turn around and go back into my room. I don't bother undressing. I just lie there on my bed, looking up at the shadow play that's still being staged on my ceiling. I know what's keeping me awake: I can't decide if I've brought home some poor confused kid, or a piece of magic. It's not the one or the other that's brought on my insomnia. It's that I'm seriously considering the fact that it might be one or the other.

4

"No, I have a place to live," Teresa said the next morning. They were sitting at the narrow table in Katja's kitchen that only barely seated the two of them comfortably, hands warming around mugs of freshly brewed coffee. "I live in a bachelor in an old house on Stanton Street."

Katja shook her head. "Then why were you sleeping in a doorway last night?"

"I don't know. I think because the people on Gracie Street in the evening seem to dream harder than people anywhere else."

"They're just more desperate to have a good time," Katja said.

"I suppose. Anyway, I was sure I'd find my word there, and by the time I realized I wouldn't—at least last night—it was so late, and I was just too tired to go home."

"But weren't you scared?"

Teresa regarded her with genuine surprise. "Of what?"

How to explain, Katja wondered. Obviously this girl sitting across from her in a borrowed T-shirt, with sleep still gathered in the corners of her eyes, was fearless, like Jilly. Where did you start enumerating the dangers for them? And why bother? Teresa probably wouldn't listen any more than Jilly ever did. Katja thought sometimes that people like them must have guardian angels watching out for them—and working overtime.

"I feel like I'm always scared," she said.

"I guess that's the way I feel, when the birds leave and all I have left in my head are empty nests and a few stray feathers. Kind of lonely, and scared that they'll never come back."

That wasn't the way Katja felt at all. Her fear lay in the headlines of newspapers and the sound bites that helped fill newscasts. There was too much evil running loose—random, petty evil, it was true, but evil all the same. Ever-present and all around her so that you didn't know whom to trust anymore. Sometimes it seemed as though everyone in the world was so much bigger and more capable than her. Too often, confronted with their confidence, she could only feel helpless.

"Where did you hear about this . . . this thing with the birds?" she said instead. "The way you can bring them back?"

Teresa shrugged. "I just always knew it."

"But you have all these details. . . ."

Borrowed from bridal folklore, Katja added to herself—all except for the word she had to get from somebody else's dream. The question she'd really wanted to ask was *why* those particular details? What made their borrowed possibilities true? Katja didn't want to sound judgmental. The truth, she had to admit if she was honest with herself, wasn't so much that she believed her houseguest as that she didn't disbelieve her. Hadn't she woken up this morning searching the fading remnants of her dreams, looking for a new word that only existed beyond the gates of her sleeping mind?

Teresa was smiling at her. The wattage behind the expression seemed to light the room, banishing shadows and uncertainties, and Katja basked in its glow.

"I know what you're thinking," Teresa said. "They don't even sound all that original except for the missing word, do they? But I believe any of us can make things happen—even magical, impossible things. It's a matter of having faith in the private rituals we make up for ourselves."

"Rituals you make up . . . ?"

"Uh-huh. The rituals themselves aren't all that important on their own—though once you've decided on them, you have to stick to them, just like the old alchemists did. You have to follow them through."

"But if the rituals aren't that important," Katja asked, "then what's the point of them?"

"How they help you focus your will—your intent. That's what magic is, you know. It's having a strong enough sense of self and what's around you to not only envision it being different but *making* it different."

"You really believe this, don't you?"

"Of course," Teresa said. "Don't you?"

"I don't know. You make it sound so logical."

"That's because it's true. Or maybe—" That smile of Teresa's returned, warming the room again. "—because I'm *willing* it to be true."

"So would your ritual work for me?"

"If you believe in it. But you should probably find your own—a set of circumstances that feels right for you." She paused for a moment, then added, "And you have to know what you're asking for. My birds are what got me through a lot of bad times. Listening to their conversations and soliloquies let me forget what was happening to me."

Katja leaned forward. She could see the rush of memories rising in Teresa, could see the pain they brought with them. She wanted to reach out and hold her in a comforting embrace—the same kind of embrace she'd needed so often but rarely got.

"What happened?" she asked, her voice soft.

"I don't want to remember." Teresa said. She gave Katja an apologetic look. "It's not that I can't, it's that I don't want to."

"You don't have to talk about it if you don't want to," Katja assured her. "Just because I'm putting you up doesn't mean you have to explain yourself to me."

There was no sunshine in the smile that touched Teresa's features now. It was more like moonlight playing on wild rosebushes, the cool light glinting on thorns. Memories could impale you just like thorns. Katja knew that all too well.

"But I can't not remember," Teresa said. "That's what so sad. For all the good things in my life, I can't stop thinking of how much I hurt before the birds came."

5

I know about pain. I know about loneliness. Talking with Teresa, I realize that these are the first real conversations I've had with someone else in years.

I don't want to make it sound as though I don't have any friends, that I never talk to anyone—but sometimes it feels like that all the same. I always seem to be standing on the outside of a friendship, of conversations, never really engaged. Even last night, before I found Teresa sleeping in the doorway. I was out with a bunch of people. I was in the middle of any number of conversations and camaraderie. But I still went home alone. I listened to what was going on around me, I smiled some, laughed some, added a sentence here, another there, but it wasn't really me that was partaking of the company. The real me was one step removed, watching it happen. Like it seems I always am. Everybody I know seems to inhabit one landscape that they all share while I'm the only person standing in the landscape that's inside of me.

But today it's different. We're talking about weird, unlikely things, but I'm *there* with Teresa. I don't even know her, there's all sorts of people I've known for years, known way better, but not one of them seems to have looked inside me as truly as she does. This alchemy, this magic, she's offering me is opening a door inside me. It's making me remember. It's making me want to fill my head with birds so that I can forget.

That's the saddest thing, isn't it? Wanting to forget. Desiring amnesia. I think that's the only reason some people kill themselves. I know it's the only reason I've ever seriously considered suicide.

Consider the statistics: One out of very five women will be sexually traumatized by the time they reach their twenties. They might be raped, they might be a child preyed upon by a stranger, they might be abused by the very people who are supposed to be looking out for them.

But the thing that statistic doesn't tell you is how often it can happen to that one woman out of five. How it can happen to her over and over and over again, but on the statistical sheet, she's still only listed as one woman in five. That makes it sound so random, the event an extraordinary moment of evil when set against the rest of her life, rather than something that she might have faced every day of her childhood.

I'd give anything for a head full of birds. I'd give anything for the noise and clamor of their conversation to drown out the memories when they rise up inside of me.

6

Long after noon came and went the two women still sat across from each other at the kitchen table. If their conversation could have been seen as well as heard, the spill of words that passed between them would have flooded off the table to eddy around their ankles in ever-deepening pools. It would have made for profound, dark water that was only bearable because each of them came to understand that the other truly understood what they had gone through, and sharing the stories of their battered childhoods made the burden, if not easier to bear, at least reminded them that they weren't alone in what they had undergone.

The coffee had gone cold in their mugs, but the hands across the table they held to comfort each other were warm, palm to palm. When they finally ran out of words, that contact helped maintain the bond of empathy that had grown up between them.

"I didn't have birds," Katja said after a long silence. "All I had was poetry."

"You wrote poems?"

Katja shook her head. "I became poetry. I inhabited poems. I filled them until their words were all I could hear inside my head." She tilted her head back and quoted one:

> Rough wind, that moanest loud
> Grief too sad for song;
> Wild wind, when sullen cloud
> Knells all the night long;
> Sad storm, whose tears are vain,
> Bare woods, whose branches strain,
> Deep caves and dreary main,—
> Wail, for the world's wrong!

"That's so sad. What's it called?" Teresa asked.

"'A dirge.' It's by Shelley. I always seemed to choose the sad poems, but I only ever wanted them for how I'd get so full of words I wouldn't be able to remember anything else."

"Birds and words," Teresa said. Her smile came out again from behind the dark clouds of her memories. "We rhyme."

7

We wash Teresa's dress that afternoon. It wasn't very white anymore—not after her having grubbed about in it on Gracie Street all day and then worn it as a nightgown while she slept in a doorway—but it cleans up better than I think it will. I feel like we're in a detergent commercial when we take it out of the dryer. The dress seems to glow against my skin as I hand it over to her.

Her something old is a plastic Crackerjack ring that she's had since she was a kid. Her something new are her sneakers—a little scuffed and worse for the wear this afternoon, but still passably white. Her borrowed is a white leather clasp-purse that her landlady loaned her. Her blue is a small clutch of silk flowers: forget-me-nots tied up with a white ribbon that she plans to wear as a corsage.

All she needs is that missing word.

I don't have one for her, but I know someone who might. Jilly always likes to talk about things not quite of this world—things seen from the corner of the eye, or brought over from a dream. And whenever she talks about dreams, Sophie Etoile's name comes up because Jilly insists Sophie's part faerie and therefore a true dreamer. I don't know Sophie all that well, certainly not well enough to guess at her genealogy, improbable or not as the case may be. But she does have an otherworldly, Pre-Raphaelite air about her that makes Jilly's claims seem possible—at least they seem possible considering my present state of mind.

And there's no one else I can turn to, no one I can think of. I can't explain this desperation I feel towards Teresa, a kind of mothering/big sister complex. I just have to help her. And while I know that I may not be able to make myself forget, I think I can do it for her. Or at least I want to try.

So that's how we find ourselves knocking at the door of Sophie's studio later that afternoon. When Sophie answers the door, her curly brown hair tied back from her face and her painting smock as spotless as Jilly says it always is, I don't have to go into a long explanation as to what we're doing there or why we need this word. I just have to mention that Jilly's told me that she's a true dreamer and Sophie gets this smile on her face, like you do when you're thinking about a mischievous child who's too endearing to get angry at, and she thinks for a moment, then says a word that at least I've never heard before. I turn to Teresa to ask her if it's what she needs, but she's already got this beatific look on her face.

"Mmm," is all she can manage.

I thank Sophie, who's giving the pair of us a kind of puzzled smile, and lead Teresa back down the narrow stairs of Sophie's building and out onto the street. I wonder what I'm going to do with Teresa. She looks for all the world as though she's tripping. But just when I decide to take her home again, her eyes get a little more focused and she takes my hand.

"I have to . . . readjust to all of this," she says. "But I don't want to have us just walk out of each other's lives. Can I come and visit you tomorrow?"

"Sure," I tell her. I hesitate a moment, then have to ask, "Can you really hear them?"

"Listen," she says.

She draws my head close to hers until my ear is resting right up against her temple. I swear I hear a bird's chorus resonating inside her head, conducted through skin and bone, from her mind into my mind.

"I'll come by in the morning," she says, and then drifts off down the pavement.

All I can do is watch her go, that birdsong still echoing inside me.

8

Back in my own living room, I sit on the carpet. I can feel a foreign vibe in my apartment, a quivering in the air from Teresa having been there. Everything in the room carries the memory of her, the knowledge of her gaze, how she handled and examined them with her attention. My furniture, the posters and prints on my walls, my knickknacks, all seemed subtly changed, a little stiff from the awareness of her looking at them.

It takes awhile for the room to settle down into its familiar habits. The fridge muttering to itself in the kitchen. The pictures in their frames letting out their stomachs and hanging slightly askew once more.

I take down a box of family photos from the hall closet and fan them out on the carpet in front of me. I look at the happy family they depict and try to see hints of the darkness that doesn't appear in the photos. There are too many smiles—mine, my mother's, my father's. I know real life was never the way these pictures pretend it was.

I sit there remembering my father's face—the last time I saw him. We were in the courtroom, waiting for him to be sentenced. He wouldn't look at me. My mother wouldn't look at me. I sat at the table with only a lawyer for support, only a stranger for family. That memory always makes me feel ashamed because even after all he'd done to me, I didn't feel any triumph. I felt only disloyalty. I felt only that I was the one who'd been bad, that what had happened to me had been my fault. I knew back then it was wrong to feel that way—just as I know now that it is—but I can't seem to help myself.

I squeeze my eyes shut, but the moment's locked in my brain, just like all those other memories from my childhood that put a lie to the photographs fanned out on the carpet around me. Words aren't going to blot them out for me today. There aren't enough poems in the world to do that. And even if I could gather birds into my head, I don't think they would work for me. But I remember what Teresa told me about rituals and magic.

It's having a strong enough sense of self and what's around you to not only envision it being different but making *it different.*

I remember the echoing sound of the birds I heard gossiping in her head, and I know that I can find peace, too. I just have to believe that I can. I just have to know what it is that I want and concentrate on having it, instead of what I've got. I have to find the ritual that'll make it work for me.

Instinctively, I realize it can't be too easy. Like Teresa's dream-word, the spell needs an element to complete it that requires some real effort on my part to attain it. But I know what the rest of the ritual will be—it comes into my head, full-blown, as if I've always known it but simply never stopped to access that knowledge before.

I pick up a picture of my father from the carpet and carefully tear his face into four pieces, sticking one piece in each of the front and back pockets of my jeans. I remember something I heard about salt, about it being used to cleanse, and add a handful of it to each pocket. I wrap the fingers of my left hand together with a black ribbon and tie the bow so that it lies across my knuckles. I lick my right forefinger and write my name on the bare skin of my stomach with saliva. Then I let my shirt fall back down to cover the invisible word and leave the apartment, looking for a person who, when asked to name a nineteenth century poet, will mistakenly put together the given name of one with the surname of another.

From somewhere I hear a sound like Teresa's birds, singing their approval.

DUST AND SAND
DAVE SMEDS

Dave Smeds *lives with his wife Connie and two children in Santa Rosa, California. Before turning to writing, he made his living as a graphic artist and typesetter. He also holds a third degree black belt in Goju-ryu karate and teaches classes in that art. He is the author of two novels and has sold short fiction to a long list of anthologies and to many magazines.*

Dabria found the stranger on her way back from the cliffs, where she had gone to gather chalk for her next dust painting. The man lay unconscious on the wet sand left by the retreating tide.

Dabria had never seen anything like him. He wore clothing even though it was not a holiday, along with a type of sandal that completely enveloped his feet. The hair she brushed from his eyes was black as the charcoal she used in her artwork. If he had been standing, he would have towered half a head higher than Old Krelall, the tallest man in her village.

She rolled him onto his back, checking for wounds, confirming that his breath flowed regularly. Despite his location, he seemed not to have come from the sea. His clothes were wet only where a far-reaching wave had just lapped against him, and his skin was free of crusted salt and seaweed. It was as if he had emerged from the sand like a newly hatched turtle.

He murmured without opening his eyes. For a moment Dabria thought he might speak, but he merely flopped his gaunt head listlessly from side to side. Pressing her hands to his temples, she found him blazing with fever.

Dragging him higher, she left him in the shadow of a clump of salt grass and hurried around the promontory to the shoals. As she expected, three of her brothers were there hunting tidecrawlers. They returned with her.

"Looks like he hasn't eaten in a year," quipped Brem, the eldest. "What do we do with him?"

"Take him to my hut," Dabria said. It was the closest building. "The healer can look at him there."

The brothers nodded. The youngest ran ahead, and by the time the bearers arrived, Neuann the healer was waiting along with Hemar, Dabria's father.

"Remove these wet garments," the healer commanded. The brothers stripped the stranger and placed him on Dabria's spare mat.

Neuann examined the stranger's mouth, ears, and glands. Her narrowed brow implied she saw no obvious cause for his condition. Though he was bony, he did not seem malnourished as Brem had implied. Forsaking common measures, the healer laid hands on his chest and slipped into a light trance. She emerged from it frowning.

"This illness is unlike anything I've seen or heard of. It is not catching, however. Provide him with rest, warmth, and water. He will recover or not on his own. This is something he has brought upon himself." Covering the patient with a blanket, Neuann hurried off, for it was nine months after the Rain Festival and two of the village women were in labor.

The brothers, needing more tidecrawlers for their feast, left soon after.

The stranger lay as if drained of life. He gave off the aura of an old man, though Dabria guessed he was no more than forty or so.

"What's this in his belt pouch?" Hemar asked. He pulled out a wooden slipcase. It opened to reveal a set of carving tools. "I've never seen metal like this in the Five Islands."

"Where could he have come from?" Dabria asked. "The Land Beyond the Ocean?"

Hemar grunted. "Even if that land supports life again, the people there would look like us." Hemar lifted a strand of the unconscious man's dark hair.

"He is a mystery, then." The thought appealed to her.

"Are you sure you want to leave him in your hut?" asked Hemar. "We don't know his character. Perhaps it would be better if he stayed in the men's lodge."

Hemar was Dabria's true-father. Of all her womb-mother's lovers, he was the one who had visited most often when Dabria and her siblings were small, bringing gifts and joining in the children's games when the women of the household were too busy. Not that Dabria was ever neglected—for most of her girlhood she had been fortunate to have five breast-mothers—but she enjoyed the paternal attention. Now that she was an unattached adult, she appreciated Hemar's undemanding presence even more. This courtship hut, for all its appeal and tradition, was a lonely place for someone accustomed to a communal household.

"And how many men stay in the lodge when they are sick?" Dabria asked. "I seem to recall you wearing out Rallea's spare mat that time you broke your leg." Rallea, one of Dabria's breast-mothers, always made room in her portion of the hut when a relative, male or female, faced an extended convalescence.

"That is different."

"Look at him," Dabria said, pointing at the pallid body of the stranger. "Even if he intended to harm me, I would be in no danger."

Hemar had to nod. Dabria had held her own for two decades against the impish harassment of five strong brothers. "I will come by every day anyway."

"I would welcome it," Dabria said, and meant it. She touched him affectionately on the wrist. He smiled at her, frowned at the sleeping man, and ambled down the path toward the lodge.

While the stranger slept on, Dabria pulled out one of her design trays. Festival week was nearing, and it was her task to coordinate the decoration of the village grounds for the Dance of the Blossom Moon. This was the third year she had won the honor, and perhaps she had become too complacent. If the elders rejected her initial design, she would scarcely have time to submit another.

She poured several handfuls of the chalk she'd gathered that morning into the tray and smoothed it into a thin layer. For her festival paintings she always used a white foundation; that helped preserve brightness and flair. Next she dipped into her urn of island soil, working it between her fingers until the tiny lumps of clay turned to fine powder. This she carefully poured into a spiral atop the chalk base.

Rust over cream. Those colors would work both in the sunlight during the children's part of the festival, and beneath the moonlight as the adults danced. Also, the chalk and clay were plentiful—Dabria had not forgotten her first festival painting, which required far too much crumbling of dried acanth leaves. Acanth leaves were the only source of the radiant brown Dabria had wanted for that design; these days she limited such indulgent choices of color to paintings that didn't have to be re-created on a scale large enough for the entire village to dance upon.

As she added accents of this pigment or that, the painting began to come alive. The hint of blue—that would sparkle in the children's eyes. The little circles of moss green—that would inspire fertile thoughts among the young women. A smile grew on Dabria's face. To create a painting was akin to creating life. A good one would make her forget to eat, or leave her young men waiting in vain for a promised rendezvous.

While she worked, visitor after visitor came to her hut, all wanting a glimpse of the stranger. After the sixth interruption she pointed out that the man needed rest and she needed concentration. With the characteristic politeness of the islands, the callers took their speculations and advice down the valley to the village teahouse.

She worked well into the evening. Finally she could think of nothing more to add to the design. The colors burst out in undiluted celebration. Any who danced the pattern of whorls and circles would be caught in its joy. Elderly men would prance, and the shyest women be bold.

After her dinner, she fetched the elders, who viewed and approved her work. Just after their visit the stranger stirred. His fever, which had eased earlier, was again forcing sweat out of him. He moaned and rolled on his side. Dabria bathed his face and chest with a damp cloth. He was still twisting restlessly when she retired for the night.

Dabria spent much of the morning down by the pools with Limron, swimming and making love. Though Abrel was the young man she suspected she'd choose when the time came for childmaking, Limron excited her more. Whenever life grew challenging, as the day before had been, Limron's playful attentions massaged away her cares.

When she entered her hut, she found signs that the stranger had awakened. His chest was once again rising and falling in the rhythm of deep slumber, but he had drunk a great deal of the water in the pitcher beside his mat, used the urine pot, and in his hands he clutched a piece of driftwood and one of his carving knives.

As Dabria eased the items from his grip, she saw that the wood contained marks. With a few deft strokes he had carved an image of an island.

Strangely, the island seemed familiar, though she had never seen that bay, and the mountain showed no sign that human inhabitants had ever thinned its jungle. She could only recall one other example of art that had ever evoked such a sense of presence—her own.

Yet this was so different from her work. A dust painting was always susceptible to the adjustment of a finger or a puff from puckered lips. Malleable, alive. The image in the wood was permanent. And it was so literal. The island resembled one she might see on the horizon of an ocean somewhere, whereas her designs were chiefly like that she had made the night before—abstract, meant to evoke moods. The carving offered no emotions; it simply recorded a view.

The carving fascinated her, though it disturbed her as well. Out of respect for his obvious talent, she took care as she set it aside. From time to time as she prepared her midday meal, she glanced at it. And at him. Despite her relaxing morning, she had to struggle to keep tension from stiffening her shoulders.

After the meal, she visited the village and set her assistants to reproducing the festival design upon the grounds. This first day, the main task was hauling more chalk from the cliffs, for which her presence was not needed, so after marking the perimeter of the design, she accepted her friend Melanya's invitation to stroll along the beach.

As they reached the shore not far from where she'd found the stranger, she almost tripped over her own feet. The formerly open sea to the west was now a narrow strait. A large island took up most of the horizon. Uncut jungle cloaked its hillsides. A bay faced the strait.

"How long has that been there?" Dabria asked.

Melanya stared at her quizzically. "Are you feeling well?"

"Perhaps not. I don't remember that island being there yesterday."

"It's been there forever. Why do you think we call our home the Six Islands? That is Robos."

Dabria stifled a wave of dizziness. As if a hand had reached into her and plucked at the threads of her memory, she could now recall an entire history of the island. Robos was uninhabited, reserved for the dead, visited only by funeral parties. It was, as Melanya said, one of the six main islands of their archipelago.

But that could not be. Robos was the name of a canyon on the island of Timmila. In ancient times its caves were used as crypts, but that had been when the people were few in number—long ago, before the custom arose that limited women to three children of the womb.

Five Islands. Her land was the Five Islands. What was happening?

Melanya gazed back with a furrowed brow.

"My mind played a trick on me," Dabria said quickly. "I'm fine now."

Melanya did not press the issue, but Dabria felt no relief. There should not be secrets between them. Melanya was to be her breast-sister. As soon as Dabria became a mother, she would join the household that Melanya and her true-sister Veya had founded. Melanya was already pregnant, and it was Dabria's fondest wish that her own motherhood would arrive soon enough that she could help suckle this first child of the family. Her falsehood troubled her all the way back to the village.

At her hut, the first thing she did was grab the stick of driftwood the stranger had carved. The image was just as she remembered—a representation of what she had seen in the ocean to the west. The "new" Robos.

She was debating whether to try to awaken the stranger when he thrashed and opened his eyes. At first he gazed blankly at the thatch overhead, but as she loomed over him, he focussed on her.

"*Hee makabbi olo retmei,*" he said. "*Aki sliff gammon?*"

She had no idea what his words meant. "My name is Dabria," she replied, merely to say something in return. "Where do you come from?"

He spouted more gibberish, growing more frantic as it became clear she did not understand. He tried sitting up, but fell back immediately. His voice trailed off, his eyelids fluttered closed, and his breathing became rhythmic.

Dabria paced around the room, feeling hemmed in by the walls, overly aware of the scent of her own perspiration. She took fresh round-nut butter and smeared it over her body until all she could smell was its rich musk. Yet that merely dulled the edge of her uneasiness.

She snatched a tray from the stack. Briskly she poured in a layer of sand, then crumpled a stick of puckerspice and threw on a dash of round-nut flour. Almost as if she were preparing a recipe to eat, she stirred the mixture in the tray until the ingredients merged into a uniform beige, not so much a design as a layer of incense.

As she achieved the exact color she was trying for, calm pervaded the room. Her nascent headache faded. The effect extended not just to her, but to everything. The stranger ceased squirming and rested peacefully.

She had resorted to such measures many times in the past. Yet abruptly she stopped stirring. The calm remained.

The calm remained. And she had brought it. Dabria set down her implement and stared at her hands as if they belonged to someone else.

Evening found Dabria sitting with Hemar outside the men's lodge. Though women were welcome at the lodge at any time, in practice they seldom visited—they could count on the men to circulate among the smaller domiciles of the women and children. Dabria, as one of the village's most eligible unpledged women, was a particular attraction. Predictably many of the young men were managing to contrive reasons to be outside—some demonstrating their agility and speed in a game of long shells, others merely strutting.

This night, Dabria ignored the show. Her father's doorstep was the place that, all her life, she had come whenever she had a problem she didn't wish to share with her mother's household—for that was the same as sharing it with everyone.

"You are not acting like yourself," Hemar commented. "Is it the stranger? Shall we move him after all?"

"Not yet. Tell me, Father—you have visited all the islands. In all the festivals you've seen, were there any as . . . moving . . . as the ones for which I've painted the grounds?"

"Of course not." He laughed. "Those are the best."

"Answer as if I were not your daughter."

He grew serious. "No, child. The festivals that you decorate are something special. You've always had talent, but since you've become an adult your paintings have gained an added quality. They never fail to engage the senses. This is not just my opinion; it is there for anyone to see. Is this not what you want?"

She gazed skyward, hardly noticing the inspired acrobatics of a pair of glow moths scant inches from her face. "Yes. I suppose it is. I just never realized before how unusual it was."

Dabria woke long before dawn. One thing after another conspired to keep her awake—first a full bladder, then thirst, then the noise of a frog near her door. The painting of calmness she had made the night before no longer soothed her whatsoever.

When sunlight peeked through the cracks in the thatch, she abandoned her mat. To occupy herself, she made several trips to the stream in order to fill the water barrel outside her hut.

When she went back inside, the stranger had thrown his coverings back. She was reminded of mornings when she had sat and admired the body of a lover in the early light. This man had a certain handsomeness—take twenty years off his age and he would be the type that Melanya favored from time to time. But whatever small amount of sexual attraction Dabria might have felt for him was buried beneath the pity evoked by his lined brow, meatless ribs, and ragged beard.

The man opened his eyes. He turned immediately to his host and said, quite distinctly, "I need your help."

Dabria blinked. He spoke the language of the Five Islands as if he had been raised in her village. "How did you learn to talk?"

He gestured feebly at a scrap of driftwood sitting beside the one on which he had carved the island. Dabria raised it up and saw it contained the image of a mouth pointed toward an ear. Though the piece was tiny and the detail scant, she recognized the characteristic lopsidedness of his mouth. The ear would be hers, judging from the gold hoops, one small, one large.

"I have no knowledge of your tongue, but from now on when I speak, you will understand."

"You carve things and they come to pass?" she asked, more for confirmation than out of surprise.

"Yes."

A shiver ran down Dabria's spine. "Are you a god?"

"Like a god, perhaps. Call me a sorcerer."

"Yet you're sick. Can't your magic heal you?"

He paused. "My magic is the cause of my ailment. The more I use it, the worse I become. But I had to risk it to find you."

Then as she had suspected, it had been no accident that she had found him on the beach. He must have arranged it from the start. "Why am I so important to you?"

He smiled faintly. "You are like me. You, too, create things that come to pass. I with my carvings. You with your dust and sand. We are a very special kind of magician."

"So it seems." She would have liked to deny it.

"You've realized it. Good." He coughed, and looked as if he might fall unconscious once more. "Will you help, then?"

Slowly she nodded. That much was clear. She had to follow this through.

"Good." He licked his chapped lips. "Listen carefully, while I still have the strength to speak. First, do you see the waterfall in the first carving?"

Dabria looked closely at the image of the island. On the face of the nearest mountain, she saw a faint notch. Though it was a single knife-stroke, it did look amazingly like a cascade.

"Hidden behind the water, in a cave, you will find what I need. Here is what you should do . . ."

She went alone, as requested. The trip across the channel was not difficult. She had learned to sail at age six, and the early morning breeze propelled her catamaran across the waves as fast as a gull could fly. She made landfall at the base of the mountain, secured the boat, and began to climb.

The thick growth, unlike the well-maintained paths on her home island, lashed her bare flanks and regularly tried to trip her, but she was young and nimble-footed, and the destination was barely two thousand paces uphill. She reached the falls before the coolness of morning had dissipated.

The passageway behind the falling torrent lay hidden within the spray, and she nearly lost her footing on the slick rock. But soon the cave opened up, its floor nearly level and lined with soft sand. She drifted inward. Right where the filtered sunlight grew almost too faint to illuminate the chamber, she saw a wall of fog.

The gray barrier was not mist; it was dry to her touch. Her hand could press no farther than the length of a finger joint, though there did not seem to be anything truly solid in the way. She wasn't quite sure why she tried; the stranger had told her she wouldn't be able to pass through in so mundane a fashion.

As instructed, she smoothed the cave floor and set about crafting a painting. Aside from the sand itself, her only working material was a small bag of dirt she had scooped up as she approached the waterfall. Within a short time, the sand began to resemble the wall of fog. The dirt became a hole within the fog.

She looked up. An opening took shape within the barrier. A dim chamber lay beyond—featureless, reeking of still air, with only a single distinct item. On the ground lay a slab of wood.

Tentatively, Dabria reached into the opening. Her hand breached the threshold. From there it felt as though she were thrusting through honey. The air clung, resisting her. Swallowing hard, she stepped in.

Everything around her swirled. The cave and waterfall appeared distant, the opening no more than a rathole. Fighting off the dizziness, she seized the board at her feet and pressed back the way she had come. The opening seemed to dodge and hop, but she did as she had been advised and never stopped walking. Suddenly she was across. The hole in the wall snapped closed, and then the wall itself dissolved, leaving a view of ordinary rock.

The wood she'd retrieved contained a scene of a beach near a set of chalk cliffs. The figure of a man stood on the sand at the edge of the surf. Dabria tucked the carving under her arm and headed home.

When she returned to her hut, the stranger was up and dressed. He had the dazed, tousled look of a man whose fever has just broken, but he was steady on his feet, and his voice was almost robust as he greeted her. He reached out for the carving.

She kept the board close to her body. The time had come for answers. "You made this?"

"Of course," he replied, lowering his hand. "It should have remained with me, but my powers were even weaker than I had supposed. When I realized it was not on my person, the best I could do was create a gateway, and send another shaper—you—to pull it across the threshold."

"Before you made this, you did not exist in my world."

"That is true. I have a world of my own."

She nodded. "This thing you have done to me—is it permanent?"

He frowned. "I have done nothing. You've simply become aware of abilities you already possessed. Yes, it is permanent." Again he reached out. "May I have my talisman?"

She surrendered it. Smiling, he sat down on the mat. She paced. "Tell me your story. Tell me how these things can be."

"My name is Evad. I was born a woodcutter's son, and inherited a hobby of carving from my father. When I was twenty, a woman called Birhea visited my small cabin. She could take a small piece of cloth and whatever scene she embroidered would come to be. She proved it first by fashioning a large tree near my home, a rare variety prized by my family because the furniture makers always paid us good silver for its hard, dark wood. The strangest part was, my father insisted that tree had been there all along. He explained that his grandfather had planted it to benefit his descendants."

"No one but shapers realize when a world is altered?"

"No one." Evad spoke with such pain that Dabria edged away from him. "For decades, I have been alone."

"What happened to Birhea?"

"She guided me through my first creations, showing me that my knives and chisels would work as well as her needle and yarn, then she left, saying she would one day return and see what I had made of my world.

"The years went on. I shaped my surroundings until they contained every spectacle, every pleasure, every facet of beauty conceivable. Still she did not come. Can you imagine what it is like, being the only real person in a land of marionettes? I craved someone of my own level, someone not created from or altered by a whim of my mind.

"Finally I learned the means Birhea had used to travel between worlds. It requires more than simply carving an image of myself into a landscape. You experienced only a taste of it today. A full crossing is much harder.

"Alas, though I visited world after world, I never found Birhea. Nor any other shapers. All those places lay unguided. Some were no more than flat plains with a single building. Some had oceans that poured off the edges, destroying the sailors who ventured too far from the coasts. Some contained only beasts, no people at all.

"I thought to myself that if I embellished these lands, perhaps Birhea would stumble across my work, be pleased, and seek me out. Nor, in truth, could I resist such a venture. Picture whole continents and peoples left to their own random fates. How could I not help them find their destinies? In a few cases I started with black void and left behind valleys and seas, nations and cultures.

"And then, my powers began to sour. Each new carving left me fatigued. Travel across the thresholds was especially taxing. Eventually my gift would work fully only when I was home. Leaving became so painful that I knew if I tried even one more time, I would die."

"Yet you're here, and alive," Dabria said. She found it hard to interrupt the narrative. When Evad spoke, his passions and experiences came across as if they were her own. It was so potent an effect that she had difficulty sorting out her own reactions to his account. It was as if he were shaping her word by word.

His voice faltered as he continued. "Yes. I am here. But at great cost. I had to destroy one of my carvings. Do you know what that means? Though I memorized every knife cut and will re-create the piece when I return, for the moment, an entire land has ceased to exist. It was the only way I could free up enough of my power to search for another shaper."

"Couldn't you have simply *made* another shaper?"

"No. I tried. I could no more succeed at that than halt my own aging. No, the only answer was to find whatever shapers might exist spontaneously. I had always focussed upon the search for Birhea, but she was either dead or deliberately blocking me. I had to widen my efforts."

Evad waved the piece of wood Dabria had fetched from the cave. "I placed this board in front of me every day, eyes closed. After many weeks, an image appeared on the backs of my eyelids. Somewhere a shaper was scooping chalk from a cliff near a beach, dreaming of other worlds, meditating on her next work of art. My hands, without conscious guidance, carved what she saw—and placed me in the scene. And there I went. Here I am."

Dabria recalled vividly the moment at the cliffs. The feeling of being . . . watched . . . was intense.

"What now?" Dabria asked. "Will you live here?"

"No," he answered quickly. "I would die if I stayed. I must go immediately, while my strength is high."

Suddenly Dabria knew what Evad would say next. "You want me to follow you."

"Yes." Evad grinned at Dabria like a child beaming at its mother. He set down the board and picked up still another carving from his mat— a new one. "After you have matured into your powers, you will be able to travel as I used to. This will guide you to me."

Dabria gazed at the carving. Her lower jaw dropped, amazed at the artistry. He'd had scarcely two hours to fashion it, yet the detail was fabulous. A cottage lay in a forest clearing. Sweet sunshine poured through the branches of the trees, brightening the lane that passed by the front stoop. To the side was a garden and an ornamental pond.

"This is my home. When the time comes, create a dust painting of this scene. Paint yourself into a spot—let us say the bench by the pond. You will be transported there."

"And then?" she asked.

"Then, with my guidance, you can resume the work I have had to abandon. You will be able to travel all the lands, setting them to rights. By the time your own powers are exhausted, we will have located other shapers and enlisted them to our cause. The universe need never lie unattended again."

Dabria touched the carving tentatively. The trees had the texture of leaves and needles, not carved wood. The cottage walls felt like sanded lumber, the chimney like stone and mortar. Evad urged the piece into her grip.

"Say you will come. It may be a year, perhaps five, before you master the means, but I will wait. Could any other goal promise so much?"

Dabria struggled to keep herself afloat within the tidal wave of his plans and desires. Standing here in the same room, his influence was overwhelming. "No, none other could," she heard herself say. "Of course I will come. In one year or five, as my talent allows."

Evad kissed Dabria on the forehead. Then, as if gaining her acquiescence had used up his last reserves, he swayed and sat down abruptly.

"I have to go now," he said. "But no matter. Eventually we will have all the time we need."

He took the carving she had brought from the waterfall. Aiming his largest chisel, raising his hammer, he struck several times with grand expertise. When he raised his hands away, the beach and cliffs remained, but the image of Evad himself was missing.

"Until we are together," he said, smiling. He was already ghostly transparent. When he had faded entirely, Dabria reached out and touched the mat. The thatch was cool, as if Evad had never been there generating body heat.

Dabria began to shake. Crawling to her bowl of wash water, she made as if to clean the spot on her forehead that he had kissed. But she stopped. No matter how much she scrubbed, the imprint of his lips would remain.

Her reflection stared back from the water. She hardly knew herself. His offer had seemed so reasonable as he uttered it. She had been right to say she would follow. The promise had sent him on his way, and only in his absence would she know her true feelings.

Now, and only now, could she decide whether or not that promise was a true one.

Sitting down, she placed all four carvings in front of her, and stared at them for a long time. The wood was firm beneath her fingers. It did not yield. How many carvings must lie within Evad's cottage? Thousands? Tens of thousands? Each affecting reality in tremendous ways. He was probably already beginning to restore the one he'd sacrificed to make the journey to the Five Islands.

What would she be like in twenty years, if she took his path?

Keeping that thought uppermost in her mind, she stepped outside and threw kindling and tinder into her cooking brazier and struck the flints. When the fire was hot, she placed the carving of Robos on the coals. As it burned, she climbed the ridge to the west, where she gained a view of the ocean.

Robos hovered like a mirage on the waves, gray as smoke. As the brazier did its work, the isle faded entirely, taking with it the nagging false history of its crypts and funerals. Dabria waved, half in regret, half in relief.

Back at the brazier, she immediately added the piece of driftwood with the mouth and ear. The board containing the portrait of Evad's home clung to her hands slightly longer—not because of the fabulous craftsmanship, but because Dabria was reminded of the passion Evad must have put into its creation. Ultimately she gave it to the fire, turning it upside down to prevent herself from memorizing its features.

She kept the remaining piece, the one from the cave. With the figure removed, the scene was nothing more or less than a bit of coastline she had known and enjoyed all her life. This she hung on her wall.

The brazier was cold by the time Dabria returned that night. She dumped the ash into a clay pot and set it aside. Many days passed before she retrieved it—days filled with good company, with dance and celebration, and with the satisfaction of knowing she had contributed in important ways to another festival. Never had her way of life seemed so precious.

Finally, one peaceful morning, she took one of her trays—she owned only five—and poured the ash into it, using it as the foundation for a painting. Then, dipping into her urns of collected pigments and sands, Dabria crafted an image of the rocky hillside across the valley from her hut, complete with its lush hanging vines and ledges of exuberant tropical growth. A few bits of charcoal from the brazier served to deepen the shadows and lend depth.

She rarely painted landscapes. Her hands wanted to burst free, craft a design, but she forced herself to be disciplined. Her skill was such that by late afternoon she had a rendering as lifelike as Evad's carving of his home had been.

And then she added to it. She took one of her rarest pigments—pollen harvested from the stamens of the shade lily—and sprinkled the rock face with dabs of bright yellow.

She went outside. There, across the valley, yellow flowers never before known on her island grew in the cracks of the rocks.

She hadn't doubted that she could do it. The sorcery begged to emerge. Yet there was only one way she could wield it and remain true to her nature.

The evening winds were picking up. Dabria placed her tray on the ground, where the riffling of the breeze would gently erase the work she had done, and sat down to admire the flowers while they lasted.

LOOKING INTO THE HEART OF LIGHT, THE SILENCE

MARK KREIGHBAUM

Mark Kreighbaum has published short fiction and poetry in a number of anthologies and small press magazines. He and Katharine Kerr are collaborating on the science fiction novel, Palace, due out from Bantam in 1996.

On the snow-covered roof of a parking garage in Toronto, Neil spoke the Fifth Word, convening the spirits of change. Shapes of color swirled around him. They drifted over the moonlit snow like fragments of a borealis. He had only moments to command them, yet he paused a moment to drink the cold wine of their light. The only love he had ever known in his life were the spirits of change, and he felt no lack. Sometimes, he dreamed about the spirits, seeing them spread across his mind's sky until the blue roof of his dreams became a tapestry of color. Only two Words remained to him, the Last Word reserved for investing his successor. Now, to his shame, he summoned purity and beauty for murder.

"Hello," he murmured to the convocation of spirits. They conjoined and melted apart, a rippling feast of silent hue. "The Lady of Situations has spoken. Her voice echoes in blood and weeping. You have heard her. You know her."

The spirits answered with a sudden blackness.

"She has used her Sixth Word. Now is the time to end her line for all time." The spirits flowed into a single form, a lambent outline of a child with eyes of jet. "Find her for me. Mark her well. Guide me to her. Let the longest war have an ending. I am the Lord of Change and I command you." Then he added, as he always did, "My name is Neil Oanly, and I ask your help."

The child-figure bowed once, low, and leapt like Prospero's Ariel into the winter night.

*   *   *

Head down, Neil trudged through the slush-covered streets of Minneapolis, collar turned up against a bitter wind. His thoughts strayed to other cities, other seasons. He was forty-nine years old, and he had seen much of the world, seeking righteous moments. In his experience, all winters were the same: ice, silence, and a lie of rebirth. Things died in winter, beyond recall.

He wondered about his family. Were his mother and father still alive? Had his sister married? Twenty years ago, he'd traded ties of blood for roots of power, and each year he felt less human, as if he were becoming one of the spirits of change. He knew little of the Lords of Change before him. Had they traveled the world as he did, hunting the Lady of Situations, following the dying echoes of her work? What did the Words mean to them? What did they mean to the Lady? He tried to remember what it felt like to laugh, to feel joy, and instead, a vision of the spirits returned, like a heroin dream.

Time passed, marked by wailing sirens and the rush of steel. The spirits would find her. They must. But not even a Lord of Change could know the hour of their return. Patience was easy for him. Neil had long since surrendered the trappings of time—he wore no watch, cared little for the names of days, and knew the month only when someone told him. He thought of himself as a ghost upon the Earth, or a lost angel.

His wanderings brought him to the Lake Street Billiard Palace, as they always did when the burden of choice lay heavy. He walked through the door. The bell above the frame sang out the first syllable of the First Word.

A nearly oppressive warmth swathed him. Cigarette smoke, jukebox standards, and laughter mingled in the air with the smell of damp clothes and spilled beer. Couples played nine-ball on a pair of the pool hall's six worn tables. A slender black man with a grizzled, neatly trimmed beard perched on a stool beside the jukebox. Smiling, he watched the customers play. When he saw Neil, the smile died.

"Evening, Mr. Oanly." The black man's voice was soft, so soft. Neil remembered when that voice had offered him the chance to do great deeds, to be more than a part-time drug dealer and full-time loser. There were times when Neil thought it was the voice of a fallen angel.

"Hello, Jamal." They didn't shake hands. Neil wondered if they were even friends. Maybe, what they shared transcended human relationships. He wondered how he would feel when his own time as the Lord of Change was done. How would he live without magic, without the spirits he loved? Jamal never spoke of it. "She's used her Sixth. I've sent the spirits to find her."

Jamal said nothing. Instead, he poured coffee for them both into white Styrofoam cups. He added cream to Neil's without asking.

"How many do you have left?" asked Jamal, voice low and smooth as the red felt on the pool tables.

"Two." Neil slid onto a stool beside Jamal. He sipped his coffee.

"Others have tried, you know," said Jamal.

"Did you?"

Jamal smiled slightly. He drank his coffee and turned away from Neil to watch the players shoot nine-ball. Neil watched, too. They were good. They believed in honest geometries and were rewarded for their faith. Once upon a time, Neil hustled people like this, took their money, sold them crack, talked them into buying an illusion of happiness. One of the women bent over the table to line up a shot. Neil felt less than an echo of lust. The Words had scraped so much of his life away.

The night wore on. The customers left. All but one of the pool hall's lights were silenced and Jamal brought out a bottle of Scotch. The two men drank without speaking. Finally, the tall black man racked a full set of balls on one of the tables, setting them up for eight-ball. The lone light, a fluorescent tube hooded by black tin, was suspended by chains above the center of the table. The light cast shadows deep into Jamal's eyes.

"Remember?" he asked.

Neil nodded. They had met here. Jamal tested him in a way that Neil was only now coming to understand after twenty years of choosing when to speak a Word that might save human lives, or doom them. The Lord of Change had to be a man without a future, an empty soul. He had lost the game, but won a direction, a destiny, and an unexpected love.

As the two men began a game of eight-ball, Neil felt something loosen inside. He had walked on the soil of every nation of Earth, but only this pool hall offered peace.

"Thought about passing on the Words?" asked Jamal. He made a cross-side bank shot, though there were easier shots on the table.

"Sure. All the time."

"Will you tell him how you used your Words?"

Neil looked down at the table. What was there to tell? Only the Last

Word mattered. And the Lady of Situations. He was coming to understand Jamal very well.

Jamal stared behind Neil. His expression was that of a child gazing through a toy store's window at untouchable treasures. Neil turned around. The spirits of change had returned, still in their golden child-form. So soon, he thought. Too soon. The messenger waited at the door, unfathomable. Did they resent slavery to a man? Why did they obey?

"She isn't helpless, even without a Word to call the spirits of binding," said Jamal.

"She has one Word left."

"Won't use it, even to save her life. None of us ever has."

Neil looked at the older man.

"I'm going to end her line forever," he said.

Jamal pushed the ivory white cue ball hard across the table, sending it smashing into a gathering of colored balls, like a fist through a rainbow.

"Her name is Constance." He returned their cue sticks to the rack, kept his back to Neil. "Give her my regards."

Neil stared at him. In the end, he could think of nothing to say. He followed the spirits of change into the chill darkness of a Minneapolis winter.

The child of light led them to a bar called Peri's. The facade was weathered to bone and the neon sign flickered. He paused outside, shivering.

"She is marked?" The spirits of change nodded. Neil bowed to them. "Then I thank you. I am the Lord of Change, and I release you. My name is Neil Oanly, and I wish you well."

They returned his bow and dissolved, like colored spheres shattered by a white light. The swirls of color danced around him for a moment, then faded into the blackness. Did they possess independent life? Were they more than spirits to command? Neil feared he would never know. He was afraid of the sorrow in Jamal's eyes. Already, the two men were becoming too much like mirrors.

"Constance," he whispered, and entered the bar.

The spirits of change had set a nimbus of red on a woman within. Neil ordered a cup of coffee at the bar and studied the Lady of Situations.

She was shooting pool with two men. He hadn't expected that she would be so young, no more than twenty-two, he guessed. She wore a leather jacket with many zippers and silver clasps. The crimson haze surrounding her echoed her dark red hair. She sank a three-ball combination with an ease that warned him. Young or not, this woman bore an ancient legacy of power.

Eventually, he made his way to the back of the bar, moving carefully through the tables. The two men were playing as a team against her and they looked like veterans of late nights in bars. Both had heavy beards and scarred faces. The bigger man wore a faded letterman's jacket from Edina High School. Neil didn't like the way they looked at her, so removed, with a drunken calculation he had seen a thousand times in men who'd dug out their souls with blunt spoons and swallowed a subtle poison to fill the chasm. Neil wrote his name on the small green blackboard beside the pool table. The men looked at him appraisingly and dismissed him in a breath. He knew he was small and homely, a metaphor for weakness. Twenty years ago, it had mattered. But the Words changed all that. The Lord of Change could not be harmed by any violence; fear never ruled his choices. He had walked through fire to speak his Second Word, rescuing an old Jewish woman who had died nine months later in a Tel Aviv–Jaffa nursing home, murdered by an Arab nurse. The nurse had been sent by the Lady of Situations.

Constance beat the two men easily and reached for the money on the rail. The older man, built like a high school fullback whose life had sunk into his eyes, grabbed her wrist and tore the bills from her grip. His friend, taller than Jamal and hard with muscle, grinned and stared at Neil.

"Why don't you get out?" he said to Neil.

Neil glanced at the bartender. He was drying glasses and watching the scene as if it were a mildly interesting television show. No one else was in the bar.

"I've got the next game," said Neil.

The Lady of Situations stepped back from the big man, twisting her wrist free of his grip. Her red nimbus seemed a cloud of blood. She laughed at them both. There was a strange echo in that laugh, as if it might be part of a Word. She shrugged and walked away from the table, turning her back on the men. But her eyes met Neil's and she smiled in anticipation. Her face suddenly gained years. He couldn't begin to guess her age now.

"Don't you want your money, bitch?"

She whipped around, pool cue held like a baseball bat and broke it across the fullback's head. He fell to the floor, his face covered in blood. His friend froze for a moment too long. She leapt onto the pool table and jabbed the jagged end of the cue stick into his windpipe. He reeled back against the wall, clutching his throat, letting out mewling sounds seasoned by blood. Neil glanced at the bartender. He was reaching for something under the bar. She was grinning down at them all.

"Let's go, Constance," said Neil. He grabbed her hand and they ran out the back. She laughed as they ran.

They stopped running when they reached Nicollet Park. She sat on the backrest of a bus stop bench.

"How did you know my name?" she asked. Her hands were buried in her leather jacket's pockets. The nimbus of red that crowned her cast a pallor over the park's chiaroscuro.

"It was on the blackboard," he said.

"What's yours, handsome?"

"My name is Neil Oanly."

"Oanly the Lonely?"

"Yeah. Like the song."

"I'm Constance Grimm. Like the fairy tales." Her smile lit up her face. She tipped her head back and looked up at the stars. The gibbous moon had nearly set. She spoke without looking at him. "Do you want to sleep with me?"

Neil's heart pounded hard and fast. He had used his Third Word to find a kidnapped college student. He found her, bound and gagged in the basement of a banker who had killed nine other young women. For a few weeks, he'd lived with her. But he never touched her, he couldn't bear it, and she came to hate him. He never listened to her life anymore.

Constance shifted her gaze back to him. The nimbus made her eyes look like pools of crimson ink.

"Don't worry," she said, softly, "I won't kill you."

Her apartment was on Minnehaha Avenue, not far from the Falls. Her door was unlocked. She lit a candle on the floor beside the door. There was nothing in the studio but a mattress and a few books. The windows had no curtains.

"Are you a virgin?" she asked.

He didn't answer. She took off her clothes, paying no attention to the unshielded windows. Her body was compact and freckled. She sat cross-legged on the mattress and brushed her fine red hair. The brush swam through the red pool of the spirits' mark.

Neil spoke his Fourth Word to a seventeen-year-old Cambodian boy who had been beaten and abused by his stepfather all his life, while his mother practiced blindness. Maybe he should have hoarded that Word to end a war or rescue children in an earthquake. The boy's change had taken him to Thailand where he ran a brothel, selling other children. The Lady of Situations had sent fire sweeping through Bangkok, and the boy died in flames. Neil had listened to his death.

He looked down at her. Now was the time. With a Word he could finish a war that had raged over centuries.

"Jamal sends his regards," he said.

The brush hesitated for only a moment. She gave a soft laugh.

"I heard your Fifth. I knew your voice when I heard it in Peri's, Oanly the Lonely." She looked up at him. "Did you think I wouldn't feel the weight of a spirit's mark?" The nimbus flared, stinging his eyes, and was gone. He hadn't known such a thing could be done without speaking a Word.

"I'm sorry," he said.

"Really?" Constance set aside the brush and pulled back the blankets on the mattress. "Why don't you join me?"

"Why do you kill?"

"Jamal told me about you." She leaned forward. "You were a drug dealer, a pusher."

"So?"

"He said you went to prison. He said they raped you there." Neil flinched. She smiled up at him. "How did you use your First Word?"

The syllables of that First Word burned like whiskey in his mouth. The spirits came, voiceless, featureless. No one in Joliet knew to mark their cells with lamb's blood and the curse spared none of them. He learned then how every life touched by a Word remains forever with the Lord of Change.

"How did you become what you are?" he asked.

"Does it matter? I'm a woman. Maybe you created me."

"Can't there be peace between us? We could do so much good together."

"You'll never understand," she said.

He knelt beside Constance and reached out to touch her face. She kissed the palm of his hand and drew him down on to the mattress beside her.

Somewhere in the hours that followed, she spoke a Word. And so did he.

In the morning, he was gone.

She rose up, naked, and leaned against the sill of the open window. The city hunched as snow fell out of the sky, flickers of cold light, like the tears of spirits.

Somewhere, out there, he was learning about change. She could hear his life, every beat of his heart.

"My name is Neil Oanly, and I wish you well," she said.

The Lord of Situations laughed.

A SIMPLE ACT OF KINDNESS

KATE ELLIOTT

Kate Elliott is the author of the Novels of the Jaran, including Jaran *and* The Law of Becoming. The Golden Key, *a fantasy coauthored with Melanie Rawn and Jennifer Roberson, will be published in September 1996. Her next solo novel,* Dragon's Heart, *the first volume of the fantasy* Crown of Stars, *will be out in early 1997. "A Simple Act of Kindness" retells an episode from* The Burning Stone, *the third volume of* Crown of Stars.

Clouds massed, black and brooding, over the hills and the great length of forest that bordered the village of Sant Laon. They sat, almost as if they were waiting, and the wind died down and tendrils of mist and spatterings of rain were all that came of them through the day. At evening mass, at a twilight brought early by the lowering clouds, Deacon Joceran spoke solemnly of storms called up by unnatural means, and she warned all the villagers to bar their doors and shutters that night and to hang an iron knife or pot above the door and a sprig of rosemary above the window.

"No matter who knocks, invite no one in. May the Father and Mother of Life bless us all this night."

So it was that not one soul saw the woman ride into town just ahead of the first fierce lashings of the storm. No one but Daniella.

The back door to the inn slammed shut and set the baby to crying, again, but it was only Uncle Heldric. His cloak seemed to sparkle in the lantern light of the hearth room of the farmhouse.

"Lord and Lady have mercy," said Aunt Marguerite, signing the circle of unity above her breast. "It looks like snow and ice on your cloak."

"And this midway through summer," said Uncle as he brushed the stain of snow off his shoulders. "'Tisn't a natural storm, Deacon was right in that." He cast his gaze round the room and found Daniella, where she sat on a stool in one shadowed corner, trying not to be noticed while she spun a hank of wool into yarn. "Girl, you take Baby upstairs and send down your brother. Seven of the sheep have got out and we must get them in before we lose the beasts to whatever walks in this storm. Night's coming on soon."

With the shutters closed and only a thin line of light showing around the cracks of the door and the window, it seemed like night already. A wind howled, whistling along the roof. Smoke from the hearth curled up toward the smoke hole in the roof, and a few flakes of snow spun into view in the patch of sky visible through the hole, only to melt at once, vanishing into the heat.

"I'll go," said Daniella. Upstairs lurked many things, not least her cousin Robert, who had been pestering her for months now, ever since her first bleeding came on her, and anyway, unlike her brother Matthias, she wasn't scared of storms. She liked them. They had life in them, even if Deacon Joceran warned that some storms had demons and other unGodly life swirling in their winds and rain. Better outside in a storm than trapped in here.

"Ach, well," said Uncle, knowing her well enough to forgive her impertinence. And she was better with the sheep, and not afraid of her own shadow, the way Matthias was. "You come, then. Put on a tunic over that. It's bitter cold out. And the sheep clipped and likely to freeze."

"It won't last," said Aunt, but she drew the circle again, not wishing to tempt the Evil Ones.

Uncle merely grunted and Daniella was quick to abandon the baby, who had stopped wailing in any case and was now busily tearing the hank of wool to shreds and stuffing bits of wool into its mouth.

"Matthias!" Aunt called loudly, through into the common room, where the ladder that reached the loft rested against one bowed wall of the long house. "Come and mind the baby."

Daniella gave one last shuddering glance at the baby and hurried outside after her uncle. That's what came of simple acts of kindness, of hiring a landless man to work a season for them because he was fair-spoken and likable and down on his luck. He had stayed the summer, worked hard for the harvest and the slaughtering, and then gone on his way . . . but it had been her cousin Dhuoda who had died giving birth to the child he had gotten on her, and who knew where he might have been by then. Perhaps getting another pretty young woman with child, and going on his way. And with Dhuoda's death the life had gone out of the house.

That was the way of it, Deacon Joceran had said, that the Lord and Lady gather to their breasts the best-loved and the sweetest, to sing as angels crowned by stars.

Outside, the slap of winter wind on her face shocked her. She stopped, staring at the dusting of snow and the long tendrils of fog that laced through the village longhouses, coating half-ripened apples with frost and withering the asperia blossoms where they grew in clumps by the back door. Then Uncle shouted at her, his words lost in a gust of wind. She hurried after him.

Four sheep had strayed out onto the commons, huddling together near the pond, and she herded them back toward the stables, carrying a half-grown lamb over her shoulders. A cloaked woman—Mistress Hilde—ran from the porch of the church toward her own house, hunched over an iron pot which she sheltered from the wind and the gentle fall of snow as if it were as precious as a casket containing the bones of a saint. Daniella smelled, like someone's breath brushing her face, a distant stench like a rotting carcass, but then the door into the stables banged open, caught by the wind, and she chivvied the sheep in under shelter. Her cousin Robert, closing the door behind her, brushed against her suggestively. She shook him off. The old sheepdog lay in the corner nearest the door into the kitchen, whining. He had urinated in the corner, so frightened that he wouldn't even move off the wet straw.

"Gruff," she said, coaxingly, "Gruff, come here, old boy." But he wouldn't come to her.

"Scared the piss out of him," said Robert, thinking it a great joke, but even so she could hear the shake in his voice. From the other side of the wall, she heard Aunt scolding Matthias, and that made her angry, too. It wasn't Matthias's fault that he was sickly, and that he'd been the one five years ago to find their Da's body in the slough after the spring rains where he had been caught in the branches and dragged under water, drowned by angry water nithies. Even Deacon Joceran had said so, that it was their revenge on Da for him building a dam and draining the south portion of the marsh for a new field. Matthias had been plagued by twitching and nerves ever since.

The door slammed open, shuddering in a new gust of wind, and

Uncle Heldric kicked a sheep in before him and passed a bawling lamb to Robert. "Still one missing, the black," he said. "She got past me, tore off into the woods." He glanced back behind him, and Daniella saw by the taut lines of his mouth and the glint of white in his eyes that he, too, was afraid, of the storm, of venturing so far away from the house, which was protected by iron and rosemary. An iron knife hung above the stable door, rosemary over the shutters that opened onto the trough.

"I'll go," she said, because she knew he would let her, however reluctantly, however guiltily. The holding would go to Robert, with perhaps a field left over for Matthias, but there would be nothing for her except the kettle, knife, and wedding shawl that had been her mother's, together with the length of green bridal cloth that Dhuoda had been embroidering in expectation of her own betrothal, whenever that might have taken place, though it never would now. Nothing else could she expect to receive from Heldric and Marguerite's family, hard as times were and burdened now with three orphans, except for a necklace of amber beads that Dhuoda had, with her dying breath, left to her cousin.

As if it were a luck charm, Daniella brushed her fingers over the necklace of beads where it lay beneath her tunic, together with the Holy Circle she had inherited from her mother's mother. Uncle Heldric handed her his cloak. She wrapped it around her shoulders and went back outside. Hunched down against the tearing wind, she walked out toward the scattering of trees, not truly a wood, so many had been cut down for firewood, that marked the farthest edge of the great forest that lay to the east.

The black sheep was hard to find, for by now it was full twilight and the ewe's coat blended in to the fog and the dark lean curves of tree trunks. But Daniella listened and heard a frightened bleating. Her feet knew the paths in this wood better perhaps than her eyes did, and she knew where the sheep wandered . . . down by the stream that wound through the wood and emptied at last into the marsh. Only one branch stung her face as she made her way through the wood and came out on the bank of the stream where the little ewe was poised between the trees and the steep slope that led down to the trickle of water and reeds that was all that was left of the stream in the summer heat.

There was no point in chasing it home. It would run off again. She lunged for it, grabbed its hind legs just as it bolted, and brought it hard to the ground, both of them together. It bleated, terrified, and voided all over, luckily missing her, but she could smell excrement and piss. The trees whispered in the wind, calling names, one name, like an old name in a dream. She got to her knees and wrestled the sheep up and over her shoulders. Unaccountably, the ewe calmed. Daniella looked up.

There, on the opposite bank of the stream, were not trees, though she had with that first swift glance thought them trees, so well did they blend in with the wood beyond.

They were creatures.

She stood rooted to the ground with terror.

Like rushes grown thick and tall, they loomed above her, whispering, dark shapes leaning over the stream like gigantic reeds bent down in a strong wind. They were darker than the twilight and an odor like hot iron swelled out from them. Their stirring and rustling made a noise like the thousands of leaves in a forest blown in a stiff wind, anchored by the distant ringing toll of a bell, caught below, as if their bodies—if they truly had bodies—rang on the earth with each step. They had no hands she could see, no faces, and yet she knew instinctively that they could both grasp and see. She took a single step back, slowly, and then a second, the poor ewe draped over her shoulders.

A sharp wind blew a flurry of snow from the heights of the pines down on her. As if lifting themselves on that wind, the creatures leapt and crossed the stream, twelve of them, at least. They brushed past her, and she smelled the liquid iron of the forge hot and stinging against her nostrils, and their whispering voices spoke a name into the wind and the sound of that name tolled on the air, like bells rung to pass a dying soul up through the seven spheres to the Chamber of Light where it would come, at last, to rest.

"Liathano."

Then they passed her, oblivious to her, to the weakly bleating ewe, and were gone, on toward the village.

Toward the village!

Daniella, shorn abruptly of her fear, ran after them, but her feet followed the worn and familiar paths, and the creatures were gone, made invisible by the twilight and the tall length of trees or by their own arts, she could not know.

By now, the village was empty, every door shut, every shutter closed, only, here and there, the glint of light showing a fire or lantern within. Only, and alone in the huddle of buildings, the door to the church stood ajar. Perhaps, as Deacon Joceran had said, the Father and Mother of Life need fear no demons, no creatures sent by the Evil Ones. Perhaps Deacon dared not shut her doors, for fear of showing fear.

Then Daniella saw a horse, standing, head down, against the wall of the churchyard. Its coat was the gray of stone, and only the saddle and the saddle blanket, trimmed with silver, and the winking lure of the bridle gave it away. No one in Sant Laon owned such a horse or such fine tack. A moment later the right side door to the church opened a bit further and a strange hump-backed Thing scuttled out, took the reins of the horse, and coaxed it up the steps in toward the church.

To profane the church . . .

But with that thought she recognized that the Thing led its horse in to safety, what safety the church might afford it. She smelled iron, borne on the wind, and she turned slowly and saw the tall, drifting shapes milling round the commons pond, as if they had lost their prey—lost the scent—there, by the water. The Thing vanished into the church, the horse behind it. Before Daniella realized she had made the decision, she settled the ewe, quiescent now, more firmly onto her shoulders and ran to the church, taking the steps two at a time. She pushed past the door just as the startled Thing reached to close the door.

Only, by the light of seven candles lit round the Altar and protected by glass jars, Daniella saw it was no Thing at all but a young woman, dark-haired and dark eyed, her skin dusky colored like bread baked too long in the oven, her back misshapen. The horse was a fine beast, big-boned but not enormous, with an intelligent head—a nobleman's mount. Tied on beside the saddlebags were a tasselled bowcase of leather embossed with griffins and a quiver full of arrows. A small shield painted black hung from the saddle. The woman wore a sword at her belt. In all things, she looked like a normal woman, except for her misshapen back and the sun-blackened color of her skin.

She looked at Daniella and then at the ewe, and she removed her hand from her sword. Moving, she slammed the door shut, and barred it.

"It will do no good," she said, clearly enough, though her words bore the accent of other, foreign lands, "but only gives us respite. They do not fear the House of Our Lady and Lord."

"Who are you?" asked Daniella, who was unaccountably not afraid of this stranger, though the woman clearly knew and expected the creatures who hunted abroad this night to follow her here. "What are those creatures? Are they hunting—" She hesitated.

"Yes," said the woman calmly enough, turning to care for the horse.

Rain began to pound on the roof above, so loud that Daniella could barely hear her words. "They are hunting me. If there is a door out beyond the altar, you should go, flee to your house. They do not know of you. They will not see you. You can find shelter in your own place, if your Deacon is wise and has told you all to protect yourselves with iron and herbs." She shifted her grotesque shoulders and with a casual gesture unhooked and shrugged off her cloak.

Daniella stared into the clear, cool green eyes of a baby.

It had a thatch of black hair but skin as pale as burnished gold, and it stared at Daniella solemnly, like a great Queen or King, marking her. It did not cry, though rain pounded loudly on the roof and a flash of lightning lit the glass windows, followed hard by the crack and roll of thunder. Daniella jumped, the thunder came so suddenly, when any natural storm would have given warning, rolling steadily toward them over the hills. The baby flinched not at all. Dhuoda's child cried at any loud noise.

The ewe bleated softly and struggled. Daniella knelt, eased it off her back, and held it tightly between her knees, gripping its neck with both hands.

Strange shadows played over the altar and the wooden benches that lined the nave. Outside, through the windows, Daniella saw lines of darkness, swaying under the rain. A bolt of lightning lit the commons, blazing, and there was a sharp snap and the smell of iron.

"Ah!" said the woman triumphantly.

But more lines of darkness crowded round the windows, seeking entrance, as if supple trees moved in on the church from the forest.

"They're getting stronger," said the woman. "Once this storm would have dissolved them. Now it barely hinders their approach." She turned her gaze on Daniella, a dark mirror of the child's gaze. "They know where I am. You must leave."

She drew from her bow quiver a staff, black wood polished to a sheen. With it in her right hand she circled the altar with measured steps, pressing her boot into the stone floor every fourth step, as if she was trying to engrain some substance into the stone. She stopped, kneeling at the point of North, and struck the staff against the stone four times, speaking words Daniella did not understand. Abruptly, the rain stopped pounding overhead and the thunder, instead of rumbling away west, simply ceased.

"Did you bring the storm?" whispered Daniella. "Are you a tempestarii?"

Although the woman knelt too far away to have heard, she answered anyway, rising to her feet and shrugging the sling that held the baby down from her back and gently setting the child, still wrapped tight, in the center of the altar between the seven candles that marked the perimeter, as if this sanctity would protect it. The child watched with preternatural calm, although it was far too young to understand.

"No, I am not. I am much worse. I am a mathematici, a magi, you would call it, who draws power down from the stars and the moon and the sun."

"Then how is it you can stand on consecrated ground?"

"Beware," said the woman, and raised the ebony staff above her head.

Fear stabbed through Daniella, and she shied away from that expansive gesture. She lost hold of the ewe just as the door to the outside burst asunder. The ewe bolted for the commons.

"Catch!" cried the woman, throwing the staff up toward the roof. The wood winked, sparked, and as darkness shrouded the church and the ewe vanished into a pit of blackness, the staff blazed with light, sucking darkness into it.

With a crack as loud as thunder it splintered into shards. The air cleared, reeking of the tang of hot iron, as the remains of the staff fell to the floor in a hail. Then it was silent. The seven candles at the altar burned peaceably, and the baby watched without a sound. By the shattered door, the ewe lay still. Daniella crept over to it.

She gasped, gagging, and clapped a hand over her own mouth. The ewe was dead. It already stank like a carcass five days old.

Outside, it was still, but trees swayed in the wind, or were there more of these creatures? Daniella backed away from the door.

"What are they?" she asked, barely able to form the words.

"They are galla," the woman said, her voice hoarse on the 'g' as if it had formed an unholy conjoining with a cough, rough and guttural, a suggestion of the creatures themselves.

"You said you are not a tempestarii. Did they bring the storm, then?"

"I brought the storm. Water can dispel them, sometimes, but they are strong in numbers this day, and strong in this world. Wind and rain can hide a trail, but they know my scent too well by now."

Daniella's gaze caught on the woman's cloak where it had been left to lie on the floor. Odd traceries decorated the lining, as if signs or spells had been sewn into it. She shivered, but it was not only the strangeness of the cloak and the woman and the shards of the black staff that littered the floor. Now it had gone winter cold again, though the storm had vanished. She braced herself against a hard swell of chill air, feeling it like a wave coming in through the broken door.

The horse neighed suddenly and kicked out, overturning one of the benches.

"Blessing!" cried the woman, bolting toward the altar, toward the child.

A blast of wind gusted into the church and that fast, like the snap of fingers, the candles around the altar went out.

It was night, black and empty. Daniella dared not move for fear she would step into an abyss, for everywhere around her it was as black as the chasm of Hell. Cold darkness poured past her like water.

But the baby cried, once, sharply. The woman cursed. As black as the air now was, the stripes of the demons—the galla—were blacker still, and by their shadows Daniella saw them struggling with the woman, writhing as if to imprison her, as if to swallow her. From the altar rose a faint gleam, like a light shielded under cloth.

It was the child.

Daniella could not leave it to die. She clamped the cloak under one arm and dashed up the aisle. Her feet knew the way better than her eyes, from the many times she had come forward to taste of wine and bread at mass.

She flung the cloak toward the woman, praying, hoping, that it might distract the galla, and grabbed the child off the altar, clutching it against her chest, tucking Uncle Heldric's cloak over it, knowing common wool could not truly shield it.

A sizzling, snapping sound, like the rain of pebbles, like water boiling onto stone, scorched the air around her. She smelled fire and the acrid scent of the blacksmith's forge. An arc of flame shot up toward the roof and the galla scattered with the tolling of bells. They scattered like grass blown on the wings of a firestorm. Heat warmed Daniella's face, then the slap of cold. Dark shapes curled around her, a ring of cold, twisting tighter, ever tighter. She felt their circle shrink. She felt their hidden eyes upon her, felt their hands grasp, reaching, touching her and insinuating their bodiless hands into her, inside her. She began to cry, soundlessly, from sheer terror. The baby did not—could not—stir, but its green eyes shone like emeralds.

"Blessing," their iron voices said. "Child born of fire and blood." And then, like Death calling her name, they spoke again: "Daniella, daughter of Leutgarda and Gerard."

And against the hard scent of iron, enveloping her, she smelled, as if it was coming from the baby, like a warding spell, the pungent, sweet scent of roses.

Fire scorched the church. The candles on the altar burst into flame, and the darkness retreated from it. But it drew back only halfway down the aisle. There the entwined galla crouched, waiting, stirring, poised to engulf their prey. Benches crashed and toppled and Daniella caught a glimpse, through the shadow of the galla, of the gray horse plunging out through the doors. It vanished into the night—only it was not entirely night. The first line of gray, heralding dawn, limned the height of the trees. It had begun to rain again outside, but softly. How could it be near dawn? How could time pass so swiftly? Yet the hint of light to come soothed Daniella's terror. Surely the sun would dispel these creatures? But the galla waited, murmuring, creeping closer and ever closer by slow degrees, their approach like the echo of drowned bells.

The woman rose from her knees with a soft moan. She was hurt. Her dark skin was scored with thin white scars, as if she had been burned by fingers of ice.

"You have my blessing," she said, and she limped over and took the baby from Daniella's arms. "I have no means by which to thank you for this kindness. You owed me nothing."

"We all owe kindness," said Daniella. "It is what the Lord and Lady grant us, to ease our pain."

To her surprise, the woman wiped tears from her scarred cheeks. "I can give you nothing that will repay you in full for what you have done. Guard my horse for me, in case I ever return and find you again. His name is Resuelto."

Daniella was too stunned to reply. The galla shifted, easing nearer, but slowly, as if they feared another blast of fire. Their voices whispered, naming, marking.

The woman ducked her head and with an efficient movement slipped a chain off from around her neck. She held it out, and the galla shrank back, the darkness retreating, bending backward, away. On the gold chain hung a medallion of beaten bronze embossed with three symbols which Daniella could not read.

"Take this, put it on. This alone will protect you."

"Protect me?" Daniella stammered.

"They have noticed you and will always mark you. You will never be entirely safe from them without this, nor will anyone nearby you.

Forgive me for bringing this trouble on you, that is all of the gift I can give in exchange for your kindness."

Daniella thought of the darkness writhing around the woman, thought of these creatures taking her and the baby, enclosing them, engulfing them, ripping life from them as they had from the black ewe, leaving a five day's dead carcass in their wake. She did not reach out for the amulet.

"Won't you need it?" she asked, thinking that no one needed her. At least this woman had a child she cared for, that was probably her own. And if she died, the child, too, would be another orphan, living on the sufferance, however kindly meant, of others.

"I must go elsewhere, where they can't follow." She hugged her child closer to her, with her free arm, and bent her head to kiss its cheek, by this small gesture revealing that she loved it, wept for it, fed it and sheltered it. As Dhuoda would have loved and sheltered her baby, though it was fatherless, had she lived.

"Take it," said the woman, and Daniella saw that she was adamant, that she would not stir until Daniella accepted the gift, though the galla whispered, muttering like bells, like words in dreams, like the language of the forest at night and all the wild places that are haunted, that care not for human kindness or human love and show no favor because, like the wood and the wild places, they cannot know a good man from an evil one.

Daniella reached out and took the amulet. The galla sighed and massed, drawing together into a great dark column, a vast funnel of night. Outside, the first pink rim of dawn rose along the treeline. The village was utterly quiet. No person stirred. Not even a lamb bleated, nor dog barked. The rain had stopped, although the sky was still dark with clouds.

Calmly, the woman gathered the child closer against her and walked past the massing galla and out the shattered door and down the steps to the lane that fronted the church. In a daze, Daniella watched her, watched the dark shape of the galla shift and turn and glide along the stone floor of the church, following the woman, bells ringing hollowly as they moved. Above, the whitewashed ceiling of the church was scorched, blackened by flame. The candles round the altar burned steadily, without flickering.

Daniella's feet seemed to move of their own accord toward the door. They echoed in the empty church, leaving the trailing sound of a second set of footsteps behind her. She emerged from the door, picked her way over the splintered wood, and halted on the steps.

The woman, cloak and bow and quiver slung over her back, still clutching her baby in one arm, knelt before a puddle of water in the lane. She passed a hand over it, palm down, and seemed to be speaking as she peered deeply into it. Behind her, the galla closed on her, spreading their cloak of darkness out to engulf her. And she was now unprotected.

Daniella opened her mouth to cry out, to warn her, but no sound came out. No sound but the scuffing of feet behind her. She turned her head to look behind her, only to see Deacon Joceran, blinking confusedly, pick her way across the entrance and halt, staring, at the black cloud that had expanded to cover most of the commons.

"They'll kill her," cried Daniella, and snapped her head back, starting down the steps.

Only to stop short, staring.

Dense fog smothered most of the commons except for a patch of clear ground around a smooth puddle. Daniella ran down the steps. The fog parted before her, and she crouched in the middle of the lane, beside the puddle, looking for remains. Surely the galla could not have utterly consumed both woman and child?

Though it rained softly, the puddle remained a still smooth surface, oddly unmarked by the raindrops Daniella felt on her head and arms and back and could see in other smaller puddles that filled the potholes in the lane. She stared into the water. There, in the clear pale blue water, she saw a reflection of the woman and the baby looking out at her, looking, peering, as if to see her, as if to say goodbye.

Then the image faded and the water turned muddy. Rain stirred its brown surface, spreading tiny ripples.

Slowly, the fog dissipated. The sun rose. Its edge cleared the trees and threw morning shadows long across the commons, striping the church.

"What has happened here this night?" Deacon Joceran asked, coming down the steps. Daniella rose. She ached everywhere, as if she had worked for hours, though it seemed no time at all had passed since she first saw the woman flee into the sanctuary of the church.

"I followed the black ewe into the woods," said Daniella, and told her the story. When she had finished, Deacon Joceran signed the circle of unity and asked to look at the medallion. She studied it for a long time. Daniella grew increasingly nervous. The church denounced magic and sorcery, all but those miracles granted to saints by the Lord and Lady and what healing magic that holy men and women of the church might use to succor the ill and dying. But magic roamed abroad nevertheless, everyone knew that, and some sought to tame it or wield it, and some sought to confine or destroy it, while the church demanded penance from those who touched it or who begged help from the magi and arioli and tempestari who practiced the forbidden arts despite the ban.

But Deacon Joceran had lived many years in Sant Laon and had never once in Daniella's memory spoken out against Mistress Hilde's potions for lovelorn lads or old Ado's reading of thunder and the flight of birds and the movement of the heavens in order to predict the weather for the farmers, especially since old Ado was always right. Once she had mildly rebuked the congregation for giving credence to a travelling mathematici who offered, for a price, to read a man or woman's fate from the courses of the sun and moon and stars, but who Deacon said was a charlatan.

Now she simply handed the amulet back to Daniella.

"These are strange and dark times," she said. "You must wear this. What will you do with the horse? How feed it? Such a horse must have grain, and there are those, alas, who will envy you the having of it, and its fine bridle and saddle. Some gifts are as much of a curse as a blessing."

The gray gelding grazed out on the commons. Like an orphaned child, it suddenly appeared to Daniella as more burden than bounty. But she rose determinedly and walked over to the horse. He allowed her to approach, but with stiff arrogance, like a noble lord forced to allow the approach of a simple farmer. One of the saddlebags was filled with more coin, coppers and silver, than Daniella had ever seen in her life, some stamped with King Henry's seal, others with that of his father and father's father, the two Arnulfs. The other bag contained a book.

Deacon Joceran walked over carefully, favoring the leg that had suffered from an infection this last winter, and when Daniella handed her the book and she opened the plain leather cover and read what was inside, she blanched. Daniella had never seen Deacon at such a loss before.

"These are terrible things," she whispered. "You must let no one see this."

"You must keep it, then, Deacon."

But Deacon Joceran closed the book and with hands trembling not with age, as they well might have, but with something else, fear or passion or some old memory, she thrust it firmly back into the saddlebag. "Once," she said, shutting her eyes against memory, "I dedicated my life to the convent, before I was cast out from the life of contemplation and sent into the world, to atone for my misdeeds. I was curious, and the old books speaking of the forbidden arts tempted me. They tempt me still, though thirty years have passed since those days. Hide it. Let no one know you have it. If a trustworthy friar passes through here, we can send it on to the Convent of Sant Valeria or to Doardas Abbey."

"But who was she, then, Deacon?"

"A mathematici indeed, child, whom we would call one of the magi. She spoke truth to you. Great powers lie hidden in the earth and in the heavens, and not all believe that the Church ought to forbid their study. I have seen with my own eyes . . . " But she trailed off, and Daniella thought that perhaps age lay heavily on the old woman as much from what she had seen as from the passing of years. "Now you have seen, and those who see are marked forever. Go then, child. Go back to your house. I will speak to the congregation of the storm and what it brought, but I pray that the Father and Mother of Life will forgive me for not telling them all that occurred in the night."

Daniella led Resuelto home and installed him in the stables next to the sheep, whom he deigned to ignore. He allowed her to unsaddle him and rub him down, but when Uncle Heldric and Aunt Marguerite ventured out, exclaiming over the dark storm that had swallowed the village for the night, he snorted dangerously and would not let them near him. Matthias was afraid to come into the stables at all, with the big horse there, and Robert, for once, was so in awe of Daniella, or so afraid of what she might have seen and what might have seen her, that he left her alone, not brushing against her hips at every chance, not groping at her budding breasts or whispering suggestions in her ear when no one was nearby to hear.

So the day passed, and the next day, and the one after that, except that strange accidents occurred in the village. Mistress Hilde's prize goat escaped and was found drowned in the pond. Uncle Heldric and Master Bertrand, their neighbor, were hit by a falling tree in the wood, crushing Bertrand's foot and breaking Uncle's left arm. Milk curdled and the hens stopped laying eggs. Churns were overturned, looms unraveled, and the candles at the altar blown out every night. Every person in Sant Laon was struck by misfortune, great or small, everyone except Daniella. Old Ado said the movements of the birds and the lizards warned of worse misfortune to come. Fog wrapped itself round the village at night and increasingly during the day, and out of that fog rose the whisper of bells and soft, guttural voices naming a name: "Daniella."

They have noticed you and will always mark you. You will never be entirely safe from them without this, nor will anyone nearby you. Forgive me for bringing this trouble on you, that is all of the gift I can give in exchange for your kindness.

At dawn on the fourth day since the storm, Daniella woke abruptly and realized that Dhuoda's child, called Blanche for her pale hair, was gone from the bed. She dressed quickly and climbed down from the loft. No one was awake yet; Uncle and Aunt snored softly from their bed by the kitchen fire, and even Gruff lay curled up asleep on the bricks that lined the hearth. She ran outside. And there . . .

There on the commons a dense blot of fog, as dark as the smoke from a blacksmith's forge, swirled round a crying, stumbling child, driving it toward the pond. Daniella cried out loud, and little Blanche, hearing her, bawled even louder and tried desperately to turn, to toddle back toward her aunt, but she could not. The galla forced her closer and ever closer toward the water.

Daniella ran. The fog parted before her, hissing, angry, and she grabbed Blanche just as the little girl teetered on the edge of the pond, her dirty dress wet along the hem.

"Begone!" Daniella shouted, forgetting to be frightened because she was so furious. She pulled the amulet out from under her tunic and held it forward, driving them away. "Begone! What right do you have to torment the innocent?"

But all they said in answer was to whisper her name: "Daniella."

The sun rose and the fog faded to patches, retreating to the wood, where it curled like snakes around the trunks of trees. Waiting. As it would continue to wait, forever, not knowing human time or human cares.

Daniella stood silently by the pond, soothing the weeping child, until Deacon Joceran came out of the church to discover what the shouting had been.

"I must leave," Daniella said, the knowledge hanging on her like a weight. She fought against tears, because she was afraid that if she wept now she would not have the courage to do what had to be done. "They will never leave the village, not until I am gone."

Deacon Joceran nodded, accepting what was necessary, what she could see was true.

Aunt Marguerite wept, when they held a council that morning in the church, Uncle and Aunt and the eldest in the village, those that had their wits about them still. Uncle Heldric offered Daniella his cloak, but he did not beg her to stay. He held little Blanche on his lap. She was smiling now, playing with his beard, and he even laughed a bit. He was fond of Dhuoda's child, what was left to him of his only daughter, favored child, the best-loved and the sweetest.

"You take my cloak," he said gruffly to her.

"You have nothing to replace it with," said Daniella. "Take my mother's wedding shawl in exchange."

"Nay, child," he replied, looking shamed by her generosity, "we have nothing else to give you. It is all you have left of her."

She gave Matthias four silver coins, which was all she could spare, knowing that she would need the rest for the care and feeding of the gelding, and Matthias sobbed as disconsolately as he had when their Da had been buried, and their Mother, dead bearing a child. He begged to come with her. Perhaps he even meant it, but with the coin he could buy himself a start on his own farm and get a wife, and like their Da he had the gift of understanding the land and the seasons, for all that he was scared of the wild lands surrounding the fields.

"You are meant to stay here," she said to him. To Blanche she left Dhuoda's bridal cloth, and to Robert, a single kiss of forgiveness.

"You must go to the Convent of Sant Valeria," said Deacon Joceran. "You must walk seven days east and ten days north, and there at the town known as Autun ask for further direction. At the convent you will find, if not protection, at least advice, for the Abbesses there are known for their wisdom and for their understanding of the forbidden arts. You must not linger too long in one place as you travel, or these creatures, these galla, may bring mischief onto the people among whom you stay, and you will be named as a witch or a malefici and driven out, or worse. Take this letter and give to the Abbess at the convent. They will take you in."

Daniella looked long and searchingly at the marks on the parchment, but they meant nothing to her, just as the book left behind in the saddlebags meant nothing.

"She will try to find me," said Daniella suddenly. "For the book, if nothing else."

"If she has the power, if she yet lives, she will find you," said Deacon, "but whether that would bode good or ill for you, I cannot say, child."

Daniella did not reply, but she felt in her heart that she left Sant Laon, the only place she had ever known, not just to spare her family, to spare the others, but to seek after that meeting, as if it was ordained whether she willed it or no.

Aunt Marguerite brought her bread and cheese, which she put in one of the saddlebags, and Uncle Heldric brought her mother's knife, which he had sharpened to a good edge. She tucked it in her belt, kissed Matthias one final time, and took the reins of Resuelto from Robert.

"Go with the Lord and Lady," said Deacon Joceran, signing a benediction over her.

"Go safely," said Aunt Marguerite. Little Blanche, caught up in her grandda's arms, began to cry, reaching her arms out for Daniella.

But Daniella turned quickly away from them and started down the lane, leading Resuelto, since she did not know how to ride. She did not want them to see the tears in her eyes. She did not want them to fear for her or grieve for her. It was bad enough that they must grieve for Dhuoda, for Da, for her Mother. Let them believe that she went with a light heart, that it was a fate she went to meet willingly. It was the only kindness she could show them, as she left them behind, probably forever.

The gelding walked with dignity beside her, ears forward, eager to explore the road ahead. She kept her eyes on the dirt lane and the wood, and as she passed under cover of the trees, she looked back once to see her village, free of any trailing mist or tendrils of fog, lying in the bright warmth of the noonday sun. The sky was clear above, as blue as she had ever seen it.

At last, with a wrench, she turned to face the road ahead once more, and she walked resolutely on toward unknown lands.

THE PEACHWOOD FLUTE
BROOK AND JULIA WEST

Brook and Julia West are a husband and wife team who write fantasy and science fiction. Julia is an anthropologist and botanist and in the Air Force reserves. Brook is a physical geographer who spent several years in Japan. Julia has been Grand Prize winner and Brook a published finalist in the Writers of the Future contest and they have sold several short stories to magazines and anthologies.

Two weeks without rain had turned the Takeda road to dust that puffed up at every step and clung to the folds of Mitaka Noriaki's patched and shabby clothing. Rice fields shimmered bright green in the heat, and the shrill buzzing of cicadas so filled the air that Noriaki could not have said when the flute player joined them. The music gradually emerged from the background drone until first Noriaki, then the other travelers, glanced back to see the gray-clad musician striding along behind them, face shadowed by a reed hat.

The flute music added to Noriaki's annoyance—awakening longing and bitter memories, reminding him why he was now ronin, a masterless samurai. Once he, too, had played the flute.

The others seemed to enjoy it; Taro the laborer's pregnant wife, Kiku, turned again to smile at the flute player and Taro, carrying bundles hung from a shoulder-pole, nodded his head in time with the music.

Rikichi, the gambler who had hired Noriaki to guard him on the road, mimed a flute of his own—much to the amusement of his friend, Saburo.

Curling his hands into fists, Noriaki suppressed the urge to shout "Begone!" at the flute player.

"Make way! Make way!" came from behind. Noriaki stepped aside and his fellow travelers scattered to the roadside. The flute player drifted after them, never missing a note or even seeming to notice the two bearers and their jolting *kago* palanquin. Noriaki almost smiled at the passenger's grimace.

The travelers returned to the road. "Must be an important samurai," said Saburo.

"Too important for comfort," snickered Rikichi. "The state of his backside showed on his face."

Noriaki fell in behind Taro and, to control his annoyance, concentrated on the bamboo-patterned cloth wrapping Taro's bundles. He found his fingers running over his sword grip—back and forth, like his thoughts. He tried to empty his mind, as the sorcerer-monk Asahiko had taught him to do in those dark days after Noriaki's dying lord had cursed him.

"Where are we?" The bewilderment in Kiku's voice—and the fact that Taro's bundles had ceased swaying—brought Noriaki back to himself. "This isn't Matsugo."

Rickety houses straggled alongside the path. Uphill, dry weed stalks stood tall in neglected vegetable patches.

Kiku hurried on down the path, hands clutching her swollen belly. "This is *not* Matsugo," she said. She stopped short before the last house—or what remained of it. It had burned to the ground—long ago, judging by the plants growing between the remnants of charred timbers. "Where are we? There's no village on the road between Kumano and Matsugo."

"Whatever village this was, no one lives here now—let's go on," Noriaki said.

"Right," said Rikichi. "This place makes my bones crawl."

Behind them on the road came the sound of pounding feet, and "Make way, make way!"

"Another *kago*?" said Saburo. "Don't often see one in a day—let alone two in less than an hour."

They moved off the road again, avoiding the charred timbers of the burned house. The *kago* looked like—it *was*—the same one. The samurai's expression had gone from peevish to apprehensive.

"Stop!" he said. The bearers set down the *kago,* eyes wide as they stared at the ruins. "You. Ronin." He pointed at Noriaki. "I just passed you but here you are again. This village, this house . . . passed them, too. Does the road circle back here?"

Noriaki bowed slightly. "I do not know. The laborer and his wife are local. They say this is not Matsugo, the village we should have come to."

The bearers, probably a relay hired at the last post town, glanced at one another and then quickly away.

The samurai grunted, looked from one bewildered face to another. "On to Matsugo, then," he said. "My message cannot wait."

Noriaki watched the *kago* disappear around a bend in the path. *Hmmm.* This was not the main road, merely a path up a valley. Somehow they had strayed from the road. He hadn't been paying attention—had merely followed Taro, trying to ignore the flute music.

"Flute player—do you know this place?" He glanced around when there was no answer. "Where's the flute player?" He looked up the overgrown path, past the burned house and weed-choked paddies. The gray-clad man in the reed hat was gone. Perhaps he lived farther up this path, and, intent on his music, they had followed him into this valley.

"Flute player? Don't remember seeing him since we stopped here to look around," Rikichi said.

"We seem to have followed him right off the main road," said Noriaki. "We should return quickly, before nightfall."

Kiku took a long, shuddering breath. "Let's go. I don't like this place." She adjusted the folds of her kimono and set off, back the way they had come. Taro, Rikichi, and Saburo followed, walking quickly and casting worried glances to each side.

Noriaki followed slowly, hand on his sword hilt again, uneasiness crawling down his spine. His training, both as a samurai and a priest, told him something was wrong. Every movement of a weedstalk in the wind, every mouse scampering across a deserted courtyard caught his eye. Something very wrong here.

"Make way, make . . ." The pounding of feet came from ahead of them this time, and the five huddled on the roadside, staring at the *kago* that stopped, without its passenger's request, in the road before them.

The samurai's face was white now, eyes staring. "*Hora!* You again. This village is accursed!" The bearers set the chair down, and he stepped out. "This is the only road, but every time I pass the headman's house, it leads back here."

"This looks like a side road," said Noriaki. "If you turn around, you might find your way back to the main road."

"True." The samurai stepped back into the *kago*, the bearers lifted it, turned, and started off.

"Wait," said Noriaki. "I think we'll see them again." The group stood quietly, breathing hard and staring around, but not panicked. Not yet.

It didn't take long. The *kago*, moving slowly now, came into view.

The bearers shook with more than exhaustion—their dusty faces were chalky with fear.

"As I thought," Noriaki said. "We cannot leave."

"*He* can't leave!" said Rikichi. "Doesn't mean we can't." He set off down the path at a dead run, Saburo trailing behind him.

The samurai stepped out of the *kago,* glanced at the running gamblers, and said to Noriaki, "Seems we are here for the night, ronin." The setting sun's rays cast copper highlights on the samurai's jacket. "The headman's house is not so tumbledown as these. All of you—better come with me."

When Rikichi and Saburo joined them, no one said a word.

The headman's house still had most of its thatch, and was ringed with a bamboo fence. But it had been stripped of furnishings, even down to screens and partitions. The samurai stalked around the building, looking for—what?

Just before sunset, Taro and the gamblers ventured into the forested hillside surrounding the village and brought back armloads of wood. They looked pale and shaken, but Noriaki didn't ask what they'd seen amongst the trees.

They laid the wood beside the clay hearth. "Here, let me do that," said Kiku. "I can start the fire and cook food—whatever food there is. . . ."

Noriaki hefted his pack. "There's food," he said.

Kiku knelt on the hearth, coaxing a tiny flame into being with flint and steel. When the kindling was well alight, she blew through a hollow piece of bamboo to strengthen the flames. Soon rice cooked in Noriaki's little pot, and the stranded travelers—including the samurai's bearers—huddled around the cheerful warmth of the fire.

The samurai came in as the rice was done. Noriaki handed the only bowl, filled with rice, to the samurai. The rest scooped rice onto bamboo leaves and ate quickly with rough-whittled chopsticks.

There wasn't much talk. Better to save that for morning, for sunlight to chase ghouls away. They spread bedding on the raised floor of the living area, and everyone lay down—except the samurai, who sat cross-legged, staring into the fire.

Noriaki lay with his back to the dying fire, watching shadows dance on the walls. None of the destroyed villages he had seen in his younger days had reeked of sorcery as this one.

A branch in the fire popped, followed by "tick, tick-tick." Noriaki came instantly alert. "Tick-tick, tick-tick, tick-tick," it sounded—from the wall before him.

Kiku sat up. "He's here," she said, her voice strained and tight. "A poverty god has taken this place. He's ruined it. That's his spider clicking in the walls."

A low voice—one of the bearers, Noriaki thought—said, "I know this village now—Takiya! Two summers ago I heard of it—the crops were dying, mice overran the houses. Onoma moved to our village from Takiya; he told me a poverty god was there. Those that stayed . . . their frozen bodies were found next spring."

Silence, except the ticking of the god's spider and the rustle of restless bodies. Noriaki knew no one would sleep with such thoughts gnawing at their minds. "If Onoma could leave Takiya, so can we. But in the morning, when we are strong. Sleep now," he said.

Noriaki dreamed. The flute wailed, its plaintive tune entwining him, drawing him on. He stumbled through frostbitten fields and tripped, fell to his knees in noisome, half-frozen mud. But the music pulled him up, drew him after the gray-clad man with the reed hat.

The mud shook, rippled, heaved upward, and castle walls rose about him. The flute music joined the smoke of the many cooking fires of a castle under seige, swirling into the cloudy sky. In the keep was a daimyo, a great lord. Noriaki watched him step out onto a balcony, as he did every night, to listen as one of his samurai, Mitaka Noriaki, played a flute.

The flute player began another tune, the notes sad and drawn out. Noriaki's heart started pounding in his chest. "No! Not again. Please go back. . . ."

Outside the castle walls, something flashed. A clap of thunder—and a musket ball slammed the daimyo back into the keep.

Traitor, whispered Noriaki's dying lord. *Mitaka Noriaki, you lured me out where they could shoot me. I name you traitor.*

"No! I'm no traitor. I didn't even know you came out to listen."

You have ended my line. I forbid you to follow me into death. I cast you out, ronin, to wander alone. I bind you to the flute. If you cast it away, it will return to you. If you break it, destruction will follow—and you will die. Traitor. . . .

Heedless, the flute music continued.

The gray-clad man's wild music swept Noriaki up, to a hillside covered with pine and bamboo, to a hut crouched in a clearing. It smelled of incense and herbs, and inside a man seeking unearned riches chanted in Chinese, the language of sorcery. He carefully scribed characters onto a slip of paper, then hung the completed talisman with others on the hut's wall. The flute music, wilder now and darker, swirled around the man. His kimono thinned, shredded, revealed an emaciated, skeletal frame. He smiled, leathery lips pulled back from cracked, yellowed teeth. The music rose to a shriek, then gave way to the tick-tick of the poverty spider.

Noriaki sat up. The moon shone through a hole in the roof, puddled silvery on the floor. Something rustled, motion in the moon pool. Noriaki snatched his pack into his lap, and mice fell out.

Kiku rolled over. She saw the mice and screamed. Rikichi grabbed a knife from inside his jacket.

"Calm down," Noriaki said. "It's just mice."

"Look! They chewed holes in my kimono!" Kiku said, voice trembling.

Rice trickled through Noriaki's fingers from a hole in his pack. He said nothing, just tied the rest of the rice up in an undamaged cloth. "Where's the samurai?" he asked a sleepy-eyed bearer.

The man looked around. "Not here."

Noriaki rose to his feet, sheathed sword in his left hand. The other travelers watched, moonlight gleaming from wide eyes. He pushed the door aside, stepped into the courtyard. Stark as an ink-painting, black and white, a darker patch of shadow. The samurai sprawled against the fence, expensive kimono tattered. Noriaki knelt, looked at a face gaunt as a starving peasant's, dead eyes wide and blank.

The bearers, standing behind Noriaki, began to wail. "The poverty god has taken him!"

"Hush." Noriaki stood, waved them back into the building. "Don't entice the god."

Kiku fed twigs, then branches, into the coals, blowing them white-hot with her bamboo tube. The other travelers crowded around, though the night was not cold. Each wanted warmth, the touch of the living.

Noriaki sat with the others, one hand on his sword hilt, the other under his kimono, on a long silken packet.

My cursed flute, so full of grief and anger. I've thrown it away many times—but it's always there in the morning. Are we alike, the gray-clad flute player and I? Was he trapped here, too? Is there a bond between us, like that which binds me to my flute?

*   *   *

The first rays of sun scaled the hills and fell on the headman's house. The huddle of sleepless travelers broke apart, yawning and scratching, but still quiet. No one wanted to go outside and see the samurai's body lying in the dust. Finally Noriaki grunted, slipped into his sandals, and stepped out.

He picked up the body, wasted and much lighter than he expected, and carried it to a dilapidated shed behind the house.

"Mitaka-san!" Rikichi leaned out the door. The excitement in his voice was unmistakable. "Kiku has an idea."

"Yes?"

"The bamboo tube we use to blow on the fire's coals. . . ." Kiku spoke quickly, in a shrill voice. "My mother told me: when it cracks from the heat of the fire, wedge a copper coin in it and throw it into the street. A poverty god is greedy and won't let go of the coin trapped in the bamboo. He follows it out of the house."

One of the bearers added, "We can purify the village with salt and rice, like New Year's Day. That drives away evil spirits—it might rid us of the poverty god!"

The rest murmured approval. Their mood had risen with the sun, and dealing with the poverty god seemed easy. But Noriaki wasn't so sure. Wouldn't the inhabitants of Takiya have tried such things? And yet the village was dead—and so was the samurai.

But he had to try, although something deep within him told him it was futile. "Very good," he said. "Do we have salt? I still have rice left." Unless the mice ate it up in the night.

"I have salt." Saburo spoke up now. "The ritual should use soybeans, too."

"Let me think." Noriaki settled cross-legged on the porch, closed his eyes, and opened his mind to the world around him. Did he really expect to fight sorcery with incomplete Shinto ritual?

He opened his eyes and met the gaze of a half circle of curious travelers. "Are you a priest?" asked Taro.

"I studied with one, once." He rose smoothly to his feet, and went inside to retrieve his pack. He untied the cloth and scooped rice into his cupped hands. It squirmed with weevils. He sorted out several handfuls of clean rice and put them into his sleeve pocket. Saburo handed him a packet of salt as he stepped back outside.

"We'll start down the road with the first house. Saburo, get some branches to use as brooms and join us there." Noriaki cut four slender pieces of bamboo from the fence, each a couple of handspans long.

They set to work on the three houses down the road, sweeping them out and, at least symbolically, cleaning them. In each, they gathered in front of the shelf where the household shrine had been and set out a bit of the precious rice as an offering. They bowed and clapped twice, then prayed to the household kami for help—assuming any kami were still in residence.

They scattered more rice around and scrubbed each threshold with a bit of the salt. They should have scattered soybeans, too, but had none—rice would have to do. They did the same in the headman's house.

"Now we need to start a kitchen fire in each house."

They walked back down the path to the first house in the village, Noriaki very aware of six pairs of eyes watching him.

He laid a small fire on the kitchen's clay hearth. He dropped a coal in the midst of the tinder and blew, first lightly, then with stronger breaths, into the fire. The kindling caught, flared.

He handed one of the bamboo tubes to Kiku, and took a copper coin from the folds of his sash. "Taro and Kiku, set the end of the tube well down into the coals and blow them up good and hot until it cracks. This weathered bamboo shouldn't take long. Then wedge this coin in it and throw it into the street. The rest of you come with me."

He did the same in the second and third houses, leaving Rikichi and Saburo in one, and the two bearers in the next. Noriaki stopped before the charred timbers of the fourth house, unsure. Should he include it? But it was part of the village as it had been. He called one of the bearers and stepped over the blackened beams to the clay hearth. The bearer seemed reluctant to follow, but when Noriaki beckoned imperiously, he entered, stepping carefully where the ronin had stepped.

Noriaki returned to the headman's hut, cut another tube of bamboo, and began blowing the coals.

"Mitaka-san," said Kiku behind him, "our tube cracked. We did as you said."

"Good."

The others soon gathered.

He continued blowing at his fire, but his bamboo tube remained whole. Noriaki still felt the sorcerous tension. "There is another house in this valley," he said.

"Mitaka-san," said Taro, "yesterday when we were gathering wood, I saw a track leading through the vegetable patches, back into the forest. Perhaps there?"

Noriaki nodded. He cut another tube and handed it and a coin to Kiku. "This fire—you know what to do," he said. He turned back to Taro. "Show me."

Taro led the way, along a bare tracery of footpath, under overhanging pine branches to a tumbledown hut.

Carefully shielding his coals, Noriaki peered in through the gaping doorway. Dirt and weeds had blown in; some animal had denned here. The scent of old incense and herbs clung to the hut. Something screamed at the back of Noriaki's mind; the poverty god had visited here first. Inside was the key to the enchantment on the village.

"*Hora!* Look what's in the back room," said Taro.

Noriaki stooped to peer in and a dragonfly darted into his face. Startled, he dropped the coals into the weeds and dry leaves on the floor. They burst into unnatural flame, and the wall caught almost immediately. He stepped back, but looked into the room as fire licked up the timbers. A skeleton lay there, surrounded by talismans—strips of paper bearing sorcerous characters and designs.

As Noriaki backed away from the flames, he brought the bamboo tube out. Stooping, he placed it at the base of the wall, and blew with all his might. Heat washed over him, the flames rose in a roar—and as he thought the skin on his face and hands would blister, the bamboo tube cracked.

Taking a copper coin from the folds of his sash, he wedged it into the crack in the tube. He turned and ran out into the coolness of the forest shadow. He hurled the tube down the path.

"Come, Taro, back to the village."

The laborer, pale with fear, needed no further urging. Noriaki followed, flinging the last of the rice and salt and chanting.

He felt nothing. No sense of relief, no cessation of his awareness of sorcery.

The travelers crowded around. "There was a sorcerer!" cried Taro. "Mitaka-san destroyed him! Now we can escape."

Rikichi set off down the path at a dead run. Noriaki watched him pass the first two houses. Unnerved by Noriaki's silence, the rest of the travelers watched the gambler disappear around the curve. They turned to look up the path and waited.

Rikichi reappeared, running.

*   *   *

A second uneasy night in the headman's house, with the poverty spider tick-ticking in the walls. There was little edible rice—what the mice left, the weevils had gotten to. Kiku curled in on herself, rocking and singing an eerie, wailing song. Rikichi talked constantly for a while, then suddenly turned and slapped Kiku. "Shut up, woman," he screamed.

Taro swung his pole at Rikichi, who ducked and ran outside.

Everyone avoided Noriaki. He sat in a corner, holding the silk-covered flute. It seemed to burn through the wrappings. He had played it when he was a young man, in his father's house. Its music had helped pass the agonizing hours during the siege of his daimyo's castle. He had tried to destroy it, pouring his guilt and anger into it when he had studied with Asahiko, the sorcerer-monk. He hadn't played it since.

The house was quiet now, except for the rustle of bedding and the tick-tick of the poverty god's spider. Tick-tick, tick-tick and, as Noriaki nodded off, a thread of music in counterpoint. The music swelled, wild and strange, and carried him to the gray-clad man in the reed hat who turned, beckoning with one hand.

Were there words behind the music? A chant? The flute player pointed, and incense rose, its scent mingled with the music. Again and again, in the five directions, East, South, Center, West, and North, the music and the sweet smoke. They tied themselves around Noriaki, seeped into his soul, wound tighter and tighter, tearing him apart. He knew this ritual.

Help me, please. Free me.

"How?"

Your knowledge. The ritual. The curse on your flute can destroy the god. Play it.

"Not the flute. I can't!"

Then you and the others will die. I can't stop him.

The music tore sight from his eyes, sensation from his fingers and feet. Nothing existed but the flute, the music, high and sweet and breathy.

The music stopped. A whisper from beneath the reed hat. *I did not play—then.*

Tension twisted Noriaki 'til he cracked like a bamboo tube.

*   *   *

Noriaki clawed his way out of the dream. No one else stirred. In the vague light of the fire's embers and of the moon through the torn thatch, he saw five sleeping bodies. Only five? Stepping quietly over the nearest sleeper, he strode to the door. Again, moonlight washed over a land of stark contrasts. The bamboo gate stood open.

When Noriaki left the courtyard, he closed the gate behind him. He trod the path, found by sheer instinct the footpath into the woods. It was dark here, with roots and fallen branches to catch his hakama trousers and trip him. But he went on, to the sorcerer's hut in its little clearing.

Two walls stood; the rest charred ruin. Moonlight showed Noriaki the storage shed in back. He walked toward it, gut twisting with apprehension, and pushed open the door.

Moonlight filled the shed like the glow of a paper lantern, silvering the tattered gray kimono that clad the skeleton at his feet. A mouse-chewed reed hat lay to one side; a bamboo flute rested beneath the outstretched fingers of a bony hand. "The god trapped you, too," whispered Noriaki. "He killed you. Why did you bring *us* here to die?"

He expected no answer. He already knew what to do. But he could not play his flute again, could not accept all that pain back into himself.

Not even to live? Did someone say that, or was it his own voice whispering within?

He almost tripped on the body lying in the middle of the path. It was Rikichi, his face a mask of terror, gold coins scattered from his fingers. The body was wizened as a hundred-year-old grandfather's.

Noriaki carried the gambler's body to the shed and laid it beside the samurai.

The sky was deepest blue, lightening toward the east. Another day. He hurried to the headman's house and slipped in through the door to sit in his corner. His hand sought the silken packet hidden in his kimono. *I must use it,* he thought, *before another dies. I am the key to this mystery. Perhaps it will ease my soul.*

Noriaki took strips of paper, a brush, ink, and an inkstone from his pack and carefully scribed a set of talismans.

He shook Taro, Saburo, Kiku, and the two bearers awake. They stared at him sleepily, muttering cross things under their breath. "Do you want to live?" His voice was harsh. "Do as I say."

"Yes, Mitaka-san." Trust and relief appeared in their eyes again, washing out yesterday's disappointment.

"Come with me."

"But . . . but where's Rikichi?" Saburo looked around fearfully.

"Dead. Get kindling, and coals from the fire. Come."

He led them a short distance east of the village, out into the dry paddies. He smoothed a patch of ground and drew a diagram. From one sleeve he took a packet of incense. "Saburo, I'm going to teach you a short chant. Kindle a fire here. When I begin to play my flute, add the incense to the fire. Then burn these three paper talismans, one at a time, while reciting the chant. No matter what I do, you remember your part."

"Yes, Mitaka-san."

He took the others to the South, Center, West, and North of the village—one at each of the five directions, each with similar instructions, then returned to the East.

Noriaki slipped the silk packet from his kimono and untied the binding cords. The covering fluttered to the ground.

The flute was carved of peachwood, suitable for a nobleman's son. He had cared for it, oiled it and polished it to a high gloss. Later, he had carved characters into the sides, and polished them, too. It was a thing of beauty, this flute.

He hated it.

He raised it to his lips, fingers fitting easily over the holes even after all these years. He drew his lips back against his teeth and blew.

A note sounded, wavery, plaintive. He moved his fingers and music rose, like the rush of hawk into sky. Aaah, the skill was there in fingers and lips.

He paced from station to station, following the ghost—a gray-clad man who walked one step ahead, playing music that rang through Noriaki's head. He followed the pattern—intricate, changeable—and felt tension in his body.

Once around the circuit; once through the pattern. Now he smelled incense, felt it twist like cords around his ankles, slowing yet dragging him on. He played, fingers moving more slowly now, wood warming beneath them, beneath his lips. Twice through.

Again, heat rising around him in waves he could almost see. He stepped, and played, though his hands felt swollen and his lips began to crack.

Once again. He lost track of his feet, his fingers. How could he play when he could not feel? But music rose from his flute, the pattern strengthened.

Then guilt rose, a wave of fire like the sorcerer's cottage burning. *My lord, I have killed you!*

Then fear. *How can I be ronin—what will I do? This dishonor—I can never return to my family.* Flames seemed to crackle all about him, singed his hair, raised blisters on his cheeks.

Anger washed over him, anger at himself for choosing to live, anger at his enemy and his daimyo for making him ronin, anger at the gods for allowing this to happen. Too much anger; it sank into his soul and split him end to end.

And feeling returned—the dusty path beneath his feet, the splintered wood in his hands. He looked down, to see his flute cracked, the characters sundered.

One of Rikichi's gold coins glittered in the dust. Noriaki shoved it into the shattered flute and threw the flute far down the path.

A cool breeze blew over his cheeks—cheeks not blistered, hair not singed. He looked up; clouds covered the sun, and moments later a fine rain began to patter down. He watched the tiny pits the droplets formed in the dust, stared in wonder and awe.

If you break it, destruction will follow—and you will die.

"I'm not dead. . . ."

Disbelief gave way to elation. "I'm free!"

Free of this accursed village, he and his fellow travelers. Free too, of the burden he had hugged to himself these twenty years and more—the guilt, anger, pain, horror. The flute had broken, destruction had followed. The poverty god that the amateur sorcerer had called into being with his greed, that he had *become,* was no more. And Noriaki *would* die, too—someday.

"We can leave now," said Noriaki.

The two bearers—whose names he had never learned—Saburo, Taro and Kiku. Chance-met travelers, and now, family, of a sort. They stared at him, wonder in their eyes.

"Gather your things. I'll join you in a moment."

He followed the thread of a path into the forest one last time, past the burned hut to the tiny shed. He stooped, took the plain bamboo flute from the skeleton's hand. "May I?" But there was no one there now. The gray-clad flute player was dead, finally dead. Free. He turned away, started back to the village—then returned for the reed hat.

THE TENTH PAINTING

THOMAS S. ROCHE

Thomas S. Roche has published fiction in anthologies such as Enchanted Forests, Gothic Ghosts, Northern Frights 4, and Blood Muse. He recently edited Gargoyles with Nancy Kilpatrick (Acer, 1997).

He rode like a thing out of Hell, leaving fires in his wake. He thundered through the worlds, aware at every turn of the part of his mind that was Theirs.

Halfway through his journey, he knew they were aware of his flight. By that time, he was far away. They could never catch up with him before he escaped.

But he rode that much faster, out of fear that he might have miscalculated. His mount changed forms as he passed through world after world after world: now a scaled lizard-thing of black beneath him, now of green, now a snake, now a horse made of steel, now a bird. . . .

He drew rein when he reached the proper place, the foot of the hill. He looked up into the cave.

He dismounted, and with a wave of his hand dismissed his mount. The creature dissolved into smoke and vanished. It would be more difficult for them to track him that way.

He moved cautiously up the hillside, approaching the cave.

He positioned himself outside the cave mouth, at the proper place, before the gaping black hole.

"Creature of the Cave," he spoke in the ancient language. "I summon thee!"

Lights began to flicker inside. There was a faint rumbling, and the mouth of the cave seemed to swirl with a haze of milky smoke. Then, slowly, her wizened form appeared, hidden in shadow and fog. The voice of an old woman, loud enough to pierce his eardrums and make his eyes water, echoed through the valley.

"Who seeks to demand service of me?" The voice was harsh, threatening.

Flames exploded out around her, brushing him with sparks.

He laughed.

"I demand nothing, old woman. Vionne, how in Hell did you acquire such a lousy disposition since I saw you last?"

Cackling, pealing laughter.

Then the fog and flame dispersed, and the shadows became more natural.

"Arundel. You *have* been away for some time. Get in here and give your old tutor a hug."

He strode into the cave, embraced her. The darkness was more pronounced, but he could see that she was in terrible shape, with wrinkled and decayed flesh and damaged features. He did not let it show that he noticed.

"Come with me," she said, beckoning him down a corridor of raw stone. "Come with me, and we'll have some food. You've been traveling long?"

"A thousand years," he grinned in darkness. "Looking for you."

"It would seem the student has surpassed his Mistress."

Arundel paused, his mouth full of bread and roasted pheasant. "I could never surpass you, lady." His mouth was full and Vionne could barely understand him. Arundel grinned wide and a thin trail of juice ran down his chin.

"You always have been a barbarian," said Vionne, laughing. "At least when it comes to food. Wipe your face." He did not move to do so immediately, so she rose from her couch, leaned over, and wiped his face for him with a white napkin. It felt very strange to have her do that.

Arundel sat hunched over the low table, a gorgeous platter of food before him. The sorceress returned to her velvet divan and stretched out.

Vionne's ancient face seemed to grow serious for a moment. "What's this I hear about you betraying the Seven?"

Arundel kept his eyes down. "It would be best if you did not ask about that just yet, lady."

"Have I suddenly been made a noble? Bah! Fine then, don't answer my questions. You never did before." She smiled a toothless smile, and

Arundel looked vaguely uncomfortable. "You can keep your secrets for the time being," said Vionne. "But you will tell me eventually."

Arundel nodded. "Soon. After I sleep."

"You seem uncomfortable."

Arundel shrugged noncommittally. "There is so much that I have to do," he said. "And it's been a long time since I saw you."

The ancient woman smiled flirtatiously, tossing what was left of her brittle, grayed hair.

"Should I assume a more subjectively pleasing form?" she asked of Arundel, who shrugged.

"If you like."

Vionne laughed, an almost insane cackling. As she laughed, her face began to shimmer, and her body to change. The shape of her curved and twisted back altered, and her gray hair slowly began to molder. It slipped out of her head in a spray of dusty strands, falling onto the ground and then rising as it became white smoke. The stained robe Vionne wore peeled off in long strips of rot, transforming on the ground into the scattered petals of white roses. The sorceress now lounged nude on her velvet couch, and her flesh peeled off and dropped to the ground, then misted into a perfumed scent of sandalwood and musk. The mouth full of rotted teeth opened slowly, and each tooth twisted and dropped, falling with tinkling sounds to the floor where they became tiny cockroachlike gremlins that ran immediately for the corners of the room, carrying crumbs that had fallen on the floor from Arundel's plate.

Around the sorceress's head, new hair flowed black and silken, cascading like a waterfall over her shoulders. The curls increased until they surrounded her face, which had become quite different. The wrinkles disappeared, the lips swelled until they were full and young and flawless, the eyes lost their watery, bloodshot quality.

Arundel had stopped chewing during the display, but he managed to start again now that it was finished. Vionne was always the overly dramatic sort.

Vionne waved her hand and a translucent, wraithlike young girl-spirit shimmered into existence, carrying a black silk robe. Vionne slipped the robe on but left it partway open. The wraith-girl disappeared.

"You are most certainly in your place of power," said Arundel.

Vionne smiled broadly. "Did you like my little display?"

With the change, Vionne had assumed a more subjectively pleasing shape, instinctively knowing what Arundel wished, though she had, in the past, held some vague disdain for this sort of appearance. She had the strange, almost translucent white skin and the blue-black lips she had favored in an earlier era, so long ago. Her eyes were the faintly glowing green he had once been fond of. Arundel knew that this form was no more or less Vionne than any other she might assume. The form of the wizened old woman had served its purpose, and now Vionne was seeking something new, with less thought to it than if she had changed her clothes. Such was the nature of her personality, when she resided in this place. He caught his breath to look at her, revealed to him on the couch. She tossed her mane of blue-black hair seductively.

Arundel sighed. "I would have liked it less . . . if you weren't trying so hard to impress me."

Vionne laughed. "Would you expect anything different of me? There will always be the balance of power between teacher and student, and . . . dominance must be established. Though I suppose I am a little bit insecure, what with the stories I've heard of your power . . . "

Arundel snorted in disgust. "If my power is so great, I wouldn't be running to you for shelter—"

He caught himself, and returned to stuffing his face with roasted meat and washing it down with phosphorescent blue wine.

Vionne leaned across the table again, touching Arundel's chin and turning it toward him.

"I know the stories," she said. "And I suspect they're true. If your powers were any less, you would be dead by now. More than dead. Don't you ever forget that."

Arundel looked down quickly, pushing her hand away, and for a moment in his eyes burned a fire Vionne had only seen once or twice before, and that she knew she would see again—soon. She did not want to stand against him in the moment that fire burned.

Vionne spoke softly now, firmly, without a hint of flirtation. "Are you finished eating, Arundel?"

Arundel wiped his mouth, then set down his napkin and nodded.

"Good, then. It's been too many hundreds of years, young student. Let's see if you've learned any new tricks."

Later, through the curtain of her hair, while she dozed he saw the black jewel of protection pulse once, cradled in the valley between her breasts; then twice, then a third time. And so on through the sixth.

He drew deeply of Vionne's scent of sandalwood and musk.

Resisting but unresisting, Arundel lifted his hand and the stone pulsed again.

He exhaled slowly, the sandalwood tickling his nose.

He had removed the stone and laid it there, knowing that the Seven would seek to contact him through it. Vionne's presence would distract them, possibly slow them down for a short time.

"Are you going to tell me the truth?" said Vionne, her voice sleepy.

Arundel sighed. "The truth, my dear, is generally less interesting than the stories which allude to it."

Vionne reached up, pulled Arundel to her. She kissed him with her blue-black lips, and the skin was cold.

"I hate it when you speak in riddles, especially since you've never been particularly good at it. Say something that makes sense for once, student."

Arundel looked at Vionne, fixing his steel gray eyes on her faintly glowing green ones. "I had a disagreement with my compatriots. I thought it prudent to leave before it was possible to invoke their wrath."

"That's why the stone was pulsing," she said, feigning indifference. "So it is true . . . what was the disagreement about?"

"The Seven seek to become One, to join in Congress and seal their minds together. I have no desire to think by committee. And if the Seven joined their minds, their power would be unstoppable and absolute."

Vionne looked pointedly at Arundel. "What stops you from wanting to have absolute power?"

Arundel sat up on the bed, wrapping the black sheet around him. "Everything. Nothing. I disagree with what the Seven do. Enforcing the laws of Sorcery—natural laws, which take care of their own—but then using these positions to twist the balance of power among all the worlds. To do the bidding of the Seven, and give them more power."

Vionne laughed lightly, for a moment taking on the look of the cynical old lady she had been when Arundel had first learned from her. "Of course, child. Are you even more stupid than you were when you were my pupil? You knew all this when you agreed to become one. And you were happy to receive what power they gave you—it was an astonishing honor!" Her face had gone somewhat pale, and the line of her lips was hardening.

Vionne sat up, pulling the sheet off of Arundel. "You were made one of the Seven at the age of 137—that's unheard of! Do you have any idea how I envied you?"

Arundel's face hardened, too. The two stared at each other, as Vionne's stone pulsed rapidly six times.

Arundel raised his hand, and the stone pulsed again.

"But they would not admit me, because of my gender, and because of politics. Well, times have changed, Arundel, and now you've come to me seeking an escape from the Seven. . . ."

"To be admitted to your Parlor," he told Vionne, his eyes dark but his face showing no anger. "I seek to gaze upon your paintings."

Vionne smiled, her blue lips twisting, and it was a strange and lovely thing for Arundel to see. "Oh, Arundel, you do have a good memory, and a good knowledge of the laws you flout. There are seven of those paintings, as well, the seven great works of Vionne Millena. And then, the eighth, the eighth painting in magic oils. And within that eighth painting is your escape, for the grasp of the Seven doesn't reach beyond the worlds, into oblivion. . . ."

"I need your place of power to escape, since my places and my strongholds are already forfeit to the Seven."

"Forfeit. This is the price of absolute power," she mused. "But I, a lowly sorceress, forever denied being one of the Seven, am allowed to keep my place of power . . . which puts you at my mercy, just now."

"Are you going to help me, sorceress? Because if not, I have business to attend to in the Parlor."

"Oh, child, you would not oppose me in my place of power. Not even *you* would be so foolish."

"But you'll let me do it," he said. "I'll be dropping by your Parlor now, and leaving the Septus. I'll be rid once and for all of the cursed Seven, and be damned with them!"

Vionne mocked concern. "Oh, but Arundel! Your contract was for life! The circle of minds will be destroyed if you leave the Septus, and the Seven will be very irritated with you . . . you will have crippled them, possibly killed them. They cannot exist as Six, and cannot close the circle while you live. And anyone who kills you, or arranges your death, is exiled from the Septus forever!"

He hadn't realized Vionne knew so much of the forbidden knowledge. All sorcerers knew a little—from shoptalk, bits of legend, ancient texts—but Vionne knew more than he had given her credit for. It disturbed and angered him.

Arundel stood, defiantly, casting the black sheet around himself. He looked at Vionne, and as she stood, her naked body was a thing of terror and of beauty. She lifted her hand and casually brushed back her hair.

"How I envied you when you joined the Seven," she said angrily. "How I wanted that place . . . "

"I'm sorry, sorceress. Are you quite finished? I have some business to attend to in the Parlor."

"Don't be so boorish," said Vionne. She turned away from Arundel and reached for her robe. Arundel turned to go, and found that his feet were frozen in place. The black sheet had curled from the bed, covering his lower body, and hardening as it swelled up over him. Arundel's naked body was immobile, and struggling was fruitless. His eyes went wide as the sheet twisted about his shoulders.

"I'm sorry," said Vionne, genuinely sad. She stood, looking at him, absently touching the black stone in the "V" of her half-open robe.

Slowly, black light pulsed out of the stone. One . . . two . . . three . . .

After the sixth pulse, Arundel instinctively sought to reply with his mind, but found that he couldn't.

Vionne lifted her hand, and the stone pulsed the final time.

"I've painted something for you," she said. "Just especially for you . . . "

Arundel was borne to the Parlor by huge numbers of pillows and blankets, immobilized by the black sheet from the bed. The bedding followed its mistress down ancient stone corridors smelling of musk and doom, sandalwood and demons. He was quite helpless.

Vionne had increased her power. Arundel never would have been taken like that in the old days. He cursed himself for his carelessness, and he knew that he had once again underestimated the sorceress.

Vionne's silk robe swelled about her, blown in the drafts that flowed through the myriad halls of her labyrinth.

When they reached the downstairs Parlor, Arundel gazed around, twisting his neck, trying in vain to move his body to get a better view. Vionne's handiwork always astonished him.

The paintings were flawless and terrifying. Perfect renderings, in oil paint and magic gems, of the matrices of each of the seven worlds. And then, in the place of honor, the eighth.

The eighth world, the place apart from the Septus. Where only Vionne had traveled, and the one place where the Seven could not exact their revenge.

By disappearing out of the known worlds, Arundel would cripple the Seven, destroy them for ever. He would take their power by vanishing while he was still one of them. They would never regain it, and he would be free—in an unknown world.

It was so close. Arundel looked longingly at the eighth painting, while Vionne walked over to him.

"No, no, no," she said. "I'm sorry, Arundel. I wish I could help you escape. But I've sworn an oath. I'm to be your jailer."

With a wave of her hand, she indicated a ninth painting. It was not a painting of a matrix, but rather of a sumptuous bedroom of velvet and pearls, with a canopied bed. It faced ominously south.

"I know it's a little much," she told him. "But I couldn't put you in a dark cell."

The seven-pointed stone of protection around Vionne's neck pulsed, slowly, six times.

She put her hand over it, and Arundel felt the pulse, the seventh pulse. It was no longer his to control.

Vionne waved her hand, and the sheets tangled more completely around Arundel, bearing him into the room in the painting.

The days blended together. She was kind enough to supply him with books, and the food was, as always, fabulous. It was delivered at regular intervals by the wraithlike girl servant Arundel had seen on the first night. She would come into view, shimmering in the painting on the wall of his bedroom that showed Vionne's work space. She would set down the tray of food and wine, and vanish.

The bed made itself each morning after Arundel rose, the covers turning back precisely at whichever moment he began to feel tired in the evening. Arundel found clean clothes every morning, laid out neatly on the divan. Vionne visited him frequently. She became a painted figure in the oil painting, then slowly began to speak, her lips moving. She would discuss matters of philosophy and politics with Arundel, but of course he could only step through the painting if she invited him.

"It's not that I'm angry with you," Vionne would say. "It's just that I can't deny the Seven. I'm sorry, Arundel, but without their power I think the Septus would fall into chaos, and would become like the eighth world. The matrix of forces that control the laws of Sorcery must be maintained as uniform throughout the Septus. You don't agree?"

Arundel would wave his hand in dismissal. "What does it matter if I agree? You've taken my place with the Seven and placed yourself as

Regent to an idiot-king! I'm your slave, nothing more than a conduit for your power!"

"Oh, that's not true," Vionne would say, looking sad.

One day, Vionne seemed excited.

"The Seven are coming here," she said.

Arundel sneered. "All of them at once? That's more than I can stomach."

"They want you to rejoin, fully. If you agree, I'll release you. Please, Arundel, be my lover. Submit to the Seven."

Arundel snorted in disgust. "Be your lover and join with the Seven? It seems unlikely from all sides. To start with, you would, of course, have to relinquish control over me."

"I suppose that would be unfortunate for me. . . ." Vionne mused as if it were the first time it had occurred to her, which it obviously wasn't.

"Of course it would. But on top of that, I don't trust you . . . or them. Not now."

Vionne began to laugh as she became a painted figure again, then faded from view. "If you ever trusted any of us, you're an idiot. But then, you know that."

Arundel read constantly in his cell, trying to find a clue as to how to escape, but Vionne had carefully selected the magic texts—they were harmless. Resigned to his fate, Arundel began to welcome Vionne's visits, and to feel a little of the old respect he had for her. He wondered, if the situation had been different, if Vionne might have helped him escape.

Vionne began to visit him every day, still wearing the aesthetically pleasing form she had assumed on the day Arundel had arrived. She was painting something in her workshop. Vionne would appear slowly in the painting before Arundel, her canvas and paints spread out in front of Arundel's cell. The canvas was always turned just to the side, so that Arundel couldn't see what was being painted. He feigned disinterest.

"They're coming soon," said Vionne one day. "The Seven will soon be here to liberate you, if you'll agree to their terms. And the painting's almost finished. Would you like to see it?"

"I'd rather not," said Arundel. "The last painting I looked at was rather an arresting composition."

"Always the art critic," said Vionne.

When the day's painting was finished, there came the hours when Vionne would step into the painting. Those hours were so pleasant that Arundel almost forgot that he and she were at odds.

"One would think you loved me. . . ." Vionne whispered at one of these times.

"Don't get any ideas," said Arundel. "But I have never seen fit to let circumstances make me miserable."

"Maybe you think I'll let you out someday."

"I try not to delude myself."

"A noble sentiment."

Vionne returned in the morning, and her painting continued.

The day came when Vionne stepped back and looked at her painting thoughtfully.

"It's finished," she said. "You should take a look at it."

Arundel looked up from the book he was reading, regarding the faintly moving form of Vionne etched in shimmering oil paints. "Am I going to be tested on this?"

"Maybe. It depends on whether you're willing to be mine."

"Yours or theirs," said Arundel derisively. "A well-groomed pet, in either case."

"Don't be so dramatic. You'll be mine," said Vionne, and disappeared from the painting. Her voice echoed after her, the voice of the crone. "When the Seven come, you'll be mine. They will too."

Arundel mused over that thought as he stared blankly at his book.

Arundel felt the six pulses, and the seventh in response. The Seven had arrived. They were with Vionne.

Arundel lounged on the other side of the room, away from the painting, disinterested.

Slowly, a figure began to take shape in the oil painting, as if being added by the strokes of an artist's brush. The figure wore a black robe and hood, with eyes that glowed faintly yellow. It took ten minutes or so for the figure to appear, and Arundel tried to ignore it.

A second figure appeared, more quickly than the first. Then a third . . . and so on, until there were six figures, all in black robes and hoods, all with glowing yellow eyes, which would have been the sign that they were all temporarily in Congress. Now, Arundel knew that the Congress was irreversible and eternal—that they were six bodies, one mind. One power. They would think as one forevermore, and for now, Vionne would be thinking with them. But the place for the seventh mind in the circle was a hole like the final setting in a jeweled crown, left empty. Vionne was only a temporary gemstone. But for now, Arundel was excluded from the loop, serving merely as a conduit for Vionne's power.

Vionne came into existence in the painting, standing behind the other six. She wore a black robe that Arundel had cast into Nowhere, and that had apparently been summoned back for her use. She had changed into the form of the crone, her hunched back causing the robe to drag on the ground.

Their voices rose in chorus.

You have betrayed us, sorcerer! It is time for you to return! Come back to be part of the Seven, and we will return all of your former honors, and forget this unpleasantness!

"I have no desire to forget it," sneered Arundel, standing before the painting. "I'm rather pleased with it, actually. Three square meals a day, and the bed makes itself! I'm rather fond of the arrangement, really!"

You're lying. You cannot lie to those who once shared your mind. Come back once, join with us, and we shall take you into our being.

"I don't think our hostess would be too pleased by that," said Arundel.

She is nothing! She will be cast aside like a stone!

Arundel shook his head. "I'm kind of creeped out by this whole thing, to tell you the truth. But if you insist . . . " Arundel vaguely nodded his head, assenting. He stood before the painting, regarding the seven figures. The one at the back nodded to him.

"Take me back," he said to Vionne, and the Seven misunderstood.

The Six opened up, their eyes becoming bright seven-pointed stars. The black robe began to shimmer on Vionne's body, as it began to come into existence on Arundel's. His clothes moldered and fell, to be replaced in a heartbeat by the robe.

He felt the eight minds around him—the Seven, including his, and Vionne's. For a moment all were in Congress, and thinking as one. Arundel could feel Vionne's strength, for they were in her place of power. Not even these six could hope to defeat her here, with all she had learned in the last few hundred years—not without Arundel's help. But only Arundel knew that.

They thought as one, and turned as one.

Arundel felt his own mind in Vionne's grasp, and in that critical moment she was in control, guided by Arundel.

Of one mind, the Seven stepped forward. Six of them faced the ninth painting; one of them faced Vionne.

Arundel brushed past the six robes and found himself before the sorceress. His bare feet touched the stone floor, and Vionne began to laugh.

Behind him, he heard the shocked exclamations of the six sorcerers.

They increased to screams of rage as Vionne's seven-pointed star that was the stone of protection began to pulse. Six times, with her eyes fluttering each time.

Slowly, Arundel raised his hand, grinning. And the stone pulsed a seventh time.

The screams faded quickly as the moving figures froze into oil paints and the yellow eyes became flickering gemstones.

There are times when he visits his prisoners, trying to see something of the compatiots he had once respected. He sits in Vionne's chair and regards the sorcerers within that oil-painted prison. Their groupthink has merged them into one ambiguous being within that frozen realm.

Vionne doesn't like him to visit the prisoners, preferring to forget about them and bask in the pleasures of her power. She has extended her dominion over the entire Septus, and there has been no bloodshed. Arundel has to admit that Vionne, a stern mistress, is much more a skilled broker of power than he, himself, would be in her position.

Arundel does not seek to increase his control of their agreement, nor to damage his lover's powers. Instead, he takes pleasure in the knowledge that the comrades he had once joined with are now nothing more than a barrel of goods to be bartered, that their forces are controlled by Vionne, for they are imprisoned in the sorceress's place of power.

Sometimes, he muses on his past and why he originally sought to cripple the Seven. Perhaps escape was not, in fact, his original goal. . . .

Sometimes, he regards the tenth painting, the one that bears a tiny, decaying cell with a hole in the corner, and which waits for him if he decides that his lover has grown corrupt and seeks to undo her. Arundel has learned much from Vionne, though, and he laughs as he muses that it would be a hell of a fight to get him in there and keep him thus, and even Vionne would have her hands full doing it. But that possibility seems more unlikely with each passing decade, and Vionne has almost forgotten that the tenth painting exists. She would laugh at her long-dead overcaution if Arundel were to mention it.

There are times—other times—when he gazes upon the ninth painting, there in the downstairs parlor, regards its rigidly painted black-robed forms, and takes pleasure in the knowledge that he, with Vionne's help, has exacted a terrible revenge.

But he cannot take pleasure in their plight, not with the tenth painting remaining behind him, its stink sometimes wafting out when he chooses to consider it.

At those times, he turns and leaves the room, drawing deeply of the sandalwood scent of Vionne's domain.

He will trust her. For now.

Vionne has once again assumed a pleasing form, and the wraithlike servants no longer bring her robes; her sheets, smelling of sandalwood and musk, tangle about Arundel's body but no longer seek to bind him.

A WREATH OF PALE FLOWERS FOR VITRI

TERESA EDGERTON

Teresa Edgerton's most recent book is her eighth fantasy novel The
Moon and the Thorn. Her habit of reading a mix of faery tales and
Victorian horror stories has more than once produced an eerily edgy
story such as the one that follows.

The Princess Vitri was dying. Everyone knew it. Everyone, that is, except for the King, who spent long hours in his
daughter's bedchamber, hovering over her bed, listening to the
sound of her breathing, his face white, his lips drawn into a thin line,
beads of perspiration standing out on his forehead . . . as if he meant,
by a sheer act of will, by the force of his formidable personality, to keep
her alive. And except for Emerald, the youngest handmaiden, who
went right on feeding, brushing, and playing with the Princess's pet
monkey, and tending the flowers in her private garden—particularly
the odd little shrub, the one with the silvery blooms, which one of
Vitri's many suitors had fancifully named "the Rose of Charun" (though
it was not a rosebush or anything like one) after the Princess herself—
just as though she expected the Princess to rise from her couch at any
moment and take her pet down to the garden for some much-needed
exercise.

Though half the court was stricken, the other half bereaved or soon
to become so, no one wore mourning. A baleful omen for the Princess,
a malignant influence—so King Jesahach had proclaimed it, and banished the color black from his presence. And on the day that Vitri's
doctors wrapped her up like a mummy in scarlet flannel and propped
her up in a chair by a roaring fire, in order to sweat the disease out
through her pores, one of them had chanced to mention that red was a
wholesome hue, much used by physicians. So now everyone had to be
dressed in crimson, claret color, vermillion, sanguine, garnet, rose

madder, carnation, coquelicot, port wine . . . any shade at all that could claim a close relationship to the color of healing.

Poor Vitri's torments were dreadful, and not least among them those that were inflicted by the Royal Physicians. For besides that they baked her in flannel, they opened a vein in each of her feet to let out the old, dead blood, dosed her with potions laced with arsenic and grains of gold, covered her with ointments of dung and powdered worms, and every day brought a new treatment, even worse than the day before. But the King suffered, too. He was always beside her when the doctors were treating her, and though he sometimes flinched or cried out at the things that were done to her, not once did Jesahach cover his eyes or turn his head, no matter how cruelly it hurt him to watch.

"You will be well, my darling. Just a few days more, my lamb," he crooned, and it was something to see and hear, that cold hard man, so tender, so concerned. He was a widower with no other children (they said that the Queen had died under the burden of his vast contempt, his crushing indifference) and the Princess Vitri was all and everything that he had ever loved.

Meanwhile, in Alöepaticum, the city that surrounded the palace on three sides, the plague raged on, and ordinary people were dying by the hundreds. The ordinary physicians and healers went from house to house, wearing charms soaked in camphor, tireless in their efforts to save as many as possible, but for all their dedication . . . for all their bleeding, purging, blistering . . . for all their laying on of hands and of stones . . . and the great tuns of barley water and hydromel that were poured down parched throats . . . still, they had only succeeded so far in delaying the inevitable.

The magicians, sages, and astrologers tried their best, too—with no better results. They scratched runes and other magic symbols on the doors of every house the plague had not touched—yet the contagion eventually crept into those places as well. They painted an immense golden pentagram on the stones of the market square. They pored over star charts, consulted papyrus scrolls, tablets of wax and of stone, and there was no counting the number of chickens, pigs, goats, and rabbits that were sacrificed to their divinations, as they searched for the cause of the fever. There had been a similar pest thirty years ago, one that had killed and killed and killed, and then ended by apparently slaying itself, because, even though no cure, no effective treatment had ever been found, it had only lasted for three months during the summer, and no cases had been reported or even suspected since. But there was some question whether this was the same disease or not—and besides, no one wanted to wait three months and see.

It was a bad time for wandering beggars and for foreigners generally; people were terrified and they were looking for scapegoats, somewhere to place the blame. A poor old man was set on and murdered by a crowd, for no other reason than because he was seen making mysterious gestures. *"Sorcery! He is cursing our city,"* howled the mob. It later developed that the man was mute, and he had only been making innocent signs with his hands in an effort to communicate.

Into this atmosphere of wild-eyed credulity and rabid speculation came a majestic stranger, who entered the gilded gates of the capital in a dark chariot drawn by six white horses. His attire was rich, all velvets and satins with strange embroideries. A visiting prince, thought some, but many who watched were unfavorably impressed by his dark complexion, his floating black hair, and a face that was cruel as well as proud. Soon the cry began and was just as quickly taken up: *"The Lord of Discord has come! Charun is surely doomed if the Prince of Eternal Night rides through the streets of Alöepaticum."*

But he was not the Lord of Discord, as they soon discovered, when he drove right up to the porch of the College of Magicians, and two white-bearded sages threw wide the iron doors of the College and welcomed him inside. He was a foreign magician named Clyssus, greatest of necromancers, who had arrived to consult with the city mages.

It had been the custom in Charun, in ages past, not to bury the dead but rather to expose their bodies in high places, that the birds and the elements might strip them clean. The broad, flat roof of the College of Magicians with its parapet and its golden tiles, had been one of those places, where the dead were laid out on platforms, between rows of ominous funeral statues. Though the custom had been long since abandoned and bodies were now decently buried under the earth, the bleached bones remained on the roof of the school for magicians, and so did the statues.

For Clyssus the necromancer, whose work was all of death, this aerial cemetery soon became a favorite retreat. When he was not down in the dark burial vaults under the building, he often took solitary walks among the iron angels and batwinged deities of a vanished religion.

Several days after he arrived in the city, he was strolling there again, this time in company with two ancient sages named Halcyon and Iliaster.

"I had hoped," said Clyssus, "to find Morphea here in Alöepaticum, and among your ranks. Either in spirit or in body. Yet for all the multitude of unseen presences which seem to inhabit this building and the vaults below, he never comes at my calling."

"He died two days before you arrived here," said Iliaster.

The necromancer nodded his understanding. The first twenty-one days after death, a spirit lingered in the Halls of Judgment, and no magician, no matter how mighty, could conjure his shade during that time. Nor could the spirit return on his own to any familiar place, no matter how fierce was his longing to do so.

"We had almost hoped that he would live to greet you. For aside from the Princess Vitri, Morphea lasted much longer than anyone else. Indeed, many here were deeply moved by how long and how valiantly he fought to live." The sage stopped in the long, misshapen shadow of one of the winged statues. "Now that he is gone, we have abandoned all hope for the Princess."

Clyssus frowned. "To live long and fight valiantly, that almost argues a natural immunity. But . . . I understood that no one had survived this pest, this plague, when it first came to Charun thirty years ago."

He was something of an enigma to his companions, this Clyssus. A dark man with an even darker calling—it seemed that his work had dyed him with the colors of mortality. Yet at the same time, he was filled with such energy, such intensity, as though, in the midst of death, he had somehow discovered the secret of increased life.

"No one did survive," said Iliaster. "And the pest never spread so far as Alöepaticum, though it took many lives in the smaller towns and villages just to the north. It is certain that Morphea was never infected, and as for the Princess Vitri, she was not even born until many years later. But you are assuming that it is the same disease, which is by no means certain."

"I am assuming nothing," said Clyssus. "Yet I keep my mind open to all possibilities." His restless movements brought him to the parapet. The great city lay stretched before him: Alöepaticum, city of granite, gold, and marble; city of temples, parks, mansions, and palaces . . . and of course, city of a thousand wretched hovels, where the poor lived in filth and degradation. But the College of Magicians was located close to the King's palace, and from a high place like this one it was possible to observe the green lawns and the gorgeous formal gardens surrounding the palace. They made a far more pleasing prospect than the homes of poverty.

In a garden of orange trees and red roses, a bird sang sweetly, a girl in a scarlet gown played with a white monkey. *So life continues,* thought Clyssus, *even in the midst of death and horror.* Then he gave a bitter laugh at his own expense, for thinking such banalities, and felt a momentary twinge of relief that he had not spoken the platitude out loud.

But the others saw him sneer and they heard him laugh. Not knowing the cause, they wondered what sort of man he was, to look out over the dying city and smile so cruelly.

"Tell us," said Halcyon hesitantly, "what spirits, demons, powers, and images you have already consulted, and which you mean to consult. We continue our own inquiries, and would not wish to duplicate your efforts."

Beside the necromancer, the two old men were pale and looked almost impossibly fragile. Like the bones on the roof, they had been bleached white by the passage of many years, dried out like husks by the hot sun of Charun.

"You cannot duplicate what I do," said Clyssus, with that same dreadful smile. "That is, I no longer seek answers among the lesser imps and jinni. Many of them appear to know *something* but are either unwilling or unable to speak. It is as though someone or something even more powerful prevents them. For that reason, I am determined to summon one of the greater powers, a very Prince of Demons, with whom I have had . . . profitable dealings before."

And he spoke a name that struck at their hearts. It was the same name that Clyssus had heard muttered down in the streets, the one which had heralded his own approach. "In fact, it may even be He who has forbidden the others to speak. His strength grows tremendously during times of pestilence and natural disaster."

Iliaster and Halcyon exchanged an uneasy glance. "We would not presume to teach you your own business," said Iliaster slowly. "But it can be dangerous dealing with the Lords of Chaos. As you know, once summoned they only depart with great reluctance. And while it is true that they cannot lie to the one who has called them, they are masters of deception, if only through misdirec—"

"I know the dangers." Though Clyssus spoke softly, his dark face was eager. "But as you say, they cannot lie. And whether or not I will be misled will depend on what questions I ask."

*   *   *

That very same evening, Vitri died. Only the King noticed when she stopped breathing, and he said nothing, stubbornly refusing to acknowledge the truth. But when one of the Royal Physicians came into the room . . . when he felt for her pulse and found none, put an ear to her chest and discovered that Vitri's heart, which had grown progressively weaker with every passing day, had finally ceased its wearisome toil . . . when he solemnly announced that the Princess was gone . . . then at last King Jesahach covered his face with his hands and wept bitterly. Turned surprisingly meek, he even allowed his servants to lead him out of the room and up to his own bedchamber, so that Vitri's women could prepare the body without interference.

Sometime during the process of laying the Princess out, somewhere between the washing and the dressing, somebody noticed that the youngest handmaiden was missing, along with the Princess's monkey. A search of the palace and its grounds followed, beginning with Vitri's private garden, growing increasingly intense as little Emerald did not turn up.

At last they found the child down in the gardens, wandering in a delirium, and cradling in her arms the rigid body of the beloved monkey. No one had even guessed that the monkey was ill. That one small death sent a cruel shock through the entire court, simply because it was totally unexpected.

As for Emerald, she wept when they pulled the tiny beast out of her arms, and grew so wild and confused in her fevered state, they were forced to tie her down to a bed with silken sashes.

In a burial vault under the College of Magicians, a deep chamber lit only by a single brass lamp fueled by the effluvium of decaying corpses, Clyssus prepared for the summoning.

In two days of intense study, he had reviewed every scroll, every tablet that he could get his hands on, every scrap of parchment or papyrus, which recorded the progress of the plague this year and thirty years past. From that mass of material he had formed a theory, a theory he meant to put to the test this very night.

By corpse-light, his dark face was solemn but no less arrogant than it had been before. He knew this was a serious, a dangerous business, yet Clyssus considered himself more than equal to the task before him.

Was he not widely acknowledged as the greatest of necromancers? A man who had, through years of searching in dark, forgotten places, discovered the secret names of countless demons, jinni, and lesser deities, before whom the spirits of the dead quailed, and whom even the Lords of Chaos treated with a careful, almost punctilious respect?

But perhaps this would be the night when he learned the wages of arrogance, the price of vanity.

With great precision he drew his pentagram on the stone floor, and filled it with many symbols: a star, a triangle, a serpent, a cross, and seven concentric circles. Outside the points of the diagram, he sketched other signs in colored chalk: an eagle, a man, a bull, a lion, a leopard. He donned a robe of white linen—the same coarse linen that was used for winding sheets—and threw a handful of acacia blossoms onto a smoldering brazier in one corner of the vault. Then he took up his gold-tipped wand and began his incantation.

There was a faint rattling disturbance among the bones of the dead, a breathless sigh from the rotting corpses, but Clyssus quieted them with a single harsh word spoken aside. Then he continued on with the spell of summoning.

"O Lord of Eternal Night, I call you. By all your many names I exhort you: He-Who-Drives-His-Horses-With-Whips-of-the-Tongues-of-Adders-And-Scourges-His-Enemies-With-Scorpions. Adzrahel. Beelzabaal . . . " The list was long, and Clyssus felt his throat grow dry reciting it, his tongue cleave to the roof of his mouth.

The demon came like a whirlwind, he came like the voice of thunder, a presence too vast for the vault to contain. He was *in* the sepulchre, but he also penetrated the substance of the walls, was simultaneously above and below, within and without . . . until Clyssus forced him into the pentagram, and he began to dwindle. Then he passed through a dizzying swift series of transformations—a wraith, a monster with gaping mouth and ivory claws, a victim of the plague, hollow-eyed and withered, too many and too various for the mind of the man to compass them all—until he finally took on a form that the necromancer knew well. A tall man with floating dark hair and burning eyes. The image of Clyssus himself.

"What do you require of me, Man of a Thousand Whispering Ambitions? What do you wish to learn of me, O Prince of Vanities?" The demon mocked him with his own smile.

For one brief moment, Clyssus hesitated. Those formless doubts which had threatened earlier now began to clamor in his brain. And yet, to summon the demon and attempt to send him away without first assigning him some task, asking some question, was a thing impossible.

With more confidence than he felt, with his heart leaping in his chest, the necromancer spoke his first question. "Why did Morphea bring the plague to Charun—and for what reason?"

The demon began to roar, and the animate hairs of his head flowed like a storm cloud around him. "O Clyssus, Clyssus," howled the Lord of Eternal Night, shaking with unseemly laughter. "That you of all men should ask me that question!"

Where black had been banished before, it now reigned supreme: black gowns, black veils, black beads, black gloves. And for Vitri's funeral, three days after her death, some of the women even painted their lips, eyebrows, and nails the same dusky hue as their gowns. But the Princess herself was dressed in white, according to tradition, and they heaped her bier with the pale silvery flowers that she loved best.

As for poor little Emerald, she had been left to die slowly in a remote region of the palace—where she was moved to keep the contagion from spreading—with only a single servant to attend her. The monkey was buried in Vitri's garden, and was slumbering far more peacefully under the earth, down among the roots of the Rose of Charun.

After they buried Vitri, after they burned their incense, made their sacrifices, and observed all the other ceremonies, King Jesahach and his court returned to the palace, where a great feast awaited them: the traditional funeral meats soaked in spices . . . cakes sweetened with honey, sweetmeats made bitter with vinegar and gall . . . and a dark purple wine laced with wormwood, that was know throughout Charun as Balm-Of-A-Broken-Heart . . . all laid out on long tables between the gilded pillars of the central hall.

The feasting began but was shortly interrupted by an unexpected procession of magicians from the College, who entered the hall in robes of purple and scarlet, and masks of beaten gold. One of the mages unmasked, revealing a tawny face and burning dark eyes.

"By your leave," said the necromancer, bowing low before the King. "I have discovered the source and the cause of the plague."

Jesahach said nothing, gave no reaction, sat absolutely motionless there in his chair. Perhaps his senses were already dulled by the drugged wine, perhaps he was only weary and grief-stricken after his long vigil, his daughter's funeral. But everyone else, the entire sable multitude gathered in that pillared hall, clamored to hear more.

"It is a long story, not simply told," said Clyssus. "Yet I will try to do it justice.

"*Many years ago . . .* " (began the magician) "*. . . there was a populous, prosperous kingdom. Indeed, in some ways the land was much too fortunate, much too prosperous. The cities were becoming overcrowded, and the common folk were breeding at such a tremendous rate that when a bad year came and the crops failed, there was widespread starvation. Now, the King of that country was a clever man, but he was not wise. Faced by this terrible problem, he did not open his vast granaries to feed the poor, for that, he considered, was only a temporary, wasteful solution. His stores would only last them a single season, and if the next year was bad and the year after that . . . well, he could easily see how a hundred thousand hungry people might eventually be tempted into mass insurrection. He thought it would be far more expedient to reduce the population quickly rather than slowly—and far more merciful, too. His ideas of mercy and expedience, you will observe, were rather unusual, but they were based on a certain twisted logic.*

"*So this King went to a magician that he knew, who was just as ruthless as the King was himself. But where the King was clever, willful, and impatient, this man was curious, subtle, and brilliant. He was one who had long since gained mastery over the Five Kingdoms of Matter: the material, mineral, vegetable, animal, and the fluid worlds. But in his manipulation of the animal and the vegetable kingdoms he had always excelled. He had already made a number of experiments in crossing species, by uniting the sperm of one with the seed of another: a lion and an eagle to create a griffon, a man and a mandrake to make a homunculus. And he dallied with spontaneous generation, as in the growth of worms out of dung, and grasshoppers and stinging insects out of the dust of the earth. But in his experiments with plants he had once come close to something that was so supremely frightening, even to him, that he completely abandoned that line of inquiry. Yet he was an arrogant man, particularly proud of those things he had created, and it did not take much urging on the part of the King to make him reconsider. So the mage began his experiments once more, and this time he met with a terrible success.*

"*The year was dying, moving on toward winter, when the magician prepared to take a journey out of the city where he lived. Dressed as a peddler, he visited a number of small towns and villages where the poor and the starving were especially numerous. In each place that he stopped, the mage left something behind: a large brown seed with a prickly exterior, which he planted in secret near the village well or fountain.*

"During the winter, the seed germinated and sent down roots, which quickly tapped into the waters below. When spring arrived, the people were surprised to discover a remarkable shoot growing in the center of their village. A shoot which became a sapling, a sapling which rapidly turned to a budding tree shading their well. And as the buds started to open, as they all but exploded into iron-colored flowers, the sap began to run, infusing the Basilisk Tree (for that was the name that the magician had bestowed on it) and the waters that nourished the tree with a deadly poison, a subtle, malignant substance which produced in its victims a sickness closely resembling the symptoms of plague."

The hall was very quiet while Clyssus spoke, everyone straining to hear what he said. Except for the King, who sat with his head down, while the color came and went in his face as the blood beat under his skin, and his eyes were unnaturally bright. Every now and again, he moved his lips, as though he knew the story and was reciting it silently, along with the necromancer.

"This scheme was wildly successful . . . " (Clyssus continued) ". . . In fact, so many died during the summer that followed, that the two conspirators became a little frightened. They decided to eradicate the menace as quickly as possible, before the trees could bear fruit and scatter their seeds. A King without subjects, they reasoned, is no King at all. And besides . . . once the wind took the seeds there was no way of predicting who might die.

"So they sent men out secretly to every town where the Basilisk Trees were growing, to uproot the trees and to burn them at once. But one of these men met with an accident along the way, was injured, and was forced to stop in another village for several weeks. Because the King and the magician had not confided in any of these agents, this man did not understand that his errand was urgent as well as secret—so it never occurred to him that he ought to send somebody else on in his place.

"When he was finally able to travel, and when he arrived at his destination, he almost began to suspect the truth, because the village was empty— empty except for deserted houses, recent graves, and rotting corpses. But he pushed the idea back into some hidden corner of his mind, rather than confront the enormity of the King's wickedness. Instead, he allowed himself to feel some relief that no one was there to report his tardiness. And of course, he pulled up the tree and burned it: roots, branches, leaves, and all, until nothing was left but silvery ashes.

"But something terrible had happened while he lay injured in that other village. The tree had produced a single fruit, and that fruit had burst open, flinging its seeds far and wide. It was fortunate, then, that the following year was a dry one, for most of the seeds fell on barren ground, where they baked in the heat of the sun until they were no longer viable. But a single seed was carried far by the wind and it fell to earth, as fate would have it, in a shaded, untended portion of a small private orchard and garden, in the palace of the King.

"Many years passed, and the seed, lying there in the dry shade, neither died nor germinated. Then a gardener came and turned over the earth so that the seed went under . . . where it found just enough moisture to live and to grow. It was never a tree, it grew into a tiny shrub instead, nor did it blossom for many more years. Yet it was able to send its roots down and out, in a vast complex network, which eventually penetrated an underground spring which fed many of the wells and the fountains in the city where the King and his daughter lived.

"Then the shrub did bloom, it was literally covered with blossoms, though not the same startling, iron-colored flowers it had managed to produce in its hardier days. These blossoms were delicate and silvery pale . . . so beautiful, indeed, that the Princess when she first saw them was utterly enchanted. She made garlands of the flowers and wore them, carried sprays of the blossoms into the palace and kept them in vases.

"And when the shrub poisoned the waters of the city, when dozens fell sick and began to die, the love that the Princess bore those silvery blossoms very nearly saved her life—as it may have saved her youngest handmaiden, as it almost saved her pet monkey. From handling those flowers with their milder poison, the two young girls and the monkey had each gained some slight immunity to the more powerful toxin that permeated the water. But the well-meaning efforts of the Royal Physicians, as they dosed her with herbs that were steeped in the deadly water, as they sweated her and bathed her, replacing her natural fluids with that deadly other, were eventually too much for the Princess. Like the magician Morphea (who had gained a similar immunity, due to his original manipulation of the seed and the sperm that produced the trees) she had lingered on, only to suffer that much longer before death finally claimed her."

When the necromancer stopped speaking, Jesahach sat silent for a long time, his cheeks still dyed with the shame of his guilt. And when he finally spoke, his voice shook—though with anger or grief no one could tell.

"It makes an interesting fable, this story of yours. But tell me: How does it end? Did the King repent? Did he not have the Rose of—Did he not have the Basilisk Tree uprooted and burned, as soon as he knew it was growing there in his daughter's garden?"

"If he tried," said Clyssus sternly, "he accomplished nothing by it. The roots had gone so deep and spread so widely, it would have been impossible to dig every one of them up, not if he razed the palace and the entire city surrounding it. And while the roots remained, the danger was not past, for the life of the tree continued, and any single root burrowing up to the surface might send out a shoot at any time, in a place where no one might find it."

Jesahach sighed deeply. "Then this King that you speak of . . . surely he commanded his magicians to water the tree with the venom of adders, that it might eventually wither and die, right down to the roots."

"If he did," said Clyssus, dark and implacable, "that was the worst of all. The essence of the Basilisk Tree is poison, and venom could only nourish it. The tree would have thrived and the two poisons married, to make something even more deadly, ten times more malignant."

Jesahach covered his eyes, and a tremor passed over him. "Was there nothing the King could do, then . . . but watch his subjects die?" he whispered hoarsely.

"There was something," said Clyssus, "but it was a terrible deed, something that only a King who loved his people more than he loved himself could have possibly found the courage to do." And he stepped forward, with a rustle of silken robes, and whispered something in Jesahach's ear. As he spoke, those who were watching saw the King's face grow progressively harder, paler, colder.

Then everyone knew that the magician had failed in his eloquence. There would be no repentance, there would be no cure. Even if a party of them rushed from the hall and uprooted the tree, the pest would continue unchecked until the end of the summer. And even after it had run its course, there would remain the terrible knowledge that some-day . . . the next year, or the year after that, or the year after that, a new shoot would push its way to the surface and the horror would all be repeated. Those who could afford to leave Charun in the meantime would do so, and those who could not would remain and eventually die. And at last, Charun and the great city of Alöepaticum would be reduced to nothing more than a vast graveyard filled with decaying corpses.

But in the morning, the King was missing from his bedchamber. And those who went looking to find him eventually discovered his body, hanging by the neck from the branch of an orange tree in Vitri's garden. There was a wax tablet lying in the grass below his dangling feet, a letter addressed to Clyssus. The message was brief: *You will know what to do.*

And indeed, the necromancer did know. With the other magicians, he carried Jesahach's body off to the college, and there they worked many wonders. First, they drained off his blood and stored it in bottles made of stone. Of Jesahach's hair they wove strong ropes, and his bones they carved into curious shapes, which combined, made charms to hang on the doors of all the houses where the plague had entered. His skin they tanned and made into parchment, on which the doctors of the city wrote spells of healing. His internal organs, along with what remained of his flesh after they had finished rendering it, were burned to ashes, and the fat and the ashes they made into ointments to soothe the afflicted. As for those bottles of blood, Clyssus and Halcyon took them to the palace, after these other things had all been accomplished, and poured them out at the base of the Basilisk Tree. When the magicians were finished, there was not one bit of flesh, not one piece of bone, nail, or hair, not one drop of blood belonging to the King which had not been given for the good of his people.

And the small stunted tree with the silvery blossoms withered and died, right down to the very tips of its myriad roots . . . the waters of Alöepaticum turned sweet and wholesome once more . . . and those like Emerald, who lay at the brink of death, suddenly sighed and relxed in the midst of their torment, and sank into a deep, healing sleep.

HUNTERS
SUSAN SHWARTZ

Susan Shwartz has edited seven anthologies and is the author of The
Grail of Hearts; *she coauthored with Andre Norton* Empire of the
Eagle. *Five times nominated for the Nebula and twice for the Hugo for
short fiction, she is currently working on a long novel about the First
Crusade.*

By the time Artemis was brought from sanctuary to
Olympos, she had formed no great opinion of any males.
Except, of course, for her brother. Even as a godling, the nectar
scarce dry on his lips, he shone like the sun and awaited only sufficient
growth to drive the Sun's fiery horses and gleaming chariot.

Even then, she knew, her brother was no fit spouse for her. He was
too bright; and she preferred the leaves and shadows of the forests and
the slopes. And then, on Olympos, Artemis gained further proof: the
example of her father Zeus and his sister-wife. As infants, she and her
brother had had to be hidden from Hera, who had unpleasant ways of
dealing with her husband's loves and, for all that she was the patroness
of childbirth, might have had equally unpleasant ways of dealing with
the inevitable offspring. Zeus's thunderbolts rarely flew to no avail.

If Hera did not punish, Hera chided, whined, plotted, and railed at
Zeus's infidelity, while he stayed as far away from the peaks and temples of high Olympos as he could. It left his wayside families perilously
exposed and had made Artemis rather prematurely wary.

The rest of Artemis's divine kin offered no better models: Hephaestos
wasted sweat and substance crafting trinkets for his unlikely wife
Aphrodite, whose white arms outshone the bracelets that she wore and
who turned her face away when her scorched, sweat-stained husband
limped into the feasts in the high-columned hall. Dionysos impressed
Artemis as a storm about to strike, music and madness combined. And
the smell of the grape that lingered about him was enough to turn even

a virgin goddess sick at dawn. Ares strutted about and blustered. Furthermore, as Artemis grew from child to maiden, he showed a dismaying tendency to try to edge her flat against a wall and fondle her slender curves. (She was not, she told him, spoils of war; and when he showed signs of disputing the issue, she had brought her knee up firmly, provoking Ares to whine complaints and Zeus to a mirth that had earned her the finest bow she had ever owned.)

Early on, she decided that Athena's way might well be hers. But Athena had little to do with other goddesses, and liked it that way. So Artemis studied her from a safe (she distrusted her half sister's thunderbolts) distance. She, too, would be cool and chaste, and honored for it. But with a difference. Where Athena cherished cities and scrolls, her path would lie in the forests and among living creatures.

As above, so below: as her brother mounted his chariot and raced across the sky, she descended from Olympos and coursed across the land. Up hill and down, through forests and fields, she hunted the wild deer with a trail of maidens of like mind. Her face was turned as often to the woods as to the sun.

The land supplied their needs. From the woods, they had their quarry. From the terraces came grapes and, in the season of vintage, wine on great occasions. They had ice-fed springs to drink and silent, hidden pools to bathe in. And they knew where the truffles were, or where they might find enough roots and leaves to heal what small harms they encountered, with some left over for their friends. They could trade game and pelts for cheese and olives from the farmers roundabout.

Artemis chose her companions from the finest maidens of the land, strong, resourceful, fit, and quick to laugh. They ran with her for a season or two or three. As girls, they joined the hunt: as women, they laid their girlhood trinkets and bows upon her altar (by now, Artemis had amassed quite a collection), and relinquished the chase to younger maids.

From time to time, Hera would tell Artemis how brave such a girl—some rustic Priscilla, Ione, or Dryope whom Artemis and those huntresses who remained virgin had seen off with tears and a wedding gift—had been and what a fine son she had (aided, of course, by Hera) brought into the world. Artemis was hardly surprised. Her hunts taught women bravery. But the sons these women bore did not interest her. Their daughters, though: let one of her former companions nurse a girl-child, and Artemis would visit and bring gifts. And, also at that time, she would mark the strongest and fairest as her future playfellows.

She could trust their mothers to prepare them and make them strong. Former huntresses made good mothers. In times of dearth, they were good providers: from their days in the wild, they knew where mushrooms and wild berries were found, or how to stalk, and kill, and dress game—and how to prepare it as well as if they had been raised at Hestia's hearth.

And because she was Artemis and immortal, the people of farm and village, who would have otherwise frowned at such wild ways, smiled when she and her maids ran by their fields, a flash of white tunics and long, slender legs. "She ran with the Lady's Hunt" became a term of praise in later years.

There were, of course, exceptions. Callisto, forced, hid her growing belly. Only when Artemis and those huntresses who were still maids stripped her was the truth known. Cast out from the hunt, she birthed a son: mother and son came to no good end—transformed to bears, they drew Cybele's chariot.

Artemis had wept, but she knew her course. Hand, foot, eye, aim, and resolve never faltered. Never forgave. Except, of course, where her brother was concerned.

And so it went for years. Artemis and her maids would hunt, tell stories and secrets in the deepest recesses of the woods, then emerge to watch her brother's flashing course across the sky. And if he smiled at one of them and kissed her face more than the others, why, that was her brother.

That she, too, might blush and smile and cast her eyes down in the presence of a man (or god) was not a thought she had. True enough, there were stories. There always are stories when the girl is lovely enough and beloved: and Artemis was both. It was only natural, she knew, that the people whose daughters hunted with her, then left to bring up a new generation, would wish for her to dwell among them and to watch her own children grow.

But it was not true that she had cast the youth Endymion into eternal sleep. What use would she have for a companion who could not get up and run? As for Tithonos, the oldest man she had ever seen, it was true she loved his music, even when his voice grew so high that it sounded like the meditations of a bat. He had loved grasshoppers, had worn, like the old Athenians, grasshoppers of gold as ornaments. And when he was so old that on his good days the most he could do was sit in the sun and sing, she would come, winded and flushed after her day's hunt, and fling herself down at his feet to listen.

Perhaps that story rose from her presence at his funeral. For once, her hair—except for the lock she had shorn in mourning—had been neatly combed and she had been robed as the goddess that she was. As the funeral pyre roared up, kindled by the sun's rays (her brother's tribute), she had sung in public for the first time, accompanied by pipers from the woods, subdued into decorum. People wept at her song and swore she was a fine musician. Perhaps that was true; but her brother was a finer one by far.

She was running one day, far ahead of the others, keeping pace with her brother's chariot, on easy, sunny ground. She ran, as she always did, without glancing aside. No other maid, human or divine, could say that. Even Atalanta, the only mortal woman half as fleet of foot as she, had glanced away, distracted by golden apples; and look at all the trouble her lack of attention had brought her—no daughters, but a son who died at Thebes.

A pack of hounds belled and dashed across her path. A youth darted after them. Man and hounds reached the quarry, a fine stag, before her maids could even nock their arrows. Artemis laughed and waved a salute. Matters might have been different had snow lain on the ground, or had they barely emerged from it into the earliest, most meager spring right before the wild greens rise and food becomes once again abundant.

But now, the year was shaping toward summer. She and her maids could well pull down another deer before sundown; and it was not as if the villagers would go hungry. She could afford to be as generous as she had always said a huntress must.

And the youth—if she must lose a quarry, it was almost a pleasure to cede the stag to him. He was tanned and tall. Save that he was mortal, he was as handsome as her brother. And though the sun had yet to strike the earth with its full force, he glowed with light and life. And that, too, was like her brother.

She smiled. He held out his hand: *join me.* Man, goddess, maids, and hounds all feasted that night and rose at dawn to hunt all the next day.

As spring ripened toward summer and the trees in the valley grew broad and green of leaf, the youth ran with Artemis's hunt. The mothers and grandmothers of the maids who ran with her came out to watch the splendid youth and the beautiful goddess, still young after all those generations. Even now, she outstripped the fleetest of their daughters. She never looked aside. Nor did she need to. For he ran with her, and she was happy to have it thus.

In the evenings or on mornings when the rain dripped from the leaves, they discovered they had interests in common: good hounds, fine weather, the proper way to kill and dress the deer they slew. The maids gave them time to speak alone. They tracked the deer. They rescued children who had climbed too high in the hills, or fallen into streams. And, when night fell, they slept on opposite sides of the fire, each with a hound or so to keep them warm. She was still Artemis, still maid and huntress; so, if the satyrs smirked at jokes more suited to a wedding than a hunt, they stayed discreetly out of earshot—or the range of a hunting bow.

In a burst of confidence, the youth had told her his true name. She locked it in her immortal heart with unexpected hopes. He was new, he said, to this part of Hellas. But since the hunting was so good and the people so kind, why, he could ask for nothing better than to stay here—at least for the summer.

And it was a golden one. If the farmwives smiled and the satyrs jested, Artemis did not notice. Or perhaps it was that she did not care—or think their jests so far amiss as they had been. Her brother kept his own counsel. The sun, as always, was in her eyes—if from a different source.

More and more fiercely Apollo's chariot shone. The summer turned breathlessly hot. Even the broad-leafed trees seemed to sigh after breath. The earth panted: Apollo drove perilously near the world as if to watch what was going on. Dogs, maids, man, and goddess hurled themselves down in their breathless shade after a morning run that the heat had cut short. The sun had kissed them all. Their eyes gleamed, and their lips had darkened till they were the color of berries before they are plucked at harvest.

After a time, the hounds took themselves off, and the maids dozed. The stranger still breathed too fast, and Artemis wondered if he suffered from some fever. She knew where grew a willow tree; and willow bark, she knew, could bring relief.

"Are you still hot?" Artemis asked her friend, who grinned response. "I know where we can cool off."

He was bronzed from the sun, and his eyes gleamed like a statue, its eyes inlaid with sapphires.

"You do?"

"These are my woods," Artemis was goaded to say. "Of course, I know the feel of every pebble and root beneath my feet. Follow me."

Easily, she rose to her sandaled feet and glanced back over her shoulder. "Unless you would rather go on burning."

He followed her. Effortlessly picking up the trail that few others could even see, she led him to the sanctuary that she had made over the generations in the woods. Over the breathless rustle of the leaves came the rush of water. She slipped into a circle of trees whose heavy branches dipped almost to the ground, and held a branch aside so he could see.

Bordered by stones flecked with what looked like gold lay a pool, rippling with leafshadow and the constant splash of water from a slender high cascade that plummeted down from a mossy cliff. Artemis could feel her skin tighten with longing for the comfort of the water.

"Let me bathe first," she said, laughing with relief. She let the branch slip back, screening her. Quickly, she stripped off her damp tunic (she would wash it later if one of the girls did not take it from her to do the task herself), hung it from the tree limb, and slipped, sighing with pleasure, into the coolness of water and leafshadow. She swam beneath its surface and emerged under the tiny falls for the pleasure of feeling the water flow down her hair and back.

But she had a guest in this place, the quietest and most secret of her forest haunts; and he must be made comfortable. Her father, after all, rewarded hospitality. So it was no sacrifice, but a privilege to emerge refreshed from the pool. She would dress quickly and leave him to his bath, too. And then they could rejoin the others until sundown, when it would be cool enough to cook and eat.

As she reached for her tunic, the leaves rustled. No wind blew. She had not touched them. It was the youth. He was watching her, and she was naked.

"Actaeon," she whispered his name. She held up a slender hand. He knew the strength in it; but he walked toward her anyhow.

She felt herself change, felt her skin flush and her body heat, deep within. She quivered as a lyre does when the deepest notes are struck upon it.

His eyes were wild, the pupils dilated as if he had chewed on the herbs it was unwise to pluck. His mouth opened, and he gasped something that might have been a prayer.

The forest ceased to move. Even the grasshoppers fell silent, forbearing to creak or leap from the tall grass. The creatures knew her from all those years. They knew when to fall silent and motionless. Actaeon, having more courage and less caution, did not.

He approached her, his eyes heating her flesh as they touched it.

"Get back. You've spoiled everything!" Her voice went up high; she was ashamed of herself.

In a moment, he would be close enough . . . close enough to touch her. Like Callisto, when they had come here, pulled her clothes off, and known in that moment that she bore a child. If he touched her, she would have to go away. She would no longer be able to keep pace, as above, so below her brother's chariot. She would fall victim to Hera's interminable lectures and Aphrodite's simpers.

She might even bear a child. Were it a son, it would need its father. And were it a daughter, it would have no huntress with whom to run. And she would not want to leave its father, who was, after all, mortal.

That was the path, she knew, that led to the grave. Oh, she didn't want to set foot on that—no matter if the grandams smiled and vowed that they would never run after the stags again, even if they had the strength and the good fortune to be asked.

They no longer wanted what they had. Let him touch her, and she might not, either.

Her bow lay at her feet, but if she bent, she knew she was lost. So she stood there, naked as a birch in winter, holding out her hands, too foolish—and too angry—even to deign to veil herself with hands or hair.

She wanted him to go away—didn't she?

What would he do? She was, still, a goddess. She could stop him. Once she regained her calm, she need have no worry about force: that was, after all, a way gods had with mortals. Look at her father or, for that matter, her brother. He wore a laurel wreath, though, relic of a maid who had spurned him, even to changing her shape. She might have eluded him, but it was Apollo who had the last word.

But this youth: what would he say? If she let him touch her, he might not be silent. And even if she refused, he might lie. And there her name would be, sullied, in the mouths of men and satyrs. Oh, Aphrodite *would* smile and run her bright, long-lashed eyes down her body, seeking for the belly swell. And Athena would sneer.

She could not bear to lose what she had gained. She could not bear that she be spoken of, looked at in that crude way. She must prevent it.

How he looked at her! As if he had long ago gained her consent—or as if it did not matter. As if she . . .

Something dark flickered in her eyes. A cold wind blew. She felt her nipples harden; and that, too, was a feeling she had known before, if never in this way. Her mouth was dry. Tears gushed from her eyes, then dried, too. She could not afford pity. Or longing.

He saw it in her eyes that she had changed. "Koré," he appealed to her. Maiden. He knew the deftness of those hands, her skill with a bow. As well hold up her hands to the Eumenides or those women who stalk the hills, brandishing cone-tipped wands and wearing blood-dappled fawn skins.

She was not maiden but immortal, ambrosial. And this . . . this rustic who toiled and sweated—so unlike her brother!—presumed to approach her as if she were some fool girl who had left the hunt and sacrificed her girlhood's toys upon an altar.

"Koré," he breathed again.

"That is my *cousin!*" she hissed. "She who lives below. Do not dare speak to me. Do not speak ever again!"

As the wind quickened and chilled, the sky darkened. She felt yet another change come over her more strongly than it did when she ran by night, caressed only by her hair and the light of the distant moon.

She stooped quickly and dashed cold water into his face.

He dropped to all fours. His legs lengthened, and he cried out one last time as his jaw jutted forth into a muzzle. His tunic split as his form altered, but he was not bare: short fur sprang out all over his body, even to where his legs joined and she dared not look.

Last of all, fine-branched antlers thrust out from his brow. A horn called across the sky. Bronze it was now, and amber. Soon the day would be over, and summer with it.

The change was complete. Only the eyes were the same—brown and liquid; yet even they, rolling up to high Olympos in desperate appeal, wore the aspect of a deer: stark terror as it senses that the hunt is up and hounds course at its tail.

But there was no recourse: gods cannot undo what other gods have done.

With a flash of whiteness, the stag that had been a man turned and fled, bounding on its slender legs on the path down which, only moments ago, a handsome youth had so confidently tracked his longed-for quarry.

Artemis thrust on her tunic. The way it clung to her flesh was an affront, and she wished she had a cloak to fling about herself.

Ahead, the hounds belled. She smiled to herself, picturing the moment when Actaeon realized that the dogs that had lolled at his feet, been fed at his hands, and slept with their sharp-eared heads resting on his breast or knee were now his hunters. Their barks and howls were a threnody for the youth who dared spy upon a goddess and approach her with lust in his eyes.

Artemis followed. She had never run so fast in her life; but for the first time, the stag outran her.

It did not, however, outrun the hounds. Or Artemis's own huntresses, wakened now, and greeting prey and familiar hounds with cries of joy and swift, deadly arrows. Three hit him in the shoulder. He tried to flee. The hounds cut off his flight.

As the hunters chased the stag, caught it, and pulled him down, she watched, one hand to her lips lest she vomit, her eyes hot with anger and unshed tears. Stag that Actaeon now was, he could not even scream. She felt the hounds' fangs as she had felt the arrows—rending her soul, if not her flesh.

Finally, the hounds reached his throat and tore it out. The crowned head dropped over the ragged wound, and the long legs kicked, then stilled.

Blood gushed upon the earth and sank into it. The hounds licked at it and at the corpse, ran in circles, barking and waiting for their master to come and feed them. When he did not, they fed from the steaming corpse, and yelped off into the night. Seeking their master.

The man gone, her maids would be safe—as safe now as she. No other would dare accost them. They had food and could make fire. Artemis slipped back into the forest. About her, leaves rustled and fell.

Tears glazed on her cheeks from which all the summer ruddiness had fled. They spilled to the ground, chilling what they touched, colder than asphodels. Through gaps in the branches, Artemis gazed up at the sky, at her brother, guiding his chariot down into the West, into Okeanos and home. He had no help for her and, though he ruled the sun, no warmth. She thought she would never be warm again.

As her tears dropped onto the grass, it froze about her feet.

Her breath hissed in the air. "I trusted you."

The wind whipped about her. The reek of blood and smoke tainted the air, along with hint of snow, whipped down from the mountain peaks.

That year, winter came early. Many people died, for Artemis had no heart to hunt for them or for herself that year.

SEVEN GUESSES OF THE HEART

M. JOHN HARRISON

M. John Harrison, one of the premier writers in the fantasy genre, is perhaps best known for his novels and stories set in Virconium, a city of many meanings.

Falkender the magician lived on an island called Ys, a little way off the coast of mainland Autotelia.

Ys, nine miles long and perhaps four across, lay like a great ship across the Autotelian approaches, to which it presented tall granite cliffs, lashed by wind and rain all winter, tawny with sunlight in the summer dawns. Sea pinks, saxifrage, and rock rose grew on the cliffs in profusion. The sandy clifftop soil was thick with yellow gorse, the spicy smell of which carried far out to sea, causing sailors suddenly to lift their heads and look for land. Coves and re-entrants dissected the granite, their steep banks on fire with monbretia and sol d'or. Inland, the long shallow bracken-filled valleys turned into dense thickets of elder, briar, and holly. Ivy clasped the trees. Push your way through, and you came out suddenly into the fields and orchards and villages of Ys.

Ivy Thorne, Wroe, Natrass Giles, names for places in a dream! Fields tiny and eccentrically shaped. Old man's beard matting the hedges. Sturdy little whitewashed houses tucked away in hollows at the junction of a lane and a stream, or planted on the brow of a hill against a stormy blue sky. Gardens full of clematis and foxgloves. A magic agriculture, which burst the churns and made the granaries creak like ships in a storm. Early potatoes, much in demand in Autotelia. Flowers less forced than persuaded under glass. Whole shoals of fish spilling like polished coins from curious tubby single-masters on to the pink stone quays on the oceanward side of the island. All this produce, Ys sold to the mainland. And though Ysians thought themselves shrewder, happier and more fertile than mainlanders, they kept an eye on Autotelia and Autotelian policy, because that was where their living lay.

Falkender lived in a village called Onvoy, in the parish of Ender Voe. His house was a great foursquare thick-walled thing of honey-colored granite; like a manse, its rooms were tall its wooden floors polished to a buttery sheen, its windows deeply recessed. But you could tell immediately it had seen better days. Look in through a ground floor window and you saw how dust had dulled the broad-striped orange and ocher rugs. How a chipped enamel teapot, pale blue, stood empty on the kitchen table. Only one live-in servant, a woman called Totty, remained. Salt sea winds had stripped the outside paintwork. The garden was out of hand: indeed there were places in it now where even Falkender didn't like to go.

Despite this—the evidence or symbol, perhaps, of a discontent he had buried as deeply as he was able—Falkender would not have lived anywhere else. Neither the magician nor his wife had been much to Autotelia, although both had relatives there. In forty years together, they had made first a romantic, then a successful, then an acceptable life on Ys: they intended to live it out.

Then their daughter Rosamund died at the end of one winter, and everything changed.

One night some weeks after Rosamund's death, Falkender had an extraordinary dream. In it, he was trying to make his way across some waste ground in a headland above a shingle beach. The air was salty, and full of a dusty, aromatic smell. The dry vegetation underfoot— heather, bilberry, myrtle—was so dense he could not walk on the ground itself, but was suspended on a kind of springy intractable mat which caught at his feet and ankles. Often he had to force his way through much taller growth, while trying to maintain his balance on a surface he couldn't really see. Panic urged him on, but the reason for it escaped him. He wasn't, for instance, being pursued. He had no idea where he was, or why. He wasn't sure if it was night or day. When he was able to look up for a moment, all he could make out ahead of him was a horizon, and a yellowish, tarry sky. The whole scene was charged with fear: but that sky had more dread in it than he had ever felt in his life before.

"A sky charged with fear!" he told himself the next morning. He laughed. "What can you possibly mean when you say that?"

He managed to hide the dream from his wife, although it woke him three or four times that week alone. She found out in the end when, trudging along under the charged and mysterious sky, Falkender missed his footing and went down. The world turned instantly to brackish water beneath him. He was drowning before he could catch himself. He woke up thinking he had heard someone scream.

"Did I scream?" he asked his wife.

She was up on one elbow, staring down at him.

"It was more like a croak," she said.

"I'm all right now."

"Go back to sleep then."

"I feel a fool," he said. "I must have woken the whole house. The world turned to water under me."

"Go to sleep now."

He shivered.

"Right to water under me," he said.

Something else occurred to him.

"Didn't I wake you?" he asked her anxiously. "Were you already awake?"

"You go to sleep now," said his wife.

He turned over.

"I will," he promised, though he didn't think he would. "I'll be all right now."

He hated to disturb his wife. They had lived together for twenty three years before he discovered she found it hard to sleep. "Once I've woken up," she had admitted, "there's no going back on it." Then laughing at his expressions: "Really, don't look so horrified. As a child I never slept. The world was too exciting, especially in the summer. I hardly closed my eyes at all until I was ten."

"But I *slept* all those years," Falkender had said: "While you lay awake."

"And you'll sleep again, if I know you."

This time though he couldn't sleep. He lay looking at the ceiling for some time, trying to remember what had been happening in the dream to make him wake up screaming. Then he said emptily:

"It was my fault Rosamund died."

He felt tears springing into his eyes.

"Hush now," his wife said. "Hush now, Falkender."

"I kept her from what she wanted."

*   *   *

What Rosamund had wanted was to do magic, and he had kept her successfully from that for perhaps fifteen years. Magic had done him no good: no good at all. "Look around you," he had told her when she was twelve years old, and full of the despair of it, full if its mad invitations, and desperately angry with him. "Do you see how well we live? Do you see what comfort we live in? Magic got us all this," he said bitterly. "It's a great trade for making money."

"There's nothing wrong with the way we live!" his daughter shouted. "I love this house!" She pushed past him and ran out into the garden. "You're just bitter because it stopped working for you."

She turned back and added: "You're just a bitter old man!"

He wasn't used to being shouted at. It made him blink. He had kept her from magic anyway, or so he thought, until inevitably he found her kneeling in the garden one summer night, her arms spread wide and some kind of white, shining frothy substance pouring down towards her out of the warm moonlit sky. She was catching it and rubbing it over her breasts. She was nineteen years old. Her face was upturned and illuminated, her eyes wide and empty. What shocked him was not her ecstacy. Nor was it his immediate sense that the rite was more difficult, more risky, more productive than anything he had ever tried. It was her nakedness. And not even so much that, as his own intense sexual reaction to it.

"It's not as if she was right, anyway," he told his wife after the funeral.

Soft rain dripped through the great yew trees and on to the pleasant shadowy pathways beneath, where in the worn wet stone there sometimes floated an image of the sky. The departing mourners talked in low voices. Falkender watched them thoughtfully. Throughout the ceremony, he had stared off between the more distant gravestones in the rainy light, his eyes hurt, hungry, expectant. As if, his wife thought suddenly, he might see Rosamund among them and not be surprised. Who knows what magicians see? Despite his age, his eyes had the intensity of a young man's. They were a startling green, a very bright green. She touched his upper arm gently.

"Hush now," she said.

"It never stopped working for me."

He cupped his hands and gazed into them intently.

"Look!" he ordered his wife.

Between his hands he had inflated a small bubble with a strange viscous surface the gelid blue color of water from some icy stream. It swelled quickly to the size of an apple. It quivered for a moment as if something was imprisoned there, or as if it was struggling to become something else. Then it grew still. A very faint impression of his daughter's face was caught in it. "Look!" he urged his wife, as the image began to fade: "She may even speak to us!" But his wife wasn't quick enough. When the ball had vanished again she advised him:

"Don't tire yourself like this."

"See!" said Falkender. "She was wrong about that. It never stopped working for me."

He saw that his wife was crying.

"I think I just lost faith," he said.

Every year of his life as a successful magician, and even in the years afterwards, the month of May had been like a door thrown down between Falkender and the truth of things. During the endless winter months he had laid the charge and lighted the fuse. In May he had seen the great green flare and soundless flash of the detonation, through which it was possible to glimpse for an instant the world that lies behind the world we know. (A world, he believed, which in some sense makes—or authorizes—our own.) In May, his magic had engaged the magic of the universe itself. In May, even now, every garden in Ys had some invention of Falkender's growing in it. A lawn like a mysterious green pool at twilight. Mists of bluebells beneath the trees. Roses with names as exotic as the flowers he had given them rioting in the sunshine on every rustic trellis. Here a yellow laburnum, there an ornamental rowan with a smell like coconut ice. Great fleshy mallows with blooms the size of a child's face. And above all, hawthorn.

Hawthorn was Falkender's mark. It was his signature. He called it "The White Tree." Children called him "the May blossom man." Everywhere in Ys in May the fields and gardens were full of Falkender's hawthorn, swagged in blossom so heavy it bore the boughs down to the ground: hawthorn which looked like white cloud in a perfect sky, or clipper ships on a green sea, or great women sailing to a wedding swathed in green satin and white lace.

But the last generation to call him "the May blossom man,"

Rosamund's generation, were grown up with young children of their own. He had made nothing new for a decade. The White Tree was his professional gift to Ys: but with Rosamund dead, Falkender found himself empty even of pride in that. Long unable to make useful magic for others, he now found himself unable to make it for himself.

Instead, he walked the island, puzzled and tired, in search of the place in his dream.

He could not get rid of the feeling that the dream hid a message—although from whom, or what, he would not have dared admit. He interrogated it nightly, as he might a messenger, using techniques he had learned when he was apprentice to the extraordinary mainland magician Thierry Voulay. "Every dream," Voulay had taught, "is a locked cave, the paradox of dreams—indeed of magic—is that to find the key you must already be inside." When that failed, Falkender simply memorized each element of the dream landscape, so he could compare them, singly or in combination, with the cliffs and headlands that he knew. The dream became a map. In this way, he learned not to fear it. As a result, perhaps, it went away.

At first he was pleased. Then, after a fortnight undistracted by it, he saw the full misery of his own condition. All along he had hoped for a message from his daughter. The dream had turned out to be only a message from himself, a way of buffering himself against his loss, a kind of senseless puzzle set by his soul to occupy his mind. Grief welled up to replace it, less like water in a spring than blood in a wound. He saw his daughter everywhere, in the condition he had last discovered her. In his memory she rebuked him: "you're just a bitter old man." He could not bear to be in Ys in May.

"I'd like to get away for a while," he told his wife one night.

"That's a good idea."

"I think I'll go to the mainland."

She stared at him angrily.

"There's grief and grief, Maklo Falkender," she said. "Have you lost your mind?"

He blinked. He touched her hand. He wanted to her to stop being angry with him: but before that he had to make her understand his emptiness, his terror. "I never minded losing the magic," he said. "But there's nothing left in me at all now. I feel my age for the first time."

"Then act it, Maklo. Act your age."

She thought for a moment.

"That would be the first time, too," she said.

Unable to answer this old complaint, Falkender was silent. Then he said:

"I thought I would go and visit the mountains."

No image whatever came to mind when he spoke the word *mountains,* and he might as well have been talking about the far side of the moon, somewhere else he had never visited. Sensing this, his wife turned away from him with an exasperated sigh. He waited for a moment, but she was pretending to be asleep. They lay there in the dark, and he tried to think of an argument to persuade her. In the end he could only repeat:

"I'd like to see some mountains."

After a long time his wife said: "They'll never let you go, anyway."

The next afternoon, wandering the almost deserted corridors of the Ysian civil service, he was gripped by the fear that he would be prevented from leaving the island because he was *too old.* He rubbed his face. He sat on a bench near a window and watched a line of watery sunshine pivot across the polished floor, until the feeling went away.

In the end he got most of his travel papers quite easily. When he met resistance, he persisted. If he was forced to, he made things up.

"My health is bad."

"You need time in a warmer climate."

"Exactly."

And in the next department:

"They have new hybrids on the mainland. Tomatoes, cooking apples, whole new *kinds* of potatoes. It's time someone from Ys went to study them."

"We mustn't let them get ahead!"

"Exactly."

This feast of invention tired him, but it produced an exit permit and a three-month visa. The actual authorization to travel in Autotelia, without which he could not buy tickets, was harder to come by.

"You seem to be unsure why you're going," the official said. She was a tall woman, ten or fifteen years younger than Falkender. Her heavily-embroidered bodice, handsome cheekbones and practical manner disconcerted him deeply. "I would be happy to write you an authorization otherwise." She held up the exit permit and visa in front of her and frowned slightly, as if her eyes would focus on one or the other but not both at the same time.

"I'm an old man," Falkender told her.

She smiled.

"Nevertheless, I would prefer you to make up a coherent story before you leave."

That evening he went up to his daughter's room and looked out of the window. The weather had taken a turn for the worse. There were high winds, sudden squalls of rain. Nevertheless, warm gleams of setting sunlight came and went unexpectedly in the garden below. He could see something moving in the wild part of the garden, where dense mutated rose briars, subject of an experiment he could never find the energy to finish, had colonized the pathways. For a moment his eyes narrowed angrily, and it looked as though he would go down there to investigate, then he shook his head and sighed and turned back to the room instead.

It was cold. Cold seemed to seep from the huge old beams and unplastered walls, the cast iron fireplace. Patches of light fell unevenly across some brocade cushions and a pile of Rosamund's clothes on the fabric-covered sofa. The dull blues and reds of the brocades were picked up in some gray wool-mix skirts, and a striped cotton jacket. A silk sash stood out, thick egg yolk yellow. Everything else seemed to soak up the light. Falkender sighted again. Nothing of Rosamund's could explain what had happened to her, not even the diary which lay open on a little intricately carved round table by the bed. In it, she had written, on the sixth of May—

"When the rosewater in this sealed bottle has finally evaporated, my love for everything will be over."

Falkender looked for the bottle, but he could find nothing like it. Rosewater! What could she have expected from magic anyway? Some stoppered but still unstable mix of opposites? Annihilation and safety? Rapture without pain, always passing yet captured forever? Sometimes he felt as if Rosamund was still in that room, occupying it as if nothing had changed. At the same time, her continued presence made it a different kind of space, faulted and unnatural: suspended, pending, as conditional as his travel warrant. What would she see if she were there? What would be worth her attention?

One of her cats—a young, sweet-natured silvertip with long legs and fur like thick cream, named by Rosamund after the magical ideogram "Seven Guesses of the Heart"—had come into the room behind him. Since her death this cat had followed Falkender about the house every long afternoon. It would roll on its back in each empty room, leap to its feet at the sound of rain on the windowsill. Now it rubbed its head against his leg. It sniffed daringly at a cupboard. It hung for an instant from the lip of an open drawer; slipped off, scattering small items—a scarf, some beads, a very small grimoire bound in wood and velvet.

"You foul demon," Falkender said absently.

The cat purred loudly. He picked it up and left the room. He stood for a moment on the landing outside, unable to manage the cat and the door.

"Hold still."

The heat which had built up in a stone house retreats on cooler days into the stairwell. Leaving the upstairs rooms, you walk into a warm twilight. Falkender was reminded, for no reason he could understand, of a summer evening he had once spent in a garden in the south of Ys. That evening was a long way away now, with its scent of laburnum, its voices from the lawn, a laugh and the clink of a glass. Looking up from—what? A book? The face of a seated woman?—from something, anyway—he had seen his daughter running to him across the lawn. In her hands she held a tiny yellow rose. She was shouting. "Daddy! It smells of *almonds!*" It had been a tranquil, almost hypnotic moment: the child, the flower, the sound of laughter. Now, as he put the cat down gently, and looked up at nothing, he found himself calmed a second time, by memory. He was falling, further and further into himself.

The next day he went back to the Bureau of Travel. He said:

"Kittens have such sweet breath."

He raised his arms helplessly.

"Then something happens. After that, nothing you can do will bring back what they were. Do you see what I mean?"

The tall woman stared at him.

"My daughter is dead. I loved her. I don't think I can live here without her. For a while I don't think I can even bear to remember her. Will you give me the permit on those grounds?"

After a long empty moment she began to write.

Some days later, at the beginning of June, Falkender stood with his wife on the worn granite setts of Limport dock, looking out over the harbor towards the Great Bay. Behind him, cottages limewashed pink and white climbed the hill in the bright cool sunshine. Clean washing cracked and flapped gaily on the washing lines. The steep little streets of shops and cafes were bustling with new arrivals—goods, animals, people dressed in the peculiar fashions of the mainland. In front of him, fifteen or twenty sails clustered together on the sheltered water, orange and blue and lime green, like butterflies with folded wings drinking from some pool in an exotic country. Eight o'clock, and the morning tide was up, though not yet full. The air smelled of tar, salt, mud. Falkender breathed it with excitement, anxiety, a curious sense of relief. He had slept badly, exhausted first by dreams of his daughter— who stared at him with a compassion bordering on contempt—and then of that haunted headland above the sea.

This time the headland vegetation was baked and dusty, the sky like a dark blue ceramic. The air seemed to vibrate with heat. Falkender toiled forward. The world went to liquid beneath him. He fell. He drowned. In this version of the dream, though, he fell not into the water but through it, *and into the landscape again.* There, he struggled towards the sound of the tide, one foot in front of the other in the dry hot smell of heath. Only to have the world turn to water once more, so that he drowned and fell back through, into the dream again and again until he woke up. This time he was screaming out loud. His wife, who had been reading a book, stared down at him helplessly. He clutched at her. He had never felt such terror and despair.

"Help me, help me."

"Maklo, what is happening to you?"

There was no answer to this, so they had clung together all night in the dark, numbly facing the monumental changes in their lives.

Now she said:

"We could walk a little. They won't board yet."

He took her arm.

"I think I'd better wait here."

She stared away from him. "If that's what you want," she said. After a moment or two she made herself laugh. "Look! My mother used to say, 'You can always tell the direction of the wind by the way the gulls face.' She was right! See? They're all pointing at the lifeboat station like wooden toys someone has arranged on the beach."

"Pardon?" said Falkender.

"Have you gone away already?" His wife asked him bitterly. Later, as he picked up his bag and waited his turn to board the boat, she said: "Why do you have to do this? I don't know what will happen to us."

Thirty or forty people were ahead of him in the queue, mostly younger people going to the mainland to find work. One or two couples had their children with them. A gull planed steeply over their heads, a precarious flash of white against the windy blue sky. The short, hacking cry of a baby seemed to merge seamlessly for a moment with the gull's repetitive wail, as if they were one species. One species, Falkender thought, raucous and scavenging; one species calling out in pain. To be human is to be mixed and miscegenated like this. To be lost.

"I look ahead," Falkender's wife said, "and I don't know what will happen to us."

"Don't worry," Falkender begged. "Please."

But she wouldn't reply to him until his foot was on the gangplank. Then it was only to repeat, "Why do you have to do this?" She clung to his arm. Her face trembled. It collapsed finally into tears. "I don't know what will happen to us."

Falkender stood on the deck among the other passengers, looking out into the great estuary. He imagined the lines already cast off, the sailors in the bows, the boat bobbing its way out, past little green islands where tangled woods and low hills came right down to the tidal water. Disembark on one of those islands, he thought, and you would find a naked boy sitting on a stone, playing the syrinx to a pure white goat. Such a boy might be part of you. You might recognize that boy as yourself, with the thin brown shoulders and black hair of long ago. Admit that, and the things which happened to you thereafter in that place would be both constructive and irreversibly transforming. You would go willingly, though in horror; return ecstatic but ruined. Magic! Suddenly he walked across the deck, down the gangplank, and pushed his way back through the crowds on the quay. His wife had already begun to walk away, up the hill into Limport. He caught up with her and took her arm.

"Let's go home," he said.

"You're a puzzle, Maklo Falkender."

"I'm an old man."

"Rubbish."

The dead Rosamund stood listlessly in her room, looking out into the garden below.

In death she was much as she had been in life; a tall young woman, with her mother's big smooth shoulders and white skin, whose hair had turned an uncompromising red the day she began to do magic.

She often found herself standing at the window, although how she got there, or where she had been before she entered the room, she was always unable to recall. There wasn't much point in it anyway. Just to look at things is never enough. She could no longer handle her favorite objects. She could no longer leaf through the grimoires. She couldn't pick up her favorite cat, or count for him the guesses of his strong, affectionate little heart—*Where will I go now? Who will go with me? What must I do there? What can I be? Who shall I love there? Who will love me?* And the seventh only a repetition of the sixth: *Who will love me?*

"I still love these curtains," Rosamund said, and was answered promptly:

"If only the room were not so small."

Was that her own spoiled voice, seven years old and never satisfied? Oh Rosamund, Rosamund! she chided herself. She was at a loss to describe her present state, but she no longer regretted it. Her last act of magic, she knew, had ended her. It had closed her off from the world. But she was no longer sure that this was to describe the operation as *failed*. It was just one unlooked-for consequence. If she cared about anything from her old life—from her life—it was that her father did not seem to be able to make this distinction. She would have liked to tell him, in the voice she imagined adults to reserve for advising other adults, "You studied under Thierry Voulay, the greatest magician who ever lived. Yet you have forgotten his most basic advice!"

It would be fatal to assume that magic enables us to see through an appearance or shadow to a reality. Magic is only a language. It speaks to us out of the duality of things. Here is the world we are born into. There is the world we sometimes glimpse behind it. Never assume that this world-behind-the-world is in any way prior to our own! It is neither more nor less. It does not generate our world. They generate each other.

Rosamund would have liked to touch her father's arm and add: "Change is not bad. It is only change. Magic is about change."

In the end, she whispered that aloud.

"Magic is about change."

Just then, her mother came into the room, and joined her at the window. Together, at first without speaking, the two women looked down into the garden below. The long, uninterrupted summer days of Ys had warmed the twilight, into which glimmered sweet william like flowers embroidered on a cushion, monbretia spears which seemed to glow pale green from within. Honeysuckle rioted over the sagging old wooden trellises, tangled amiably with the long elegantly-winding runners of an albertine rose, whose petals were a kind of deep salmon pink at the base, fading almost to white at their tips. Drugged by its heavy scent, a few late bees flew in and out of the honeysuckle then away, in low arcs over the grass, where the cat Seven Guesses of the Heart stalked and startled them with sudden leaps and twists and darts.

Further away, in the more formal gardens, thin mist the color of milk, which for an hour had waited among the great dark trunks of the cedar trees, now breathed about the sunken lawns and white stone balustrades. It lay more thickly in the wild part of the garden where, in the theater of Maklo Falkender's failure, among the mutating roses, the dense thickets of brambles, the bindweed and nettles the height of a man, something seemed to move when you watched.

After a moment, Falkender himself came into view. Mist lapped about his feet as he crossed the lawns. He was wearing a long robe of gray silk and carrying a rosewood staff.

The dead girl watched. The dead girl sighed. The dead girl tapped upon the windowpane. For the hundredth time she failed to attract the magician's attention. For the hundredth time she asked her mother: "When will he let himself see me again? He passes me on the landings, he crosses me on the stairs. He comes into this room every afternoon and allows himself to pretend I am not in it."

And the mother, who heard her daughter's voice sometimes as the whisper of a leaf on an unswept stair, sometimes like the clear voice of any other young woman, advised:

"Hush now."

"When will he acknowledge me?"

The mother put her arm round her daughter's shoulders and pulled her close, so that their hips touched warmly in the cold room.

"Give him time," she said.

She laughed softly.

"Look!" she said.

Down in the unruly garden, the magician had raised his staff. Magic began to flow from him into the darkening air, delicate and hesitant as soap bubbles from a ring. "Look! Look!" Hip to hip, mother to daughter in the empty room, the women watched Maklo Falkender confront in the only way he could the tangled foliage and unkempt pathways of his own heart.

COPYRIGHTS